DELIVER US

A Kingdom Fantasy Novel

Jim Doran

ISBN: 978-0-9601017-2-6

Cover design by: Daniel Johnson
Library of Congress Control Number: 2021904890
Printed in the United States of America

To Carla and Ken Graham, makers of dreams, fufillers of wishes, believers of magic.

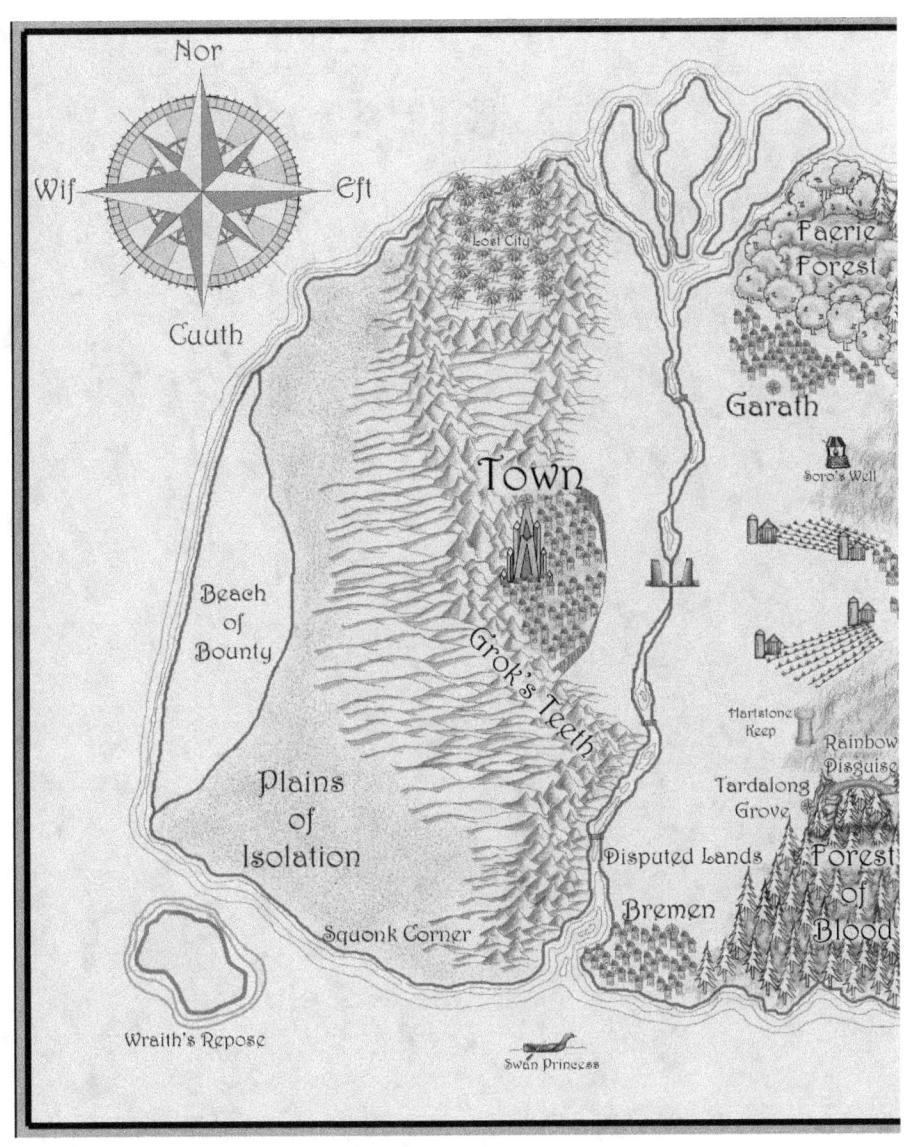

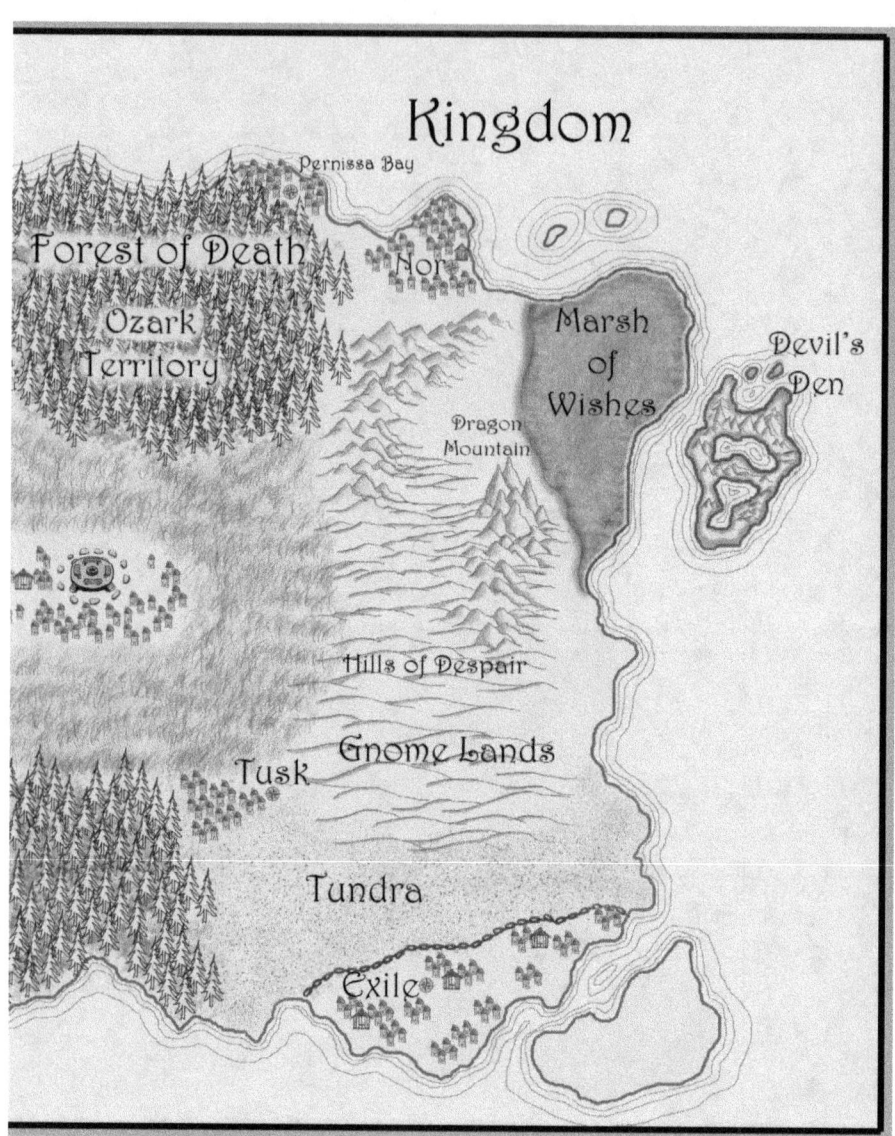

Kingdom

Pernissa Bay

Forest of Death

Ozark
Territory

Nor

Marsh
of
Wishes

Devil's
Den

Dragon
Mountain

Hills of Despair

Gnome Lands

Tusk

Tundra

Exile

Every war when it comes, or before it comes, is represented not as a war but as an act of self-defense against a homicidal maniac.
- George Orwell

"We will not leave each other," said Snow-White.
"Not as long as we live," said Rose-Red.
- Grimm's Fairy Tales, Snow White and Rose Red

CONTENTS

PART ONE

The Part One Cast of Characters

Earth Citizens:
Harold Saturn - Earth author and data scientist, aka Hero.
Sondra Saturn - Earth author and chemist aka ?
Alice - Descendent of Wonderland Alice, Traveler. Fairy tale: *Alice in Wonderland.*
Sylvia Swonewith - Earth politician and former social worker.

Kingdom Royals:
Penta Emily Corden - Kingdom queen, eldest, teleporter. Fairy tale: *The Maiden without Hands.*
Beauty Corden - Kingdom princess, adopted daughter of Penta, aka Shaina. Fairy Tale: *Beauty and the Beast.*

Helga Helvys - Kingdom queen, second oldest, warrior, cures curses. Fairy tale: *The Marsh King's Daughter.*
Danforth Tyreeph - Kingdom prince, bard, former earth resident, married to Helga.

Valencia Arkenson - Kingdom queen, third oldest, match girl, luckiest. Fairy tale: *The Little Match Girl.*

Cinderella (Radiance) Hartstone Jolly - Kingdom queen, fourth oldest, events organizer, charmer. Fairy Tale: *Cinderella.*
Roger Jolly - Kingdom prince, army commander, one leg, married to Cinderella. Fairy Tale: *Cinderella* and *The Steadfast Tin Soldier.*
Cuthbert John Jolly - Kingdom prince and son of Cinderella and Roger, aka Cutlass John.

Snow White Whisper - Kingdom queen, youngest and fairest, cannot be harmed by weapons, aka Coal. Fairy Tale: *Snow White and the Seven Dwarfs* and *Snow White and Rose Red.*

Kingdom Citizens:
Celeste Constellation - Kingdom pixie and royal spellcaster.

Planet Constellation - Kingdom pixie, deceased, sister to Celeste, parallel to Sondra Saturn.

Graddock Elston - Kingdom rogue, Valencia's companion.

Grr - Kingdom suitor to Princess Beauty. Fairy tale: *Beauty and the Beast*.

Rose Red Fyrekilm - Kingdom archer, Snow White's best friend. Fairy Tale: *Snow White and Rose Red* and *Little Red Riding Hood*.

Lyken - Once huntsman to Snow White, doorman to the queens. Fairy Tale: *Snow White and the Seven Dwarfs*.

Ozark the Mighty - Druid, most powerful magician in Kingdom.

T. Pennilane - Kingdom selkie, Cinderella's best friend.

The Dwarf Brothers - Snow White's Seven: Ox, Squirrel, Fox, Hedgehog, Turtle, Rabbit and the youngest Dear (renamed from Deer by Snow White). Fairy Tale: *Snow White and the Seven Dwarfs*.

1 - THE START OF
THE LETTER

Dear Godson,
  The hour has come for me to put to paper the most significant fairy tale of your life. While you are not of an age to read it yet, tempus fugit—*time irretrievably progresses—and I shall keep this story waiting for you until the proper moment occurs.*

  I foresee in your life a day when the fairy tales your parents tell you will sound old and tired, and you will reject them and their gift of fantasy. You will think believing in pixies and giants, magically gifted monarchs, and immortal love versus evil silly. "No such things exist," others will tell you. "No one is good without stain or irretrievably wicked."

  People will educate you, and they will proclaim how important their lessons are, and how you will be a better person if you only follow their instructions. I trust, however, you will know better.

When they explain something that doesn't ring true, my dear boy, simply pretend their ramblings are worthy of your consideration, and parrot their ideas back to them.

Let them wallow in such trivialities. Do not forget the lessons you learn at first are always the most lasting and authentic. With that perspective, I write this account, though it divulges a secret I would rather keep hidden from you. But as with all confidences, we should always reveal the ones that matter.

This is a tale of Kingdom, the fairytale land disclosed in the books on your shelf. I noticed the last time I visited you the bindings on the Kingdom books were dusty. For shame! Contained herein is a tale from the perspective of the principal people involved so that you may have more insight than my limited viewpoint on the matters that transpired. The novel is so personal that the story was never meant to be published, but I believe you should read it. I will conclude this letter at the end of my tale, and once you finish it, my sincere hope is that this volume takes a prominent place on your bookshelf, and that it's never laden with any dust other than fairy dust...

Harold

The best fairy tales end with a romantic kiss—this story starts with one.

Sondra, my wife of three years, straddled my legs and pressed her lips firmly against mine. She pulled my hips closer to her body while simultaneously pushing my head back with her forward motion. My spouse maintained the pressure longer than usual before slowly drawing away her lips, first her top one, then her lower. She quirked an eyebrow. "Shall we?"

I took a deep breath. I had been reading in my writing room when my wife entered and gave me her "good night" kiss, her flirting taking me by surprise. She had come in, shut the blinds so no suburban busybody could see us in our new starter home, and sidled up to me in my office chair. Then, without warning, she affixed her lips to mine. Next, Sondra stood, holding my hand, and backed up one step. My arm extended to her, my eyes wide with expectation, when my cell phone rang.

"Ignore that!" responded Sondra, but she was too late. Out of habit, I glanced at my mobile sitting on my desk and grunted at the caller display.

"The phone says the call is from the Fifth Precinct Police Station." I made a face. "It could be important."

Sondra shook her short, black bangs from her face and stepped backward, directly in front of a bookshelf. Bookshelves surrounded us with only my writing desk in the center. On my laptop, my newest Kingdom novel waited for me to continue writing. Sondra clutched her peek-a-boo purple nightgown closed, body stiffening. "Police? What could they want?"

I ran my hand through my close-cropped hair and examined my buzzing phone. "It could be your brother."

"What has Jim gotten himself into this time?" Sondra frowned and waved her hand in the air. "Let him sit in jail for the night. His timing sucks."

"Sondra, really. I have to answer it."

"You can bail him out yourself then," said my wife. "I warned him the last two times."

She walked over to a hobbyhorse leaning against the wall. Then she stroked the toy she had named Bree, her eyes glued to its mane, but she didn't leave the room.

I tapped the speaker button. "Hello?"

"Hello? Hello? Did I get through?"

A high, reedy voice gushed through the speaker into the room, words tripping over each other, as I struggled to identify it. The voice sounded familiar. I dared to hope it might belong to someone I knew. Someone connected to the novel I was writing. "You've reached the Saturns. Who is this?"

The voice raised an octave, light and airy. "Is this Hero? Have I found you?"

Sondra's head turned sharply to me and then her glance descended to a paperback sitting on my writing desk. The front cover of the book depicted five women dressed in medieval clothes holding pennants. Most people thought my novels were fantasies, but the truth was I based them on my real experiences in an alternate world known as Kingdom, where I had united five fairytale queens. When I had first traveled there, I was renamed "Hero."

Sondra pointed at the cover. "One of the queens of Kingdom," she whispered.

Wow, Sondra, I would never have guessed, considering I wrote two novels about them. I reached for my nearest floor-to-ceiling bookcase, picked out another book of Kingdom, and flipped it over. A second depiction of the queens graced the back cover. "Cinderella?"

"Do I sound like her?" asked the phone voice. "Really, Hero, you can do better."

A background voice interrupted the call. "Miss! You've been arrested. You shouldn't spend your one call on a guessing game."

The original caller responded. "Well, my friend called an old phone number, and you wouldn't let her call another one. The injustice of this place! If I were in charge of your world...er, this place...such a travesty would not occur."

She had, meanwhile, forgotten she was speaking to me. Sondra corrected me in a low tone. "Lisp, Harold. Cinderella has a lisp."

I bit my tongue. I hadn't noticed Cinderella's lisp for a while. When you come to know someone, a lisp is easily overlooked. I ran through the queens' voices in my mind and matched one to my mysterious caller. "Valencia?"

"Correct! I am imprisoned, waiting for you to do something with water," she said.

"What?"

"Something about bailing. The only thing I know how to bail is water. I don't quite understand it, but Alice can't talk to you because she used up her one phone call, you see."

"Alice is with you?"

Sondra's bare feet shuffled across the hardwood floor. "Explains how Valencia made it to Earth."

I addressed Valencia. "I understand what I need to do. I should be over in about…fifteen minutes. Did they mention how much this is going to cost?"

I winced when Valencia quoted a number. The queen spoke to someone on the other end. "I have a golden necklace with a ruby, but I must keep it. Oh, you could have my silver ring. Retrieved from Sweena's Kiss, a haunted mountain in—"

"Lady, I told you before. We ain't a pawnshop."

I rubbed my head. "Tell him I have enough to bail you out. I'll come right over."

"Graddock's here, too. I'm afraid our arrest is all his doing."

"I can't wait to hear. Sondra and I will be over."

Valencia's voice lost its mirth. "Yes, we have…troubling news. We shall see you soon."

Resigned, Sondra marched toward the door. "I'll go change. Meet you in the car."

I exited our house ten minutes later and walked to my wife's Malibu, color faded, and rust spots ignominiously displayed. I climbed in, threw Sondra's Dow Chemical badge sitting on the driver's seat into the cup holder, turned over the engine, and flipped on the headlights. They lit up our new home's dirty blue and white siding.

While I waited, I thought about how difficult crossing from Earth to Kingdom was. When I had first gone to Kingdom to help the queens ascend, a ghost had escorted me there. The second time, a sorceress had whisked me there and placed the queens on Earth. That time, Sondra had followed me to Kingdom using her magical hobbyhorse, Bree.

The front door slammed shut and I spotted my wife in a long, tan overcoat with faux-leather, olive-green boots, and umbrella hanging from her arm. She rushed to the passenger side and jumped in while placing the umbrella next to the seat. "Not the way I expected to spend a Friday night." She indicated the yellow umbrella. "I brought this in case we have a sudden spring storm. Wouldn't want rain to land on our fairy-tale queen."

"You know Valencia's not like that."

I set my phone in the holder affixed to the windshield while a mapping app calculated directions. After backing out of the driveway, I started off west toward the police station. "I'm sure she's not here to visit."

Sondra gripped the door armrest. "Slow down. Yes, I'm sure it's something important, but here we go again. Good thing Kingdom needs a chemist from Dow and a data scientist from IBM to save their world. Again."

"Come on, Sondra. Don't be like that. You enjoyed your visit to Kingdom, too."

"Yes, I thoroughly enjoyed when an evil sorceress turned me into a pixie and I couldn't turn human again."

I didn't respond.

Glancing my way, Sondra said, "Sure, I would like to return to Kingdom but not tonight. It's funny. I wonder what our neighbors would think. We attend block parties like everyone else, have jobs, keep our house in relative order. What would they imagine if they found out we visit a fantasy world and rub elbows with fairytale characters they grew up with?"

"They know I write books," I interjected.

"They don't believe the stories real," said Sondra. "You think they'd believe you helped five sisters become queens? And that I saw your adventure through the eyes of a pixie named Planet?"

"And that—" I swore and swerved to avoid a braking car.

Sondra barked, "Cat's piss, Harold, watch out!"

I hadn't been paying attention. After I took a deep breath, I said, "Yeah, we're Mister and Missus Boring with a capital B. I'm more interested in how Valencia got here. After my first visit, I thought I would never go back. Now that I know that you can cross worlds—"

Sondra's foot stomped on an imaginary brake pedal. "Will you slow down? And it's called 'Traveling,' not crossing worlds."

So she was suddenly an expert. I'd been to Kingdom one more time than Sondra, but she'd spent time with a Traveler. "Yes, Traveling. Now that I know people exist called Travelers who are able to bring people from world to world, I hoped we might go back one day. We're aware of Alice, for instance."

Sondra pointed ahead. "Don't run that light!" She exhaled loudly. "Crossing worlds reminds me. You know, everyone else received a new name when they went to Kingdom, but I didn't, and it kind of sucks."

Oh no. Not this again.

She continued, "It's unfair! Planet renamed you Hero when you went to Kingdom. When I went there, everyone still called me Sondra. Where's my new cool name, huh?"

"Saturn is a pretty cool name," I said.

"That's my real surname. I want a new one. What goes with Sondra Saturn? How about Sundread Saturn? As in, people should dread sundown when Sondra's around. My tagline even rhymes."

I changed lanes. "That's ridiculous."

"Right, because *Hero* is such a regular name."

I followed the GPS voice from my phone and turned off Andersen Street. "I don't like this bit Valencia delivered about 'troubling news.' I have a feeling something's wrong. This time, I'm afraid that whatever's in store for us, we won't come up with a happy ending."

2 - TROUBLING NEWS

Sondra

That's how he ends a chapter? In his James Earl Jones voice, he says, "This time, we won't have a happy ending." You know what? He's right. We won't wind up with a happy ending because he's going to kill us with his driving before we even get to the station.

Anyway, Mr. Dramatic to the left of me continued nearly hitting cars and not paying attention to the basic rules of the road until—a minor miracle—we made it to our destination. Whew.

After we inquired about our three criminal friends, Harold and I filled out the paperwork and presented our credit cards to provide bail for them. When I asked about the legal charges, the desk sergeant looked over the paperwork. His response was "destruction of property." He proceeded to tell us the address where the police had found Valencia and the others. Harold glanced at me. The street number and name he mentioned was our old condominium address. We had moved out four months before.

We waited another hour for the police to process the paperwork—mostly because Valencia was recorded as Valerie —but then Harold and I spotted her through a pane of glass. She spotted us too, smiled and waved, a strange gesture in a police station. A minute later, she exited ahead of a large man and a red-haired woman. Valencia, a queen of Kingdom, normally in flowing dresses for balls or a sturdy jerkin for adventures, was dressed in a pink blouse with black slacks. Behind her walked a tall, broad-shouldered man, rippling muscles, clean-shaven but with unruly black hair. The last person in line was small in stature with long, red hair and blue eyes.

Valencia ran up to Harold and hugged him and then kissed me on the cheek. A little unexpected, I admit, but welcome. Tears shined in her eyes, and a smile highlighted her freckles. "I'm so glad to see you. More than you know."

Graddock grabbed Harold's hand and shook it vigorously. "You people here greet others like this, right?"

Arm nearly pulled from his socket by the muscular citizen of Kingdom, Harold winced and responded with a "Yes."

The redhead hung back, and I nodded to her. "Hello, Alice."

"Sondra."

Harold unclasped his hand from Graddock's grip and examined the ginger-haired woman. "So, you're *the* Alice? From Wond—"

Alice interrupted him. "Not here."

Harold broke out in a grin. "It's nice to finally meet you."

Alice pulled nervously at the hem of her green turtleneck. "Likewise."

Valencia brushed back her straw-colored hair. "We need to hurry to your house. We have much to tell you. Let us not tarry."

The sergeant at the desk looked up at the word "tarry" while handing a duffel bag to Graddock, and Harold put a hand on Valencia's back and guided her out the door, the rest of us following. When we walked outside, Harold unlocked my car with his fob. "Climb in."

Graddock stopped dead in his tracks. "I am not willingly entering one of those beasts again. The transport here was bad enough."

Valencia grabbed his hand. "'Tis called a *car*, Graddock. A car is not a living thing, but a vehicle Hero controls."

Graddock hesitated but allowed himself to be led in and sat down in the back seat, placing the duffel bag on his lap. Valencia patted his arm. "You are in safe hands."

I snorted, thinking of Harold's driving.

I couldn't help myself. I watched the back seat through the rearview mirror and had a good view of Valencia seated in the middle. Graddock was as pallid as milk, and his mouth puckered as if he had drunk the same liquid, but after it had spoiled. Harold started the car, and when it moved, the other man closed his eyes and uttered something under his breath. Valencia grabbed his hand while her other hand fiddled with a tiny pendant hanging off a golden necklace. Harold and I knew about their not-so-secret-but-they-try-to-keep-it-quiet romance as revealed in letters we received from Kingdom.

While the car pulled away, I realized how little time Harold and I had spent with the three people in the back seat. Harold and I had spent the most time with Valencia, but had interacted seldomly with Graddock. And this was the first time Harold had met Alice.

Harold said, "Hey, Graddock. Did Alice tell you my world knows Valencia as the Little Match Girl, and Alice as Alice in Wonderland? If people knew they were riding in my car, they would flag us down for autographs."

"What is an autograph?"

I turned around. "People on Earth ask others for their

signature to prove they've met them."

Graddock clutched the seat in front of him, knuckles whitening. "I have been on many adventures with Queen Valencia. Would they want my autograph too?"

Valencia put her hand on his knee. "I told you, Graddock. What happens to us in Kingdom makes an impression on Earth, like a ripple on a pond, and authors here think they are creating something original, but they capture some details incorrectly. Unfortunately, they didn't write down your part in my story."

"She means you're a nobody here," snapped Alice.

Valencia moved her hand to Graddock's and squeezed after he frowned. "I would want your autograph."

"No one had better ask for mine. I'm not *the* Alice in Wonderland," said Alice. "The first Alice in my family line was Alice in Wonderland. I am only a sixth generation Alice."

Yeah, yeah. She really had a chip on her shoulder about not being the original Alice. "I told you that, Harold."

Alice shrugged. "People often call me by that title, considering she and I were both Travelers."

"Has Wonderland been discovered in Kingdom yet?" Harold asked.

Alice exchanged a glance with Valencia. "No."

"Do you go there often, Alice?"

The red-haired woman examined her hands in her lap. "Let's not talk about Wonderland. We have more pressing matters."

"Kingdom. Let us...let's go back to your home, Hero, and discuss it," said Valencia. "I do not wish to speak of it in this car."

That name! Now tell me, why does *he* get to be called Hero? I mean, Harold is very cool. I love him more now than ever, but that Planet renamed him and no one thought of a slick moniker for me I find so unfair. "Please don't call him Hero here," I interrupted. "You can call him Hero when he's in Kingdom. Here, he's Harold."

Harold visibly suppressed a smile, no doubt because he knew how much his Kingdom name irked me. He asked, "Is everyone well?"

Valencia looked down for a moment. "Let's talk at your home," she mumbled. "So when did you move? We were standing outside of your dwelling deciding how to find you when Graddock broke a window."

Graddock grunted. "I figured we might discover a clue as to your present whereabouts if we could get in."

Alice crossed her arms. "I tried to tell Muscle-Brain here the idea was stupid."

"I am not a...Muscle-Brain...and the move brought Harold and Sondra to us."

"At great cost to them," Alice snarled. "The Traveler's Guild is not going to look kindly on me after this."

Valencia put a hand on the Traveler's arm. "Oh, Alice, the police said it was uninhabited, and if we pay for the window, they'll drop all charges. I doubt none of us will suffer any long-standing consequences for our escapade tonight."

Alice snorted. "You're lucky they bought my stupid story about Graddock shadow boxing and striking the window accidentally. Well, sort of bought it. They still arrested us."

I said, "We sold the house where you were arrested. Alice has been faithfully relaying your correspondence from Kingdom, but the last letters were forwarded from our old address. I don't have your address so we couldn't let you know we had moved."

Alice unfolded her arms. "I'll give you my address. You have your own way to Travel to Kingdom."

I shook my head. "Don't you know? Riding my hobby-horse to cross worlds doesn't work. I've tried many times, often to my embarrassment. I miss Celeste. Her letters are too brief. I long to sit and talk with her."

A passing streetlight reflected the twinkles in Valencia's eyes. "Celeste is well. She talks fondly of you often, Sondra. I am sure she would love a visit."

"After our quest," reproved Graddock.

Valencia patted her guard's knee. "Of course, Graddock. Sondra, have you experienced anything unusual after your last visit from Kingdom?"

"No, nothing unusual."

"I thought since you transformed into a pixie in Kingdom and then back to your human self, some part of the magic might have lingered."

"My pixie condition resulted from a curse, and Helga removed it."

Harold winked in the rearview mirror. "Not all of it."

I held up my finger, index not the other one, in front of my husband's eyes. "What did you write, Ducky?"

Valencia put a hand over her mouth, suppressing a smile. "Harold's letter said your heart beats loudly when he kisses you, just like when you were a pixie in Kingdom."

I slapped Harold on the arm. "Why did you write that?"

"Because it's true. The last time we were in—"

Ahhh! Harold! What were you about to say in front of everyone? "Shut it!" I ordered.

"In the park." Harold eyed me with an "I wasn't going to say where we really were" expression. He certainly had seemed as if he was about to, and I noticed Valencia blushing, seeing through the fib.

She switched the subject. "Tell me, do you keep in touch with the ladies who journeyed with Harold to Kingdom last time?"

The conversation shifted to a group of women the queens had met during their last adventure on Earth. Harold tried to interrupt to press for news from Kingdom, but I wasn't about to allow him to speak again. Not after that last statement. I prattled on, occupying the rest of the trip with mundane gossip of our mutual, Earth-bound friends.

After we arrived and parked, I led our three visitors inside through the living room and dining room to our most spacious quarters at the back of the house. The entertainment room held a couch and loveseat positioned to face a fifty-inch, free-standing television and tables with our Kingdom books —ideal to read under the clerestory. Graddock set his duffel bag near the fireplace.

Valencia stroked the wood paneling. "This is cozy. What a wonderful home."

Harold uttered a command and music played from strategically placed speakers. "It's no castle, Valencia."

Valencia squinted at Harold. "I love my castle because it's my home. Not for the size, but for the people who live there. I sense love in this house, too."

"I'll put on tea," I said. "Would you like that?"

Graddock looked around the Saturn house and stepped tentatively on the linoleum, bouncing up and down on it. "I would prefer wine."

Alice cleared her throat. "Wine is common in Kingdom, but usually you wait for the host to offer it on Earth, Graddock. I'll have tea."

Valencia ran over and turned on the faucet in a half-bathroom off the back room. "Graddock, really! Behave! Now come here and look at this."

I headed for the kitchen. "No problem. We have wine."

Valencia excitedly explained indoor plumbing to Graddock while Harold joined me in the kitchen. "I wonder who's threatening Kingdom this time?" I whispered. "Maybe the Big Bad Wolf? Oh, I forgot, you defeated him the first time you went there. Maybe Dame Gothel?"

Harold retrieved wine glasses from a high shelf. "Nice. Don't forget Cinderella and Snow White's stepmothers nearly killed me the last two times I was there. Kingdom's enemies are nothing to laugh at."

"True, but don't the queens know by now how to protect themselves? Why bother us?"

"You're upset because they interrupted us."

I retrieved a corkscrew from a drawer. "Not even an 'I'm

sorry.' It's only...is this our life now? Are we going to spend our time chasing the Gingerbread Man? Just when it seemed that we were settling in and establishing ourselves, Kingdom pops up."

"From my perspective, Kingdom brought us together." Harold crossed his arms. "And Kingdom kept us together."

I pulled the cork from a bottle of wine. "Go out there and entertain our fairy friends."

Harold turned back at the doorway. "I think Alice would punch you if she heard you calling her a fairy."

I threw a towel at him as he walked into the entertainment area. Through the doorway, I heard Graddock address my husband. "Harold, I can see the stars through that hole in your ceiling."

"It's called a skylight," Harold explained. "It's deliberate."

Graddock nodded and turned to the television. "This is a curious painting, Hero. Why did you encase it in ice?"

Harold said, "Television on."

When the screen came to life, Graddock jumped back. On the television, a topless, suntanned woman, lying on her stomach, looked over her shoulder and raised her eyebrows seductively. Graddock's jaw hung open.

From out of my line of sight, I heard Valencia snap. "Turn that off. Really, Harold, what were you watching? I wish that Earth would learn a little modesty. Half the girls run around *en déshabillé*!"

Harold blushed. "That wasn't on when I...never mind. Television off."

The visitors and Harold sat down, and I bustled out with a tray of cups of tea and glasses with white wine. I maneuvered around the furniture and handed out cordials to Valencia and Graddock. Graddock held up his glass, raised an eyebrow, and flicked a finger against it, making it ring. He shrugged, satisfied. Valencia smelled hers and dipped her pinky finger in it. She tasted her finger and then sipped, nodding appreciatively.

I sat next to Harold, my hip brushing his. "Tell me about Celeste."

"The queens first. Jeez, Sondra," said Harold.

"Celeste is like my sister. She's the court magician, protector of the queens, Planet's sister, and my best friend. She's a better sister than Karen." Our three visitors looked at me curiously. "Karen's my actual sister. Let's hear about Celeste first."

Valencia lowered her glass after a sip. "Celeste is fine. She's become even more accomplished in magic since you've been there. Turducken's been a big help to her."

Out of the corner of my eye, I noticed Harold tense his shoulders when Valencia mentioned Turducken the elf. Yes, that was his real name. Some people have ridiculous names in Kingdom, but Turducken is a sweet elf about two feet high and a cutie-pie. However, Harold has some stupid rivalry going on with Turducken that only exists in his head.

Graddock added, "Surprising for a pixie." Valencia flashed him a look, and he held up his hand. "Pixies are highly magical, but she's accomplished in spells unknown to her species—that is all I mean. She surpasses many in the mystical arts and is a welcome ally on the battlefield."

Alice asked, "Shouldn't we talk about—?"

Valencia shook her head at her companion. "Give me a moment before we start discussing our purpose here. I'd rather catch Harold and Sondra up a bit. Since you've been gone, my eldest sister has found and adopted a teenage girl. We think she is Kingdom's version of one of Earth's famous fairy-tale queens."

Harold stared over the rim of his glass. "Which one?"

Valencia sipped her wine. "The one you call Beauty. From the tale Beast and the Beauty?"

"Beauty and the Beast." I tucked my legs under my body. "I wondered if more fairytale princesses would show up in Kingdom."

"Beauty lives up to her name," Valencia said. "She's a

wonderful niece, and we all love her. Beauty has the ability to change someone's appearance to reflect who they are inside. Ugly but kind people look beautiful, and those of a sinister nature look evil. 'Tis similar to Cinderella's gift."

"Her gift, like those of the queens, proves her worth as a princess," Graddock added. "All the queens have their own unique abilities. Beauty can project one's inner nature on their outer appearance."

"And Grr—he who you call 'Beast' in your stories—is a worthy companion," said Valencia.

Alice sipped her tea. "Earth has it right. He's like half-animal."

Valencia shook her head. "He's a lovely boy and devoted to Beauty. When they marry, he'll be a blessing to our family. But we must switch the subject to someone else you know, someone dear to all of us. We're here because of my youngest sister, Snow White."

Harold looked at me from the corner of his eye. Now I regretted making fun of him and his "not a happy ending" remark. The sorrow in Valencia's eyes spoke volumes, and I tensed. "What's wrong with Snow White?"

Valencia's voice became as soft as taffeta. "The time has come to tell you what has happened."

She swallowed and closed her eyes. Graddock put his empty wine glass down. "I can tell it, Valencia."

His tone was gentle, but Valencia raised her hand. "I must tell it. 'Tis important they hear it from me. I was there for most of it."

When Valencia opened her eyes, tears rolled down her face. Both Harold and I started and looked at each other. Cheeks sunken in, Valencia took a deep breath. "I am afraid your friend, my sister Snow White, is dead."

3 - SNOW DRIFTS

Five days earlier

A pale, young woman raced over Kingdom's landscape on the back of a black steed with a golden horn in the middle of its forehead. She rode across the Waste Lands toward the center of Kingdom, hugging the edge of the Forest of Blood, past a row of trees whose roots broke the surface then burrowed back into the soil, making the horse and equestrian's progress treacherous.

The mount, however, adeptly avoided the tangles and loops beneath his hooves, keeping his rider from harm. She patted the side of the animal's neck, urging him forward. "Hurry, Neighsayer. I wish to make the Inn of Five before night-fall."

"Shall not be easy, Queen Snow White," Neighsayer grumbled.

She stroked his mane. "You are so negative all the time, dear one. We are not far from our destination. The timing should not be a problem for a royal unigard like you."

"Pardon my saying so, but if you had not negotiated that last bit between the gnomes and garboles, we would have departed sooner."

Snow White sighed. "The job needed to be done, my good Neighsayer. After all, I am the royal ambassador."

Neighsayer leaped over a bramble. "But will the factions ever stop fighting each other, my queen? You and your sisters ascended six years past and yet these two parties still quarrel."

"Indeed, but 'tis the way of the world. We would have no use for ambassadors if the situation were any other way." She huffed out a breath and then inhaled deeply. "I agree that I long to be at home, serving the poor with my sister Valencia, and helping her provide clean water to our beloved citizens."

The equine rolled his eyes. "The ditches that hold the iron rods buried below the soil block the inroads leading to the royal city of Town. It shall slow me down tomorrow."

"Piddly-poo," said Snow White. "A minor detour. You are a unigard, faster than your cousins the unicorns and unicenses. You always make a mountain out of an anthill."

Snow White allowed the unigard to focus on his task as she pictured the reunion with her other four sister queens. They were all back in the castle now and hadn't been together in three months while off performing royal duties.

As Snow White rode across a field, she spotted a pack of tardalongs—the furry beasts that transfixed their victims with spotlight-like eyes. These raced ahead now, right next to Neighsayer.

The queen had no time this day for their petty savagery. Strange how, six years past, she would have been terrified by a single tardalong, and now they hardly concerned her. The unigard galloped forward, leaving the creatures in the dust.

Neighsayer dashed up an incline, and the fairest queen raised her head to the sun. Snow White welcomed the heat on her face after two days of thunderstorms. She closed her eyes and smelled the loamy dirt, the pine scent of the forest, the faint acrid trace of wyvern droppings.

The queen took in both the pleasant and unpleasant smells with relish. Cocking an ear, she couldn't discern any flapping of the wings of her friends, the birds. Odd. Usually one of her feathery darlings flew close by, but today the air was entirely still, as if, other than the tardalongs, something had warded off all living creatures.

Mount and rider crested a hill and Snow White urged Neighsayer down toward an expansive plain where she spied three elderly women struggling with a cart and a broken wheel. For once, the queen wanted to act out of character by riding past and pretending she hadn't noticed them, but she immediately admonished herself. The poor needed her, and one day she would be an elderly woman as well and would require someone young as she was now to help her.

She directed her horse to the three women and hailed them as she approached. Their faces had deep wrinkles, and the hair on their heads was stringy and white. The first lady had a large, hook-like nose, and a rotund body. Another one had snake-like slits for eyes, conferring an evil countenance to her features. Snow White again corrected herself that looks could be deceiving. The woman's narrowed eyes were probably due to her advanced age. The third, leaning on a birch tree staff, adjusted a hat on her head.

The hat woman spoke with a raspy voice. "Hail, my queen. Will you help a few, defenseless old crones?"

Snow White nearly said "I'll," but contractions were out of style in Kingdom. "I will be glad to do so."

The women all gasped and stepped back. They stooped over in an effort to bow. Snow White dismounted. "Please, do not strain yourselves attempting to show me honor. I will help and then I must be on my way."

She walked up to the wagon and examined the wheel as the beak-nosed woman clapped her hands. The hat woman said, "We are honored that you would bother to help out your most insignificant subjects."

Snow White examined the wagon's underside. "No one is insignificant in Kingdom." Her forehead wrinkled in concentration. "My good ladies, something is amiss here. I do not see how this wheel ever fit on this axle."

She turned back to the women and found them surrounding her. All three crones put their hands out and placed them on Snow White's body then spoke words she didn't understand.

Snow White stood and stepped away from them. "What is this?"

The one with snake eyes cackled at her, a disturbing laugh full of malice, and Snow White's skin broke out in goose bumps. The woman in the hat pointed at the queen and displayed a toothless grin, leering in a disturbing manner. Snow White hugged her arms in defense. When she touched her skin, she found in place of her soft and pliable arms, unfamiliar bony limbs. She pulled away her hands and gasped.

Her arms and hands were covered with age spots. Her hands went to her face and her fingers patted wrinkles beneath her eyes and above her drooping jowls. They had taken her youth from her in seconds! Tears filled her eyes, and her vision blurred.

"What have you done?" Snow White screamed.

The obese, frizzy-haired witch cackled. "Looking-glass upon the wall. Who now would not be asked to a ball?"

Neighsayer galloped up, creating a barrier between the witches and Snow White. "Mount, my queen, and let us depart from this unfortunate scene."

Snow White set her hand against the horse's side and his black hair turned gray. The horse, sensing something pass between them, pulled back and whinnied. Snow White stepped away, raising her hands into the air. "No!"

"Yes, dullard queen," hissed the hook-nosed hag. "Your touch now ages others. The horse is fortunate and will probably survive, but as you grow older in the upcoming days, your touch will become more deadly."

The frizzy-haired one giggled. "Your touch reduces friends to bone and then you will be quite alone," she shrieked.

In a wisp of smoke, the three women and their cart disappeared. Snow White trembled, and for a brief moment, wondered if she'd just had a terrible nightmare. Then she held out her arms and examined her aged limbs once more. Her hands again sought for her face and uncovered the same mass of wrinkles she had found before. Her quivering voice cut across the stillness. "What have they done to me? Neighsayer, what have I done to you?"

"Do not worry about me, my queen!" exclaimed Neighsayer. "Mount, and I shall ride through the night to return you to Celeste. She shall have spells to restore you."

Snow White shook her head. "I cannot do so without risking your death. And I left the ring I use to communicate with my sisters with the garboles as a gift of friendship. You must ride on, my dear Neighsayer. Go away from me back to the royal castle."

"Why have they done this?" asked Neighsayer. The loving ungulate's eyes filled with tears.

Snow White brought to mind the latest laws and battles to see if they were the cause of the trio's maliciousness. She was less concerned with the age spots, wrinkles, and white hair than with the reason the women would cast such a powerful and terrifying spell on her.

Snow White turned south. "I do not know why, but I must seek isolation in this direction. You must go now. I will send messengers ahead of you explaining my condition to my sisters."

Neighsayer stomped his hoof. "But—"

"And that is a royal order, Neighsayer. Go!"

Snow White's mount whinnied and galloped off east. After watching him make his way, she took a few steps herself. She turned, undecided which trail would be less inhabited, knowing she must not cross anyone's path. Neighsayer might not die but her touch had led him to the brink of death. Snow White couldn't chance an ill of this sort with anyone else, deciding to drift along the back roads to isolation.

4 - REFLECTION

"**B**lue hair, Celeste?"

"I like it, Ma."

Penta Emily Corden, eldest of the queens of Kingdom, sat next to Celeste Constellation, her pixie court magician. They were drinking tea with Celeste's mother, who had come for a social visit. Ma Celeste floated in front of her daughter in the sunshine filtering through the royal castle window. The light shone brightly on the maternal fairy as she scrutinized her blue-haired, grimacing daughter. Ma Celeste reached out and lifted a curl. "But your golden locks, my dear. What of your beautiful, golden locks?"

Penta adjusted her long, sky-blue skirt to suppress a grin. The royal magicians all deferred to Celeste for her knowledge of spells, and the monsters on the battlefield trembled when she started an incantation. Described as "the pinnacle of the mystic arts," Celeste now floated uncomfortably before her mother. Everyone has someone they answer to.

Celeste shifted her shoulders in her silver, form-fitted dress. "A goblin archer last week aimed at Cinderella, thinking she was me. I need to stand out, be a target to keep the queens safe. Hence, blue hair."

Celeste hadn't revealed to the queens the reason behind her hair color change, and Penta regarded her court magician with gratitude. Celeste's mother, though, didn't share Penta's sentiment. "You may be the queens' defender, but you aren't invulnerable, my dear. I certainly do not want Cinderella hurt, but you are an important part of the queens' royal advisors. Why not mimic Snow White? She cannot be harmed by weapons."

"You think a goblin archer could hit me, Mother? Truly, you ought to have more confidence in me."

Ma Constellation's lower lip protruded. "And now you sound like your bragging father. He is impossible to take to parties these days. They all want to invite him, but he will only talk of you and how you halted the march of the Rock Trolls on the Island of Pikripsky."

Celeste closed her eyes in embarrassment. "That was over a year ago."

Penta set down her teacup, enjoying this conversation between Celeste and her mother. She had never entered into this type of mother-daughter rapport with her own mother, having been kidnapped as a baby. She did occasionally slip into mother mode with her sisters, however, much to their displeasure. Cinderella had once told Penta to save the Mom stance for Beauty. Of course, mother mode with Beauty, her adopted fourteen-year-old daughter, came as easy as sliding into a golden slipper.

A blue jay landed on an open window and started singing. Celeste looked at the rude bird in annoyance and tried to focus on her mother, who prattled on about how her father had argued with the mayor for refusing to erect a statue of Celeste in Faerie Forest. The blue-haired pixie whistled sharply at the bird, but the fowl chirped something that made both women stop. A chill ran through Penta at their expressions. "What is it?"

Celeste held her finger out to the bird. "What do you mean Snow White is in trouble?"

The bird sang a few more notes and hopped onto Celeste's finger. Celeste answered with a whistling response. The warbler tilted its head, and the pixie shook her finger. The bird flew away as Celeste turned to Penta. "We must go to Snow White immediately."

Her mother, having heard the bird's discourse, nodded. "Indeed. You have no time to waste."

Penta's hands, always gloved, reached for Celeste, and she used her natural ability to teleport away.

Penta and Celeste appeared on a plain east of the Forest of Blood; their eyes peeled for Snow White. The bird had specified this location—at a broad, flat, area with a tree line in the distance, away from people. From behind, Snow White hailed them with a warning.

"Stay away!"

Penta turned around and found her sister huddled in a ditch a few yards off. Crouching, Snow White had her arms wrapped around her body with her head slightly raised. At first, she appeared normal, dressed in her favorite riding clothes. Then Penta spotted the wrinkles on her sister's face and arms along with white hair hanging down from under her hood. Penta ignored Snow White's warning and stepped forward with the royal pixie following her.

"On your life, stay back, Penta!"

The tone tinged with panic, Snow White's voice jarred

her elder sister. Penta halted three feet from the ditch. "What happened?" she demanded.

Snow White described her encounter with the witches. "My curse, the aging, spread to Neighsayer. He survived, but the witches say he will be the last. I fled to a place far from civilization, skirting around Tusk and then came here. As for Neighsayer, he is making his way to the palace. I couldn't even pet him good-bye."

Snow White buried her face in her arms, and her body convulsed in sobs. "I do not know why they have done this to me."

Penta's fingers pulled on the tips of her right-handed glove. "Your gift. You cannot be harmed, but the witches overcame your natural defense and aged you."

"Let me try a spell to reverse the effects," suggested Celeste.

The pixie threw her arms in the air and golden light emerged from her heart. The light made a circle around Snow White, then entered her chest. Snow White placed her hands over the location where the beam had pierced her. The wrinkles and age spots remained on her skin.

Celeste's wings beat rapidly. "Let me try a more powerful spell."

The pixie flew closer and gestured frantically, murmuring chants. A brilliant golden ray appeared and enveloped Snow White. The light crackled with power as Celeste spoke words neither queen understood. Then, without warning, a sharp sound like a gunshot exploded near the fairy and Celeste flew backward, the golden light extinguishing. She struck the ground in a puff of dust.

Penta hastened to Celeste's side. The pixie was conscious but holding her head. Penta grasped the fairy's tiny hand. "What happened?"

Celeste shook her blue curls. "This is foreign magic. I have never been rebuffed in such a manner."

Penta scooped up the dazed pixie and held her aloft. "If

you don't know a counter-curse, I'm troubled. Where could these witches be from?"

Celeste shook her head in frustration. "Perhaps the netherworld where only demons dwell."

Penta pursed her lips together at the answer. She and her sisters had faced an adversary that they had banished from Kingdom when they became queens. "Perhaps a wish from Valencia would restore her?" One of Valencia's gifts included the ability to precisely word a wish on a wishing stone.

"Perhaps," replied Celeste.

Penta turned back to her sister who had tears rolling down her face. Snow White wiped her eyes on her sleeve. "You must go. 'Tis as I feared. I am beyond hope. Warn the others not to come to me."

Penta put a hand on her hip. "Until we find a way to reverse it."

Snow White didn't reply.

Celeste touched Penta on the shoulder. "Return me to the castle so I may conduct research. Snow White, do not despair. I will do everything in my power to remove the spell."

Snow White said, "Go with her, Penta. We cannot take the chance the curse will transfer to you."

Jaw set, Penta used a colloquialism she had picked up from her time on Earth and pledged, "I won't leave you, kid sister."

Again, tears filled Snow White's eyes. "You must. Not for my sake, but for Kingdom's. I will find a place in the woods and make my way further to the sea so as not to run into any of Tusk's citizens. Now go, before I spread this curse."

Penta ground her teeth. Her sisters, knowing of this, would want to see Snow White. As for Penta, Kingdom had to come first, even at the cost of her sister's safety.

"I will be back, and soon." Penta raised her hand in fond farewell, and she teleported away with Celeste.

Not much later, Penta gathered the remaining three queens in the throne room to explain to them Snow White's condition. The throne room was the largest room in the royal castle, made of marble floors and stone columns. In the center, the monarchs had placed their five thrones on a dais in a semicircle. Each queen had designed her own throne to her own style, but one element was present on all five—a plaque. Each chair had a rectangular placard proclaiming the owner's name.

Helga, Cinderella, and Valencia sat on their thrones while Celeste, invited to join them at Penta's request, hovered outside of their gathering. Helga gripped the armrests of her wooden throne. The vertical pieces of the back of the chair were assembled from boards on various ships Helga had captained. "My ability removes curses. Take me to her," demanded Helga.

Celeste floated closer to Helga. "Recall that some dark magic, like a sleeping hex, is immune to your ability. This is no simple curse. I strongly suspect if you touch Snow White, she will age you."

Penta, pacing to and fro, spoke before Helga could respond. "If Celeste's magic will not work on Snow White, then you trying your natural ability is not worth the risk. You'll be dead, and Snow White will remain in the same state."

Helga appeared to be on the verge of rebuffing her sister, but she remained silent. Cinderella, whose throne was a swing hanging from a silver frame, scraped her slippered foot along the floor. "We need a more certain solution."

Helga brushed aside her black bangs. "I will consult the

army scouts and see if they know anything about the witches. I'll capture the hags and force them to throw a counter-spell."

"Excellent," said Penta. "But be careful."

"They will be unconscious before they realize I am there."

"I'll use a wishing stone," Valencia piped up. "Perhaps one of the wishing gems."

Penta looked at Celeste. "What do you think?"

The pixie turned her attention to Valencia. "The gems are limited to Kingdom's rules. We need something foreign to our world to counteract the curse."

"I will use one anyway," said Valencia. "We lost the Sapphire of Fortune three years ago, but I have the Onyx of the Elements."

Penta licked her lips. "I know you and Graddock recovered the onyx at great cost."

Valencia, seated on a simple wooden chair, folded her hands. "I'm the best at wishing on wishing stones. I'll use it on Snow White."

"But it disappears after a wish is made on it, whether it works or not," said Penta.

Valencia shrugged. "The onyx's innate ability is to provide the bearer with favorable weather. It's not one of the more powerful wishing gems. If the onyx doesn't work, I will consult ancient tomes. I will search for a countermeasure, something not of this world."

Helga stroked the wooden trim on her armrests. "If anyone will find the answer, sister, it is you. You are the most learned scholar in Kingdom."

Penta walked up to Cinderella. "You and I shall go on a quest."

Cinderella brushed back her curly hair. "You wish to see Ozark, but you know the rules, Penta. I'm the only queen allowed in Ozark's territory because I'm his—"

"Adopted daughter," finished Penta with a sigh. "Yes, I know." She wrapped her finger around one of her long, russet-colored strands of hair. "These witches might come for him."

"Then for me to go alone and not transgress Ozark's wishes would be best." Cinderella bent over and looked at Valencia. "Thanks for the word transgress, sister. I've added it to my vocabulary list."

Penta regarded Snow White's throne, a mammoth log with a carved-out inset. "Ozark, the most powerful magician in Kingdom, may know something we can use to reverse Snow White's curse. I'll teleport you to his border."

Cinderella stood up from her swinging throne. "Groovy. That one I learned from Hero years ago."

Helga said, "Cinderella! Our sister is in peril. Don't take this lightly."

Cinderella bit her lip. "I'm sorry."

Penta tugged her white gloves tighter in a nervous gesture. "She uses slang to cope, Helga," she explained. "But now we all have our tasks. Good. Then we are adjourned."

Penta stood in front of her own marble, bejeweled throne and held out her hand to Cinderella. Her younger sister grabbed it and the two queens disappeared.

After Penta and Cinderella landed outside of the boundary to Ozark's territory, Cinderella hurried across the border and made her way deep into the Forest of Death where Ozark ruled. For her part, Penta paced under the forest canopy.

Someone summoned Penta on her ring and she at first expected the caller to be Cinderella, but it was Valencia. Valencia's voice floated up from Penta's finger. "Penta, I have tried the onyx, and Celeste teleported to check on Snow White. It didn't reverse the aging."

"Did you lose the onyx?"

"I did," she answered. "I'm sorry."

"If a wishing gem won't work, I'm convinced Helga's ability won't either. We must make sure she doesn't try to remove the curse on Snow White."

Helga's voice came from the ring. "I'm listening in. I won't try something rash, Penta."

"First time for that," murmured Cinderella's voice from the ring.

"Cinderella!" rebuked Helga.

Cinderella continued on, ignoring her sister. "I wish you could see Ozark's hut. It's made of tree trunks and branches, all living, including the vines he wove to make a hammock. I'm entering now. I'll return in a few minutes."

Penta tracked the sun's progress while she waited. She was certain fifteen minutes had passed and still no Cinderella. Where was she? Then she spied her sister weaving through the trees on her way back. Cinderella shook her head as she approached Penta. "Ozark has sensed that a trio of magicians with hellspawn power have come to Kingdom. He has told me to seek out artifacts that transcend Kingdom's magic to counteract their spells. Artifacts not crafted within Kingdom like Zyrax's treasure chest."

"The chest was buried in the mythical Underworld. We're not likely to find such a place or such a relic." Penta ran a hand through her hair. "What about our abilities?"

"He said they won't work."

Penta wrapped her finger around a strand of her hair. "Will he help us?"

Cinderella lowered her head. "He's a sick man, Penta. I fear he isn't long for this world." Tears began to stream down her face.

Later in the day, the funereal council of queens elected to meet in quarters crowded with furniture, a room known for its intimacy. Penta sat in a fauteuil with pale-violet upholstery. Valencia and Celeste gathered around a table with Valencia's hands resting on a large, open tome. Helga paced about the room.

Cinderella stood next to a small fireplace arranging the small ornaments on the mantle, an act that she insisted settled her nerves. She had stooped down and smeared soot under her eyes. Cinderella regularly dirtied her face to detract attention from her exquisite features in deference to Snow White. Cinderella claimed it ensured the people wouldn't argue who was the fairest in Kingdom. Now, she dropped her arms to her side and described her encounter with Ozark. As she finished, her lisp was pronounced, demonstrating her anguish. "And so, we parted, and now, within the same day, I find both Ozark's death near and my sister's life endangered."

Cinderella's body tensed, and Penta teleported next to her sister, hugged her, and guided Cinderella's head to her shoulder, allowing the younger woman to weep. Cinderella tried to catch her breath. "My tears are not befitting the occasion."

"Tears are windows to the soul." Penta stroked the back of Cinderella's neck. "We share your grief. You demonstrate you're the bravest of us by showing how you feel."

Cinderella sniffed and pulled away, wiping her eyes. Penta held her sister queen's hand and turned to the others. "Helga, any news?"

Helga moved a chair out of her way, scraping it against the floor. "No. None of our scouting parties in the region have seen the hags."

Valencia, eyes on her book, flipped a page. "'Tis our worst fear. Three women have struck a deal with our demonic adversary and have brought spells here previously unknown to our world."

Penta released Cinderella and addressed Valencia. "And what have you found?"

"Nothing yet, sister, but I haven't read all the books on my list."

Penta took her seat again. "Celeste?"

"I have thought deeply upon the situation." Celeste

floated above Penta's chair. "Helga's gift is the greatest coun-termeasure to a curse, as her ability was divinely bestowed. But if Helga cannot touch Snow White for fear of contract-ing the disease, I wonder if she could use another way to cure Snow White from a distance."

Helga stopped walking and stared at Celeste. The pixie continued. "The monks at St. Isadora's monastery have an an-cient ritual called Reflection. Reflection allows the caster to have her soul step out of her body for self-examination. Two halves of a person co-exist apart—in the form of the mortal body and the soul-body. The soul, for all intents and purposes, is a body. It may experience the five senses, be seen, and touch others, but is immune from poison, curses, and disease."

Penta clasped her hands at her waist. "And the downside is...?"

"The sins of the host stains it," said Celeste. "The trans-gressions manifest on the skin as green spots. The more sins you have, the more spots. Certain monks would rather not have that exposed."

"Are you sure it's safe?" Penta asked.

Celeste answered, "I am confident it is. I have witnessed monks who were empowered by a Reflection spell cure people with diseases and curses with no side effects. Shall I prepare the spell? If I start now, I will have it ready by sunrise."

Helga asked, "Can we use our abilities in this state?"

"I've read tales that the soul-bodies can cast spells." Celeste lifted her chin. "I believe you could remove Snow White's curse."

Helga moved toward the pixie. "Then I vote aye."

Penta ground her teeth. Helga often applied titles to herself: Helga the Light-Bearer, Helga the Peacemaker, Helga the Goblin-Crusher. Once she had called herself Helga the Foolhardy. That title seemed appropriate to this situation. "You are rushing into this, Helga. Certain magic, even if it is light magic, is forbidden for good reasons."

Helga leaned against a nearby table. "For Snow White, I

would bare my soul to all of you."

The other two queens quickly voiced their approval. Penta grimaced at Helga. "Sister, you are too critical of yourself, and the Reflection spell will add wood to that fire. If we all had your ability, I would be the recipient of the magic, but as it is, I vote for it."

The next morning, Penta teleported the queens and Celeste to Snow White's hiding place. They spotted her in the distance. Their sister's white hair was tangled and dirty, her clothes ripped, her lily-white hands covered in grime. She sat on the grass and stared dispassionately at a mound of dirt as if transfixed by it. Tear streaks were the only clean part of her dusty face.

Cinderella gasped, and Valencia put her hand over her mouth. Snow White's shoulders slumped, her mouth hung open, her eyes glazed over. She didn't acknowledge her sisters though they stood in her view.

Penta called to her, but her summons didn't even warrant a glance. Instead, Snow White focused on the pile of dirt in front of her. She cleared her throat, but her voice remained raspy. "He was a farmer. He had a wife and two sons. When I was sleeping, he thought I had been attacked and wanted to help me."

As one, Snow White's sisters took a deep breath.

"He said his name was Luriday. He told me before he died." Snow White paused. "I don't have the strength to cry anymore."

Penta released an unsteady breath. "'Tis not your fault, Snow White."

"I was not careful enough. 'Tis agony. My touch ages and kills others quickly but I live on, aging more slowly but inexorably marching to my death as well. I'm doomed to witness the results of my curse inflicted on others."

Helga nodded to the pixie. "Celeste, begin the ritual."

Celeste started to mumble words and make gestures while Valencia stepped forward and explained the Reflection ritual to Snow White. Snow White wiped her face, careful to absorb every word. As Celeste finished the ritual, the fairy asked Helga to lie down. Next, the pixie placed her palms on Helga shoulders and continued to incant the spell. Helga convulsed once, and then her skin stretched outward as a second body arose from the first.

Penta expected the skin of the recipient of the spell to be translucent, but it remained the same as usual. The only difference was Helga's soul-body was nude.

Briefly, everyone except Helga looked on, fascinated, but they all lowered their eyes for their sister's modesty's sake. Helga tilted her head. "'Tis not as if any of you have not seen me without clothes before." She peered down at her body. "Oh, the markings have caused the delicacy, I believe."

Green spots, like measles but the color of moss, spread freckled across her body. Helga touched one of the spots and rubbed it, but it remained. "I shall not remove them *that* way, assuredly. As you see, I'm not the woman I claim to be."

Cinderella lifted her chin. "None of us are, dear sister. Certainly, my soul is more spotted than yours. None of us think the less of you."

Celeste waved her hand and produced a durable, white robe. Helga accepted it from the master spellcaster and slipped it on, tying it in front. "You should think less of me. However, my misdeeds are not my purpose here."

She strode toward Snow White. The youngest sister placed her hands on top of the mound of dirt. "I'm fearful. If you become infected, I'll never forgive myself."

Helga continued forward. "I'm more worried about

green spots than age spots."

Helga crouched next to her youngest sister and placed her hand on Snow White's cheek without hesitation. The youngest sister closed her eyes and leaned into her sister's hand, and sorrow overtook Penta as she watched the scene unfold. Snow White, the perennial provider of an abundance of hugs and greeting kisses, intensely desired a human touch.

Helga closed her eyes and took a deep breath. Fifteen seconds passed. Thirty. After a minute, Snow White opened her eyes. "It's not working."

"Give it time, sister." Distress filled Helga's response, unusual in her voice's normally steady timbre. "I can feel my power flow from me to you."

Helga placed her other hand on the opposite side of Snow White's face. Another two minutes passed. Snow White lowered her head. "It's not your talent that's at fault. Lifting a curse has never taken you this long."

After a further minute, Helga pulled back and frowned, speechless. Her eyes moistened with her misery. Without a word between them, the two came together again in a loving embrace.

The spectators hung their heads, wiping away tears of frustration and despair. Penta wanted to comfort their sister, to hold her like Helga, but didn't dare draw closer. She knew the others shared her dilemma. Celeste had her hands over her mouth. She lowered them to speak. "Helga, you must return to your body now. The spell ends soon."

Helga parted from Snow White and brushed back Snow White's hair. "I love you, dear sister."

"And I you." Snow White stood and faced them. "All of you."

Helga walked slowly back to her body and reclined into it, matching her pose. Her soul and body united once again.

Cinderella called to her sister. "I will not leave you. I'll be your constant companion from this point forward."

Snow White brushed the tears from her face. "Your

words comfort me, yet your remaining with me is not fair to your family. My best friend, Rose Red, won't stay away, though she too has a family. Let her come to me. Rose will help me with my plan."

Penta asked, "What plan?"

"I will journey with Rose to the coast, and she will ensure no one will approach me. Her eyes and ears as an archer are attuned to people moving at far distances. Please tell the dwarfs of my condition and ask them to make a boat large enough for me to sail away on. I will meet them at the shore to the sea directly ahead of this location and will send birds to guide them."

Cinderella stepped forward again, realizing full well what her sister intended. "You cannot."

Snow White put up her hand. "Do not step closer, Cinderella. I will board the ship alone and sail for an isolated island. I shall send birds to Celeste to inform her where I am located, and she shall hide it from external eyes. Once there, I will live out the rest of my days, however short they may be."

Helga rose. "Snow White, you know I have sailed around Kingdom and no uninhabited islands exist close to the mainland. If you survive long enough to reach such an island, you'll have no supplies. You're almost certain to die from drowning, sea creatures, or thirst."

Snow White returned her gaze to the mound. "I'm aware of it."

The sisters all protested at once, but Snow White stood and lifted her chin. "I anticipated this. I'm still a queen of Kingdom, and I still have the power to make a royal edict."

Cinderella crossed her arms. "Only if it passes by a vote."

"Cinderella, you forget that only one of us is required to proclaim a threat to Kingdom. You yourself proclaimed your stepmother a threat in order to imprison her. As such, I proclaim myself, Snow White, a threat to Kingdom. My punishment is banishment."

The sisters all cried out again and Snow White slowly

shook her head. "I say it again. I am a threat to all living in Kingdom. My condition has now killed an innocent man. Something must be done. Penta, do what is right and take them away and return to me with Rose. You always put Kingdom first. I trust you will do that now."

Penta opened her mouth to protest but sighed instead. She requested the other queens join hands to form a circle, working to convince Cinderella for over a minute. When at last they grasped each other's hands, they left Snow White behind.

5 - WHITE SAILS

Snow White's steady hike to the coast made her bones ache and her legs stiff. If she had had her youthful energy, a journey of this distance wouldn't have been a problem, but her feet throbbed now, and she tired easily. How awful she had been to the elderly, not understanding the great struggle traveling could be, that something as simple as walking required an effort. When older citizens had come to the castle to see her, she had acted as if their pilgrimage was a pleasant stroll, without recognizing how much they had sacrificed to visit there. If only she could go back, if only she could be cured, she would treat them differently.

She glanced at her companion, her best friend, no, her sister in soul if not in family. Rose Red Fyrekilm marched alongside her, twenty yards away, her eyes watchful for any approaching citizen of Kingdom, her hickory bow slung over her shoulder. Snow White had grown up on a farm, and her nearest neighbors were Rose Red's family, the Schells. Snow's mother, Faye, had turned crueler and crueler Snow's entire life, but the Schells remained true to Snow White, and their house was her safe haven.

After Hero had found Snow and helped her become a queen, Snow White had worried Rose would distance herself —but the two women had remained true to each other and to the roots of their friendship. Rose Red continued to call Snow White "Coal," her childhood nickname, when they were alone. In return, Snow White was one of the few allowed to call Rose "Red."

In the later years, when the two were admiring the new birds in the castle aviary, walking through the gardens, or chatting in Snow White's bedroom, Rose would give her frank opinions on the queens' newest edicts and describe the people's sentiments toward them, whether positive or negative. And when Snow White went to Rose's cabin, she pretended she was no longer a queen but merely a simple neighbor, come to visit the people she loved most in the world: Rose; her husband, Lolander; and their son—Hildegrant, the boy Snow loved above all other children.

Snow White halted to catch her breath, and Rose stopped beside her without a word, turning around to make sure no one approached from behind. Snow White recalled the scene the day before, after Penta had transported Rose here, and how Snow White had needed to invoke Lol's name to keep her friend from approaching. Rose had broken down, sobbing after exhausting every question about a cure. Composing herself, Rose had said, "You have asked me to accompany you to the gallows."

"No, 'tis only banishment," Snow White had answered.

But Rose's brow had wrinkled. "No, Coal. Do not lie to me. Not now."

And Snow White had not responded. They had walked

in silence and in brief discourse after that, and Rose had done what the queen had asked of her. She played the role of sentinel, guarding the rest of the world from the queen. Snow White trusted her friend above all others in this regard. Rose's skill at archery excelled even that of Snow's sister Helga, especially when the matter came to firing arrows to ward away strangers.

Rose's head swiveled as she took in their surroundings, a hilly, grassy plain with a few trees of stunted growth. One larger oak spread its leaves at the bottom of a steep incline, and Rose's eyes settled on it. "I recognize that tree from my travels here. Coal, we are about a half-day's journey to the coast."

Snow White straightened from her stooped position. "Let's take cover under the tree for the night, Red. I'm tired."

While the queen hobbled toward the oak, Rose Red gathered sticks on the way. "I will build you a fire while you rest."

"The curse is only partially at fault for my fatigue. I'm exhausted because I've let everybody down."

Rose picked up a half-dozen branches on the way to their resting place. "You have not let anyone down."

"All of this could've been avoided if I'd passed by the hags."

Rose, taking up Snow White's cue to use contractions, responded, "And they would've found you, or one of your sisters, and inflicted the curse at that time."

Snow White hung her head, white locks hanging down and covering her face. "Then I'm grateful they chose me. If they had selected one of my sisters, she would be dead now."

Rose arranged the sticks into a small pile. "I've been thinking about these witches during our march. I believe they chose you so that you would suffer the longest. 'Tis one of the most diabolical plots I have come across. Be assured, I'll find them and make them pay for it."

"Don't go near them, Red. Don't make me command you."

Rose didn't respond. Instead, she gathered more kindling and dry debris to place on top of her small pile. She reached into a pouch on her belt and removed two pieces of flint and struck them together. Sparks flew down onto the branches. Rose blew on the struggling flame and watched it grow. The tiny tongues of fire danced in Rose's pupils when they beheld her friend. "I cannot bear to see you suffer, Coal."

Snow White bit her lip. "I chose you for your company and to prevent others from coming near me. But I had another reason I thought you suited for this task. Of everyone I love, you alone are the only one who can bear this burden."

The flame wavered and caught on a small pile of leaves, gaining strength. Rose, still watching her handiwork, choked out a response. "You're confusing strength with an absence of feeling. I'm not heartless. Watching you in this condition, understanding what's next, is agony."

"Red, I'm sorry. If I had known my request would affect you in this way—"

"How could it not? I have no sister but you. All my most joyful moments include you. You tended to me when I was ill, remember? You knew my heart belonged to Lol before I did. You helped me see the error of my ways when Lol and I almost parted. You were my maid of honor and took care of my parents when I went on my honeymoon. You released me from your service when Lol was wounded in your quest for the throne. You were the first one I told when I was pregnant."

The fire sparked, and Rose leaned away from it. Snow White walked toward the flames, careful to keep a wide berth from her friend. "You don't know how much you've meant to me all my life," Snow White said.

Worry lines creased Rose Red's forehead. "I've given you nothing in return. You've shared your riches with me. I married Lol. I had a child. I know this was your heart's desire too. And I know with whom. You should've told Dear."

Tears escaped from Snow White's eyes and her chest heaved with emotion. "Don't remind me of unfulfilled wishes.

You think, if I could go back in time, I would've made the same choices? But all things happen for a purpose, and at least I won't leave behind a widower or an orphan."

Rose Red picked up sticks for a second campfire, her own. "So you say. Yet, my heart will be orphaned when you sail. I must take revenge for you, Coal. Give me your blessing to hunt the witches."

"*Don't* kill them, Red."

"I promise nothing."

"I could order you."

"You wouldn't dare."

Snow White held her hands out to the blaze. "I told you about the Reflection spell and Helga's green spots. I've thought about my own green marks. My specks represent the people I've killed or wronged, or peccadilloes that seemed right in the moment, but were paths to more serious transgressions. Don't place a green stain on your soul on account of me, my dear. I beg you."

Rose didn't reply.

In the morning, the queens and their family and friends sat at the dining table looking at each other through tired, bloodshot eyes. The servants had cleared their breakfast, but those gathered continued to sip their morning tea. The queens, Prince Roger, Prince Cuthbert John, Prince Danforth, Graddock, and Princess Beauty were all present, along with a human-sized Celeste.

Tangled hair, dark circles around their eyes, wrinkled clothes, and drawn expressions all told the tale of how the queens had spent the prior eight hours. Prince Roger set down his teacup. "Did any of us find any rest last night?"

All shook their heads in response, except Penta, who spoke. "We stayed up trying to find ways to help Snow White. My sisters and I would appreciate any counsel now, as our options are limited."

Graddock nodded his head at Penta. "We're all loyal to Snow White. Even to death."

Roger eyed Graddock. "Of course we are. As if you needed to say it."

Cinderella put her hand on top of Roger's. "At this time, dear one, we need to hear it."

Penta eyed her daughter, Beauty, who had a special relationship with her Aunt Snow White, being closest to her in age. Many nights Penta would have to retrieve Beauty from Snow White's room, interrupting their conversation—and Penta knew full well her daughter shared confidences with Snow White that she wouldn't with her. Penta felt pleased that Beauty spoke highly of Snow White's concern for others and emulated her compassion when listening to others' grievances.

Beauty dabbed at her eyes. Penta wanted to reach out and embrace her, but she had to be queen now, not mother. "Sisters, what have we found out?"

Valencia put her right hand to her forehead. "I shall go first, but I am afraid I have poor news. I have read half of *Sir Tristam's Guide to Kingdom*, the unabridged version, not the tale told to children. Anyway, I have not found a place in Kingdom yet that will heal Snow White."

Penta nodded at her. "Don't despair, Valencia. Helga?"

Helga brushed her hair from her eyes. "I have flown on a wyvern to our generals. No one knows anything about the hags, I'm afraid. I have summoned the dragons to aid me in looking for the crones. Good-Baer and his sister Paidae have come, but I can't be in multiple places at once."

"I will fly on Good-Baer, Tootsie," said Danforth.

Helga's cheeks colored at her husband's pet name for her,

but she smiled gratefully.

Penta turned to Cinderella. "Any news from Ozark?"

Cinderella put down her teacup. "I stayed with him all night. He slept on and off. We made a short list of possible items from outside of Kingdom that could be a key to healing Snow White. We don't know the location of any of the items, though, but if they can provide any hope..."

Penta leaned forward. "I will take any chance."

Cinderella nodded her agreement. "Our list includes the treasure chest of Zyrax, the sword Cusp, and the orbs of Sarsaparilla." She held up her hand. "Do not be vexed at the last one. We only discussed the white orb not the dark one. The white orb's and the treasure chest's whereabouts are unknown. And Cusp lies beyond our reach. The sword comes to you, not you to it."

Danforth leaned toward Helga. "I'm not familiar with any of these items. What is the sword of Cusp?"

Helga rubbed her husband's arm. "I sometimes forget you are from Earth. Cusp is a holy blade, supposedly the sword Mykhael the Archangel used to subdue the devil. 'Tis a divine sword, endowed with a spirit of its own. One of Kingdom's leaders, King Leopold the Magnificent, wielded it. In his thirty-three-year rule, Kingdom knew unprecedented peace. Legends say any wound using Cusp, no matter how small, is instant death. Cusp could assuredly remove Snow White's curse if we had it, but it vanished at King Leopold's death."

Penta stood. "We all have much to do."

Beauty rose from her chair. "Except me. For my part, I will write Aunt Snow White and tell her I am praying for her."

Penta's eyes filled with tears as her daughter stood and hurried away. After the young princess left the room, Helga broke the silence. "The girl may have chosen the best course of action."

That night, Cinderella, Valencia, and Penta gathered, leaving Helga to rest. Cinderella had had no luck finding the lost artifacts. Valencia had found one annotation about a healing waterspout in Sir Tristam's guide that she was now cross-referencing with an ancient manuscript. Penta had teleported across Kingdom, seeking the wisest men and women for their counsel.

"I have found nothing I did not already know," said Penta. "Although a curious event occurred in Bremen when I was visiting Sagely Nawbarker, our friend the cobbler. Someone delivered statues of the queens, but only of three of us. The artist did not identify himself. It's a good likeness of me, of Helga, and of you, Cinderella."

Cinderella yawned. "I didn't commission an artist."

Valencia creased her brows. "Nor I. Odd. I wonder if Snow White had them fashioned to surprise us."

"Tis a mystery for another time," commented Penta. "Our task grows ever more desperate."

A guard announced Prince Danforth, and the swarthy prince entered, striding along in leather riding boots. The expression across his brown complexion foretold his news. He began to bow before the queens when Penta stopped him. "Forget ceremony, and tell us what you've found out."

"Nothing you want to hear. I flew over the eastern... eftan...half of Kingdom today but I didn't spot three hags together. If I had found them, Good-Baer would have taken care of them."

Penta covered her face with her gloved hands, and her breath hitched. Danforth cleared his throat. "I have other news. The dwarfs have built a vessel and are sailing it around the edge of the coast."

Valencia brushed her hair away from her face. "So soon?"

Danforth regarded a spot on the floor. "Dwarven magic. I watched the construction for a few minutes. The seven of them have been working night and day."

"They deserve to be knighted," said Cinderella. "Why haven't we done it before?"

Penta sighed. "Because sometimes tragedy is required for us to see clearly. Danforth, when you return to your room, tell Helga to be ready in the morning. Snow White will be at the coast, and if the boat is magical, it should reach there tomorrow."

Danforth nodded, and Penta turned to her sisters who regarded her with panic. Penta closed her eyes. "We are nearly out of time."

Mid-afternoon the next day, Celeste received a message from a robin that Snow White had approached the coast and the dwarfs were nearing her location. At the rate they were sailing, they would reach Snow White just before nightfall. Celeste informed the queens, who hung their heads in despair and misery. Then, after a couple more hours of no progress, Penta gathered them all, including Celeste, and asked them to join in a circle.

The queens found themselves on a rocky beach with the dwarven longboat on the edge of the rocks, tied to a tree. The queens and Celeste appeared next to Rose Red. The seven dwarfs, all named after animals they resembled, remained off to the side, heads lowered. The salty spray of the water hung over everyone as they sought Snow White, who emerged from behind a boulder. "Be forewarned, sisters. My age has increased."

Her sisters couldn't repress their horror at Snow White's situation. The youngest queen's rheumy eyes stared back at them, and her wrinkled face struggled to form a smile while the recesses on her skin were like the surface of the moon above Kingdom. Her left eye drooped, and her white hair hung in clumps and tangles in stark contrast to its normal obsidian shininess.

Cinderella wept, and Valencia held a hand over her mouth. Gulls cried in the distance, putting into sounds what the queens didn't dare to express.

Celeste swallowed back her tears and spoke. "Snow White, my dear. I am going to cast the Reflection spell on you so you can approach us. 'Tis a complex spell, I'm afraid, so you will only have minutes."

Snow White nodded her understanding. "Long enough to say farewell."

Celeste recited the ritual, and Cinderella stepped forward. "You must not leave. We will find a cure."

"Do not step any closer! My suffering is nothing compared to how I would feel if one of you were cursed by my hand. Instead, let me embrace each of you for the last time."

The queens lined up youngest to oldest, and Penta guided Rose to the end of the line—the last to say goodbye. Celeste made a motion, and Snow White reclined on the ground and lay as still as death. After a moment, she rose from her body like one renewed. She held out her arms and marveled at her younger self with fewer than ten green spots blemishing her skin.

After slipping on a robe, Snow White approached a human-sized Celeste first, much to the pixie's surprise. Snow White leaned over and hugged her. The pixie wept on Snow White's shoulder while Snow White said, "I am not afraid of death. I know your beloved sister is there, awaiting me. The thought of her fills me with comfort."

Snow White left the pixie and moved on to the dwarfs, standing in two rows. She kneeled before each one, said his name, and hugged him. When she came to Dear, clearly her favorite, she trembled. His face lit up. "Do you recall how we used to tell jokes to each other when you hid at our cottage?" he asked. "I have a joke for you."

Snow White tilted her head. "This is no time—"

"What is a late furry creature called?"

Snow White shook her head.

"A tardy-along." He raised his eyebrows. "Tardalong?"

The youngest queen barked a short laugh and then exploded in giggles. When she tried to catch her breath, she snorted through her nose and all the dwarfs smiled through their tears. Snow White had hugged Dear's brothers with warmth, but she pulled Dear to her fiercely. "Oh, what a horrible joke. I command you to never tell it again."

She pulled away from the dwarf, who choked back his tears. "As long as I live," pledged Dear.

Reluctantly, the queen released him and wiped away her tears. She hurried over to Cinderella, took Cinderella's hands to draw her close, and hugged her. When they parted, Cinderella's tears streamed down her face. "Ozark is dying. You're dying. I lose not two but three—my father, my sister, and my best friend. The last two in one person."

"I'll pray for Ozark's soul," promised Snow White.

"How can you think of him when you suffer so?" asked Cinderella.

"Thinking of others is a balm to me. My grief is hard to bear when I consider only myself."

Snow White placed her hand on her sister's cheeks and moistened her fingertips with Cinderella's tears. She then wiped away the ashes on her sister's face. Snow White looked Cinderella directly in the eyes. "Now *you* are the fairest in the land."

Snow White lingered a moment but next moved on to Valencia. She reached into her pocket. "I have something for you. Something I have carried since we met in Exile."

She revealed a burnt match and handed it to Valencia. Snow White said, "With this match, I gained a sister, Little Match Girl. It's one of the most precious things I carry."

The smallest queen received the match and held it to her heart. She wiped her eyes as she spoke. "I read as much as I could in the library. A tome speaks of a legend, a waterfall that can wash away any curse. No one knows precisely where it is, but if you found it, it would cure you. The waterfall exists in the sea, not on land, and it's not of Kingdom origin. You still have a chance, Snow White."

Snow White wrapped her arms around Valencia. "Leave it to you, my brilliant sister, to have hope in these times. I trust you completely. In what direction should I sail?"

"I...don't know."

"Use your gift and choose one."

Valencia raised her trembling hand and pointed outward to the sea in a southwestern direction. "That way."

Snow White smiled at her. "That is the way I'll go."

She moved onto Helga and enfolded her sister's hands. "Helga the Light-Bearer."

"More like Helga the Grief-Bearer." Tears streamed down Helga's face. "I have tried to find the witches to reverse the spell, but I've failed you."

"Not in the least. You have never failed me, nor do you do so today. Don't forget. You are Helga the Honorable. Helga the Curse-Lifter." She paused and added a title Helga had never given herself. "Helga the Holy One." Snow White embraced her. "I wish you health, happiness, and my blessings, unworthy as they are."

"I'll miss you," said Helga. "You'll never know how much."

Snow White released Helga and turned to Penta, who heaved with such emotion that she gasped for breath. "Kid sister, I can't bear it," said Penta. "I've let you down. I was supposed to ensure you lived happily ever after, as in Hero's stories."

Snow White wrapped her arms around her older sister. "But I *have* lived happily ever after. When was I in want, or miserable, or suffering with you at my side? I was a queen—better yet, I was a benevolent ruler. You taught me how to lead. You taught us all. Penta, you made my happily-ever-after possible."

"But I should've looked out for you."

"You speak like my mother, yet you are but my sister. Motherhood suits you, but let it not lead you to despair. Our own mother would be so proud of you. She knew best that we all must die someday."

When they parted, Snow White said, "Good-bye, big sis."

Penta couldn't answer; she was too choked with tears.

Snow White then faced her best friend, Rose Red. Rose shook her head, still in shock, unable to cry. Snow stepped forward, but her friend stepped back, out of her reach. Rose said, "Do you remember our promise? You said, 'We will not leave each other.'"

Snow White responded, "And you said, 'Never so long as we live.' The promise ends here, I'm afraid, but we will continue to uphold it in paradise."

"I won't say good-bye. You can't die this way, Coal."

"Please, Red, do not let me leave without embracing you and saying farewell."

"'Tis not fair."

"No, but even life in Hero's fairy tales isn't always fair," agreed Snow White. "My last request is to hold my best friend once more and remember the love we've shared."

Rose hung her head, and Snow White rushed forward and hugged her, planting a kiss on her lips. "When my life was nothing but misery, you made it worth living. If I die, I die knowing someone loved me when I needed her the most. Do not reflect on the injustice of my suffering, my dear. Reflect on what you meant to me, and I hope, what I mean to you."

Rose started crying, unable to respond.

Snow White released her and returned to her body. Instantly, her elderly frame shook and re-animated. As she rose, everyone noticed a figure near the body—Dear, the dwarf. He reached out and took Snow White's hand.

She snatched her hand away quickly. "Oh, Dear! What have you done?"

Dear reached again and put his hand on hers. The hand showed immediate signs of aging. "I will not have you make this journey alone, my queen. You are too precious to me for me to live without you."

Snow White's tears rolled down her face. "You should not have! My Dear, I will be the cause of your death."

"Not you, but the curse," he said. "If I can bring you comfort in your final hours, then my life will be complete." The dwarf blushed. "You...you are and have always been...the desire of my heart."

Snow White cried harder. "You should have had a life with a nice sturdy wife, a blushing bride with a full beard, and young, happy children. 'Tis unfair, my Dear, for me to be the object of your heart."

"Has Hero taught you nothing? True love may not be fair, but 'tis always beautiful."

Snow White leaned down and tilted her head, and her lips met Dear's. She closed her eyes at her first romantic kiss, binding her to him until they died, as was Kingdom's custom. When they parted, she continued crying but said, "Hero's story had a handsome prince rescue me. And now it has come true."

They held hands and walked together to the boat. Holding Dear's hand, Snow White felt her elderly face shine with serenity. The dwarfs stood aside, each one a proper distance from her, but standing at attention, loyal to their queen to the end. She proceeded up the gangplank to the small ship, and

Dear cast off. Snow White turned around and faced the shore.

"It's true the world can be cruel, but I believe in people, and most of them are kind and merciful. I've been cursed for three days, but it's nothing compared to the six years I've spent with my sisters, the six months I spent with my beloved dwarfs, and the lifetime I spent with my Rose, my best friend. I am the most fortunate of all because of the tremendous affection you have each shown me. I love you all."

Snow White raised her hand, and the boat, piloted by Dear, headed in the direction Valencia indicated. Those on shore watched her sail toward a setting sun, quickly becoming a silhouette, the boat shrinking into a smaller and smaller shape, and then disappearing in the sun's dying haze.

6 - PENTA REVEALS

After returning to the palace, the queens each mourned Snow White differently. Cinderella read correspondence from Snow White received during times when they were parted. Helga cried on Danforth's shoulder, Valencia used her matches to light candles in the chapel, and Penta broke the news to Beauty.

The queens had agreed to separate, then come back together later in the evening.

When they later gathered in the throne room to determine what to do next, Snow White's empty chair carved into a massive tree trunk served as a reminder of how much they had lost.

With Celeste's magic, the queens sent a message all over Kingdom relaying Snow White's fate and the deadly threat of the three hags. They were careful to describe the three witches in detail, using Snow White's description of them. The citizens loved the fairest queen, and the queens feared mobs would hunt innocent elderly women in their thirst for revenge.

The people of Town, Kingdom's royal city, gathered outside of the castle that night. The tradespeople closed all taverns and businesses. Bakers, merchants, blacksmiths, painters, soldiers all stood next to each other in the courtyard. A group of young girls dressed as Snow White, her fans, stared up, tear tracks running across the powder on their faces. Everyone present held aloft a candle, illuminating the darkness. The queens stood on their balcony, observing their people, as a sea of small flames lit up the front lawn and extended down into town. Overwhelmed by grief, Cinderella turned away. Valencia said, "I doubt Snow White knew how much she was loved."

The following day, while Penta and Valencia were questioning a council of mages on the details of an aging spell, a voice cried out from Penta's ring. "Penta, my queen. Help us!"

Penta recognized the voice as that of Sagely Nawbarker, a friend and a cobbler of Bremen. "What has happened?"

"The statues I told you about transformed into three elderly women. They are here killing people with magic."

Penta gripped Valencia's wrist and they both teleported to the throne room. Penta then vanished and reappeared with their two other sisters and Celeste within seconds. They quickly formed a circle and Penta grabbed their hands, transporting them to the center of Bremen.

Bremen, primarily a merchant town, featured wide dirt streets surrounded by wooden buildings. The queens appeared on a central road. As their eyes adjusted to the bright sunshine after the dim room, they heard the sounds of screams and running footsteps.

Between buildings a street over from where they stood, they spied a merchant with his hands raised in the air. Lightning exploded from out of their view and struck the man. He shook violently, foam dripping from his mouth, and dropped to the ground.

Celeste reduced herself to her pixie size and zipped past the queens to the next street. The queens chased down a narrow alley after Celeste. When they arrived, they spied three elderly women along the street watching townspeople run for cover.

A hag with a long, crooked nose, puffy eyes, and sallow skin flicked her fingers and emitted a blast of lightning at a barmaid hiding behind a wagon. The witch wore a folded-over, dusty hat and a hoop earring in one ear. A second crone, an obese woman with frizzy hair, squeezed her fingers together as an elderly peddler howled when her arm snapped in two. The third old witch, a thin woman with a sharp chin and slitted eyes like those of a snake, cupped her hands together. She blew blue smoke at a teenage girl who gagged and wrapped her hands around her neck.

Before anyone could speak, Celeste gestured, and a golden, glowing ring appeared around the hags. The victims scrambled away, while the witches turned toward the pixie and the queens. Wicked smiles creased their ancient faces. The magic-wielder with the hat spoke first. "You have arrived. We wondered how many we would have to kill to gain your attention."

Penta stepped forward. "Who are you? Why are you doing this?"

The woman with the hat chuckled. "Penta Emily Corden, we do not answer to you nor your sisters. We know you act like a queen, and think yourself above everyone, but you are not above *us*. Nonetheless, we are not without manners."

The witch who wore a hat stepped forward, curtsied,

then spat at the queens. The spittle landed at the queens' feet and sizzled into the ground. "Picana, lead witch."

The sharp-chinned wielder of magic stepped up next to Picana. She also curtsied, then made Kingdom's rudest gesture at the queens. "Tomana."

The third witch edged between the other two. She bowed instead of curtsied, turned around, and released gas as Picana chuckled. The flatulent witch then faced the queens. "Mya."

The queens, never ones for pompous acts or proper manners, were still outraged. Cinderella's lisp was noticeable when she shouted. "You will address the leaders of Kingdom with respect!"

Tomana mocked her. "Cinderella Jolly, the belle of the ball, sistersth."

Valencia's nostrils flared. "You know us. Tell us why you have cursed our sister and killed these people?"

Picana cackled. "Why, Valencia Arkenson, we only murdered people to summon you here. Let their deaths be on your heads."

Tomana nodded. "We had to do something to pass the time."

The frizzy-haired hag, Mya, clapped her hands. "Wait. Bore. Kill. More!"

Picana patted her neighbor's arm. "Yes, dear. We do like to kill."

Helga pulled out her flail with a spiked ball attached by a chain. The points on the ball had been blunted to avoid drawing blood from her opponents, yet the Nor queen was a master of the weapon. Dressed in her finest chain armor, she marched forward. "I assure you, this is the last time you shall murder anyone."

Picana turned her attention to Helga. "You are Helga the Brave, Helga the True-Hearted, Helga the Light-Bearer. The elves made your armor, did they not? I like armor because it likes lightning."

Mya raised her hands, and Celeste's golden ring of magic dissolved. Picana pointed at Helga, and lightning exploded from her fingertips, engulfing the warrior queen. The witch cackled. "How is that for bearing light? Lightning, that is."

Helga screamed in agony, dropped her flail, and clutched at the air. Immediately, Celeste waved her hand and the lightning dissipated. Trembling violently with the aftershock, Helga slumped to the ground. Cinderella and Valencia ran to assist her.

Readying a spell, Celeste spoke in a language unknown to the queens. Picana nodded her head at the fairy. "Ah, the poxy pixie Celestial."

Tomana spoke, and as she did, the words appeared in midair out of her mouth. "Ineffectual, impotent, useless, weak."

The words, when spoken, materialized in the middle of the air, flew at Celeste, and struck her. Each word hit her like a blow and knocked her backward. The hag Tomana advanced, yelling at her. "You couldn't save your *sister* and now she is *dead.*"

The words "sister" and "dead" sprang from the witch's mouth and pierced Celeste's body then dissipated. The pixie cried with pain as blood flowed down her side and leg where the harsh words had stabbed her.

Mya gestured, and a giant hand appeared above Celeste. Abnormally large fingers carefully pinched Celeste's left wing and held her up by it. As it did so, Celeste's body slumped. She was conscious but her arms hung at her sides. Shock and distress overtook her features. "My queens! I…I am helpless."

Penta disappeared and quickly appeared behind Picana with a cudgel in her hand. She swung it but it evaporated as Mya laughed. "Eyes behind, eyes before, cannot beat the witches' score."

Cinderella squared her shoulders and pointed at Tomana. Her target glared at the queen and spoke in a low voice. "Your ability to make me follow my conscience won't work on me. I rid myself of that burdensome trifle long ago." She gestured to the rhyming witch. "Sister?"

Mya balled her fists and then opened them in a sudden movement. Cinderella shrieked in terror as popping sounds like firecrackers emerged from her own hands. Her digits twisted, and she wailed in pain, all of her knuckles broken.

Picana turned around to face an astonished Penta. She took hold of the queen's throat and applied pressure. Penta, though, grabbed the crone's gnarled hands with her gloves and squeezed hard. The queen's metallic hands were stronger than most in Kingdom, and her ability to pry apart her opponent's fingers caused the hag's eyes to widen. Picana opened her mouth in response and a small scorpion scuttled out of it. The arachnid launched itself at Penta, stinging her on the face.

Helga slowly stood, shedding her mail with help from Valencia. Valencia turned toward the witches and reached into her pocket, holding up a circular, smooth stone. She mumbled and pointed at Picana, but her efforts only resulted in a flash of light and the sound of a crack of a whip. Valencia stepped back, surprised.

While the failed wish didn't affect the hags, it kept their attention on the queens. Behind the evil trio, a unigard with a rider rounded a corner at the far end of the street. The horse's hooves made no sound.

Picana shook her head at Valencia. "Your wishes won't hurt us. We have magical protection. How would you like to join your simpering sister as an elderly maid? No, I don't believe that would bother you as much as it did her. Perhaps I can cut that pretty brain out of your skull?"

Mya blew on her open hands and created a large sphere containing multi-colored leaves. She flung her hands and the sphere floated above Valencia and then popped, raining the leaves down on the wish-bearing queen. These leaves, however, had razor-sharp edges. One sliced across Valencia's hand, leaving a thin line of blood; another cut open the material on the shoulder of her dress.

Valencia retreated from the leaves, which rose back into the air and followed her. Helga had nearly removed her armor. Penta's face sported a purple bruise that spread with thin filaments over her cheeks as she stomped on the scorpion that had attacked her. Cinderella ran at the witches, holding her fingers at her sides. Agony etched on her face, she lowered her head as if to butt the old hags like a goat.

Seemingly amused, the witches looked on as the unigard galloped nearer. A green-cloaked stranger readied an arrow in her bow and aimed it at Picana. The arrow sprang from the weapon, while the missile multiplied into two others, each one aimed at a crone. The arrows, in the wink of an eye, burrowed into the backs of the three witches, tossing them forward onto their faces.

The unigard pulled up in the middle of the street, the newcomer remaining on its back. The green-cloaked stranger held open her palm, and the arrow buried in the witches disappeared, then reformed into one missile in the archer's outstretched hand, bloody from three deadly hits. The bodies sizzled into smoke and vanished.

The queens looked to their rescuer, who tucked away the arrow. She reached up and pulled back her hood. Rose Red sat expressionless on the horse's back. "You are welcome."

A cheer arose, and the citizens of Bremen lifted Rose Red onto their shoulders and carried her to the queens. They set her down in front of the sisters, and Rose, grim-faced and solemn, lowered to her knees and bowed her head.

Celeste, now free of the witch's spell, touched Penta's face, eradicating the scorpion's poison. Penta's eyes remained on Rose Red. "You killed them."

Rose Red said, "As it is not war and I am not a soldier, by your own laws you must charge me with murder. Arrest me and take me to the royal castle."

Shouts of "no" and "spare her" arose as the queens looked on uncomfortably. After Celeste healed each queen, Penta held out her hand. "Rise, Rose Red. Follow us."

When the queens, Celeste, and Rose Red all took each other's hands, Penta teleported them to the throne room. Without a word, the queens ascended to their thrones and sat down, contemplating the green-cloaked archer. Celeste exited rapidly.

Rose Red stood before them. "Announce my sentence."

Penta set her hands on her cream-colored chemise and leaned forward. "How did you know they would attack in Bremen?"

"The statues appeared around the time the hags encountered Snow White," replied Rose Red. "I followed my intuition and assumed they were connected to the witches. I have been watching Bremen closely."

Cinderella's eyes shifted to the archer's quiver. "You have a weapon that belongs to us."

"Indeed. Snow White gave me Lycrotta's Arrow when the bandit uprising occurred near home." Rose retrieved the arrow and held it out to the queens. "I return it now to you. I did not steal it. Surely you know I could not."

"Yet you did not use it the way Snow White intended, to disarm your targets," said Penta. "She specifically asked you to refrain from seeking revenge."

"She did, and I specifically ignored her. My plan was to kill the vermin responsible for her death, and no power in Kingdom would sway my decision."

Penta leaned forward. "Rose, you know full well how much we abhor killing as a solution to a threat. You were involved in our coup d'état and followed our orders not to kill then. Your place was not to decide whether the witches lived or died."

Rose shuffled. "I did it in honor of my friend."

"Honor?" Helga's voice rose. "Putting an arrow in the crones' backs? Disobeying your queens? Ignoring your best friend's instructions? You call that honorable?"

Rose said, "I knew you would sentence me. You believe that taking a life for a crime, even one this monstrous, is rarely necessary. I believe it too but not this time. I had to take action."

Valencia gripped the armrests on her throne. "What about your family? What about Lol and Hildegrant?"

"My husband knows. He attempted to dissuade me."

Penta stood. "And your child? Were you thinking of Hildegrant when you set out to do this? You have put us in the heartbreaking circumstance of having to sentence you, separating you from your family, Rose Red."

"I knew what would happen when I made my choice," Rose answered. "When it comes to children, we do not always think rationally, but I am a better mother to him for killing the witches than holding my hand. You must send me to prison. I do not blame you and gladly go to Kingdom's dungeon to await my fate."

Cinderella put her hands on the sides of her face. "Why did you do this, Rose Red?"

Rose Red had held her composure until that question. Now her face fell, and she struggled to regain her calm. "I lost my queen, my friend, my sister at the same time. 'Tis too much to bear. In her memory, I did the one thing I could do. I prevented the death of the rest of her beloved sisters. Snow White would have wanted me to give my life for you, and so I have."

Before the queens could respond, the rings on their fingers and Rose's made a noise. The sound of an elderly cackle resounded loudly throughout the room, echoing across the chamber. Penta held her hand out and regarded the ring as if it were a venomous spider. "Who is this?"

"Why, I introduced myself to you earlier. Picana, lead witch. I'm standing in the courtyard of your castle."

Helga sprang from her throne and ran for the door as fast as a cheetah rushing toward its prey. She lifted her flail above her head as she exited the room. Penta gestured to the others to gather around to teleport them to the courtyard.

"Oh, don't bother coming to us," laughed Picana. "We'll

be gone by the time you reach here."

Penta addressed her ring. "You're dead."

"You want to see death? We left you a present in the courtyard. Ah, here comes your sister."

Penta again went pale and grabbed Valencia's and Cinderella's shoulders to teleport, but a new voice from her ring interrupted her. "Oh, Redeemer, how...?"

"We're coming, Helga."

"Don't!" A gagging sound. "I saw them vanish. They're still alive."

Penta paused, and then Helga said, "They disemboweled a number of our soldiers out here."

Penta's lip trembled. "How many?"

"Perhaps thirty? I will call for others to remove the dead, then join you."

The sisters stood looking at each other. "How did the witches survive?" asked Penta.

Rose Red was the first to blush red with fury. "Return Lycrotta's Arrow to me. This time I will guide it through their hearts."

Penta turned sharply to her. "No." She shook her head. "You are excused from sentencing. You have killed no one."

"But—"

Penta held up a finger. "That is a royal order, Rose."

Rose folded her arms.

Penta addressed the ring. "Helga and Celeste, meet us in the consultation room. I'd rather be there right now than here."

Penta put her hand on her sisters' shoulders, and they teleported and landed in another room, a more compact one, with a table, chairs, and sideboard. The queens sat at the table, and Celeste appeared just as Helga entered.

Helga dropped a note on the table they were gathered around. "They left this behind. 'Tis their terms. They say we are welcome to rule this land as long as we don't interfere with their activities. They want access to toads, newts, leprechaun gold, troll toenails, goblin skin, and pixie scalps. And they demand ten newborns a year."

Celeste clasped her hands together. "All ingredients for powerful, dark magic. How can I stop them? I could not even protect you!"

Penta said, "'Tis curious they were resistant to your magic. They avoided your detection and removed your defense spells."

Celeste lowered her head. "You need someone better to guard you."

Penta brushed back a lock of hair. "We want you to protect us. I trust you above all."

Cinderella's lower lip trembled. "But what are we going to do?"

Penta's gloved fingers played with the lace on the end of her sleeves. "The first thing we are going to do is research these hags. A way to defeat evil always exists. They boast of their invulnerability, but we know they lie. Heaven's rules dictate we are all frail in some aspect."

Helga turned to Celeste. "Do you know of a spell that allows a person to live forever?"

Celeste shook her head. "No. We who were destined to perish must die eventually."

"Demons and other creatures inhabit the next phase of life and they cannot die." Helga leaned forward. "Are we sure they don't belong to that class of creature?"

Celeste lifted her head. "Their spells indicated they were human. All species put their mark on magic—human, pixie, elven. If these three were demons, their brand of magic would reveal it."

"So, they can be killed," said Penta. "Perhaps if they are killed a second time, they will remain dead."

Helga set her elbows on the table. "We need to find a way to confine them, not kill them."

"Agreed." Penta cinched the cuffs at her wrists and then loosened them. "I am trying to establish the range of their power. If they can be killed, they can be confined, or perhaps reduced in power some way."

Celeste regarded Cinderella. "We need to travel to Ozark. I need his help."

Cinderella reached across the table and placed her hand on Celeste's. "Celeste, he is ill. You are now Kingdom's greatest magic-wielder. Not Ozark."

Valencia peered into the pixie's eyes. "Celeste, you must deliver us from these women. If not you, then who?"

Cinderella lowered her eyes to a small drop of wax on the tabletop. With her index finger, she scratched at the wax while Valencia grabbed a lock of her own hair and rubbed it between her fingers. "I wonder..." Valencia said.

Valencia looked up, eyes alight. "How did these three escape Ozark's attention? They must have Traveled here from another world. Earth."

Cinderella stopped her chore and regarded her sister. "But, Valencia, 'tis impossible. We have been to Earth. No magic exists there."

"Do not forget our powers worked on Earth," replied Valencia. "Perhaps Earth has magicians hidden from its citizens."

Again, Penta pulled at the strings attached to her cuffs. "Valencia, you are without a doubt the most inspired of all of us. Yet as a resident of Earth for eighteen months, I must disagree. If magic-wielders reside on Earth, they are that world's greatest secret."

Valencia tried to interrupt, but Penta held up her hand. "With how information flows so freely and in the open there, I don't believe a spell-caster lives on Earth undetected."

Valencia folded her hands. "We must try."

Penta smiled at her sister. "I am not dismissing the proposal. Your intuition, as usual, serves us well. You have sparked an idea that has perhaps a better chance of success."

Cinderella leaned forward. "And what is that?"

"We must find a magic-wielder greater than Celeste outside of Kingdom."

Valencia sighed. "But you just told us no such person exists on Earth, or if he did, he would be hard to find."

Penta gazed at Helga, who raised her eyebrows while the rest regarded the two, expecting one of them to speak. Penta said, "I have a confession to make. When I leave Kingdom with my friend Alice, we do not always go to Earth. In fact, Earth is not our usual destination."

Cinderella looked puzzled. "Where do you go?"

"Valencia, Cinderella. More worlds exist than Kingdom and Earth."

Helga's face lit up. "Glinda!"

Valencia blinked rapidly. "Where is Glinda?"

"Glinda is not a place. She is a person," explained Penta. "Glinda is a magic-wielder in another world, a world Helga and I visited years ago."

Shocked, Cinderella turned toward her sisters. "Helga. Penta. Why did you not tell us?"

Color rose in Helga's cheeks, but Penta spoke before Helga had a chance to defend herself. "Don't be angry with her. I swore her to secrecy as part of my arrangement with Alice in order to Travel. My adoptive father lives in Glinda's world, and I visit him there."

Torchlight sparkled in Valencia's brown eyes. "What about Hero? Would he know of this Glinda?"

Penta tilted her head in an encouraging way. "With his study of fantasy literature, I have no doubt he has read of her and her world of Oz. Glinda is a popular figure on Earth, a good witch, and more. She is the essence of magic herself. Oz is unlike Kingdom. Magic is more commonplace there. Ordinary people use it all of the time without casting spells. And the absolute best magic-wielder in Oz is a witch of indeterminate age, pure of heart, named Glinda."

Valencia asked, "Is she as good as Celeste?"

"I would welcome it if she is," Celeste interrupted. "This is not a competition."

Cinderella lifted her head hopefully. "Do you think convincing this Glinda to come here will be possible?"

"We will contact her," Penta said. "But I like Valencia's idea as well. I think, before going on to Oz, we should make a stop at Earth and pick up our specialist on fantasy. My intuition is not as sharp as Valencia's, but it tells me we'll need him."

"And her," added Celeste, the pixie's eyes twinkling.

7 - WE'RE OFF TO SEE THE...WITCH?

Harold

Valencia finished her tale and set down her wine glass. Everyone had shed tears throughout the story, and Sondra had stood and hugged Valencia when she described the queens meeting with Snow White for the last time. Overcome by emotion, Valencia released my wife and left the room.

When Valencia returned, she continued the story of Snow White's departure in halting sentences, staring at us with red eyes. She ended her narration on hope: hope Sondra and I would know about Oz, hope I would have the Oz books at the ready, hope Glinda would come to the immediate aid of Kingdom. Valencia folded her hands, teary-eyed and pale.

"Will you help us?" she asked.

I made my way to Valencia and embraced her. "Of course, we will. We can't leave you in the lurch. 'Leaving you in the lurch' means to leave you in an unfortunate situation."

Valencia wiped her tears away after we separated. "I know what it means. It's on Cinderella's list."

Sondra turned to Alice. "But, Alice, you know the Oz stories. Why come to us?"

Alice sipped from her second glass of wine. "I know about Oz, but I'm a Traveler. I'll help and offer information. Though you and Harold aren't Travelers, you've Traveled across worlds. You're allowed—" Alice made air quotes around the word 'allowed.' "—to make a significant difference. Because of the Guild rules, Travelers aren't supposed to change the worlds they visit."

Valencia moved to the love seat and squeezed in hip to hip next to Graddock. "However, you told Penta the Traveler's Guild wouldn't mind helping us."

"Absolutely," said Alice. "The witches aren't from Kingdom, and we need to set things right. Their presence there resembles a foreign organism without its own predators invading an ecosystem. They'll upset the balance, perhaps leading to the end of that world. The Guild sent me to Kingdom once Travelers stationed there reported the witches had returned. I met with Penta a few hours after the queens decided to involve you, Harold—and Sondra. We left earlier today."

Sondra shook her head. "I still don't understand, Alice. If you know about Oz, why didn't you tell them about it yourself? Why involve us?"

"I never read the books," said Alice. "I've only Traveled to Oz."

Alice then lowered her gaze and shook her head, seeming to regret what she had just revealed. "Yes, some years before, I went to Oz. I haven't been back since."

I leaned back in my chair. "Why not?"

Alice sighed. "I knew this was going to come out at some

point. The truth is I'm banished from Oz indefinitely. Oh, stop looking at me that way. What I did was minor."

Valencia spread out her arms. "Banished from a world? Was it by the Guild?"

"Not them. Glinda."

Sondra rubbed her forehead. "So how are we supposed to get there?"

"You've forgotten my power, Sondra. I only escort people to other worlds as long as we're not on Earth. Whether I had been banished or not, you'd have to find another way to go to Oz. But even if I could take you there, I'd need to leave before Glinda sent her flying monkeys after me."

Sondra peered over her wine glass. "Flying monkeys? I thought the Wicked Witch was the one who had flying monkeys."

"The book is different from the version popular culture knows," I said. "The monkeys obey the wearer of the Golden Cap. But how would Glinda know you're there, Alice?"

Alice rubbed her temple with her index finger. "How doesn't matter. Glinda will know we're there the instant we arrive. She knows everything about Oz."

"Is she going to hold it against us if you help us?" Valencia asked.

Alice sipped a little more of her wine. "The books don't do Glinda justice. She won't hold my minor offense against you, because she's friendly to people in distress. I wouldn't be surprised if she knows why you've come."

I laced together my fingers. "Is she a Traveler?"

Alice stared at her glass. "Glinda is not a Traveler, but she has Traveled. She probably knows more about the worlds than any actual Traveler. She is Glinda the Good Witch, an exemplary witch with strong morals. She banished me, but she doesn't dislike me, because she knows I'm a decent woman. Glinda says she has exiled me for my own good. You have to understand, Glinda's not a person—she's the essence of positive magic. Ageless, powerful, but humble, approachable. She is unique across the worlds."

Valencia tilted her head forward. "She will help us?"

Alice ran her finger around the rim of her glass. "I believe she will."

I put my chin on my palm. "You keep saying 'worlds.' Do you know of more than three? I've always assumed Wonderland is in Kingdom but is it a separate world?"

Alice drew in a sharp breath. "The Guild wouldn't like it if I told you." Yet she nodded her head.

"And others exist?"

"I shouldn't say."

Valencia came to Alice's rescue. "Clearly she's not comfortable revealing more. Let's focus on our quest instead."

Sondra set down her wine glass. "Harold can go to Oz, and I'll go to Kingdom to help my sister, Celeste."

Valencia jutted out her chin. "You most certainly will not go to Kingdom. It's far too dangerous."

"But—"

"I won't have it, Sondra! Celeste would be enraged if I sent you to Kingdom. Don't cross her. You'll accompany us to Oz and then return here. Hero...Harold, you have the Oz books?"

"Of course."

Valencia stood. "I should go read them then. We'll set off in the morning."

I nodded to the front of the house. "Then let's go into the library and talk."

The rest of the party went to bed while Valencia and I spent the next three hours, pouring over the Oz books, focusing on Glinda. We talked until early morning after Valencia had to nudge me when I fell asleep researching a name in *The Patchwork Girl of Oz*. After I awoke, Valencia rested a hand on my shoulder. "You need to rest."

"I'll be fine."

"No, I insist. If I were queen here, I'd order you to go to bed."

I shut the book. "Maybe we both better sleep for a few hours. After all, we're Traveling tomorrow."

"Harold, I've been thinking. Perhaps you should remain here."

"What? Why?"

"Because the journey is dangerous," replied Valencia. "No one wants to see you or Sondra in harm's way, but I have another reason. I hope I'm not intruding here... Are you and Sondra in a good place?"

"Sure. We love this house."

Valencia flexed her fingers. She had a habit of rolling a match between her fingers, and I recognized she was repeating the motion sans match. "I meant..."

"Our marriage? Don't worry about us. We're good."

Valencia stopped moving her fingers. "I am happy for you two. Do you remember the two statues outside of the palace? Of you and Planet holding your arms out to each other?"

I blushed. "Yes. Jeez, don't bring that up in front of Sondra. Even though Planet and Sondra look the same, she's not Planet. She isn't thrilled about the statues' poses."

"Then she'll be pleased to know Celeste threw a spell to change the statues. They no longer face each other. Celeste commissioned a sculptor to build a statue of Sondra to go with yours. Her spell made the original statues move and reposition themselves, and now your statue is embracing Sondra's. Planet's statue is more majestic, not like the real Planet assuredly, but the time has come for legends to replace reality."

"That sounds nice."

Valencia's fingers fiddled with a chain, and she pulled out a pendant with a ruby inset. "The result is how everything should be. Yet, my intuition is telling me our trip to meet with Glinda may be better if you do not come with us." She thumbed the ruby. "Were you and Sondra in the middle of an argument when I called? She was quick to want to separate from you. Is she still struggling with the fact that she and

Planet are so similar? What did you call them? Parallels?"

I gulped. What did she intuit then? "No. Sondra's at peace with being a parallel. Did you know I thought up the word 'parallel,' and now Alice's Guild is using it? Alice told me she's aware of other parallels other than Planet and Sondra. Remember Roger's parallel the last time you were here?"

Valencia dropped the necklace pendant down under her neckline. "What a mess that was. But Harold, is this a good time for you and Sondra to visit Oz?"

I regarded Valencia. She herself was the daughter of my dead sister's parallel. When I had first met her, I had been struck by how much she resembled my sibling, Lauren. I thought back to when I'd met Valencia and we'd had a private conversation on a ship in Kingdom. Valencia had shared a secret with me then, an innermost fear. I was shocked at how much she trusted me. Perhaps I should return the favor.

"Sondra and I are trying to have a baby. However, our efforts aren't going well. So far...nothing."

Valencia clasped her hands together, eyes alight with hope. "I'm sure it will happen in time."

"Maybe not. We've seen a fertility doctor. Our chances are much lower than those of a typical couple. Not zero, but not good."

"You keep trying." A little pink colored the queen's cheeks. "This couldn't be too large of a burden?"

I leaned back on my hands. "You'd think trying to have a baby wouldn't be so hard. But, in reality, it's become a chore. Certain times of the day are optimal, certain times of the month. Yeah, I can see it in your expression. No sympathy, there, but secretly, and this is something I haven't told Sondra, I'm sort of relieved."

"Relieved?" Valencia's eyes widened.

"Maybe I'm not father material."

A gentle smile blossomed on Valencia's face. "I don't believe it for a second. If it's meant to be, you and Sondra will welcome a wee one someday, and you'll be the best of fathers."

Tired and abashed that I had revealed the truth, I lied, "You're probably right."

Valencia recognized the fib, and she accepted it gracefully. She dropped her attention to the book in her hands. "I am of two minds about asking you to join us. I don't want you or Sondra to be hurt. I've seen enough suffering these past five days for a lifetime. Yet my intuition is at the same time saying you should join us on the quest."

"I'm a good luck charm," I joked.

"No, you're similar to a blind spot in Evil's eye. Our enemies never see you coming. We need that now more than ever. But I must warn you. My intuition is at odds with itself. Part of me wants you to come with me, but I'm also worried."

I stood and stretched. "I'll get you a sleeping bag. You'll sleep next to Alice in the living room?"

"No, I'll sleep with Graddock in your second bedroom."

I smirked.

"In a separate sleeping bag." Valencia blushed. "Remove your crass thoughts, *s'il vous plait.* We often sleep side by side. Graddock is my guard and a gentleman."

I opened my mouth to respond, but Valencia glared at me. I switched the subject. "I'll dig out the sleeping bag."

We were all up early the next morning, and I made pancakes for everyone. After drowning his food in maple syrup, Graddock declared the "meal of fluffy bread" was quite good. Alice had communicated with the Guild during breakfast, reporting they would reimburse me for the bail money. After I cleared the table, Graddock hoisted the blue-and-white duffel bag he had carried into the house last night. "Time to change into our Oz clothes."

He unzipped the duffel and handed a bundle to each of us. I accepted my pile of clothes and unfolded them. "Where did you find these?"

Alice said, "I selected garments for you. You must blend in."

We each retreated to private corners of the house to change into our new attire. I slipped on an orange shirt and a purple vest. My upper articles of clothing seemed normal when compared to the bright-red breeches for pants and white stockings for socks. To complete my wardrobe, I placed a top hat on my head that had small bells hanging down from the brim. The bells jingled as I left my bedroom.

Sondra emerged from the bathroom. "I look ridiculous," she complained.

In fact, she did. She wore a mint-green onesie with bright orange boots the toes of which curled at the end. A sunshine-colored taffeta collar encircled her neck. On her head perched a pink feather headdress. Her garments contrasted with her glasses.

I chuckled and reached for my phone. "I'm going to take a picture."

"I'll break the camera first and then your nose."

We proceeded downstairs, and Sondra went to the library to retrieve her hobbyhorse. I went into our living room where I found everyone dressed and ready to depart. When Sondra joined me, she whispered a comment to me about each one. Valencia wore a pink and white gingham dress with pink stockings and white, feather-covered boots ("oh sure, she makes it work"). Graddock had on a powder-blue coat over a silver shirt and blue breeches with flat shoes ("he looks better than you"). Alice had on a green blouse with gold stripes, a white skirt over lime-green stockings, and ankle boots with a gold bandana ("why couldn't I wear that?").

"Alice, you're coming with us?" I asked.

She smoothed out her blouse. "Guild rules. If I'm stuck

there for some reason, or Glinda allows me to stay, I have to look the part. We're all dressed as visitors to the Quadling country. We'd never pass for natives but will resemble other Oz residents."

Sondra knitted her brow. "Wait, the Quadlings?"

I said, "Glinda lives in the south of Oz. She oversees the Quadlings."

"I thought she was in the Emerald City," said Sondra.

Alice shook her head. "No, Ozma lives in the Emerald City."

"Who the hell is Ozma?"

I grabbed a book and showed Sondra a map of Oz. "Ozma's the true ruler of Oz. She was introduced in the second book in the series, *The Marvelous Land of Oz.*"

Alice said, "Focus on the word 'Quadling,' and you'll end up in their region."

Sondra's shoulders slumped. "We aren't going to the Emerald City?"

"This is not a joyride, Sondra," said Alice.

"Nothing wrong in a little sightseeing," murmured Sondra.

Alice addressed the rest of us. "As I said last night, I cannot Travel with others off Earth, only off other worlds. Sondra will need to conduct us one by one to Oz."

Sondra held up the toy horse. "This isn't going to work, Alice. I've tried to ride this horse since we returned the last time. It never took me anywhere."

"I can help you. You lacked a purpose before. Your totem won't work to go visiting. The hobbyhorse conducts you in a time of real need. We are in need. Take Graddock first, in case you miss and end up somewhere else."

"Miss? What do you mean by miss? Cat's piss, Alice!"

Alice touched Sondra's arm. "You'll be fine."

Graddock frowned at the wooden pole with a cloth pony head as he and Sondra mounted it, with my wife in front. She closed her eyes and jiggled the handle up and down as if it were a real horse galloping. Nothing happened. After a few minutes, Sondra opened her eyes. "See?"

Alice pressed together her lips and exhaled through her nose. "Don't you want to help Kingdom? Try harder, Sondra."

"I am trying."

Valencia eyed me, and I recalled my promise from the prior night. The queen bit her lip. "I am sure you are, but something is holding you back, Sondra."

"Nothing's—"

She stopped herself and dropped the stick horse. "Be right back."

She scurried out of the room and up the stairs. A couple of minutes later, my wife ran back down with a purse slung over her shoulder. "All set."

Alice put her hands on her hips. "A purse will stand out."

"As if the clothes wouldn't. No arguments. I'm bringing it."

She mounted the hobbyhorse again, and again Graddock swung his leg over the stick. Sondra had barely shut her eyes when the stick horse expanded into a living, chestnut-brown stallion, Sondra's Traveling companion. Everyone else stepped back as the horse, named Bree, took up most of the room. The steed crouched and leaped and disappeared in mid-air.

Valencia cheered. "We're off to Oz."

Alice squinted at the location where Bree and his riders had vanished. "Or somewhere."

"Alice, I have full confidence Sondra went to Oz," Valencia said.

Three minutes passed, then five. I clasped my hands behind my back. Damn, my wife made me nervous with her cockiness sometimes.

Without warning, Sondra and Bree appeared again, and the animal transformed back into a stick horse. Sondra regarded us with a broad grin. "Our destination certainly appears to be Oz."

Alice climbed on the hobbyhorse behind her. "I'm next, in case you Traveled to another world by mistake. I can teleport us to Oz from wherever you went."

Sondra's eyes twinkled. "Wait until you see it, Harold! The real Oz makes the movie look like a grade-school play. The trees are—"

"Let's go, Sondra," Alice urged when securely on Bree. The horse appeared again, and the riders vanished after the steed took a step.

Once Valencia and I were alone, the queen turned to me. "What did she put in her purse?"

"I have no idea. Fertility pills?"

Valencia was in no mood for humor. "What kind of an adventure do you two think you're going on? I don't have a good feeling about it, if you get my meaning."

"I'll talk to her," I assured the queen. "Whatever it is, it won't get in the way of the quest."

"Please be careful. I'm panicked about Kingdom, but now I have a second concern."

"Valencia, please don't—"

But Sondra materialized again with her reverted hobbyhorse, beaming like a lighthouse on a clear night. "It's Oz. Alice confirmed it. Harold, I can't wait for you to see it."

"I'm next," said Valencia. "I hate to say this, but I'm fearful the horse may not continue to work, and I must be on this quest."

"Of course."

Valencia climbed onto Bree behind Sondra, and they vanished. My wife made Traveling look easy-peasy. I waited for their return. Two minutes stretched to four. Then six. I started pacing the room, waiting.

Sondra appeared next to me, hair ruffled. "Get on!"

"What's—?"

"Now!"

I jumped on. Sondra gripped the stick horse and gritted her teeth. "We're in trouble."

8 - DECOYS

Prince Roger crossed his arms and scowled at the six dwarfs gathered in a semicircle around him. A porter had escorted the weathered and downcast men into his room fifteen minutes before. His guests had then described why they had called upon the prince.

The dwarf with a white tuft of hair scratched his elbow. "It will work."

Another of his visitors, this one skittish, rubbed his hands together. "With the wyverns, ye could be there in a couple of hours."

"I know, Squirrel," said Roger. "Tell me again how you found this out. I do not want to walk into a trap."

A red-haired dwarf stroked his goatee. "After the witches took our beloved Snow White from us, we established a network of dwarfs to be on the lookout for them. We regularly contact each other using our picks in the caverns through the underworld of Kingdom. To communicate, we use a specific sequence of taps and pauses known only to dwarfs."

Another dwarf, his hair standing on end, shuffled nervously. "We are wasting time. The message we received told us the witches are on the coast near Faerie Forest, camping for the night. If we hurry, we should be able to find 'em and take care of 'em."

The prince unfolded his arms. "Why tell me and not the queens?"

Fox, Bull, Hedgehog, Squirrel, Turtle, and Rabbit exchanged uneasy glances. Roger nodded his understanding. "You do not want the witches captured, do you? You have something more final in mind. The queens would never allow it, but you think I may agree to your little scheme. And I may be able to recruit others."

Bull scraped the bottom of his shoe against the floor. "Kingdom adored Rose Red for her act of courage, but her arrows must have missed their mark. If Rose has another chance, she may finish 'em off."

The dwarfs closed in on Roger—their eyes demanding revenge for Snow White's death. Rabbit thumped his foot. "'Tis not only for Snow White, ye know."

Roger lowered his head. "Your brother Dear will be missed. The simple gesture of taking Snow White's hand was the most heroic act I have heard of in a long time."

Turtle leaned against a wall. "Perhaps if ye convinced only one of the queens without the others knowing?"

Roger rubbed his beard. "God's heaven, which one? Valencia would be the most likely to keep secrets from the others, but she is gone. Helga is our best warrior but despises killing. Penta abhors murder as much as Helga. And do you propose I go to Cinderella with this plan? Her wrath, since she is my wife, would be the worst of all. 'Tis why I am not king. I hate such decisions."

"Rose Red taught us to show no mercy with them," said Hedgehog. "And she was right."

Roger retrieved his shoes and slipped them on. "You are in luck. Danforth and Rose Red are both in the castle tonight and may be convinced to participate in your plan."

Bull grunted. "Does Rose Red have Lycrotta's Arrow?"

"'Tis locked away. I cannot access it, nor anything in the queens' treasury." Roger strode across the room to the door. "Let me consult with Danforth and Rose. I will have an answer for you at the next bell."

A few hours later, Roger, Danforth, and Rose made their way through the forest. Roger had his longsword drawn, Danforth carried a cudgel, and Rose slung her hickory bow over her shoulder. As they approached a clearing, Roger spied the witches huddling around a campfire.

Roger motioned his cohort back into the forest. The trio retreated until they stood out of earshot behind a row of pine trees. Roger crouched down. "I know we agreed to find them, but now is the time to decide. Do we attack?"

Rose reached behind, whipped out an arrow, and slotted it into her bow. "We are committed, are we not?"

Roger shifted his gaze between his companions. "We may face severe penalties if we kill them."

Danforth stroked his face. "We have to survive first. You both know I'm not a fighter."

"But I trust you, Danforth," replied Roger. "We have the element of surprise."

Rose put her hand forward, palm down, inviting their mutual pledge. "For Kingdom and her queens."

Danforth swallowed and placed his hand on top of hers. "For Kingdom and her queens."

Roger shifted and stood. "Danforth, if Helga is mad at you in front of others, I have fought with her long enough to know she will admire you if we are successful. Nothing will temper Cinderella's reaction, though. This assault may be the end of my marriage."

Rose creased her brow. "Remind her these wolves invaded Kingdom, and her son, Cuthbert, will never talk to his

Aunt Snow White again."

Roger rubbed his jaw for a few moments but then placed his hand on top of theirs. "For Kingdom and her queens."

Once more, the three approached the camp. The witches sat around the fire, not talking but gazing at the flames. Danforth used a signal from Earth, counting with his hand. He held up three fingers, then two, then shouted, "one." The heroes of Kingdom rushed into the clearing, weapons poised to strike.

The witches were ready for them and turned toward their three attackers. The crones smiled, revealing vast crevasses in their teeth. "Did you honestly think you could surprise us?" Picana asked. "We have been watching you in the fire!"

Roger swung at the witch with the frizzy hair, Mya. She held up her hands, and Roger's blade became mist, leaving him with nothing but a handle. "God's heaven!" he cursed.

Danforth raised the cudgel over his head to strike Tomana, but she clapped her hands. His cudgel enlarged, and the weapon's weight pulled Danforth backward, toppling him. He landed on his back with a grunt.

For her part, Rose let loose an arrow at Picana, but Picana shook her head, as if to indicate she wouldn't be killed the same way twice. The arrow curved downward and embedded in the ground at her feet.

Roger dropped the handle of his sword and reached for a knife until a shudder passed through his body. His hands released the knife. Horror-struck, he raised his right hand to examine his fingers, which were pulled back into his palm like deflating balloons. No discomfort accompanied the sensation as, in seconds, his fingers became nubs and his arms began to repeat the same process. His limbs retracted into his torso, creating thin folds of fat as if his bones didn't exist. While his arms retreated, his calves began to shrink in the same way.

Picana pointed, and a wave of lightning ripped through Rose, who screamed in agony, unable to release the grip on her bow. Danforth started to rise to his feet, but at that moment, Tomana held a white dandelion to her lips and blew on it. The fuzzy seeds struck Danforth with the sharpness of needles, drawing blood.

Roger's arms collapsed into his torso. "Release me from this spell."

Tomana lifted her chin. "As if I would obey you. How about I watch while you fold into nothingness instead?"

While his companions screamed in pain, Roger dropped to the dirt. Though but a torso, he glared at the witches. "You shall not win. The queens will defeat you."

Picana sneered, "So say all dying heroes."

Only seconds later, six voices shouted behind the hags. "For Snow White! For Dear!"

Six dwarfs slid from the shadows from the other side of the encampment. Six knives held by six small hands plunged, two per witch. Knives sliced through their hearts and lungs, and the hags screeched.

After the witches fell to the ground, Roger's torso sprouted his arms and legs. The electricity surrounding Rose ceased, and the dandelion seeds vanished. Tomana fell forward, landing on her face while her blood spilled over the grass. Blood poured from Picana as well, but she made a slicing motion with her finger at one of the dwarfs. Bull grabbed his throat, choked, and collapsed in the clearing.

With a dying gesture, Mya clenched her fist, and Hedgehog screamed, grabbed his side, and fell over, convulsing. Mya's eyes rolled up into her head, and Hedgehog stopped shaking but moaned in pain. All at once, the witches' bodies became translucent and dispersed into the air.

The dwarfs ran to their fallen brothers to assist them, and the leporine man of the brood, Rabbit, wailed as he leaned over Bull. Fox confirmed Hedgehog was unconscious but alive, as he picked up his brother and held him in his arms.

The four remaining dwarfs gathered in a circle around Bull. Each put a hand on his brother while tears rolled down their faces. They sang a hymn, a deep melodic dirge, and Roger, Danforth, and Rose observed an ancient ritual of their champions' kind, the dwarfs guiding their dead brother to his final resting place.

Penta shook her head in shock at Roger's report, not trusting her ears. Bull dead, the witches dealt with, Danforth–no fighter—in mortal peril. The prince had not only dismissed consulting the queens but had joined with others to kill the witches.

Cinderella resembled a volcano about to erupt while Helga's blank expression didn't convey her inner thoughts. Penta held up her hand. "I would like a brief recess to mourn Bull and collect my thoughts. Meet us in the throne room in thirty minutes."

They all gathered as requested after a half-hour had passed. With two thrones vacant, and Cinderella sitting in a small chair in front of her swinging throne, the chamber seemed off-kilter to Penta. Helga sat on her throne with her arms crossed. Cinderella turned away from Roger, red-cheeked and shaking. Rose, Danforth, and Roger stood at attention. Penta gripped her armrests and leaned forward. "Do you think they are truly dead?"

Roger licked his lips. "I do."

Cinderella addressed Rose, ignoring her husband. "You killed them before, yet they lived again."

Rose said, "I must have only wounded them."

Helga said, "All three of them? You only wounded all three of them? With Lycrotta's Arrow?"

"You were there," answered Rose. "You know I pierced

them in the same place. If not a critical wound for one, it would not be a critical wound for three."

"While I hope and pray they are dead, I worry they are still living. Without corpses, 'tis hard to believe them vanquished." Penta rubbed her eyes. "My hope still lies with Valencia."

Rose lifted her chin. "I cannot speak for the others, but I knew what I was doing. I defended my homeland, my beloved Kingdom. You call it murder, but I disagree. If those damn hags appear again, I will be there, on the front line, killing them again and again until they stay dead."

Penta slammed her fist down on her armrest. "Rose Red!" she shouted. "Your revenge for Snow White's death has consumed you. Have you no concern for your immortal soul?"

"They are evil, Penta! My soul is in no jeopardy."

Helga's stare bored into the archer. "You are no paladin, Rose."

Rose Red turned to the warrior queen. "I never claimed to be a holy knight. You lost a sister! How could you not understand my predicament?"

Helga shook her head. "And now, my family has turned to murder in some ill-plotted offense. Exactly the opposite of what Snow White wanted."

Penta nodded to Lyken who stood at a far door of the room. "Rose, you and the dwarfs are not the only ones who loved Snow White. I called in a favor from Alice and had a Traveler bring someone here from Earth to attend her memorial service. She's been listening in on one of my rings. Perhaps she can talk sense to you where we have failed to do so. Call in Sylvia Swonewith."

The door opened, and Sylvia Swonewith stormed into the chamber, cheeks blazing. Rose paled at the sight of the Earth resident striding forward, hands clenched. Sylvia had stood in for Snow White in the past under Rose's guidance, and the three of them were close. Sylvia marched toward Rose Red.

Rose licked her lips. "Syl, you do not understand. I must

—"

Sylvia, taller than the others, held up her hand. "How dare you? How dare you besmirch *her* name by becoming a killer? Should we change the title of your fairy tale to 'Snow White, Deceased, and Rose Red, Killer'?"

"Syl...you have not faced them," whispered Rose.

"One thing Snow White taught me, taught all of us, is every enemy has a weakness. You could have captured them, Red. You could've aimed at their hands."

"Their magic is powerful—"

Sylvia stepped forward. "So powerful that they turned your soul black? And Bull?" Sylvia gasped and cried.

Rose's teardrops fell to the floor, and Roger hung his head. "He died a hero."

"Bull dead." Cinderella gripped the folds of her night robe, knuckles white. "What would Snow say?"

Roger threw back his shoulders. "In our defense, we attacked the witches for Kingdom. Do not deny those hags were the largest threat we have ever encountered. We knew the consequences. If you want to throw us into the dungeon, we are ready. But we three would do it again."

Penta winced when Cinderella leaped from her chair. Flushed, Cinderella yelled, "And what of us? In all your secrecy, did you forget the little fact that two of you are our husbands and one of you is our dear friend? You could've been killed like Bull. Your disregard for our law is one thing, but to risk your lives without telling us?"

Roger startled Penta when he yelled back. "As if you do not risk your life every day for Kingdom. How do you think I feel when I see you, my love, walk onto a battlefield without a weapon? You are a queen of Kingdom. One thousand soldiers should be between you and the enemy, and I should be in front of all of them."

Cinderella stepped forward and poked him on the breastbone. "Have you lost your mind? I have my God-given ability to keep me safe in such a situation. How could you be so cavalier with your life as to act as a decoy for the dwarfs? You, the love of my life? And what of our son, Cuthbert?"

"Who do you imagine I was thinking of?" Roger argued. "What kind of world will Cuthbert have if these witches survive? 'Tis why I did it. I have lived in a free and wonderful world since you became a queen. If I have to die to return joy to you and all the children of Kingdom, then so be it."

Cinderella stepped back and squared her shoulders. "You disobeyed the law, your queen, and your wife. You can't get away with it."

Penta stood. "Enough. Sister, please listen to me and return to your throne. Let's take a moment of silence to reflect on the situation."

Cinderella twisted on her heel and again settled in her small chair. She glared at Roger, a vein throbbing in her temple. No one said anything for a long time until Penta broke the silence.

"I absolve the dwarfs of all blame. I cannot do anything else given the death of Bull. For the three of you, censure. Two days. Sisters, will you join me?"

Shock stole over Cinderella's features. Penta twisted the ends of her left glove with her right fingers. "We gain nothing by punishing them," said Penta, looking from Helga to Sylvia to Cinderella. "They will receive their punishment in private, I expect."

Cinderella said, "But, Penta, they planned to murder the witches. They considered no other option."

Penta hung her head. "Yet Prince Roger is right. If I cannot protect Beauty, if you cannot protect Cuthbert, what good are our laws? I vote for censure and absolution."

Helga snorted. "Aye."

"Cinderella?"

Lisp pronounced, she said, "I abstain."

"Then the motion carries, and you three are free. Please leave while I discuss this further with my sisters."

Rose Red, Roger, Sylvia, and Danforth proceeded out of

the throne room as quickly as decorum allowed.

9 - A FYTE

Harold

I inhaled the sweet scent of cherries, sensing the smell before my eyes adjusted to the brilliant sunlight of my surroundings. My first breath in Oz was as pure as mountain water, a natural phenomenon this land apparently shared with Kingdom. Thick woods stood guard on my right, embowered with fiery-red and ocean-blue leaves. The dense line of woods had a break in the middle for a fully grown cherry tree in the center. A gurgling rill, the flapping of birds' wings overhead, plus a soft breeze ruffling luminescent grass blended to make a harmonious melody.

Ironically, I couldn't enjoy any of my surroundings, because the minute I arrived, my attention turned to a skirmish nearby. Graddock, red-faced with exertion, lifted a frantic man made of metal with thin limbs and a funnel for a hat

—The Tin Woodman. Graddock held the metal man over his head, about to hurl him against one of the trees. The muscles of the man from Kingdom bulged with the effort while The Tin Woodman's arms and legs flailed in a manner like that of a spider on its back. From somewhere close, voices chanted, "Fight. Fight."

"Put him down!" Valencia shouted.

A similar tin woodman, but this one dressed as a soldier with a rectangular cap on his head and a sword attached to his belt, stood over an unconscious Alice. The tin soldier dropped a flower near her head. "The poppies work on them, Nick." His name, of course! The Tin Woodman's full name was Nick Chopper.

Nick Chopper waved his bird-like arms. "Help, Captain Fyte."

Graddock had paused at Valencia's order. He turned to his queen and regarded her with a question in his eyes. "These monsters mean to kill us."

The captain withdrew another poppy from a knapsack at the same time Sondra dug her heels into Bree. The horse galloped straight for the captain made of tin, distracting him from Graddock. Sondra plucked the flower from the tin soldier and crumpled it in her fist.

Valencia ignored our arrival and marched up to Graddock. She pointed downward. "Restore him to the ground."

Weighing her command, Graddock gritted his teeth but then lowered The Tin Woodman. Across the path, Bree reared up, Captain Fyte cowered in front of the steed, and I slid off the horse's haunches, landing on my rear end.

"Fight. Fight." That murmuring again.

"All of you, stop!" cried Valencia. "For once, I wish I had Cinderella's power. She could force all of you to listen to your consciences, and then you'd know brawling is pointless."

All heads turned toward Valencia. Sondra placed a gentle hand on Bree, calming the horse. Graddock squinted at The Tin Woodman, and Captain Fyte scrambled away.

Valencia threw back her shoulders, and her queenly manner shone as bright as the sun emerging from a cloud. She spoke to The Tin Woodman. "We haven't come to hurt anyone. Your attack on us is unwarranted. Let's discuss your grievance like civilized people."

The woodsmen eyed each other while Sondra dismounted and Graddock crossed his arms. I stood, brushed the dirt off my red pantaloons, and with a shock spied mouths on enormous cherries. No eyes or noses, the mouths had been egging on the battle. When the cherries noticed I had spotted them, all their mouths grinned at me. I shook my head. "What happened?"

Graddock leaned toward The Tin Woodman. The metal gentleman quaked in the Kingdom rogue's shadow. Graddock said, "Alice and I were waiting for Sondra when this thing—" indicating The Tin Woodman— "came from the forest with his ax raised. He ran at us and screamed. Alice tried to stop him, but the other one strutted over and grabbed her wrist. Then Valencia and Sondra arrived."

Valencia poked Graddock on his chest. "Nick didn't swing his ax, and he stopped when Alice spoke to him."

"But, my queen, he threatened me. You distracted him, allowing me to gain the advantage. Otherwise, he would have killed me."

Valencia turned sympathetic eyes on The Tin Woodman. "He's as timid as a church mouse and shaking like a wet dog in the cold."

Graddock gestured to Alice. "And what of our guide?"

"'Tis a poppy, a flower of Oz that creates drowsiness, nothing more," replied Valencia. "I read about them last night."

As Valencia finished speaking, Alice sat up, holding her head. "Stupid poppies. I'm fine but must depart."

Captain Fyte pointed at Alice. "This one said she shouldn't be here."

The Tin Woodman spoke, his voice gentle and pleasing. "Captain Fyte and I were returning to the Winkie country when you appeared from nowhere. Raiders have used this path before to steal from our land. They have taken something precious from a friend of mine." Tears rolled down Nick's tin cheeks, and Graddock's lip curled, making me grin.

Valencia stepped toward The Tin Woodman. "You are Nick Chopper, correct? You're a good man and a friend of Glinda's. We seek her."

"To attack her?" growled Captain Fyte.

Puzzled, Valencia observed the other tin soldier. I said, "He's Captain Fyte, a friend of Nick Chopper's."

The captain gripped the hilt of his sword. "How do you know who we are?"

Valencia pointed at me. "My friend is an oracle, and he has taught me about your world. Please, I beg you to help us. If you could show us the way to Glinda's castle, we would be in your debt."

The tin woodsmen exchanged a glance. Nick Chopper said, "We'll do better than show you, we'll accompany you. I've not visited Glinda for a long time."

Valencia inclined her head at Nick. "My sisters know Glinda. We aren't enemies. We are ambassadors from another world."

"You are more than an ambassador," remarked Graddock.

Valencia ignored him. "We are visitors who wish only the best for Oz, but we need Glinda's help. Our world is in danger."

"Danger?" Captain Fyte puffed out his chest. "Are you from Ix, Ev?" His eyes narrowed. "Or the Nome Lands?"

"None of them," answered Valencia. "I'm afraid you may not have heard of my world."

Alice peered into the sky. "I must go. The monkeys will come for me if I remain. I'll see you on Earth, back at Hero's and Sondra's."

Alice had used my otherworld moniker, and I beamed

with pride. Alice tossed her ginger-colored hair over her shoulder and disappeared, which caused the tin woodsmen to step back. Captain Fyte again put his hand on his sword. "What manner of a witch is she? Good or wicked?"

"She's not a witch, but she's good," I replied.

Valencia approached Nick Chopper and held out her hand. "Let us be better acquainted." She introduced herself and the rest of us. When she came to me, she called me 'Hero' though Sondra rolled her eyes. When she said Sondra's name, Nick didn't hear it right and asked, "Sanders?"

"Sondra," my wife replied.

I smirked. "Perhaps Sanders could be *your* off-world name."

"Shut up."

"What's wrong?" I put a hand to my chest in mock offense. "Didn't we receive a box of Sanders chocolates last year? You've got brown hair and are kind of nutty on the inside."

"It's a stupid name." Sondra turned to Nick. "You may call me Sundread Saturn." I shook my head.

Valencia explained Kingdom's peril and why we sought Glinda. The woodsmen changed their attitude once they understood the situation. Nick shouldered his ax. "I am sorry for mistaking you for raiders. Welcome to Oz."

He then turned to Graddock and held out his hand. "My apologies."

Graddock shook the hand, staring at the tin fingers wrapped in his.

Nick nodded his head to point down the road. "Glinda's castle is in this direction. If we begin now, we should arrive before evening."

"We could ride Bree," suggested Sondra.

Nick eyed the horse. "Sanders, I am afraid no horse can bear me, and we can guide you. We're right outside Rigmarole Town. You don't want to wander in there. An instant headache, those people are. Captain Fyte and I will step lively because we never tire."

We started and observed the enchanting sights of Oz while we made our way. We passed small, hut-like houses, from which the residents emerged and pointed at Nick Chopper and Captain Fyte, ignoring the rest of us. The Quadlings were about four-and-a-half to five feet tall. Pointed hats sat on top of their round heads, and the caps shadowed their ruddy faces. They dressed in a variety of clothes, but red dominated all other colors.

We traversed fields until we entered a forest of red trees. When asked, Nick explained the leaves' color never changed, unlike autumn leaves on Earth. Their natural color was vermillion, matching the same hue as the bark of the trees they grew on.

Graddock insisted Valencia ride on Bree, and Valencia agreed but insisted Sondra—or should I use her new off-world name of Sanders now—remain on his back. Sanders and the queen both rode side-saddle to take in the surrounding Quadling countryside. All of us pointed at the many spectacular sights we spotted.

Valencia, to pass the time, asked Nick about the raiders. He explained, "The raiders are mysterious strangers who come from nowhere, steal Oz's treasures, and then vanish, similar to the way your friend Alice did. They're brutish and once stole the hands off the lady I love."

"What happened?" I asked.

"My love is named Tristalynn. One day, a raider came and snuck into her chamber, tied her up, and stole her hands. Her hands were the prettiest in all of Oz."

The entire party examined the woodsmen's hands, and it dawned on me where I had seen a similar pair. The tin hands were a replica of Penta's. Valencia gulped in recognition. "What would anyone want with her hands?"

The Tin Woodman replied, "If you had no hands and you attached hers, they would follow your commands."

Valencia closed her eyes. "And when did this occur?"

"Several years ago, perhaps three," Nick answered.

I calculated quickly. Penta'd had her hands for at least seven years so they couldn't be Tristalynn's, but they could perhaps be those of some other tin woodwoman's. Penta was always guarded about where she had obtained her hands, wearing gloves to avoid calling attention to them.

The Tin Woodman said, "Anyway, Tristalynn would not marry me without her hands because she thought she was unworthy without them. No effort on my part could persuade her to matrimony, and she retired to a cozy corner of Winkiedom, leaving me with a broken heart for the second time."

Valencia shook her head a little to warn us all not to speak about Penta.

As we traveled, the Quadlings continued to stop and wave at us, thinking us visitors from another corner of Oz. Every time I moved my head, the bells on my hat would jingle, and Sanders would smirk. Ridiculous clothes!

After finally rounding a tall mountain, we came upon a castle. Nick pointed his ax at it. "Here we are."

The white marble of the walls shone in the fading sunlight and highlighted the turrets that extended outward at odd angles instead of skyward. Without support, they should have collapsed, but I had to keep reminding myself this was Oz. Every window in the castle was a different geometric shape, and none of them lined up with the others. Perched on the roof, a red flag hung limply on a pole.

A stream flowed toward the castle and around it in a circle, but no drawbridge extended from the entrance. Outside the main door, a young lady with red hair and a flowing, gauzy gown waved to the group, beckoning us forward.

"Who is the woman at the door?" asked Valencia.

The Tin Woodman lifted his funnel hat off his head and tipped it. "It's Glinda. You're expected."

10 - AN UNEXPECTED
REQUEST

Sondra

The Kingdom couple, Oz residents, Hero—as promised, I will refer to him by his otherworld name now—and I traversed a broad field of heather nearing the castle and moat of clear water. Glinda pointed at Nick and Fyte, and the two woodsmen floated over the water to the narrow strip of ground next to the Good Witch.

Graddock hailed Glinda. "Have we a dry way to cross, m'lady?"

Glinda gestured to the stream, a playful smile on her lips. "Step on the water. The moat will support you as if it were the ground."

I couldn't see the bottom of the stream. The water tumbled past as fast and slippery as an eel. Valencia returned her attention to the witch. "We can't swim across?"

Glinda's hair moved away from her face though the air was still. "Dear me, no. Walk across. If you try to swim across, the water will pull you down and drown you in seconds."

Valencia and Graddock squeezed each other's hand while I blew my pink feather out of my eyes. Hero bit his lip. "If you're supposed to be good, why test us this way?"

"Crossing isn't much of a test if I gave you the answer." Glinda winked.

Valencia stepped to the edge of the water. "Who will go first? I am willing."

Graddock put out his hand. "Allow me, my queen."

Glinda's eyes flashed at the word "queen," but she didn't register any other emotions. Graddock walked to the trench and hovered the toe of his boot above the rolling liquid. Glinda retrieved a slim, white wand from a hidden pocket. "Please be careful. The water will pull you under if you're at all hesitant. Walk as you would on dry land."

Graddock closed his eyes then stepped forward. His foot landed on the water's surface, and he took six quick steps and mounted the other side. Glinda addressed him. "Wasn't so difficult now, was it?"

I crouched down. "Must be a non-Newtonian fluid. When we step on it, we compress it, and its viscosity changes, supporting our weight."

"Or it's magic," said Valencia.

Valencia and I followed, and when Hero, who went last, arrived at the other side, Glinda turned and opened her door, pocketing the wand. "Well done. Now follow me."

Valencia walked behind her, matching her long strides. "Do you know who we are and why we are here?"

Glinda stepped into the interior of the castle. "I have a theory as to who you are. I know you're seeking my help."

When we emerged from the long hallway, Glinda and the woodsmen continued into the center of her castle, but the rest of us halted, stunned by the scene before us. Hero is the writer who employs flowery language, but I'll do my best to describe what we saw. The "room" was more of a courtyard than a chamber; cloudy mist replaced the walls, grass replaced the stone floor, and the ceiling was open to allow the sun and the sky to sparkle overhead. Animals roamed around the room with natural predators and prey—such as a coyote and a rabbit—lying next to each other.

Floating in the air at the four compass points of the room were fireplaces with no flues, rotating slowly like a single carousel, with fires on either side. A red fire blasted warm air, while on the other side, a blue flame kept the yard cool. A golden tent with red poles stood in the middle of this unusual yard. The flaps on the tent were rolled back, revealing multiple oversized cushions. Glinda and the two woodsmen lowered themselves onto three broad pillows.

Viewing the courtyard produced an electric tingle through my shoulder blades. When I'd first arrived in Oz, the same sensation had rippled through me. I tensed my back until the feeling disappeared. I'd worry later about what it meant.

As we non-natives entered the room, four silver statues intercepted our progress. Humanoid-shaped but without clothes or faces, they presented their arms to each of us. We each took the arm of a simulacrum and allowed them to escort us to the tent. Graddock and Valencia sat on separate cushions, but Hero and I shared a large mauve pillow. Two identical twin women soldiers stood behind Glinda, on the alert.

Glinda spread her arms in a welcoming manner to Valencia. "Since I sense you are a true queen and not one like so many others by name only, I invite you as a dignitary into my castle and to be seated in a place of honor. However, since you are not my queen, I hope you will excuse me if I present myself to be your equal here in my royal chamber."

Valencia stood and curtsied. "I'm not a queen of Oz, my

hostess. I'm not insulted by the seating arrangements here."

This answer pleased Glinda, and in response she lounged back on her cushion. "Though you are desperately trying to blend into Oz, I suspect you are from Kingdom, at least some of you. The clothes are typical Traveler garb and easily spotted by one who knows of the different worlds. You must be Queen Valencia. You have Queen Helga's chin and similar eyes to Queen Penta. The other three of you queens look different from one another but are all quite pretty."

Valencia blushed. "My two younger sisters are far more beautiful than I am." She faltered, thinking of Snow White. "At least, my sister who is alive."

Glinda's smile vanished when Valencia hinted one of Kingdom's queens was dead. Valencia proceeded with the introductions. "This man beside me is Graddock, my guard, also from Kingdom. The woman on my other side is Sondra and her husband, Hero."

"Welcome Graddock, Hero, and Sanders."

What! Will everyone keep mistaking my real name for that stupid one? I cleared my throat. "Sundread, please."

Valencia ignored my comment and got down to business. "We need your help. Please be patient and hear us out."

"I'm Glinda the Good Witch. If I deem the help you require as worthy, I will be most willing to assist you."

Valencia repeated her story to Glinda who grew more and more concerned while the Kingdom queen recalled the events of the past two weeks. When the narration came to the part of the witches returning to life, Glinda crossed her arms and scowled. Valencia explained why Hero and I had accompanied her and then finished with a plea. "My sisters believe you to be the most powerful magic-wielder across all worlds. We would be in your debt if you could travel to Kingdom and work with Celeste to deliver us from these witches."

Glinda unfolded her arms. "No."

Valencia's head jerked at the rebuff. "No?"

"No, I am not the most powerful of magic-wielders.

Some wizards and witches are more powerful than I am. I know of the three witches you referenced, and I could defeat each in a magic duel individually. However, they would be the victors when working together."

Valencia licked her lips. "But...perhaps...you and Celeste together would be more formidable."

Glinda's eyes sparkled. "I like your mind, Queen Valencia. You are an alert and wise woman. You do your sisters justice. Yes, I'm sure Celeste the Extraordinary and I would be worthy opponents." She folded her hands and grinned.

"You know Celeste?"

"I've never met her, but I'm aware of her. Someone of her talent cannot go unnoticed by witches, sorceresses, and magicians across the worlds. We good witches have titled her 'Extraordinary,' as her accomplishments deserve."

"She was not effective against the witches," remarked Valencia.

"Appearances are deceiving. Do not underestimate Kingdom's pixie defender. The hags are expending a lot of their magical energy to undo her spells. They may belittle her, but they view her as a threat. Don't be discouraged."

Valencia asked, "So, you will help us?"

Glinda produced her wand again and regarded it. "Yes and no. Take your choice."

Valencia's eyebrows rose. "I choose...yes?"

"You need help in two ways, but despite all my magic, I can only be in one spot at a time."

Valencia tilted her head, puzzled.

Glinda ran her fingers along the length of her wand. "Let me explain. Only three witches comprise a coven, and their order is important: Picana; Miasis, or Mya; and Erotomana, or Tomana. I've been watching this trio grow in skill and cunning. All at once, an unknown force made them thrice powerful, and I believe the increase is due to a dark deal with an evil presence."

Valencia pressed together her lips and then spoke. "We

are a particular target of the devil."

Glinda's eyes narrowed at the last word. "Whether the force is the Devil or a devil, I can't say. What I know is the time was coming for the hags to die in their world. I carefully watch over Oz but leave the other worlds to my companion mages. I suspect the witches left their world and Traveled to yours, trying to find some way to extend their lives. The fact that they did not die after your friend killed them is of paramount concern to me."

Valencia said, "The only types who come back from the dead are the unliving, zombies, and the like."

Glinda tapped her index finger against her cheek, deep in thought. "They aren't zombies, I assure you. How they manage to stay alive is disturbing. Hmm. We can't hope to win without knowing more about them. Everyone has weaknesses. They do as well. One path leads us to their home world to find a hole in their armor. The other path leads us to Kingdom to stop their antics before they destroy all you hold dear."

Valencia wrapped a drawstring on her dress around her finger. "We have to know what will defeat them."

Glinda sat up on her cushion. "I agree, which is why I will go to their home world of Astage, make inquiries into their past with an imp I know, and hopefully return with the knowledge to defeat them."

I adjusted my glasses. "And what will we do?"

Glinda regarded me, eyes dancing. "Why, wait here, of course. None of you are magic-wielders. Keeping Valencia out of Kingdom is for the best. While I don't think slaying another queen is their goal, they might be tempted to bring the number down to three, one for each of them to contend with. In this case, a fourth queen in Kingdom is dangerous."

"You will go to their original world and find out about them?" asked Hero. "But that could take years!"

Glinda brushed a curl away from her forehead. "While I don't keep watch over them, I have tracked them. Their condescending attitude makes them careless, and they think I didn't notice their wickedness. They have forgotten the other meaning of 'good' is *exceptional.* I've had them in my purview for a while without their realizing it. I know their world, and I know someone who can help us."

"You're a Traveler?" I asked.

Glinda slipped her wand back into her sleeve. "No, and we need a Traveler. I will lift Alice's banishment from Oz. The girl has done many good deeds since her transgression, and I believe she's learned her lesson. I will call her tonight, and she can take me to my destination and then return to you. I can come back to Oz without a Traveler."

Valencia stood. "But you must leave as soon as possible."

"I understand. However, reaching Alice will take time. I'll need the evening. You may as well spend the night here."

Valencia's shoulders slumped. Glinda stood, approached her, and placed a hand on the young woman's arm. "Be comforted, Queen Valencia. I will obtain news from Kingdom first and relay it to you. If the situation is dire, I will change my mind and go there promptly."

Valencia agreed to the terms with a nod. Glinda gestured toward a guard. "Please show these visitors to the guest rooms."

Before we left, I had an important question to ask the Good Witch.

Harold

Glinda nodded for us to follow the guard out of the royal chamber, and we stood and started to walk behind her, but Sanders held back. She said something to Glinda I couldn't hear. When Sanders caught up, I asked, "What was that about?"

She took my arm. "I asked if Oz had running water."

"The first question you ask of Glinda the Good is whether or not her palace has running water?"

Sanders pouted. "Men don't understand. These things are important!"

After viewing our luxurious rooms consisting of canopy beds and one of those fireplaces with the red and blue flames, the four of us gathered in Valencia's room to discuss our next step. The idea of sitting around vexed Valencia, and she paced the room, reflecting on how to be more useful.

A guard knocked on Valencia's door, announced supper was ready, and guided us to a narrow dining hall with long windows overlooking the Quadling countryside. While we waited for the servants, Glinda entered the dining hall. Her contacts in the Traveler's Guild had reported the three queens were safe. Valencia's eyes showed relief when she heard the witch's good news.

We consumed the food, a delicious combination of loaves of bread, jams, and soups. Glinda sat at the head of the table, radiant in the candlelight.

Graddock spread white jam on purple bread. "Glinda, have you Traveled to this Astage before?"

"Yes, I have Traveled to most worlds. We have a resident Traveler here named Dorothy Gale, but she's off on a mission with Ozma."

Hero chewed a bit of bread. "Alice is reserved about the worlds. Can you tell us more? What is Astage like?"

"Some worlds are fantasies—Oz and Kingdom. Some are similar to Earth, while others are far more dangerous. They all resemble Earth in some way. The worlds are similar to points on a map. Kingdom and Oz are straightforward paths. Trying to journey to Astage requires world jumping—going from one point in one world to another point."

Sanders stirred her soup with a silver spoon. "I didn't get Bree to work back on Earth. If I had..." She gulped.

Glinda's eyes sharpened. "You might have ended up on a random world, unable to return home. Better for you if Alice accompanies you."

After dinner, we went to our respective rooms to try to

sleep. After freshening up in the adjoining bathroom—with its running water—Sanders and I slid into a "triple-king" bed, a bed so large Sanders could roll over twice and still not reach me. Despite the fact we had more than enough room, we held each other beneath the silky sheets. While we snuggled, Sanders' heart pounded louder than scientifically possible. She rolled her eyes. "Not again. I thought my heart only betrayed me in Kingdom."

"It's because we're in Oz," I assured her. "By the way, I love you, too."

I fell asleep in her arms, lulled to dreamland by the steady beat of her heart.

I'm a heavy sleeper, but this night I awoke by chance to spy Sanders slipping out of the room. Puzzled, I followed her through the palace and was about to call out to her when I spotted her sneaking into the open-roofed room where we'd visited with Glinda. I hung back when I realized Sanders had arranged to meet with someone. Someone "good," I assumed.

I approached the partially opened door and peered through. The flaps of the tents were up, and Sanders stood with her back to me inside the enclosure. Glinda, a head taller than my wife, towered over her. The witch wore a beautiful white night robe compared to Sanders' baggy candy-cane-striped pajamas she had found in a drawer. Sanders bowed her head. "Thank you for meeting with me. As I said, I had a personal matter to discuss with you, and I wanted to be discreet."

Glinda's eyes flashed. "Your exploits whether as Sanders, the pixie, or as Sondra Jean Saturn, the scientist, haven't escaped my notice either."

Sanders took a deep breath. "My husband once told me about something in Oz called the Powder of Life. This powder brings to life inanimate objects like a sawhorse, right?"

Glinda's demeanor grew solemn. She nodded.

Sanders reached into her purse and retrieved an object and held it up. "Can I borrow just a little of it to bring this to life?"

She presented a Pinocchio doll to Glinda—a toy I recognized. The wooden toy had been in the Saturn family for decades, passed down from father to son, mother to daughter, or in her case, father to daughter. The family legend was Pinocchio's author, Carlo Collodi, commissioned the construction of a few of the dolls after he had written his famous fairy tale. He had gifted the wooden dolls to his family and friends. I knew this Pinocchio had started Sanders' interest in fantasy.

Glinda observed the doll. "And why bring it to life?"

"I have my reasons."

Glinda's fingers brushed the doll's nose. "They are personal, I assume."

Sanders said, "Yes, all I need is enough powder to bring it to life. I'm not trying to recreate Pinocchio. I wouldn't call my little one by that name."

Her features softening, Glinda said, "Unfortunately, I shall not grant the request. The Powder of Life is a powerful magic item and not for recreational use."

"It's not for recreation, I promise," replied my wife.

"Sanders, I thought you were going to ask me for something else."

"What?"

"Don't you realize you are practically radiating magic?"

Sanders stepped back and then thrust out her chin. "I thought Helga removed the curse that turned me into a pixie."

Glinda held up a placating hand. "Queen Helga the Light-Bearer removed the curse that kept you from returning to your human self at will. Like it or not, the spell that first transformed you into a fairy only awoke something already present in you. Then its latent magic fell back to slumber."

Sanders crossed her arms. "I still don't understand."

Glinda put her hand on Sanders' shoulder. "You have magic, Sanders. Magic's essence is in your blood. On Earth, you can't tap into it, but on other worlds…"

Sanders didn't answer her.

"You've felt it," said Glinda. "Haven't you?"

Sanders closed her eyes, and in a flash, her back rippled, and a beautiful pair of pixie wings emerged. They spread behind her, unfolding like petals on a flower. She glowed a faint blue. I swallowed a gasp.

Sanders set down the doll and shrunk to pixie size. She put her hands on her hips. "Happy? Now I'm stuck again."

"No, you aren't," Glinda replied. "The darkness of the spell cast on you, the curse, wasn't making you a pixie. Your inability to remain human is what Queen Helga removed. You were born human, Sanders, and on Earth where you are known as Sondra, you are fully human."

Sanders bobbed in the air. "I can be a pixie here and still return to Earth?"

"Precisely. Only on magic worlds will your pixie abilities be present. In other words, depending on the world's level of magical essence, you may not be able to use your full powers or any powers at all."

Floating, Sanders circled the Pinocchio doll. "I know so many spells. I can animate it myself now."

Glinda picked up the doll. "Animate it? Yes. Bring it to life? No."

"What do you mean?"

Glinda tilted her head. "Only the divine has the power to impart free will. All spells and items, including the Powder of Life, are limited to animation, not life."

Sanders floated in front of Glinda. "Then do you know of a spell that would increase our chances of having a child?"

Glinda heaved a weary sigh. "Yes. A spell exists that guarantees a woman to become pregnant after relations with her husband. But Sondra, the cost is too great."

Sanders returned to her human form. "You're not powerful enough to throw it?"

"I will not cast it." Glinda handed her the doll. "The incantation is complex. Only the most advanced spellcaster would dare try it. And there's an element to it..." She shook her head. "I'm sorry, Sondra, but you'll have to keep trying without magic."

My wife's shoulders rose and fell. She trembled and then wept. "I'm sorry I'm crying, but if you knew why, you'd understand."

"Don't be embarrassed by the gift of tears, my dear," replied Glinda. "Tears are the refreshing rain the soul provides the body and mind."

Spying on Glinda and Sanders was not my finest moment, so I retreated down the hallway. I returned to bed and closed my eyes, reflecting on Sanders' request. I knew I should feel bad for my wife, but instead, relief washed over me thanks to Glinda refusing to throw a fertility spell. Letting out a shaky breath, I thought about being a father and the high standard of parenthood. I still wasn't sure I was suited to it.

Sanders returned ten minutes later and reclined in our massive bed. She sniffled a couple of times and rolled away from me, pulling away sheets. I nearly rolled over and put my arms around her but refrained. If she knew I was awake, she might know I had been spying.

Early the next day, a woman soldier came and roused the party. After she showered, Sanders again remarked how wonderful having running water in Oz was. The showerhead was an enormous daisy that rained water from its pores. Refreshed and dressed in more ridiculous clothes, we waited for the soldier to return. When the sun topped the horizon, we followed an escort down to a garden with a mammoth hedge maze behind the castle.

As we strolled after the guard, Sanders manifested and unfolded her wings. I acted surprised. "What happened to you?"

"Glinda showed me how to restore my wings before you woke up. I can use my power here and in Kingdom without staying a pixie."

"You avoided the pixie thing before."

"Because everyone thought I was someone else." She stroked the membrane of her left wing. "Now they know me as Sanders the Pixie. My magic might come in handy." Thankfully, she had dropped the Sundread moniker.

We spied Valencia and Graddock near the entrance to a large hedge maze seated on a bench. As we approached, the queen stood, her mouth agape at Sanders' wings. After we all greeted each other, Valencia said, "Hero, would you mind accompanying me into the hedge maze? I have something important I wish to discuss."

Sanders eyed me, retracting her wings to her human form once more. I nodded and followed Valencia into the entrance of the hedge maze.

11- THE PERFECT HIDING SPOT

A teenage girl sat legs crossed on her queen-sized canopy bed with gold posts and taffeta shears. The posts extended eight feet into the air and held up a white and gold tulle covering. The rest of the furniture: a five-tiered set of double dressers with brass pulls, a sensational carved antique wooden desk, and a bookcase full of parchments, all surrounding her bed in a mammoth room outfitted with historic wall friezes—everything fit for a princess.

The girl brushed back her bangs, revealing more of her forehead. Penta sat across from her, positioned in the same manner but with her hands resting on her legs. Gloveless, Penta's pink fingers drummed on her leg.

"Do you think the witches are dead, Mom?" asked the girl.

Penta stopped moving her hand. "I wish the dwarfs

hadn't resorted to such violence, certainly, but I hope so, Beauty. Never forget, we queens don't end a life unless our own lives or the lives of others are in imminent danger."

Beauty bit her lip. "When *will* I be a queen?"

Penta placed her hand on her daughter's. "Don't rush it. You'll be queen soon enough. Enjoy being a fairytale princess for now."

Beauty lowered her eyes. "But am I a real fairytale princess? I'm adopted. The whispers from the servants say differently. I have no right to become a queen."

Penta grasped her daughter's hand. "Nonsense. Hero's world transcribes events in our lives to stories they call fairy tales. Your story is one of the most famous of all. 'Beauty and the Beast' is better known on Earth than my own tale, 'The Maiden Without Hands.' Who is Beauty if not you and the Beast if not Grr?"

"You renamed me Beauty," protested the girl.

"I placed it before your birth name of Shaina and renamed you Beauty because your life mirrored Hero's story. A maiden held captive in a castle and a gentlemanly yet primal suitor are all elements of Earth's fairy tale."

Beauty regarded her brown toes. "In his tale, the beast is her captor, not her friend. And Hero's Beauty was a different color."

"Hero's stories don't always have the details right. And what of this?" She held up her other hand, also of human flesh.

Beauty replied, "Ordinary magic-wielders could accomplish as much."

Penta shook her head. "Only the prophesied queens have abilities without casting spells. Even Celeste has to draw upon a reserve of external essence to use her magic. We use our gifts without limits. My teleportation, Aunt Cinderella's charm, Aunt Valencia's fortune are all gifts. You also have a gift."

"A useless gift. How will it help when we're facing an army?"

"You have a wondrous gift. You view the world as beautiful. When you will it, others view it the same way you perceive it. You don't perceive Grr as a beast—you see him as a true gentleman. And now we all see him as if through your eyes. You don't regard my silver hands as ugly constructs the way I do, and now I don't either. My hands don't only look different than before—they feel different too."

Beauty shrugged. "I can make people look different, but what's the use?"

Penta cupped a hand under her daughter's chin. "Do you think that's your gift? Beauty, you see the inner person. You perceive their kindness and then project it as beauty so the world may observe it. Don't you realize how powerful your ability will be when you become queen and you want to persuade others to your side? And we haven't touched on the benefit of transforming your perceptions into reality. Restoring my hands to me is a gift the entire royal treasury couldn't accomplish."

The edges of Beauty's mouth tilted upward. "Your hands revert when I'm not around, though."

"But as you've grown older, my hands have retained their altered state from a farther distance," said Penta.

Beauty clutched a bedsheet in her fist and squeezed. "But, Mom, with these witches...I don't know if I could've done anything useful if I'd had to face them."

Penta removed her hand from on top of her daughter's. "I'm grateful you didn't have to. You'll be queen soon enough, and then you'll have your own challenges."

A pair of dryads stepped aside, allowing Cinderella and

Cuthbert to enter Ozark's hut. Chests and shelves adorned the small interior, supporting various small wooden household items. Cuthbert reached for a wind chime made from an ash tree and brushed it with his fingers. The ornament made not a sound; instead, it illuminated the room with a dozen colors. Noticing the color blast, a sprite doctor rose to her feet from the side of Ozark's bed, nodded, and excused herself.

Lying on a thin covering of leaves, Ozark looked like the husk of a man he was before, the former fire in his eyes now only embers. He managed a smile. "Forest Lily."

Cinderella's eyes welled up with tears. "You have not called me Forest Lily in some time."

"You commanded me not to," he whispered. "Now that I am on my deathbed, will you be severe with me?"

"Of course not."

The druid's eyes shifted to his other visitor. "And hello, Cuthbert John."

"Thank you for not calling him Cutlass John," said Cinderella. "His father started the nickname, and I fear it will follow him."

The old man managed to snort. "This coming from one whose name was Radiance but who now goes by Cinderella. Have you heard mothers name their daughters Cinderella now? The name no longer means what it once did."

Cinderella approached and kneeled by her stepfather's side. "I am sorry I have not visited you recently. I did not know the illness had progressed this far."

Ozark's eyes softened. "You are a queen of Kingdom. Your duty lies with your people. I wish your adopted sister, Pennilane, would stop hovering over me. She makes me nervous. Please send her away on some quest."

Cuthbert giggled. "Auntie Pennilane, the seal."

"Selkie," corrected Cinderella. She turned to Ozark. "In truth, she loves you dearly."

"Help her, Cinderella. She is not as misanthropic as she pretends to be." Ozark's attention shifted to Cuthbert. "But you came here for a different purpose, true?"

Cinderella bowed her head. "Yes. I need you to throw a protection spell on Cuthbert."

Ozark closed his eyes. "The witches. But they are dead, are they not?"

"I do not believe it for a moment," declared Cinderella. "If they could come back once, what would stop them a second time?"

"Agreed."

Cinderella stroked her father's arm. "With your enchantments, I will not worry about his life."

Ozark shifted, and a few leaves from his bed fell to the floor. "He is safer under Celeste's protection than here."

Cinderella clasped her hands together. "Please. You must be able to do something. Hide him somewhere safe."

Ozark's eyes widened. "Hide? A possibility." His head turned slightly to Cinderella's son. "Would you like to stay here in disguise?"

"Would I?" The child's grin nearly reached the end of his face.

The old druid closed his eyes. "But do I have the strength for such a complex spell?"

Cinderella cupped a hand behind her son's neck and urged him closer. His hair color and texture shined in the candlelight as a copy of hers. Cinderella said, "Others did not call you strong only because of your power. You are more than a spellcaster."

"I am afraid not, Forest Lily. I'm but a spell-wielder."

"Protector, defender, strategist, advisor...and father."

Ozark brushed Cinderella's cheeks with his fingertips while Cinderella leaned into his touch. Ozark said, "I will transform him into a commoner and hide him among the people. I will keep his location hidden from you in case they peer into your mind."

"Why a commoner?"

"Evil is blind to the potential in those they think beneath them." Ozark closed his eyes. "A lesson Wickedness will never learn, much to Righteousness' credit. Now then, kiss your boy good-bye and leave him with me. You will not see him again until this trouble has passed."

"Not yet," said Cinderella. "My visit is twofold. I am here to be with you, Father, and to give you comfort in any way I can. Cuthbert, kiss your grandfather, then go outside and talk to the dryads. I want to be alone with him."

Cuthbert followed his mother's instruction and skipped outside. Ten minutes later, the druid summoned him inside for the transformation.

When Cinderella returned to the castle, she found her sisters, Roger, and the other royals gathered at a dining table. Roger stood. "Has Ozark hidden Cuthbert then?"

"Yes," Cinderella snapped.

Roger placed his hands on his hips. "And where is he?"

"Safe," she answered.

12 - AN EXPOSED ROCK

Harold

I caught up to Valencia and strolled beside her deeper and deeper into the maze. She didn't hesitate when she turned or chose paths, moving forward with a single-minded purpose. When we were out of earshot of her guard and my wife, she stopped and crouched down, spotting an object wedged in the bushes. She reached into the brambles and retrieved a gray stone with glittering silver specks and held it up. "An Oz wishing stone." She grinned ear to ear. "I'll take all the luck I can uncover on this quest."

Valencia's lucky feeling made her a human homing beacon for wishing rocks. She had a personal goal to collect the most powerful wishing stones in Kingdom to keep evil people from wishing disasters on others.

She pocketed this stone and turned to me, growing serious. I had a flashback, recalling when I had first met her, and we had talked privately on a ship in Kingdom. She had the same trusting expression on her face. "Hero, I want you to return with Sanders to Earth when Alice arrives.

I stepped back. "No way. We're in this together now."

Valencia grabbed my arm. "Listen to me. My intuition tells me the two of you are headed for danger. Something terrible is about to happen to you two, and I can't bear to think of it."

I noticed the dark circles under her eyes; she'd had a rough night. I put my hand on top of hers. "It's us, remember? We've fought demons together. Sanders and I have squared off alone against a powerful witch. We can handle it."

Valencia pulled away. "These hags are different. The witch you faced before had some scruples. These three crones would consume Kingdom in fire if they thought it served their purpose."

I removed my hat and scratched my head, bells jingling. "You'll need every friend you have if these three are more powerful than Glinda. You said before your intuition indicated you need us. Why the change of heart?"

Valencia rubbed her hands together. "The little I slept, I dreamed of Snow White. She was drowning in her boat, screaming for help."

"Oh my God. I'm so sorry."

"I woke and called for Graddock. He comforted me, but I wasn't able to return to sleep." She heaved a deep sigh. "Snow White would never forgive me if you or Sanders came to harm."

"And she wouldn't forgive me if I went home and you came to harm," I replied. "So we're even. I'm the blind spot, right? And now Sanders has magic. We can help."

Valencia observed the grass, the edges of her mouth turned up. "You two are an inspiration to me, you know? Hugging each other. Kissing. Sitting in the same chair. Your closeness to each other...I wish..."

"I'm sure you and Graddock are close in private."

Valencia's thoughts showed on her face. I winced. Maybe not.

The queen bit her lip. "I know I shouldn't say, but I wish that lug of a man would relax around me. Graddock is attracted to me, but he's guarded and avoids physical contact. He claims he cannot be passionate around me because he believes he can't be a prince."

I squinted in the Oz sunshine. "Why not? Graddock is prince material."

She smirked. "Trust me—he's not. Graddock cheats at cards, he threatens everyone who disrespects me instead of shrugging it off, he visits The Thirsty Wench—don't ask, it's exactly what you think it is. Others tell me about his exploits and have tried to persuade me to avoid him, but I can't separate from him."

I crouched down and caught her eye. "Because you love him."

She nodded, tears in her eyes. She blinked them away. "What am I doing? I shouldn't be telling you this. This quest of mine has completely scattered my thoughts."

I held out my hand. "Hey, I'm your friend. I won't say anything to anyone. You know Sanders and I are struggling with having a baby, and now I know you and Graddock need a little encouragement. Friends trust each other with their secrets."

Valencia grabbed my hand. "You don't think yourself a hero, but you're wrong."

We embraced and then made our way back through the hedge paths. Valencia's "lucky guesses" enabled her to walk through a maze without becoming lost.

When we left the hedge maze, we observed something

that destroyed whatever equanimity I still possessed. Graddock and Sanders were off to the side. Sanders was resting on the ground, her hands behind her, head tilted backward and eyes half-closed. Graddock sat behind Sondra, straddling her, arms around her waist. Graddock's lips touched the back of Sondra's neck again and again, and she released a long, pleasurable sigh.

"Shock" would be too small a word to encompass my thoughts at that moment, and I think Valencia shared my inability to believe what we were witnessing. I was so stunned I couldn't speak or move. We observed Graddock again firmly but passionately kiss the back of Sanders' neck, his lips taking a moment to tease another gratified sigh from my wife. Valencia's head trembled from side to side like a leaf shaking on a tree when a breeze ruffles it. She drew in her breath.

"Graddock!"

Valencia's voice cut across the verdant lawn as a butcher's knife slices through fresh meat. The guard turned his attention to her and glared as if she had no right to be here. Annoyed, Graddock gestured with his head for Valencia and me to go away and leave him and Sanders alone. When Valencia's face hardened, her guard resigned himself and drew back from my wife. Sanders opened her eyes slowly, irritation written across her face. When she noticed me, she appeared nonplussed. She observed me the way someone regards a house chore she was obligated to perform.

Wearily, Graddock rose to his feet. "My queen," he said, his flat tone tinged with disappointment.

Sondra

I gotta tell you, I was more than pissed. I was cat pissed. I finally got that hunk of a swordsman to myself, and we came together like two interlocking puzzle pieces. The man has a body that would make Roman gods jealous, with the face of the actor Kris Heavens. You know what I'm talking about. He said I looked tense, so I asked him for a backrub, and the rest is history. And the first time his lips touched my neck? Let's say the kiss was the type I felt all the way down to my purple-painted toenails. And then *she* had to come along and ruin it.

Valencia's mouth opened and closed. Arms straight at her sides, her face was as red as lava about to burst out of a volcano. Hero started to say "What the..." before Valencia nudged him, cutting off an offensive word. She's such a child!

Valencia recovered before Hero. The words then poured out an octave higher and twenty decibels louder. "Graddock! How dare you? You are my guard and— How could you do this to Kingdom?"

I pitied Valencia. She was so beneath my league that the situation was embarrassing. "Your simple feelings for him are common knowledge, Match Girl. He's traded up for a real woman."

"Sanders!" Hero bellowed loud enough for a rock at Graddock's feet to jiggle. "Godda—"

Valencia's hand clamped over his mouth. The queen bristled. "And you! You are married to Hero. You're a hussy of the first order."

Oh, yeah. I sort of had forgotten Hero was my husband. Graddock's muscles distracted me. But Valencia was one to talk. "Hussy? Me? Isn't it your custom to obtain your sisters' permission before you play tonsil hockey with others? Graddock's crush on you is over. We love each other now."

Red-faced, Hero's body shook. He'll get over it, though, after the divorce. But for now, he pointed at me. "Did you throw a pixie spell and mess it up? You and Graddock hardly know each other."

I smirked. "We're getting better acquainted every second." I made a shooing motion. "Go back to talking in the maze. We want to be left alone."

Given Valencia's expression, I was glad she wasn't holding a gun. She said, "Of course we won't. You can't possibly be attracted to each other. We were only gone for—"

Valencia's aposiopesis was taken up by Hero, who finished her sentence. "For ten minutes? Fifteen? How could you fall in love...or whatever the hell you call *that*...without magic in such a short time. Think about it!"

I hardly listened to my ex-husband, or current husband, I *guess*. Valencia marched toward us across the lawn. I murmured to Graddock. "I'm going to kick her ass and then she'll leave us alone." He grinned in response.

But she didn't attack me. She moved toward the wiggling rock at Graddock's feet. The stone moved back and forth as if trembling or...giggling?

Valencia lifted her boot and brought it down on the stone in one swift motion. The rock screamed and erupted in a flash of light. In its place stood a small being, a boy sprouting goat ears.

The newcomer turned to jump through a hedge, but Valencia grabbed his left ear. "Who are you?"

"Alas! A wandering merry-maker of no consequence," he replied.

She twisted his ear, and he wailed in pain. The boy screamed. "Unhand me, woman! I have not harmed e'en a petal on a flower to warrant such ill-treatment."

Valencia gritted her teeth. "Fairy, if you do not tell me what you have done, I will twist another part of you more sensitive than your ear."

The boy paled. "Puck's my name, and I have administer'd a small spell while your party reclined in relaxation. A minor jest."

"I do not think it a funny jest," said Valencia, tugging his ear. "And I suggest you undo your spell immediately."

"You jest yourself? You su-jest?"

Valencia grabbed the other ear and twisted.

"How, woman! You will have me deaf afore the sun sets."

"Then do as I say!" Valencia's directive would command a lion.

Puck grumbled something under his breath. He reached

in his pocket and produced a vial filled with a liquid. "Allow a single tear of this to drop on closed eyes, and all shall be as it once was."

Valencia swiped the liquid out of his hand and commanded us to stand before her with our eyes shut. Her order, forceful as that of a commander in the army, was not to be crossed, so we lined up. I decided her potion wouldn't matter. True love won't be denied.

Valencia applied a single drop to each of our eyelids and then said, "Open your eyes."

When I followed her instruction, I blinked rapidly. What had I done? I looked from Hero to Graddock and back to Hero, my face turning radish red. I opened my mouth to speak to my husband, couldn't think of what to say, and turned to apologize to Graddock. But I should apologize to Hero first, right? I didn't know what to do.

Graddock blushed under my scrutiny but regained his composure and turned from me, rushing to Valencia and kneeling before her. "My queen, I do not know how to beg your forgiveness."

Valencia spun to Puck, but the fairy was gone. She shifted her attention back to the rest of us, eyebrows still knit. Graddock, head lowered, trembled before her. Awkwardness as thick as pea soup smothered us.

Hero said, "This has happened before in a play called *A Midsummer Night's Dream*. They couldn't help it, Valencia."

What a weird thought, but at least he wasn't yelling. "What's a Shakespeare character doing in Oz?"

My question went unanswered, for Valencia addressed Graddock. "Follow me. Give the Saturns their privacy."

The queen's guard stood and followed Valencia into the hedge maze where she and Hero had just emerged. Hero cleared his throat and caught my eye. "Well, how exciting."

I folded my arms. "I don't know what to say. We were sitting on the ground talking when I noticed the rock appear. I was about to say something, and then..."

I couldn't go on. Instead, my face flushed again! "It's not my fault. I was under a spell."

Still, Hero didn't approach me. I wanted him to embrace me and tell me he understood. I needed that moment. Instead, he snapped at me. "I'll have the image of Graddock fondling you for the rest of my life."

Thanks, husband. "It meant nothing to me."

He eyed me. "You had a look in your eye I haven't seen in a while."

I knew *that* expression—physical yearning. "You're mistaken. If Valencia hadn't called…"

He leaned away. "Am I? If our bedtime activities were dancing, they'd feel more like square dancing than dirty dancing if you get my meaning. Making love is no longer spontaneous or sensual. Lately, we've been so focused on our plans, we've forgotten about *us*. Maybe we ought to focus on each other again?"

"I'm not going to put aside our dreams for the future," I replied. "You know how I feel about having a baby. If only it would've happened by now."

"But it hasn't. It may never happen."

That statement hurt. I stepped forward and slapped his arm. "Don't lose hope now."

Hero rubbed his chin. "We have to face facts. And the doll in your purse. Really? Asking Glinda for the Powder of Life?"

"You were there last night! You spied on me."

"What were you going to do with a living doll?" he asked. "Hide it away on Earth? Don't you think it would be a little strange if we're having dinner with friends and a Pinocchio doll walked out in the middle of our meal, asking you to play with it?"

"I had a plan."

His right eye twitched. "You and your plans. You didn't talk to me about it at all. How could you ask her for the Powder of Life and not consult me?"

I struck out my chin. "The Powder of Life was Part One of my plan."

"I figured. And who was going to turn him into a real boy? Does such a spell exist?"

I gulped. "It's beyond me."

"You don't even know if it's possible? And if it was, who would you get to enact it?"

I turned away, and a burning sensation formed behind my eyes. I wouldn't cry. I wouldn't give him the satisfaction. "I haven't figured it all out yet. I don't plan everything out to the tenth degree the way you do. I felt, in my heart, I would make everything work."

He closed his eyes and stepped forward. He knew how much he was hurting me. "Sondra—"

I put a hand on Hero's chest, and the simple gesture was the right thing to do. His body relaxed, guilt etched in his face for his earlier statements. I licked my lips. "I love my job at Dow. I'm good at it, and I don't want to quit, but I also want a family. We've tried and tried, and I'm becoming desperate, Harold. I'll start with a Pinocchio doll if I have to."

"I prefer the old-fashioned method."

I rolled my eyes. "I do too, but Mr. Old-Fashioned is taking his sweet time. We started a year ago! I have friends who started after us and have their babies now. Why don't men understand this?"

"This isn't a race." He sounded regretful.

"I know, but what if it never happens? What if we can't have children?" I asked, tears gushing into my eyes. "God, Harold, I love you, but I've always dreamed of having a family. This isn't simply, 'Now that you're married, the time has come to have a child.' It's important to me in a way I can't describe." I couldn't suppress the waterworks running down my face.

I rarely have vulnerable moments with anyone but Hero. He knows this, and to his credit, he stops arguing when it happens. Pushing aside his irritation, Hero stepped forward and hugged me. "I love you," I said.

"I love you, too." He stroked the back of my head. "But perhaps...perhaps we're not ready for a child."

I pulled away. What was this crap now? "We talked about this. We said we were ready and wanted to have a family."

"I know. And I think you'll be a great mom." Hero took a deep breath. "I'm not so sure about me, though, as a father."

I put my hand on his cheek. "Stop being silly. You'll be a wonderful dad. Don't worry about it."

His forehead wrinkled at my statement. "I just don't think—"

Footsteps sounded at the hedge maze. "Quiet," I said. "I hear Graddock and Valencia."

I wiped my eyes while the guard and queen stepped back into view. Valencia arrived first, her complexion pale and her lips pressed together. A few steps behind her walked Graddock with his attention remaining fixed on a point to the left of the monarch. Valencia approached us, and I could instinctively tell Valencia and Graddock had not made up. The queen hung back, avoiding eye contact with her guard.

Graddock stepped forward and bowed low to me. "Please pardon my offense. As you know, I was not in my right mind."

I bowed my head. "And as for what I said, it meant nothing."

Graddock turned to Hero. "I have always considered you a good man. As such, my behavior was—"

"Over and done, Graddock. Over and done," Hero said.

I caught Valencia's eye. Oh, this wasn't going to be easy. I straightened up. "You know I would never do anything to hurt you."

Valencia nodded but didn't respond. This particular queen used to have a chip on her shoulder against pixies. Apparently, crumbs of that chip remained.

Not long after apologies were given and mostly accepted, a small horse with two riders made its way toward us. I blinked twice while it approached but should've remembered I was in Oz. An animated sawhorse carried Glinda to us with another rider, Alice, on its back behind the Good Witch. The two of them arrived, the little wooden legs moving fast. When they dismounted, the riders stared at us.

"What happened?" asked Glinda.

Hero stepped forward, hoping to avoid the question with another question. "What is Puck doing in Oz?"

Glinda put a hand to her temple and rubbed it. "What did he do?"

"We'd rather not discuss it," snapped Valencia. "Other than to say he's caused considerable embarrassment."

Glinda inclined her head toward Valencia. "I apologize. Puck is from Astage, the home world of the witches. He has a wealth of information, and I traded his knowledge of the witches to permit him to spend two hours in Oz. The good news is his information is excellent. I found what I was searching for—a way to defeat the witches of Scotland."

"Scotland? The Scotland on Earth?" I asked.

"The Scotland in Astage, not on Earth," Glinda clarified. "Now gather around."

Valencia eyed Graddock, and he approached Alice. "Begging your pardon, Miss Alice. I would appreciate it if you would take me back to Kingdom."

I couldn't believe Graddock was going to abandon the quest. My husband eyed the guard's sword. "But Graddock, you can't leave. You're Valencia's guard."

Graddock didn't speak, so Valencia answered for him. "He may depart. If the witches still threaten Kingdom, he is better stationed there. I have you and Sanders for guards."

I crossed my arms. "But we're not fighters the way Graddock is. We could use a prince on our side."

Wrong thing to say. Valencia and Graddock's body language spoke encyclopedias. Graddock said, "I will send another guard in my place. I am no prince."

So that was it! The throne or the dude. Tough choice, Valencia. The queen's body posture and expression were as stiff as those of a mannequin. She said, "He leaves."

Alice didn't question the command. Whatever she said would only have added to the awkwardness. Instead, Alice walked over and took Graddock's arm, and they disappeared.

Valencia turned to Glinda. "Now tell me how we defeat these damn witches."

13 - A FISHY SITUATION

I n the morning before dawn, Penta, Cinderella, and Helga
gathered for breakfast in a circular room extending from
the castle on the east side. The windows had a delightful
view of the free-roaming bestiary. The walls and the ceiling
were constructed of square glass panes, a rarity in Kingdom.
Sunlight poured in and provided illumination to an elegant
U-shaped table, allowing the queens to view each other and
converse.

After the three queens were seated, servants carried in
trays of various fruits and slices of bread and set plates before
the monarchs. The table, large enough to seat five queens and
one guest, was only half-occupied.

Cinderella stared at the vacant seats. "We need a smaller
table."

Lifting a golden fork to her lips, Helga eyed a piece of
melon on its tines. "Valencia will return, Cinderella."

Cinderella observed the empty chair to her left. "But

Snow White never will."

The spiked fruit hovered before Helga's lips. "Have courage, sister."

Cinderella snapped, "Get real, Helga."

Outside, a muzzled dormadog roamed past the window behind Penta. "The witches are making us anxious and short with each other. We fear to hope Valencia has found Glinda and she will help, or to hope the witches are dead for good," the gloved queen said.

Cinderella reached for a serving spoon. "For my part, I cannot hope. I have returned from visiting Ozark whose life hangs by a thread. I don't know the whereabouts of my son." She dropped her chin. "And I have lost my beloved sister. I feel her absence more today."

Penta picked at her breakfast. "Snow White's loss has affected us deeply, 'tis true."

A giraffe and a squonk strolled by together. Amused, Penta observed the creatures, when she was interrupted by a voice from her ring. "Queen Penta. Please answer if you are there!"

She lifted the ring to her mouth. "Elisa? From Pernissa Bay?"

"Yes. We are under attack."

Penta's jawline hardened. "By whom?"

"The witches!"

Helga slammed down her utensils. "I knew it. Six dwarfs are unlikely vanquishers of such a powerful adversary."

Penta stood. Cinderella and Helga rushed to her side and grabbed her hands. They teleported to Celeste, described the situation, and reached for her hand to create a daisy chain. All united, Penta teleported everyone to Pernissa Bay.

The queens found themselves in the center square of town an hour before the first rays of sunlight had a chance to shine on the buildings. The little fishing village had sprung up in the last four years as a restful retreat outside of Nor on the north coast of Kingdom. They spied Elisa across the way, the ring still at her lips. Before they could converse with her, screams originating from the docks down the street caught their attention.

Elisa rushed across the road to the spot where the queens appeared. "My six brothers have gone to help. The witches and others came from the water."

Helga removed a flail from her belt. "Others?"

Elisa never had a chance to answer the queen. Creatures with human bodies but enlarged fish heads rounded a corner down the street. The marine bipeds' bulging, dead eyes stuck out of either side of their narrow faces that connected to necks thin at the base of the skull and broader at the shoulders. The bizarre beings carried fishing poles on their shoulders like rifles, and they were casting them down the street. Lines unspooled from the rods, and the hooks landed on people. Paralyzed, their targets fell, and the fish-men hauled their captured victims in the direction of the water.

Swinging her flail above her head, Helga charged forward while Penta vanished and reappeared between the creatures and the sea. Cinderella raised her hand and pointed at the strange beings.

Elisa put her hand on Cinderella's arm. "Save your strength, my queen. The witches have formed men from the fish in the sea. The vile sorceresses enacted this deed while floating over the ocean."

The fish-men ignored Cinderella's ability, having no conscience, and continued to collect people on the street. Cinderella reached for the dagger in her hilt to protect herself when Penta materialized next to her. The high queen gasped. "Hundreds of the fish-men and their captives are assembled on the beach. The villains are dragging the people into the water and drowning them."

Cinderella grew pale. "Send me back to Kingdom, and I'll gather Roger and the army."

Penta nodded and touched Cinderella, teleporting her to the royal palace. Elisa retrieved a short blade from a loophole in her belt. "Did you see my brothers?"

"They have transformed into swans and are snipping the fishing lines with their sharp beaks," said Penta. "Their quick thinking is saving lives."

Penta unsheathed her knife. Yelling, Elisa and the queen rushed toward the fracas.

Penta retreated to the royal palace after fifteen minutes of battle. Under the portcullis, she spied Roger. He stood on a platform in front of a squadron of soldiers poised at attention in the courtyard.

Penta stepped up next to him and cupped her hands around her mouth to address the troops. "The hags have returned and are now converting fish into men. They are attacking Pernissa Bay. Do not engage the witches. They are only jeering at our efforts and creating more fish-men. We are outnumbered, but we must fight them. Do not waste your energy killing the creatures unless your life is in peril. Focus on severing the fishing lines to save as many of our citizens' lives as possible."

Shouts of affirmation followed her speech. She held up her hands. "Are you ready?"

The soldiers raised their weapons and screamed a war cry.

Penta hopped off the block and touched Roger, sending him to Pernissa Bay. She then ran up and down the troop formations brushing the ends of her fingertips along each officer's shoulder, transporting them all to the north coast to follow Cinderella's prince. Cinderella stood in the back of the army and held out her hand. Penta grabbed it, and the two queens whisked away.

The combat raged on all day with wave after wave of fish-men marching out from the ocean. Fishing lines crisscrossed over the town of Pernissa Bay, similar to spider webs in an abandoned room. At one point, Cinderella nearly drowned until Helga came to her aid. Helga saved numerous lives, but the screams of those silenced by gagging on water echoed all across the city as the hours passed.

People were saved and hooked again, over and over. Some were rescued multiple times only to lose their lives later on. Penta herself had kept a teenaged Hansel from drowning to Gretel's relief. After hours of liberating the community's members, the weary soldiers severed lines more slowly.

As the sun started its descent for the day, the witches approached Penta. Picana flicked her fingers, and the queen's arms rose into the air against her will. The witch leaned toward her. "Not to worry. We aren't going to hurt a hair on your pretty head. We have come to talk of your surrender."

Penta glared at them. "Your fish-men will have to kill me first."

Tomana cackled. "Over five-hundred-thousand fish swim in Kingdom's ocean for every person on land. You'll never succeed."

Penta glowered at them. "Better everyone dead than my serving as your slave."

Tomana reared back. "Do my ears deceive me? And they say I am ruthless?"

"You are battle weary." Picana flicked her finger at her fish-men. "We shall call off our army. Take your sisters, return to your castle, and discuss the terms of surrender before tomorrow morning."

Tomana narrowed her eyes. "Don't entertain any idea of moving everyone out of the city. We have placed a curse on the residents. Only you and the soldiers may leave."

Picana flashed a toothless grin. "We shall expect white flags over Pernissa Bay tomorrow."

Penta's nostrils flared. "We will never submit."

"Did we neglect to say?" Picana set a finger on her chin. "You may have noticed today the fish-men targeted the men and women of the village. Tomorrow, they'll target the children."

Penta's face pinched in terror. "Not the innocents. Leave

them be."

"The children, Penta, every one of them dead by tomorrow night," sneered Picana. "And I predict their parents will succumb to the same fate when they follow them to the sea."

The witches screeched with laughter and disappeared, while the fish-men all performed an about-face and marched to the water. Cheers from the townspeople rose into the air when the fish-men retracted their lines and retreated. Penta knew better. She fell to the ground and covered her eyes, weeping.

14 - THE THREE DOORWAYS

Harold

We sat down in the Oz garden and gave Glinda our full attention. With the sun shining on her pale complexion, Glinda waved her hands and the ants scurrying around us grew three times their regular size, standing on their hind legs. Their faces transformed to display the features of the three old witches: one grew a pointed chin; one's antenna formed a hat; frizzy hair sprouted from the third.

Glinda brought her hands together then arched them downward as if constructing a rainbow. Small, colored orbs encircled her head. "At the start, all three witches were once human girls. You must understand they are mortal with normal, yet twisted, souls. Because of this, the fact that they are cheating death is troubling."

The grass formed a tiny cauldron, and the three ants gathered around it, clicking with glee.

Glinda regarded the ants. "Even when they were young, they were not good girls. Picana, the leader, was born to a family in Northern Scotland. Oldest of the children in that brood, she murdered her brother after the town promoted him to mayor instead of her."

A blade of grass took the form of a tiny, green man. The hat ant clicked its mandibles and snapped it in two.

"Myiasis, or Mya, also hailed from Scotland. She had a natural inclination for magic, and she spent her early years in a loving family. Unfortunately, a mosquito stung and infected her with a deadly disease. She survived but lost her sanity in the process. From that point on, mischief and torture consumed her mind."

Glinda pointed at the ant with the sharp chin. "And the third, Erotomana, or Tomana, was a neighbor of Mya and her brother Hale. A cold girl, Tomana showed tenderness only to Mya's brother. Hale, for his part, didn't return her affection. To torture her brother, Mya threw a love spell on Hale, and for a few days, he and Tomana were happy together. When the spell wore off, Hale rejected Tomana. Tomana's heart broke, and her conscience darkened.

"Seeking revenge on Hale, Tomana begged Mya to teach her magic and found herself an apt pupil. Tomana became a powerful witch in quick measure and threw a spell to have a horse toss Hale and break his neck. Mya clapped when her brother's neck snapped."

This time, a blade of grass took the shape of a boy. The tip of the shoot turned sideways with an audible crack, and the ants shook with glee.

Glinda's orbs bobbed around her head like bees drunk with honey. "Mya's delight at her brother's death caused her family to disavow her. Tomana inherited her family's estate, so she took in Mya. Tomana threw a bonding spell on Mya with a connection as strong as family, making defeating Mya hard while Tomana's magic protects her.

"The two of them gained a reputation for being cruel witches, and Picana sought them out. She desired, more than anything, to be in control of everyone, and she realized power like that only came with the dark arts. The three formed an alliance. Mya and Tomana weren't ambitious, so Picana became their leader. Ironic then that although Picana worked hard to become a mighty magic-wielder, she was not as powerful as Mya or Tomana."

The three ants came together, chittering at each other.

"These three swore sisterhood to each other and became a coven," continued Glinda. "The coven spent many years performing malicious deeds, cursing farmers and spreading the pox. They were an evil, notorious trio, but Picana wanted more power. She knew Mya, in particular, was capable of much more and didn't realize increasing Mya's abilities was dangerous. To this day, Picana doesn't understand the consequences of her actions if Mya doesn't stay in check. Recklessly, the witches made a deal with the devil."

An enlarged beetle scurried to the ants and stood on two legs. It towered over the ants, glaring down at them, and crossed all its appendages—an imposing figure.

The small circles around Glinda's head flashed a fiery red and then regained their multi-color palette. "Picana, Mya, and Tomana were given a task to gain the devil's favor. You have to understand the devil to understand his request. He gave them a challenge to hurt them not only during the trial but for the rest of their lives. He loves to watch people suffer from regret and indecision...to struggle with temptation. His request? To birth babies and abandon them."

"He didn't ask the witches to actually sacrifice their children?" I asked. "Sounds more devilish if he had."

Glinda said, "Killing a child is an act one cannot take back. The devil cannot tempt you to restore its life. Abandoning a child carelessly and willingly is something quite different. The temptation to return for an abandoned child would be constant."

The beetle clicked its jaws and gestured to the ants who bowed to it in worship. Valencia put a hand to her mouth, and Sanders sucked in her breath.

"For the three witches, killing their offspring would've been much easier," said Glinda. "Evil witches delight in killing children, but to have to suffer through nine months of carrying a baby, to overcome a mother's preference for her child, and then to abandon it without any remorse..."

"...is truly evil," finished Valencia.

"Some mothers choose to separate from their newborns for the good of their children," remarked Glinda. "Their act of separation is a mature decision, often to the babe's benefit. However, a woman who casts away her child as if she's kicking off a worn-out shoe is evil to her core." The Good Witch lowered her head, frowning.

"How they came by these children is a tale better left for another day," she went on. "The infants, all girls, were born of the seed of unsuspecting men. Shortly after their birth, the devil commanded the evil child-bearers to abandon their children, never to seek them out or reconcile with them. Without remorse, they followed his instructions to the letter."

The ants twitched, and their abdomens grew large. They produced larvae and drew back from their offspring, repulsed. Then the ants picked up their newborns and raced to three separate anthills, descending into the ground below.

Watching the action of the supposed witches, Glinda continued, "In return for their passing the test, the devil gave them the power of the creatures of hell. With that, they became the most powerful coven in Astage. The witches killed Picana's and Mya's remaining family. Picana wiped out the town that had denied her the position of mayor. The three overshadowed Scotland like a dark plague."

The ants emerged from underground and came back together, gathering around the grass cauldron.

"Why did they leave Astage's Scotland?" I asked.

Touching her orbs, Glinda made each sphere illuminate brighter. "Astage is not as rich in magic as Kingdom is. They lusted for more power. As for the daughters, Puck told me the witches' offspring, while not being witches themselves, were born with natural abilities, much like Kingdom's queens. They each have a unique magical talent. I sense the hand of a benign Higher Power in this. Puck has heard rumors the daughters are considerate and courageous young women."

Three ants with wings emerged, one each, from the three anthills. The winged offspring approached the enlarged ants from behind. While smaller, the three ant children didn't falter in their progress toward those gathered around the cauldron. Before the smaller ants attacked their mothers, Glinda waved her hand and transformed them all into regular-sized ants. The insects scurried away.

Valencia sat up on her haunches for the last part of the speech, visibly excited by the prospect of defeating the evil coven. "The daughters...do they live near Scotland or will we have to journey far?"

Glinda regarded her. "You're willing to collect them and direct them to fight their mothers? This quest is far from a fait accompli. You have to find them first. They may not believe in witches, even if they are aware of their own abilities. And they may not want to leave their homes to battle their powerful mothers. If you happen to overcome all of this, you still don't know how to defeat them. The daughters will have their talents, but they remain susceptible to the hags' spells. The witches will be thrilled to kill their offspring."

Valencia stood. "I love a challenge."

Glinda's orbs revolved around her head more quickly. "A challenge it is, assuredly. I would call it a fool's errand if the hand of God were not in it. Furthermore, I have not told you the most difficult part yet."

"Which is?" asked Valencia.

Before Glinda could answer, Alice and a companion appeared. The woman behind Alice, dressed in a leather vest, thick pants, and knee-high boots, held a spear. I recognized her as Pennilane, a selkie from Kingdom and Cinderella's best friend. Her stark-white whiskers and mahogany-colored face greeted us with a grimace. Her hair was longer than I had seen it before, coming down to the middle of her back.

The two newcomers made their way to us. Pennilane appeared ill at ease but relieved to see Valencia. The selkie kneeled before her queen. "At your service."

"Stand. Do not worry about formality on this quest. What is the news from Kingdom?"

Pennilane recounted the past events in Kingdom, and Valencia wept when the selkie described Bull's death. The queen summarized the story Glinda had just finished. She turned to the Good Witch. "You were about to tell us why our task would be difficult. Please continue."

Glinda waved her hand, and the orbs vanished. "The devil is a Traveler. He didn't want the witches to leave their children in the world of Astage. He accompanied each hag to a different world and demanded she leave behind her newborn. Knowing how difficult Travel is, he seems to have decided that keeping the daughters far away was in his best interest. To defeat the coven, you will have to Travel to three different worlds, find the daughters, and convince them to journey to Kingdom and risk their lives."

Valencia put her hands to her face. "Why didn't you tell us this when we started? How will we find the worlds? And if we do, how will we find the daughters within an entire world?"

Glinda floated backward. "In this, at least, I can help you. I know the worlds the daughters call home. Using my quill as a totem, I'll create three portals to these worlds and cast a spell to place you within the vicinity of the daughters. When you arrive, you will inquire whether the residents know of a young woman with unnatural abilities."

I asked, "How far away is a 'vicinity' precisely? Ten miles or ten feet?"

"I measure it in time. Within a ten-minute walk."

I rubbed my chin. "And you'll accompany us there?"

"I think it's better if I go to Kingdom where I can help Celeste."

Glinda shook her wand three times, and it turned into a quill. She stepped away from us and drew three door-sized rectangles that shone in the daylight. The Good Witch gestured, and three doorways materialized. Nothingness surrounded the entrances. I recognized the darkness as the Void from my Travels before.

Glinda turned back to us. "Are you ready?"

Alice stepped away while Pennilane gripped her spear. I stood next to Sanders as Valencia examined the doorways. "Indeed. But we number only five. One will have to cross over alone."

Alice cracked her knuckles as if readying for a fight, "I am used to Traveling solo. Tell us which worlds are beyond the doorways, and we'll adjust to being shy a person."

Glinda nodded. "Beyond the first doorway lies a land draped in shadow. Chronologically, this world is later than Kingdom, but in Earth's past. Residents call their world Morbidum."

Alice eyed the doorway. "The Guild knows of Morbidum. Travelers avoid it because of its dreary atmosphere and tragic events. We labeled it a land of misfortune. It's not all doom and gloom, however. You're likely to find roaring fires in the hearths of cozy homes within small villages. They gather and tell each other ghost stories. Magic exists there, but subdued, dark magic, not comparable to the spells of Kingdom."

Glinda pointed to the second doorway. "The second world is Janay. A world in a similar time as Morbidum but vastly different living conditions."

Alice lit up at the name of this world. "A passage to Janay! I've heard rumors of this world, but the Guild hasn't found a way there yet."

Glinda said, "Janay is a land of bounty, of festivals, and chance encounters. You'll find a world on the verge of the Industrial Revolution. 'Tis a delightful world of sowing and reaping, dancing and merry-making."

Alice's eyes twinkled. "And romance, so I've been told. One can't help but fall in love there."

I asked, "The third?"

"I daresay the third is the most dangerous," said Glinda. "I have not visited there nor had any wish to. It's a world called Cixxes."

Alice gasped. "No! Of all of the worlds, why is that one of our destinations?"

Valencia asked, "What is Cixxes?"

Alice, white as the moon's surface, turned to the queen. "Cixxes is a world set in Earth's future made up of a variety of dangerous continents. Far from the future utopia people long for, Cixxes is a world where its citizens suffer from mechanical tyrants, alien overlords, evil governments, or oppressive technology. Travelers do not go there for pleasure, and only on targeted missions." Alice's voice trembled.

Valencia put a steadying hand on Alice's arm. "Have you been there, dear Alice?"

"Twice. I almost died each time."

Sanders took her glasses from her pocket and put them on, examining the Cixxes portal. "Does magic exist there?"

Alice clasped together her hands. "Unknown. Some say technology opened a channel for evil magic to enter Cixxes. Ironic, isn't it? We believe magic belongs to the past and advanced science to the future. In Cixxes, magic is as difficult to determine as technology because they seem the same to us. Rumors persist that magic exists there but is disguised as technology."

Sanders stepped closer to the Cixxes doorway. "If magic is there, my pixie powers will protect me. If it's not magic, I'll rely on my scientific knowledge. I'm the most suited for this world."

Alice protested, "Cixxes is not what you expect it to be. Pollution makes some areas unfit for living, and in other sections, people are treated worse than animals."

Sanders leaned forward, trying to view more of the Cixxes world through the doorway. "The scientist in me is curious to see a potential future Earth."

I stepped next to my wife. "I can go with you."

Alice shook her head. "No, you need a proper guide in Cixxes. No Traveler goes there alone. The Guild sends five or six of us at a time, the 'safety in numbers' theory. Some expeditions have never come back."

"We cannot all go," said Valencia. "We've spent too much time in Oz."

Alice ran a hand through her strawberry-colored hair. "I'll go with Sanders. If we stick to the purpose of our mission and you can place us close to a daughter, we'll get in and out quickly."

Pennilane said, "Then it's settled. I'll accompany the queen to Janay as this seems to be the safest world."

Valencia shook her head. "No, I shall go to Morbidum. 'Tis the ideal world for me as I am the most fortunate of people. If my luck holds, my ability and the world's influence will counterbalance the ill."

Pennilane stepped toward the first doorway. "I shall accompany you there."

Valencia put her hand on Pennilane's shoulder. "No, you must go to Janay with Hero."

The selkie's whiskers quivered in revolt. "I must protest, my queen."

"Pennilane, the world's misfortune may not work on me, but it will on you. You must accompany Hero."

Pennilane breathed through her nose. "Janay sounds as though Hero shall be safe there."

Valencia approached me. "Hero, my intuition says your mission may not be dangerous to life, but it may put your marriage at risk. Pennilane, above all people, will keep a watchful eye on you. She's the perfect partner."

Pennilane said, "But you are unprotected, my queen."

"Your concern for me is touching, Pennilane, but don't forget I'm not defenseless," replied Valencia. "I'll go to Morbidum alone."

Glinda nodded. "My magic will dress you when you step through the portal so you will blend in. The spell I've cast is powerful and will cost you most of the day to Travel there. You'll arrive at dusk. You won't be able to return through the portal, however. The passage is one way."

Sanders patted her stick horse. "Not a problem. When Alice and I find our daughter, we'll travel back to each world, using Oz as a hub."

"And I can transport people too," said Alice. "Sanders and I will try to finish first and join Valencia as soon as we are able. I've never Traveled to Janay. Getting there might be hard for us."

Glinda said, "I'll place the route in your mind, Alice, so you may jump to all three. The landing point in each world shall place you near members of your party."

Pennilane stepped up next to me, and Valencia advanced to her doorway. I leaned over to Sanders and held out my right hand. "Be careful."

Sanders took my hand and squeezed it. "You too."

Glinda spoke again. "Valencia, while I will go to Kingdom and join your sisters to help, I will take precautions and remove the witch's history from my memory to keep our knowledge secret from the hags. They excel at mind reading. I'll remember that you're on an important quest but won't know where or why."

Valencia squared her shoulders. "Then let us all be off at once. Pennilane, I order you to listen to Hero. You must fit into the world and not attract attention. Hero, heed Pennilane. She will guard you against yourself. Sanders and Alice, if Cixxes is too dangerous, return, and the rest of us will accompany you.

I hope the matter does not come to that as I have been away from Kingdom for too long as it is. Have faith! We will see each other soon."

After her speech, Valencia stepped onto her path and walked through her doorway. Alice and Sanders were the second ones to enter their world, and Pennilane and I proceeded through our portal last.

15 - THE GOOD AND
THE EXTRAORDINARY

In the royal castle, Penta, Cinderella, and Helga sat on their thrones, discussing the witches' terms for their surrender. Joined by Rose Red to sit in for Snow White and Celeste for Valencia, Penta repeated the witches' demands. Helga said, "Their terms of surrender are not terms at all. If we agree to them, the witches will run amok in Kingdom."

Cinderella rubbed her puffy, red eyes. "How many children do you estimate live in Pernissa Bay?"

Celeste held her index finger up in the air and acted as though she were pressing buttons. "Four hundred fifty-two under the age of thirteen."

Helga placed her hands on her knees. "Even if only one child is affected, I will not forfeit a single youth to these hags."

Cinderella nodded. "I wasn't suggesting we sacrifice the children. I'm only trying to understand how many we stand to lose."

Rose Red sat back in Valencia's wooden chair. "The witches will use this decision against us. If they slaughter the children, they will announce to the townspeople that we knew it beforehand."

"Of course," said Penta. "The children's deaths will be on our heads."

"I couldn't live with myself." Cinderella stifled a sob. "What are we going to do?"

Helga reached out and grabbed Cinderella's hand. "We'll fight them, of course. We need rest to fight them for as long as it takes."

Penta drummed her fingers on her marble throne's armrest, "I know we're all tired, but we must continue our discussion until we have our course of action. We must think of a solution other than engaging them in battle. They must—"

A knock interrupted the high queen's statement. She turned to the door and sucked in a quick breath. "In all of our days of ruling Kingdom, we've never been interrupted while in council. Only the people who wear one of my rings have stopped us while making battle plans. Lyken knows this."

Helga pulled out her flail with the spiked, iron ball. "It's them."

"*They* don't knock." Penta raised her voice. "Who dares to interrupt us?"

Recognizing the high queen's frustration, Celeste transformed to pixie size and flew to the entrance to the room. "I will answer it." She slipped through the crack under the door.

Penta focused on the debate and leaned forward. "We disguise the children."

Helga swung her flail back and forth like a pendulum. "The witches will see through it."

Penta continued, undeterred. "With the children disguised, Celeste transforms plants to look like children. She could—"

"Celeste will use up all of her magic on a doomed plan,"

said Helga.

"Damn you, Helga! Give me a chance to explain myself."

The blood drained from Cinderella's face, and Rose Red sat back, stunned. Helga replied, "Penta, I wish to go to the chapel, pray, and retire. You and I aren't ourselves. We need to reflect. End the council."

Penta slapped her hand down on the armrest. "I will not end the council unless one of us comes up with a plan. I will entertain anything, including killing the witches."

An awkward silence filled the room. Cinderella leaned forward. "From the start, we agreed, as fairytale queens, we would not consider killing as an option. Taking a life belongs only on the battlefield and as a last resort."

Penta let out a long breath. "I didn't mean what I said." She closed her eyes and put a hand to her forehead. "Helga, perhaps you are right."

Celeste reentered and flew up to the thrones. "I have told Lyken we were not to be disturbed, but he said a stranger has come to our door and wishes to address us." She presented a card.

Penta read the card, eyes widening. "Send her in."

Celeste waved her hand, and the doors opened. Lyken stood outside, and he gestured for someone to enter. A cloaked figure dressed in blue walked into sight and entered the room. The person lowered her hood, revealing her long, red locks. "I am Glinda the Good. I'm here to help."

The sorceress of Oz observed everyone around the room and curtsied elegantly. Penta and Helga rose and approached her as if she were an old friend. Penta reached her first, and surprise registered on the Good Witch's pale features when the queen hugged her. "Your timing is perfect. You're most welcome to Kingdom."

After Penta released her, Helga walked up and offered her hand. Glinda pressed it while addressing Cinderella. "I have met your sister Valencia. Unless I am mistaken, you're a queen of Kingdom."

Cinderella came close and presented her hand. "Welcome. Your reputation assures our friendship."

Glinda took her hand. "A pleasure to meet you. My friend Dorothy has told me your tale. She admires you dearly."

Penta introduced Glinda to Rose Red next, explaining her presence. They greeted each other cordially. Glinda then marched over to Celeste and curtsied in front of her. "Am I in the presence of Celeste the Extraordinary?"

Celeste stepped back at the introduction. "I am Celeste Constellation, the royal magician."

"Your deeds are known beyond Kingdom's borders, and the magic-wielders across the worlds know you by the appellative 'the Extraordinary.' I am delighted to meet you at last."

Celeste lowered her head. "I am not so extraordinary. I cannot overpower three simple witches."

Glinda took her hand. "You underestimate these three. They're far more powerful than they appear."

Penta threw back her shoulders. "But now, we have Glinda, and we have the advantage."

Glinda released Celeste's hand. "I'm afraid not. I cannot defeat them alone."

Helga's and Cinderella's faces fell. Penta blinked in disbelief. "What do you mean?"

"As I told your sister, I'm not as powerful as the hags."

Penta reached up and twirled an end of her hair. "We sent Valencia to find you, but while she has succeeded, all was for naught."

Glinda shook her head. "Not for naught. You sent for me to help you with the witches, and I certainly will assist you. I will occupy them for as long as I can while Valencia finds the means to defeat them."

"What is Valencia doing?" asked Helga.

Glinda opened her mouth then touched her chin. "I... I don't know. I've erased that memory from my mind. The witches are excellent mind readers, so I didn't want to take the chance of their gaining information from me. If Valencia is not here, then she must be doing something important."

Doubt blossomed on the queens' expressions.

"Worry not!" exclaimed Glinda. "My advice is to trust your sister. She and her friends have great resolve. I think our chances of success are fair."

Helga drew back at Glinda's declaration. "Fair, Glinda? We are talking about Kingdom's fate!"

"Helga, nothing is certain in life. You know this. I would presume to say, before I arrived you would have put your chances at nearly hopeless. If this is the case, you should be encouraged."

Helga pointed at the exit to the room. "The witches have raised an army from the fish in the sea. They plan to drag all of the children back to the water to drown them tomorrow."

Glinda narrowed her eyes. "Despicable hags, but don't worry. Celeste and I will counter their threat."

Celeste perked up. "We will?"

Glinda smiled, eyes dancing. "We have much to discuss. We shall enlighten each other, but I feel much better about our chances of success with you here."

Celeste's blue aura glowed. "I look forward to it."

Glinda swung her attention to the queens. "I shall be able to defend Kingdom and prolong this conflict with the witches, but the fate of this world rests in your sister's hands. Are there any more capable?"

The queens didn't respond. Glinda continued, "Queens three, supporting Valencia is the most important thing we can do right now."

Penta nodded. "Agreed. I call an end to the council. We leave the defense of Pernissa Bay to Glinda and Celeste."

After the council disbanded, Helga proceeded to her suite in the castle. Each queen had her own sitting room, bedroom, and lavatory decorated to suit her taste. Helga had grown up in Nor, and her people had constructed Helga's furniture in a Viking style. Their masterpiece was a queen-sized, boat-shaped bed narrowing at the feet to a masthead of a dragon.

Helga entered the sitting room, a cozy chamber with a fireplace, a heraldic rug, two chairs, a small table, and a divan. On the walls hung axes and swords Helga had used in significant battles.

At this moment, Danforth sat on the divan and plucked a lute, a glass of red wine on a table next to him. When Helga entered, he set the instrument down and stood. They came together in a friendly embrace, and Danforth rubbed her back. "You looked as if you needed a hug."

After the two broke apart, the warrior queen related what had transpired in the council room. Danforth took her hand. "This will all work out, my love."

Helga removed her hand, crossed the room, and peered out a window. "I've been reflecting a lot on a particular matter. Ever since Celeste cast the Reflection spell on me, I've wondered whether I am worthy enough to defeat these witches."

Danforth walked up behind her. "You'll defeat the witches. I have complete confidence in you."

She turned to him and flushed. "Why does Evil have the upper hand this time? I ask myself, 'Where is the Creator?' I refuse to believe the Creator has abandoned us in our time of need. The problem must lie elsewhere."

Danforth lifted an eyebrow.

"With me, my dear," Helga said. "The problem is me. I have become corrupted. You should have witnessed the green spots on my skin. They covered me like roaches."

She put her hands on either side of her face, and Danforth placed his hands on hers. "Tootsie, you are Helga the Paladin. Perhaps a regular person would be a deep shade of green."

"Snow White was almost spotless."

Danforth rolled his eyes. "I'm sure on the precipice of death we're all remorseful for the wrongs we've done. Helga, my beloved, I cannot imagine the loving Creator you believe in would desert you."

"I don't sense the Creator's presence." Helga took a deep breath and released it. "Perhaps...I am not worthy."

"Helga—"

"I also fear my sisters' judgment when it comes to the witches, particularly Penta."

Danforth asked, "What do you mean?"

"Her time with the Paisleys on Earth has changed her significantly," Helga responded. "After she came home, she adopted Beauty. Her concern for Beauty—and children in general—clouds her judgment."

"She's a wonderful parent."

"No doubt, but Penta's no longer objective in Kingdom's affairs. She crossed me today in a way she's never done before. I know she had her daughter in mind when she spoke harshly to me, picturing Beauty in Pernissa Bay. Yet her words cut me."

Helga slumped and regarded her boots. "My sisters think because I am the fighter that they cannot hurt my feelings. True, I guard my feelings, but not in front of them. I wept as much as they did for Snow White. Yet they still think I'm thick-skinned."

Danforth cupped her chin and lifted it, meeting her eyes. "I know better."

Helga put her hand on his cheek. "If Valencia fails, I will need to find something to defeat the witches. As you would say on Earth—it's all riding on me."

Strolling next to her daughter in the garden, Penta finished telling Beauty about the battle of Pernissa Bay, keeping to herself the witches' threat to drown all of the town's children. Wide-eyed, Beauty didn't interrupt the story while they walked the perimeter of the hedged enclosure. When Penta finished, her daughter asked, "And Elisa and her swan brothers are alive?"

"Yes."

Beauty stroked the branches. "And the witches will return on the morrow? What has the council decided?"

Penta plucked a dead branch from the hedge. "Fortunately, your Aunt Valencia sent us a powerful magic-wielder from another world—as Hero is from another world. She's going to fight the witches tomorrow."

"A magic-wielder from another world? May I go tomorrow and watch her?"

Penta's fingers clenched the branch in a stranglehold, and her knuckles whitened. "'Tis far too dangerous."

Beauty leaned away from her mother. "You think I'm a child."

"You are a child."

Beauty threw out her hands. "One year, and I'll be of marrying age. I'll be Snow White's age when Hero arrived in Kingdom!"

Penta threw the branch to the side. "On Earth, the age of adulthood is as late as eighteen."

Beauty's lower lip stuck out. "We're in Kingdom, not on Earth."

"Beauty, I've had a long day, and it's not yet nightfall." Penta rubbed her eyes. "Please, let's not have this discussion now."

"You may as well put me in a convent for the rest of my life," snapped Beauty.

They came to a corner of the hedgerow, and Penta led the way. "You are a princess of Kingdom. You attend balls and festivals and travel everywhere and receive the best education I can give you. How can you say I shelter you?"

"You never let me do anything significant for Kingdom." Beauty lowered her eyes. "I should be on the council in Snow White's place. Rose Red isn't a princess."

Penta's nostrils flared. "We've discussed this. You would be a target on the council. I won't let that happen."

Beauty reached for her mother's pink hand and lifted it. "I have my ability."

"It will not help us tomorrow." Penta's voice was shrill.

Beauty glared at her. "You thought it special a few nights ago."

Penta pulled away her hand. "I'm sorry, Beauty. Please, excuse me. I've seen many people die today. I can't have this discussion now."

Beauty's features softened. "Okay, Mom. I'm sorry, too. But one day, I hope you'll let me share your burden. I can't be your little girl forever."

Penta put her hand on Beauty's cheek. "I know."

Sunlight shone down Pernissa Bay the following morning. Eerie silence shrouded the town. A few dogs roamed about, nosing around in the debris left by the prior day's battle.

The witches appeared as the sun tipped its hat above the horizon line. They floated on the water like three ghosts seeking a house to haunt. The hags left the sea and entered the town from the north. Tomana crossed her arms. "Where are the queens? They are such an obdurate bunch!"

Picana adjusted her hat. "My spell keeps the towns-people stuck within the borders of Pernissa Bay, and I'm sure all of its residents are huddling against its southern border. It makes no difference. Our fish-men will travel the length of the town and drag people back to the sea."

Mya danced from foot to foot. "Children sigh. Then they cry. Children hide. Then they die."

The witches raised their arms, and row after row of fishmen emerged from the sea until they filled the main road. The hags moved to the front of their squadron and led them into the town, making their way to the main thoroughfare. The trio arrived at a bend in the road, a short zigzag before they resumed their southern march, where they came upon a solitary figure standing in their way. Celeste, their sole opponent, waved childishly at them.

The royal pixie stood resolutely fifty yards down the road. She smiled and clasped her hands behind her back as if they had caught her out on her morning constitutional. More curious, she wasn't glaring at them or paying them any particular notice. Celeste observed a bird land near her, and she whistled to it.

Picana found her voice first. "Fairy, begone. We have bested you at every encounter. We shall do so once again if you cross us."

Celeste put her hands together as if praying, and mumbled a few words. Her hands glowed blue. She parted them and began pointing at a fishman next to Mya. She indicated her target, and a popping noise sounded where he stood. In his place, a fish fell to the street. The witches blinked while Celeste pointed to another fishman near them. Pop. Fish. Pop. Pop. Pop. The smell of raw fish filled the air.

"What is this?" cried Tomana. "How does she know the counterspell? How does she know magic hidden from Kingdom?"

For once, Mya was silent and grave. Picana watched while fishman after fishman transformed back into his original form, flopped on the ground, and then remained still. The head witch curled her lip. "Enough! We attack."

The witches advanced down the street, crackling with energy. Celeste paid them no attention but continued to point at the fish-men. The trio gestured, sparks emerging from their fingertips when, from out of nowhere, a giant cube surrounded the witches. A thick, viscous liquid filled the interior of the cage. The hags found themselves preserved in the middle of the cube, unable to finish their spells or move. They glared at Celeste, who ignored them and continued to transform the fish-men one by one.

From behind the coven of witches, Glinda the Good drifted into view and observed her captives. Their eyes, enclosed in the jelly, enlarged a tiny fraction. Glinda grinned at their shock. "I understand this spell will slowly wear off in a day, and then you will be free. I also realize my little cube incantation won't work again. You'll think of some other scheme as, you understand, Celeste and I know how to undo this one."

Tomana's lip quivered, and Glinda noticed the movement. "If you could talk, you would be telling me how hopeless my presence is here, how you three are more accomplished in the dark arts than I am in white magic, and how eventually you will see Kingdom's destruction and mine along with it."

Glinda showed her hands opening and closing like two mouths. "Blah. Blah. Blah. We all know I cannot defeat you, but I can counter you, and furthermore, I can instruct Celeste.

I have a willing student on my side."

Picana's jaw tightened. Glinda patted the cube. "I say farewell for today, and I hope you'll consider departing this world the way you came. Your absence would be to the benefit of all."

Glinda waved her hands, and the square containing the frozen witches flew from Pernissa Bay over the ocean and out of sight.

Celeste had spent the entire speech pointing at the standing fish-men who continued to regress to their initial state. Glinda joined her, and within minutes, a heap of fish lay in the street, more than enough to compensate for the local fishermen missing a morning of work.

Glinda turned to Celeste. "I threw a spell so the queens could watch you triumph over the crones. Let me show you what they saw." She swung her hand in a circular motion, and in the center, the morning encounter between the witches and Celeste occurred again. "Right here, you smiled," said the Good Witch. "You're so serious, Celeste. A smile becomes you."

"I have not had much to celebrate lately."

Glinda took the pixie's hands. "We shall not celebrate, but we can hope. You have exceeded my expectations as my pupil. Let's return to the queens and plan our next move."

16 - MORBIDUM

Valencia walked down the mist-enshrouded forest trail, avoiding the puddles and holes in the slime-encrusted path. Trees stood on either side like guards at a formal ceremony, barring passage in any direction but forward or backward. Knowing the portal to this world placed her close to a witch's daughter, she proceeded forward, following her intuition.

Amused at how Glinda's spell had dressed her, Valencia regarded her mud-splattered ivory frock with its puffy short sleeves and lacing around her wrists. She adjusted a white cap on her head held in place by a drawstring tied under her chin. A breeze ruffled some of her exposed hair. Her mid-ankle buttoned boots were scuffed and ragged.

An owl swooped overhead, and the queen ducked as the bird glided between the trees. After the owl passed her, a small animal's death cry pierced the usual nocturnal whispering, squelched by a sharp sound like a twig snapping. Valencia grimaced and spied the silhouette of a beast deep in the forest staring back; the animal's eyes shone without blinking. The queen rubbed her ruby necklace between her thumb and fingers while speeding along the trail.

Past a small bend in the road, Valencia spied the tip of a mansion's gable over the trees. She hurried along the lane, accidentally stepping in a puddle. Around the crook in the trail was a cast-iron gate with pointed and rusted finials at the top of each post. Valencia slipped through the gate's opening toward the large manse obscured by the mist.

Unlike the ancient manors of Kingdom, this compact, chestnut-colored construction boasted newer lumber and stone. The three-story house supported a gable on each of its ends, with a third and tallest gable projecting up from the rear. The mansion's horizontal windows grew increasingly narrow the closer they were to the middle of the house, giving the dwelling a beady-eyed look. The final assembly reminded the queen of a multiple-eyed monster observing its next meal. Valencia clicked her tongue. "*Tres impressionnant.*"

Advancing to the front door, Valencia lifted a knocker and let it drop. She placed her hand on her chest, her fingers rubbing her conspicuous ruby. Valencia decided to present herself as a simple maiden, not a rich lady, and removed the necklace with the ruby and placed it in her pocket. Her fingers brushed the wishing stone she had found in Oz, and she pulled it out and examined it. "You made the journey too, little one? My luck also holds here, it seems."

She waited a long time until a man opened the door for her, and the queen pocketed the stone. A gentleman, dressed in a black suit coat with a red ascot, had answered her summons. He had sunken eyes and was as bald as a croquet ball. The queen took a deep breath. "Excuse me, sir, but I'm lost and wondered if you could help me."

"You aren't expected," the man said. "But you may come in. Name?"

"Valencia Arkenson."

The man stepped aside and allowed Valencia to enter the manor. The entrance displayed a stuffed raccoon on a shelf, its teeth bared, and ledges holding snuffed candles. The dark-paneled walls created an illusion of a smaller room on the inside than outside.

They walked down a hallway, slightly more illuminated than the foyer, toward the back of the house. Her host remained silent, guiding her forward.

"I am sorry, sir. I didn't mean to disturb you. Mister?"

"Lyndon. The butler."

"Thank you. Whose mansion is this?"

"Peter Harcourt Marstings. The master is out but will return in two days. He's buying a lost La Tour and has invited potential art critics and historians to await his arrival. In his absence, Peter's guests instructed me to invite anyone seeking shelter inside and to the parlor. You're welcome here and may spend the night if you wish. Your presence, it seems, was predestined."

They entered a large chamber in the back of the mansion lit by candles in three silver candelabras, a light not strong enough to illuminate the entire area—most of the upper portion being therefore cast in darkness. Valencia blinked while taking in the rectangular parlor.

A fireplace stood guard at the far end, displaying a low flame, providing little in the way of heat or light. Three end tables stood along three of the walls holding small sculptures. A skull with glass eyes and dotted lines on its cranium sat atop a bureau. Two paintings hung on the wall—one of a young lady on a swing kicking off a shoe and the other of a dead woman floating in a brook.

In the center of the parlor, a man and woman sat on a settee across from another seated man. A fourth person, a woman, towered over the gathering. All turned to regard Valencia when she entered.

Furthest away, the standing woman straightened her black, broad-shouldered dress, a white layer of material hanging down from her waist. With a drawn-out face and concave cheekbones, the woman glowered at Valencia at first and then flashed a tight-lipped smile. Over six feet tall, she commanded Valencia's attention first.

On the settee rested a swarthy gentleman and a veiled lady. The man wore his hair parted down the middle and tied back in a ponytail. He nodded Valencia's way. The woman, slight of frame with a pillbox hat and a thick veil over her face, folded her gloved hands on her lap.

Across from this couple slouched a small man, dark-haired, with a precise mustache to offset his unkempt hair. Rumpled clothes hung on his slight frame, and from his sleeve draped an arm holding a tumbler.

Lyndon announced, "May I present Valencia Arkenson."

The gentleman with the ponytail rose to his feet and approached the queen, a black cape with red lining flowing behind. He took her hand and kissed her fingertips. "It is my honor to make your acquaintance. *Je m'appelle* Count Brahm Cupsince."

Valencia, often treated cordially in her own country, found this man's elegance rivaling the nobility in Kingdom. "Charmed."

The count turned and said, "My companions...they are not as hospitable. Please excuse their rudeness, but know that *l'habit ne fait*—"

"*Pas le moine,*" finished Valencia, recognizing a common Kingdom colloquialism meaning, in this case, their elegant clothes didn't automatically instill manners.

The count set his hands on his black breeches and inspected her. "Have I met a compatriot of my beloved home, France? You certainly are pretty enough to belong there, but I do not detect an accent in your English."

Valencia remembered Hero asking her if she was French when they had first met. She didn't know what French was until he explained it referenced a country in his world. She detected the count's accent now and hoped to speak with him more.

The slouching man shook his drink. "Rummy! Two of them!"

The woman seated on the high-backed chair stood and curtsied to Valencia. She wore a golden, off-shoulder dress with a low décolletage. A small rose-colored, half-cape accented her dress, reminding Valencia of a red and golden sunrise. The lady said, "I apologize, but I have a most dreadful condition where I cannot expose my face to the light, even candlelight. My name is Beatrice. Beatrice Rappaccini. Art student. Please, join us."

"Dunno why she'd want to be here," said the man with the tumbler after taking a drink. "Hardly a party."

Count Cupsince took Valencia's arm and led her to the man. The spirits from his breath hit her like a wall two steps before she stopped in front of him. Cupsince made the introduction. "May I present Allan Usher, an art critic. Please forgive him. He has met with some misfortune recently. As have we all."

The man glared at Cupsince, and with an unsteady hand, put down his glass. He stood and bowed to Valencia. "A'plogize. Your servant."

He didn't kiss her hand but squeezed it. She nodded at him.

The count turned Valencia toward the last person to be introduced, gesturing to the remaining guest. "And this is Ms. Zephyr."

The woman sized up the queen, her eyes beginning at Valencia's feet and rising to her face. "Zariah Zephyr. Artist and art historian."

Zariah reached out and grasped Valencia's fingertips before the queen could stop her. "You have long fingers," she observed. Zariah met the queen's eyes while rubbing her fingernails. "Artist's fingers."

Valencia took a step back and pulled away her hand. The count said, "Now, Zariah, behave."

"My hands are my life." Zariah lowered her chin and winked at Valencia. "I expect yours are too."

Cupsince clapped his hands. "We are diversely located. I call France my home. Dear Beatrice is from Italy, Allan from Baltimore, and Zariah from Boston. And, my dear, where do you hail from?"

"An island." A lie. "My father was exiled there as punishment." A truth. "I'm afraid I am a little backward. I didn't grow up in society."

Cupsince put his arm around her, and Valencia tensed her shoulders. He breathed in deep. "Do not tell me any more. We were discussing the spiritual world before you rapped on Peter's door. Zariah and Beatrice believe in a world beyond ours. Allan and I are of a different opinion. If a world exists where our spirits go, why has no one ever communicated with us?"

Zariah smirked. "Perhaps you were too busy admiring the living. The dead escaped your notice."

Cupsince ignored her. "We were talking about how to contact the spiritual world. However, holding a séance with an even number of people is dangerous. We needed one more. And then you knocked on the door. The mysterious stranger." He raised an eyebrow. "And a lovely one."

Valencia blushed at his flagrant flirtation. Cupsince gestured to a chair. "Would you be willing to join us in exchange for shelter and sustenance? I am Peter's lifelong friend and lord of Marstings Manor when Peter is abroad."

Valencia's eyes darted back and forth. Beatrice or Zariah could be one of the hags' daughters. She needed to come to know them and gain their trust. "I would."

Cupsince nodded to her. "I'm most grateful." He clapped his hands together. "Shall we commence with the séance then? I shall go to the game room and obtain a table suitable for the event."

The count left the room, and Valencia took a seat opposite Beatrice. Without warning, a big black bird swooped down over Valencia's head from one of the room's dark corners. The creature roosted on the frame of a large mirror.

Zariah cursed. "Damn that bird. This is your doing, Allan, bringing your pet here."

Allan's eyes turned to slits. "It's not my pet. The sooner that demon is gone, the better."

Beatrice's veil moved when she spoke. "Didn't you say it talks to you?"

Zariah laughed, but Valencia scrutinized the bird sitting atop a large, golden-framed mirror. The bird cocked its head and returned her stare. Deliberately, it moved its head from side to side to regard the entire party.

Allan held up his drink at the animal, as if toasting it. "I dreamed it talked to me."

Valencia said, "'Tis a raven."

Zariah put her fingers together in a steeple formation. "Yes, Allan's familiar. It has been following him around since..."

Valencia and the bird engaged in a staring contest until the queen turned away and noticed Allan had drained his glass, slumped in his chair, eyes unfocused. Valencia touched his arm. "Perhaps you should retire?"

"Ish alright. Sides, I want to torment Peter's guests more. Did you know Zephyr learned to paint in a circus? It's why her art is sho terrible."

"Bastard!" she snapped, then grinned.

Allan chuckled, but Valencia didn't find the banter funny. He continued, "Beatrice is not only an artist but a killer as well."

Beatrice's head jerked. "Lies!"

Cupsince entered carrying a long table. "Who lies? We have chairs!" He laughed at his joke.

The count placed the table in the center of the room. "I called the damned manservant Lyndon to help, but I can never find him when I need him."

All but Beatrice moved chairs around the table to seat

five. Cupsince walked to the fireplace and put a large grate in front of it. Shadows and a draft descended on the parlor at the same time.

"Everyone take your seats," said Cupsince. "We're ready."

Count Cupsince, Beatrice, and Allan sat in a row on one side of the table. Valencia and Zariah sat on the other side—Valencia across from Beatrice and Zariah across from Allan. Cupsince snuffed out the candles on the table with his thumb and forefinger. When he extinguished the last light, the room went as dark as the bottom of a well. "Let's begin! Put your palms flat on the table."

Beatrice exhaled. "How do we start?"

"We choose someone to contact," replied Cupsince. "The only qualification is the spirit must be dead. Does anyone have anybody in mind?"

Zariah cleared her throat. "Lenore."

Beatrice gasped, and Allan swore. The profane word he had used jarred Valencia. Kingdom's customs would never permit Allan's interjection in polite company. The darkness obscured her vision, but she could still observe Cupsince's head droop. His voice startled her. "Damned unfunny, Zariah. You forget, she was also Peter's cousin."

"And intended for me," growled Allan. "Name another."

Zariah leaned forward. "And why not her? She has a headstone in the back like the others."

"But no body lies in the grave," remarked the count.

Defeated, Allan sat back. "Fine. Anything to get thish madness over with."

Cupsince slicked back his hair. He proceeded in a flat monotone, all levity vanished from his voice. "Very well. We'll call upon the spirit of Lenore to attend to us. Lenore, if you can hear us, send us a sign."

In the darkness, Valencia couldn't discern the expressions of anyone around the table—only their outlines. Most of them shifted in their chairs while waiting. Zariah leaned right and left. Beatrice lifted her hands from the table and crossed them in front of her chest, shivering. They waited five minutes, then ten, in utter darkness, in oppressive silence, in fearful reflection.

Beatrice's voice cut through the silence, muffled behind her veil. "Allan, *svegliati*. Wake up. You're snoring."

Zariah drummed her fingers on the table. "I can't blame him."

Cupsince called out once more. "Lenore. If you are out there, if you can hear us, we ask you for a vision, a word, anything."

The plea was met with stillness, silence, the inexorable sound of solitude as if the party guests were trapped in a grave. A sense of wrongness hung over Valencia—the opposite of her lucky feeling. When she thought she couldn't stand it any longer, a rapping on the wall originated near the fireplace. After the knocking, something dropped to the floor with a thud.

"Something else is in this room," breathed Beatrice.

The count rubbed his chest. "It's not from beyond the grave. It's that damned raven."

He didn't sound convinced, and Valencia and the others turned toward the chimney. Another tap, two seconds passed, and then a fluttering of wings.

"I'm going to capture our little winged fiend and eat it," grumbled the count. "The bird will pair nicely with the merlot."

The joke served to break the tension. Valencia relaxed for a moment, but the respite was over before it began. A shadow rose behind Allan, and Valencia's eyes widened. Living in Kingdom, she had encountered many eldritch beings. The presence of this one didn't rattle her as much as it seemed to bother the others. The queen called out, "Who are you?"

The silhouette stopped growing and moved swiftly. Allan emitted a pained grunt, his chin dropped to his chest, and the being behind him reached down and set its hands on

165

his shoulders. Allan pitched forward, and the shadow pulled him away from the table. The drunkard toppled off the chair and onto his back. The creature shook its head. Beatrice screamed, and in an instant, the dark shape shrunk down, melting into the shadows.

Valencia stood, unwilling to trust her eyes. She had encountered bizarre beasts in Kingdom, but Morbidum was nothing like her home world. "Something attacked Allan. He is hurt."

Beatrice moaned. "What spirit is in the room with us? Begone! Begone!"

Valencia, never without her matches, retrieved one from a pocket and struck it against the table. Its head flared while she held it out toward Allan to view the scene. Beatrice cried out. Allan lay on the ground on his back, eyes open, a knife planted in his gut, and blood pooling around his body.

Valencia lit a candle. Beatrice had retreated into the darkness, raising her veil but not revealing her face. Zariah was seated still as a statue, arms on the table, staring at the empty chair across from her with wide eyes.

Over the years, Valencia had encountered many horrific, supernatural monsters. She had survived many snowy nights with zombies roaming about in Exile. She had battled a half-harpy, half-bird creature and a giant, telepathic spider in Kingdom. Yet, a spirit taking vengeance on a man seated so close unnerved her. She relied on her experience as a queen to rise to the occasion. Valencia handed a match to the count. "Light all the candles, *monsieur*."

The count lit three more candles, and he and Valencia walked over to examine the art critic. The count reached out and put his hand on Allan's chest. He shook his head.

Beatrice moaned again while Zariah took a deep breath as if coming to terms with Alan's death. Cupsince exhaled forcefully, and the candle flame wavered as a result. "Who did this?"

Beatrice returned to the candlelight with her veil restored. "Not one of us! I couldn't see anyone precisely, but if any of us had stood and moved, we all would've seen it. Was it the spirit?"

Zariah stood and pointed to the door. "While I know the spirit world exists, I don't think we should blame specters. The door is open. Could someone have crept in while we were distracted and murdered him?"

The count eyed the door with fury. "Where is Lyndon?"

Zariah unsheathed a knife from a belt that Valencia hadn't noticed before. The four-inch blade was as sharp as the crescent moon's tip. "I shall go and find him."

She exited the room, and Valencia noticed the raven again. The bird peered intently at the dead man and opened and closed its beak without making a sound. The others obviously observed it too, and the count went to seize the bird. However, before Cupsince could grab the raven, it flew off into a remote corner of the room.

Valencia walked around the table and put her hand on Allan's shoulder. "The poor man."

"I want to leave the room," said Beatrice.

The count took her arm and hooked his elbow for Valencia. The queen pulled back. "One moment."

She crawled under the table and peered down at a puddle of dark liquid. "'Tis blood."

"Is it significant?" asked Cupsince.

Valencia scooted back from under the table. "I wonder..."

The queen held out her arm, and Cupsince hooked his elbow around hers. The three party guests crossed the hallway into a smaller sitting room, and everyone took a seat around a circular table. Cupsince went to a cupboard and pulled out a decanter with glasses. He poured drinks and handed them out without a word. Valencia drank the cordial he offered, expecting wine. She nearly gagged but let the potent brandy slip down her throat.

Cupsince set down his glass on the table with a bang.

"What if it wasn't Lyndon?"

Beatrice asked, "Valencia, you were on the other side of the table. What did you see?"

Valencia said, "A large, dark form rose behind Allan and grabbed him."

Beatrice's gloved hands shook. "Perhaps it was a demon."

"It was no demon," said Valencia. "You doubt me, but I am not jesting."

Before anyone could challenge Valencia's declaration, Zariah rushed into the room. "Lyndon is gone. I sent a maid to fetch the constable."

The artist grabbed the decanter out of Cupsince's hands and poured herself a drink. She tossed it back without hesitation and then took a deep breath. "Clearly, he killed Allan."

"Impossible," said the count. "We would've seen him when we lit the candle."

Valencia eyed the aristocrat. "The match's light didn't extend to the floor. What if he had crawled in?"

"Lyndon? Crawling?" asked Beatrice through her veil.

"None of us was close enough to stab Allan except Valencia," said Zariah. "And she didn't move through the entire séance."

"Our hands were all above the table." The count nodded in Zariah's direction, agreeing with her. "One thing is certain. You must all spend the night. I'll lock the mansion securely this evening."

Valencia folded her hands. "Are you sure this is wise?"

"With a maniac on the loose, I couldn't let you leave. *Qui vivra verra*," he murmured.

The others didn't comprehend his dark quip except for Valencia. An idiom meaning "time will tell" but whose actual words were "who will live, will see" wasn't humorous at all.

The constable came, and his men carried away Allan's body, promising to start a hunt for Lyndon when they left. He departed with a tip of his hat. Count Cupsince escorted the ladies to their rooms on the third floor. Valencia's quarters looked out on the main gate. She sat at her window for over an hour, unable to lie down to sleep. The soaring trees beyond the mansion's fence gave her the impression of a haunted grove, reminding her of the cursed cul-de-sacs of Kingdom's forests. Valencia was not one to shy away from the woods, but this world's vast expanses of gnarled trees resembling tortured souls unnerved her.

She spoke aloud to herself. "Graddock. We shouldn't have parted. I need to talk to you most of all."

The clock downstairs rang the midnight hour. After its final chime, a footstep in the hallway caught Valencia's attention. She crept to her bedroom door and put an eye to the keyhole to spy who was out so late. A maid and Count Cupsince stood in front of an open door leading to stairs up to the servant's quarters. Valencia turned and put her ear to the hole to listen in. She had not forgotten her mission to find one of the daughters of the witches. Perhaps the daughter was this maid.

The servant whispered. "Tomorrow night?"

"Assuredly. *Adieu*, my sweet. It was lovely."

"That it was."

Valencia returned to peeking through the keyhole while the count took his companion in his arms and dipped her. The maid sucked in her breath in anticipation. Cupsince leaned down, kissed her forehead, and proceeded to kiss her face down the left side, ending with her lips. His hand wandered over her body, lifting her petticoats, rebuffed by the crinoline underneath. His lips lingered on hers, pulling back slowly, skin stretching between them. The maid appeared to be deliriously pliable, mesmerized by the count's touch, ready to follow his every command.

Valencia held her breath as the couple parted, and the maid lifted her skirt and ascended the staircase. The count's pale, Gallic profile watched the servant's shadow moving up the stairs before he reached to shut the door. He cocked his head and turned and faced Valencia's door. Valencia drew back, holding her breath, her eyes darting to a key on a ledge near the unlocked door. A footstep from the hallway prompted Valencia to pick up the key, jam it into the lock, and twist it.

Click.

Silence reigned in the hallway after she locked her door. She imagined Count Cupsince staring at the door—through it —into her room, and she pressed her knuckle to her mouth. Then, with a rustling sound of his cape, his footsteps receded into the distance.

Biting her lip, she lay down on the bed but didn't fall asleep for hours.

17 - CIXXES

Sondra

Alice and I stepped through the door into a cobble-stoned alleyway between two brick buildings. At first, I thought we had crossed into the wrong world. Both four-story buildings displayed mismatched bricks, gray and red, covered in soot. The bumpy street had a gutter on either side with a trickle of water running down the trench. My nose wrinkled at the smell of sewage and urine.

To my immediate right, I spied a four-panel door with a transom window. At the end of the alley stood a gas lamp—its wick flickering and casting shadows. Halfway down the narrow lane hung a yellowed poster on the right wall. The rectangular sheet's calligraphic font, reminiscent of a sign from the eighteen-hundreds, was entitled with one word: "Report."

An oval, pencil-drawn eye took up most of the surface area on the poster.

Before we could move, my stick horse flung itself out from where I had strapped it to my belt and landed on the ground. It clacked on the cobblestones, and Alice sucked in her breath at the ruckus it made. The toy enlarged and expanded into the living form of the steed. Bree shook his mane at his newfound freedom, turned to me, and nickered.

I reached out and petted the horse while Alice peered down the alley. The Traveler placed her hand on my arm. "Control your horse, Sanders, and get it back to its original state. If someone sees it, we're going to pay dearly."

While Alice tried the door and found it locked, I stroked Bree's mane. "Here, boy. Calm down. I'll call you later, and you can take us back to Oz." Bree's eyes rolled at my gentle touch.

Alice eyed the poster and flattened her back against the same wall it hung on. "Get against this wall!"

"Alice, what happened? How did we miss Cixxes? And why did Bree appear?"

Alice flung out her arm and pushed me up against the bricks. "When a Traveler carries a magic totem to another world, it sometimes actuates on its own. And for your information, we *are* in Cixxes. We're standing in a dangerous place."

Bree nodded at me and then shrunk into his stick form. I caught the pole before it dropped to the street and tucked him in the back holster I had made for him. "What? This looks like the past."

"We're on a continent known as Centrania in a city called Lymton. One of the worst areas." Alice glared at the nearest edge of the poster. "And that's saying something in this world."

Colors shone on the opposite wall, and I realized I was the source of the reflection. I examined my clothes. Alice and I were both wearing silver shirts with colored electrical lights spinning across them like meteorites crossing a night sky. My top tucked into tight-fitting trousers that hugged my legs, while the lights ran up and down the sleeves and pants. Clear boots encased our feet, and an ivory bonnet covered my head.

I noticed something move in the alleyway, and my heart skipped a beat. The painted pupil of the eye on the poster shifted and looked down the alley our way. Goosebumps erupted down my flesh when the eye enlarged as if trying to see something out of its view. Us.

Alice grabbed my hand. I wanted to curse but was too frightened. The baleful eye continued to stare down the passageway and then, after an extended minute, turned its attention to a pedestrian on the street. A woman in a wimple and an old-fashioned coat with laced-up brown boots strode along the lane.

As the lady scurried past, the eye followed her movements step by step. Across the street, a man in a stovepipe hat heading in the opposite direction stopped in his tracks. He struck a match. The eye winked at him, and he returned the motion. He couldn't spot us further back in the shadows of the alleyway.

The man ran out of our view. Moments later, a woman's shriek cut through the air, a discordant sound in the otherwise still night. Alice's hand tightened on my fingers when, across the alleyway, the door opened soundlessly. The figure of a woman stood in the shadows.

As one, Alice and I darted across the passage without the eye spotting us. We entered the building, and the woman who had opened the door shut it, careful to lift it to avoid its scraping against the ground and alerting the eye. When she closed the door, I noticed Alice bracing herself to attack our rescuer.

The woman turned a dial on a lantern, which then illuminated a small foyer. The entryway contained only wooden stairs leading upward. Dark, paneled walls sealed us inside.

The woman leaned against the door to the street. Slightly younger than Alice and me, she let her crystal-blue eyes bore into us. "Who are you?" she demanded in a slightly British accent.

Alice replied, "We're no one. You never saw us."

The woman squinted at my handbag. "I know what you are. Travelers. I once encountered a Traveler at my job. I'm a court stenographer."

I grabbed Alice's arm. "Where are we exactly?"

Alice moved so the woman couldn't ascend the stairs. "Think *1984*, *Brave New World*, Zamyatin's *We*. Centrania inspired portions of those novels."

Though I knew *1984* by reputation, I had never read it. I braced myself, ready for anything.

The woman twisted her short black hair with her thumb and forefinger and then rubbed the freckles on her cheek. "Follow me if you want to stay alive."

Alice made a "puh"ing sound. "I'm not following you anywhere unless you prove I can trust you."

The woman's shoulders tensed. Her off-shoulder, light-gray blouse rippled down to her purple petticoats, ending in ragged, black boots. Electrical impulses zipped up and down her skirts. Her sudden rigidity drew my attention to her upper torso. A tattoo of a cougar in profile stood etched on her ivory shoulders. The animal had the same color eyes as the woman. The stranger flexed her arm, and my jaw dropped when the cougar turned its head and gazed at us.

"That's awesome!" I blurted out.

My exclamation made two things clear to the Cixxes woman—the tattoo had been the source of my surprise, and I had never previously seen a tattoo move. The woman grimaced. "You've never been here before, have you? I suggest you follow me. Quickly."

She hurried up the stairs, brushing past Alice. While she climbed, Alice held out her hand to restrain me. "Her tattoo isn't awesome. It's common. The ink is infused with microscopic circuitry that reacts to her brainwaves. Now focus. We're in danger. Didn't you read *1984* in college?"

"I was busy earning my biology and chemistry degrees. Liberal arts weren't at the top of my list."

Alice lowered her hand. "Universities should require students to read *1984*. All of the science in the world isn't going to save you if the Center is running it."

"Skip the literature lecture. What is the Center?"

"Every continent has a ruling party. The Center is an oligarchy of unknown people who consolidate Centrania's power. Everyone is a spy, tattling on their own family for a favorable position. Trust is hard to come by here."

I eyed the stairs. "We have to trust someone. Otherwise, how will we find the daughter? If something happens, we'll Travel back to Oz."

Alice bit her lip. "I've been to Cixxes twice. Both times bad things have happened. Be extra careful."

We ascended the stairs with Alice leading the way. The paneled walls of the building sparkled without dent or blemishes. Movie-set walls, not historically-accurate.

The woman waited for us on the fourth-floor landing. "I'm not a spy, and I won't turn you in. I knew you were coming, which is why I came out so quickly. I'll explain in my apartment."

Alice climbed the last two steps. "What about the viewer in your apartment?"

"I bypassed the viewer. The Center could imprison me for tampering with it, but I knew you'd arrive."

Alice's eyes narrowed. "How?"

"I dreamed about it. Follow me."

A clock chimed nearby, muffling Alice's response to the woman. While the timepiece tolled nineteen times, the woman rushed down a wallpapered corridor and stepped through a narrow doorway. As we followed, I noticed the doors had no markings on the outside. "No numbers on the doors?"

Alice grabbed my arm to urge me forward. "No one visits people here. The Center knows where everyone lives."

"No locks either," I observed.

Alice said, "Door handles monitor a combination of

your pulse, body temperature, and a dozen other biometric readings. Cutting off someone's hand to use their fingerprints to enter won't work."

I leaned toward one of the handles. "Cat's piss. Color me impressed."

At the doorway, Alice snorted. "*Don't* be impressed by this place, Sanders. You're going to get us killed if you're too busy admiring technical advancements."

The woman entered, and Alice and I followed her inside. My companion grabbed me and flattened me against the wall.

We stood in a cramped apartment furnished by a nineteenth-century-styled divan with discolored cushions, two wooden chairs, a table, and pea-soup-green carpeting. An open doorway led to a spacious kitchen. I repressed an urge to hold my nose at the moldy aroma permeating the room. A painting hung on the wall—the room's sole decoration—a man's portrait with his flesh melting down his face and leaving his exaggerated eyes staring back at the observer. Both disgusted and interested in the painting, I leaned forward to examine it, but Alice shook her head. "Camera," she mouthed.

The woman stood before the painting and made a gesture to it. "Don't worry about them." She pointed at an inset in the far wall that showed a cube and a pyramid on a ledge. "I bypassed it."

Alice stepped into view of the painted man's eyes but kept her attention on the gadget. "An interference pyramid. Highly illegal."

The woman set down the lantern on the table. "Many people have them these days. It replays a three-day loop of me cleaning my apartment and watching the telebubble. That's all they see now. The pyramid will provide us with privacy." The woman pointed to the only other door in the room. "My bedroom is in there. The pyramid jams the signal in there too. You can set your pack in this room."

As I set down my bag and Bree, I made an observation. "Your teeth are blue!"

The woman twisted her hair with her forefinger, revealing her faint blue teeth. "Thank you. The government calls it shade sixty-seven, but people call it robin's egg blue. Isn't robin a funny word? Now, follow me."

The woman led us into her bedroom, which was a simple affair of a bed and wardrobe, along with a wall-mounted screen displaying the alley with the eye poster. After we entered, the woman shut the door by touching her midsection, her fingers dancing on the lights. One more swoop, and music roared to life in the front room, a tuneless, discordant chiming of bells that made elevator music sound like a Mozart concerto. Then our rescuer turned her attention to us. "Who are you?"

Alice peered at a painting here of a three-eyed man, the third eye set on the bridge of the subject's nose. "You first."

"No way to treat someone who has saved your lives. I'm 07151823051212."

I observed the resident's twin bed with thin sheets and rubbed my hand along the bedpost. "Can't we call you something else?"

The woman blinked. "A name?"

Alice moved by the door to the sitting room, blocking it from the owner of the apartment. "Addressing each other by name here is illegal."

The woman brightened. "When I was young, my papa said I reminded him of his mother. He said not in looks but temperament. He whispered her name to me. Julia. I could be Julia."

"Julia? Ever hear of Winston Smith?" asked Alice.

Julia bit her lip. "No."

"How very curious. Not quite *1984* then."

Julia clasped her hands behind her back. "Tell me, where did the horse go? For that matter, where did you come from?"

Alice's eyes narrowed. "My mom and dad."

"How about a straight answer?" Julia snorted. "The Center tells us matter transference is at least thirty years away. How they would know, I have no idea. What are your real names?"

I put out my hand. "This is ridiculous. My name is Sondra, and my companion wouldn't tell you her name if you tortured her."

"Hello, Sanders," said Julia, to my surprise. Why did everyone insist on calling me that?

Julia ignored my hand, and I dropped it. She said, "You're unfamiliar with Centrania. I can help you survive here."

Alice leaned against the wardrobe. "What's in it for you?"

I turned to Alice. "We have to trust someone here. Why not her?"

"Because she could easily turn us over to *them*." Alice nodded in Julia's direction. "And she knows who I mean. We could end up at The Body, The Mind, The Soul, or The Choice."

"What are those?" I asked.

Alice said, "Government departments where they torture citizens. They drive people insane in The Mind, and they give people choices to induce overwhelming guilt in The Choice. In The Body, they physically torture citizens, often to death. And then there's The Soul."

I didn't trust the sound of a place called The Soul. "What happens there?"

"Emotional torture. Often people commit suicide when they're released." Alice cast a worried glance at the door to the living room. "I want to check the pyramid. Make sure it's legitimate."

Julia snorted. "If the pyramid didn't work, the Center would be here by now."

Alice walked to the doorway. "I'm not taking your word for it. I'll be back."

After Alice left, I turned to the screen. The eyeball darted left, sending a chill down my spine. "You saw us arrive?"

"Yes, but I expected you," she said.

"Tell me about this dream you had."

Julia put her hands on her blouse, and the lights avoided her fingers. "I guess I have to trust you first? Fine. I've had prescient dreams in the past."

I rocked back and forth. "Sounds like an ability."

"An ability? I have abilities. One I can control."

"What is it?" I asked.

"When I lie down, I can imagine a story and then transmit it into the minds of others who are sleeping. The Center hasn't found out about it yet."

I leaned against the bedpost. "You project dreams into others while they sleep?"

"Vivid ones. Most people are convinced their dreams signify something important when they awaken. I once managed to free myself from a spy this way."

Now for the clincher. If Julia answered my next question affirmatively, we would have found our daughter. "Julia, are you an orphan by chance? Were you abandoned?"

"Yes. A family adopted me. At age sixteen, I left my home and joined the courts as a stenographer."

Excellent. Glinda's spell had led us directly to the daughter. "Were you born with these abilities?"

"I've always had them to some degree. The power to control dreams became heightened after...they took me to The Choice."

I leaned forward. "Listen, we're trying to find someone, and I think it's you. Will you go with us?"

"You mean, leave Centrania?"

"No, I mean leave Cixxes." I stepped toward Julia. "We can take you to an entirely new world. My friend is a Traveler. We came from nowhere, right? We can disappear as easily. All you have to do is climb on my stick horse with me, and we'll leave this place."

Julia bit her lip, considering. "Could you describe this world?"

I again extended my hand, palm up. "Rows and rows of

trees, green grass, blue skies. Castles. And people who allow you to say what you think, even if it's not the way they think. It exists far in the past."

Julia's eyes glazed over, picturing it. My hand, untaken, drooped. "Robins fly there, too," I added.

"They exist?"

I withdrew my hand. "As do evil women. In particular, your mother. We're here because of her."

Julia's nostrils flared. "She was a Traveler and abandoned me here? In this place? I could've grown up somewhere else?"

"As I said, she's evil," I replied. "We're asking you to go to this world and confront your mother."

Julia's eyes narrowed. "I have a few words for her! What does she think of me?"

"She would murder you if she found out you left Centrania."

Julia huffed. "I won't give her the chance. May I stay in this robin world permanently?"

Just then, Alice entered the room. She walked over by my side. "What did you tell her?"

I repeated our conversation. Alice said, "And now she wants to go to Kingdom? Permanent relocation of people across worlds is discouraged."

Julia's cougar tattoo glared at us, baring its teeth.

I nudged Alice. "But possible. We both know people who've done it. I'm sure you can stay in Kingdom."

Julia reached out and took my hand and squeezed it. "Then I accept."

Alice said, "Julia, will you excuse us for a moment? I want to talk to Sanders alone."

Julia backed against her dresser. "Why?"

Alice replied, "Just a small detail about Traveling."

Julia wrinkled her brow but walked through her bedroom door, shutting it behind her. I pumped my fist. "This has to be a world-record accomplishment. We solved it in minutes."

Alice scowled. "She may be a fake."

I jerked my head away. "What?"

"Sanders, she would say anything to get out of here, and I don't blame her. This world is terrifying. Imagine if she happened to spot us in the alley on her telebubble. We appear, and then your horse transforms. Maybe, with her knowledge of Travelers, she made up a lie about manipulating dreams. In Centrania, hell in all of Cixxes, good people sell their own families to avoid suspicion. I've seen it myself."

I brushed my fingers on the bedpost. "I say we take the chance anyway."

"You want to travel back to Kingdom, have her face the witches, and then find out she's a phony?"

I adjusted my glasses. "I hadn't thought of how desperate people would be to leave. But I think she's the right one. What would you suggest?"

Alice pointed to the living room. "The pyramid is fully functional, so we're relatively safe here. I say we put her to the test."

I gripped the footboard. "And if she fails?"

"I've seen that look on Travelers before when they find oppressed people in other worlds. You want to believe she's the daughter because she's in danger. You want to save her from all of this. But we have to be sure about her." Alice paused and then slapped her hands together. "I've got it. Let's make her prove it. We'll go to sleep and have her transmit a dream into our heads. One we're both in."

Her idea sounded good to me, so we left the bedroom and entered the living room where an alarmed Julia paced around on her green, moldy carpeting. Her voice had a higher pitch when she addressed us, tinged with hysteria. "You *are* taking me with you, aren't you? You promised."

Alice stood next to the pyramid object. "We want a demonstration of your abilities before we leave."

Julia's head swung between us. "What demonstration?"

"We want you to project a dream into our heads."

"But...I can't do it while you're awake."

I jerked my thumb toward her bedroom. "Then we'll go to sleep. It might take us a while. I'm a bit wired, but eventually, we'll fall asleep."

Julia's tattoo twitched its tail. "You have to be in REM state before I can do it. We won't leave until morning then."

Alice challenged her. "Can you do it or not?"

Julia set her chin. "Yes, I can do it."

I toed the spongy, green floor. "Alice will take the bed. I'll sleep on the floor in here, and you'll stay awake. When we're in REM state, project the dream then wake us up."

Julia sat down on the divan. "I will create a dream of this world you described. At least, the way I imagine it. You two will be together and be able to talk to each other. Will that suffice?"

Alice walked to the bedroom door. "Peachy keen."

I lay down on my side, and the fungus smell assaulted my nostrils and irritated me. I should have been used to it by now, but this close to the ground, it stank worse. Minutes crawled to hours while I shifted to get comfortable.

"Are you asleep yet?" asked Julia at one point.

"No."

"Your friend is."

"I'm trying."

I tossed and turned, and from nowhere, a wave of lightheadedness enveloped me. The gossamer fingers of sleep switched off my waking mind. I breathed deeply and let slumber overtake me at last.

I found myself in a field. The grass was long, and the warm wind blew my hair. The light stroked me with its rays —a sunshine massage. Nearby, a tree line enclosed me in a field. I watched while people wearing the clothes of Centrania emerged from the woods, stretching out their arms to the sun.

I noticed a butterfly on my wrist. It folded its wings and then expanded them. The insect melted into a tattoo, but didn't stop its motion. Julia had given me moving ink.

"Hey!"

I turned around and spotted Alice approaching me. She said, "She didn't depict Kingdom accurately, but she's legit. I think the vulture-like bird in the elm tree is her version of a robin. Let's wake up and go."

We nodded and the scene dissolved. However, I didn't find myself on Julia's floor. Instead, I was holding a teacup in my kitchen, an altogether different dream, but I couldn't speak. As in nighttime visions, reason and logic succumbed to chaos, and I had forgotten Julia or her talents. Voices came from my living room; one of them was Harold's.

I walked out to the other room and stopped dead. Harold sat on the couch next to a woman holding a baby—his baby—I knew the baby belonged to him as sure as I knew my own name. Beside him, a woman swaddled the baby, rocking it and lightly pressing her finger to its chin. The woman's features and body shape mirrored my own, except she was younger. Was I looking at myself or having an out-of-body experience?

No, not an out-of-body experience. Oh, God! My throat closed around a cry. The teacup tumbled from my fingers. Not a dream but a nightmare!

I sprang awake, breathing heavily with the cry still threatening to emerge. Wearing a silver shirt with dancing lights, Julia crouched next to me and leaned back. She nodded at the bedroom. "Hush. Your friend's still sleeping. I just woke you."

I reached for my forehead and wiped water from my face —sweat and tears. I gritted my teeth and narrowed my eyes at Julia, but my host paid no attention to me. Instead, she made a motion to the adjacent kitchen and mimed eating, pointing to the kitchen door.

I grabbed tufts of green carpeting. Why had Julia given me a second dream? And what did it mean? Was it real? Harold had shared the nightmare as Alice had shared the Kingdom dream. I cleared my throat. "What was the meaning of the second dream? Why did you do it?"

Standing in the kitchen doorway, Julia pressed her lips together and then spoke. "Second?" She tilted her head. "Oh, I told you I had oneiromancy. Occasionally, people near me have a prescient incident. I can't control it. You had the first dream, right?"

I stood and followed her, my vision a bit blurry. I'd retrieve my glasses later. "Yes, but did you create the second dream?"

"I caused it, but not intentionally. I have no idea what happened."

"If others were present in it with me, did they experience the same visions?" I asked, entering the kitchen.

"Yes, that's the way it works. You're taking me now, right?"

I sat down at the dining table. "When Alice wakes up."

Julia reached into a small compartment, retrieved a plate of instant food, and set it down in front of me. Canned tuna. This was future food? Julia walked into the sitting room and then brought my hobbyhorse back to the kitchen. "Does this horse work only for you, or will it work for anyone?"

I shoveled the tuna in my mouth. Tasteless. "Only me. The toy's a totem that will transfer you across worlds."

"Will it take us to this utopian world?" asked Julia.

"It will transport us wherever I want to go. The other woman can take us without the totem." I kept Alice's identity hidden.

Julia stroked the stick horse's thread mane. "Fascinating."

I noticed a change in my host's mouth. "Julia, you whitened your teeth. They're no longer blue."

"I want to blend in." She mounted the horse. "All we have to do is put our legs around it? Like this?"

I reached for the horse and gripped the horse's mane. "Yes. All three of us. Get off it."

Julia said, "Can you prove it?"

I sighed and thought of the dream about Harold and the woman who resembled me. With my thoughts, Bree transformed into a horse. "Now get down—"

I realized Julia's plan a second too late. In the living room, through the doorway, I noticed the inset in the wall. The cube sat alone—the pyramid no longer placed next to it. My eyes widened while Julia leaned forward on Bree. "Goodbye, Sanders."

I heard the clomping of boots out in the hallway rushing toward the door. Bree took a prancing step, readying to move. I jumped up to mount my horse, but I was moments too late. The steed started to gallop and vanished, leaving me behind as Julia's door exploded inward.

18 - JANAY

Harold

I stepped through the door to Janay and onto a rutted road in the middle of a field. To my right, the terrain had rolling, small hills in the distance, and a succession of willows and birches lined up on my left. The last rays of the sun shone at the horizon, illuminating water on the grass and puddles in the path from a recent rainfall. A light breeze whipped back my hair and brought the smell of heath from somewhere in the distance. No house or building stood within sight.

A pair of tight boots pinched my feet, and a stiff shirt rubbed against my skin. Baggy pants with breeches, a blue waistcoat with a mauve vest, and a white ascot completed my attire. I held my arms out to admire my clothes, and then I spied Pennilane out of the corner of my eye and stepped back, stunned.

The selkie stood next to me in an ankle-length, egg-shell-white dress with a large crimson bow. An elegant shawl lay around Pennilane's shoulders, revealing her dark-brown skin. Ruby-colored gloves covered her hands and the lower part of her arms, and she had gained height in her red riding boots. Glinda's spell had styled the creature's hair in ringlets piled on top of her head with a flower arrangement pinned to hold it up. One loose curl dangled down near lightly applied eyeliner encircling her eyes.

Pennilane flipped her gloved hands over and back, examining both sides when I addressed her. "Look at you, Pennilane."

She examined an object on her belt, a fan. "What about me?"

"You look fantastic."

Pennilane's whiskers bristled. "As if I care what you think. I am not here to attract notice to myself, and I do not care for compliments from a man." She narrowed her eyes. "And a married man at that."

I held up my hand. "Don't worry. Not interested. All I'm saying is you've transformed like your friend, Cinderella."

"I do not care about how I look. This appearance is not my true one. I am not fond of my human shell, and I long for the days when I may return to the sea as the seal I truly am."

I turned away from her. "Got it. Sorry I complimented you."

"You should be." Pennilane rubbed her whiskers. "Be forewarned. I will be watching your every step."

"Oh, rapture," I replied. "Retract your whiskers, and let's go. The first place we come to, we'll ask about a woman with abilities."

Pennilane and I began our journey toward the west and the remaining light. Our boots splashed puddles and sunk into the mud along the way, and I had to extract my footgear from the muck more than once. We strolled along the road, and the hilly terrain to the north flattened into a plain. Pennilane re-examined her gloves. "What is our relationship? I refuse to be your wife. Shall I pretend to be your sister?"

"Why not? We don't look anything alike, but I will say my family adopted you."

Pennilane's head snapped in my direction. "How about if you are the one who was adopted?"

"Sure."

We walked for half a mile without speaking until a stone wall with a gate came into view. A well-polished plaque on the wall announced the estate's name. I bent forward to read it in the darkness. "Pemberley. The daughter is probably inside."

"We are not invited." Pennilane's eyes followed the long chaise road leading to a building in the distance. Several carriages and their uniformed drivers waited outside for those who were obviously guests inside for the evening.

"Leave it to me."

She acquiesced, and we advanced to a well-maintained mansion that, back home, I'd more likely tour than crash a party. I estimated the white, Greco-Roman styled estate held at least twenty rooms among its three stories. Music drifted from the rear of the residence, and I whistled. "I think we're at the right place."

Pennilane grunted. "A wise conclusion as the mansion is the only place around."

I reached for the gold knocker and let it drop. In a moment, a man opened the door dressed in a black suit coat with gray pants. He used his sloping nose to peer down at us. "Your card?"

I didn't expect this question, and I fumbled for a response. Pennilane nudged me aside. "We do not have a card. We wish to speak to the lady of the house if you please."

The man spoke with a clipped British accent. "Highly irregular. If you do not have an invitation, I shall have to ask you to leave."

Pennilane squared her shoulders. "We have urgent information to share with her. She will want to talk to us. If you send us away, I will return with people of noble bearing and create a scene, ruining your party."

Pennilane must have had Valencia in mind when she mentioned "noble bearing," and the words affected the doorman. Class mattered this far in the past. The man grimaced but gestured for us to enter. We stepped into a large room with a grand staircase in front and exits to our left and right. The man retreated while we listened to music from the back of the building. Heels pounded against the floor timed with the rhythm and interspersed with the indistinct murmuring of conversation. A party was in full swing.

The two smaller doors on either side of the room were nearly indistinguishable from the walls. While the man hurried up the staircase, a door to the left of us opened. A short woman dressed as a maid and carrying a large tray of slices of bread and cheeses rushed into the room then hurried to the opposite door. Adjusting the tray to avoid dropping it, she stopped for a moment and caught sight of us. The uniformed servant turned toward us, eyes widening, and she and I spoke at the same time.

"Sondra!"

"Harold!"

I stepped toward her. "What are you doing here? I thought we left you—"

I didn't finish my sentence because the maid's eyes rolled up into her head, and she swayed back and forth. I rushed forward and extended my arms to keep her head from striking the floor. Pennilane was next to me in an instant, catching the tray and examining the unconscious woman. "What is *she* doing here?"

"I don't know. Maybe she found her witch's daughter?"

Pennilane scoffed and set the tray on the ground. "We have only now arrived."

I scowled at Pennilane. "Why is she masquerading as a

maid? How did she pull that off so fast?"

A woman with dark hair and sharp eyebrows entered the room. "What happened to my maid? What did you say to her?"

The woman marched to her servant's side, grabbed her hand, and rubbed it while glowering at us. I stepped back, shocked at the familiarity between the woman of the estate and Sondra. "I don't know. She fainted in front of us."

The hostess rubbed her cheek, and the maid moaned. The woman said, "Cassie, can you hear me?"

Pennilane nudged me. "Cassie?"

At the name, I examined the woman and noticed the maid was younger than Sanders. My wife was twenty-five, but the girl in front of me was somewhere around eighteen. I should've realized it before, but her maid uniform and unexpected entrance threw me. Now I knew what was going on. "Parallel," I whispered to the selkie.

Pennilane returned her attention to the unconscious maid. "Like Planet?"

I nodded.

"I don't know what you two are babbling about over there," said the hostess. "But I do not appreciate strangers coming into my house and frightening my maid."

The prone woman's eyes fluttered open, and she regarded the woman next to her. She spoke in a thick Cockney accent. "M'lady. I don't know—" She stopped, gawked at me, and huddled closer to the lady of the house. "How can it be?"

Pennilane crossed her arms. "My question as well."

I whispered to Pennilane. "Parallels are people with the same genes but born in different worlds. Crap, you don't know what genes are, but what I mean is they look the same but don't act the same, like having a twin in a different world. I thought Sondra had only one parallel, the pixie Planet in Kingdom, but I was mistaken."

Murmuring, Pennilane asked, "But then how did she recognize you?"

I shrugged then raised my voice and addressed the maid. "You've seen me before."

The maid gripped the hostess's sleeve. "It's impossible."

The woman of the estate held her servant. "Cassiopeia Yarkus, what has he done to you?"

The majordomo entered the room while the maid shook her head. The hostess helped her to her feet. "John, please take our uninvited guests into the study." She glared at me. "You will remain there."

John led us down the right hallway and into a spacious room with bookshelves and a broad, mahogany desk in the center. The majordomo lit a lamp on a shelf and shut the doors behind us, locking us in. Paintings and crossed swords hung on three of the walls as the fourth had windows overlooking the grounds. Pennilane stood next to the window, its glass displaying initial raindrops of a developing storm. "I can smash this window if we want to leave."

"Why? We've found the daughter."

Pennilane placed a knuckle on her chin. "You think the parallel is the daughter?"

"Yes, I do. It makes sense, doesn't it? We're fortunate to find her so quickly. If we can have a few moments alone with her to explain what's happening—boom! We're out of here."

Pennilane put her hands behind her back. "Or boom! Your plan goes awry as it often does. I should be the one to discuss the matter with her. You do not have a good track record with women who resemble Planet."

I twisted my wedding ring. "Come on. I'm married to Sanders."

"Exactly. Cassiopeia may tempt you away from your true love. Have you not told me parallels share many qualities with their twins? This maid could persuade you to leave your wife."

"I think you're making too much of this."

At that moment, the door opened, and a man stepped inside. Tall with striking features, dark well-combed hair, and a square chin, he wore a red waistcoat with small silver buttons. His pants extended to the ground over high polished black boots. He entered the room with the superior air of the owner of Pemberley.

The lord of the manor examined us at first without introducing himself or speaking at all. He spent more time sizing me up, and I straightened up from my slouch. To talk to Sanders' parallel, I would have to endure this man's scrutiny.

The man rubbed his clean-shaven chin. "What is the meaning of your intrusion into my estate and scaring our maid senseless? I have never witnessed such ungraceful manners in one dressed for so formal an engagement. State your business here, sir."

"We didn't mean to scare her." I licked my lips. "My sister and I are searching for someone. Your maid...uh, maybe."

The master of the house scowled. "If you think I would be so thick as to allow you to talk to Miss Yarkus again, you take me for a fool. While I do not have any particular affection for my servants, they are under my care and provision, and I take responsibility for them. This particular maid happens to be close to my wife."

Pennilane set her hand on the window frame. "And what does the servant girl say?"

At this point, the hostess entered and shut the door behind her. She tapped her husband on the shoulder. "Cassie wants them to remain. This is a queer situation."

The man grimaced. "I would rather turn them out."

She leaned close to him. "Mr. Darcy, as she is my maid and not yours, and as we've taken her—"

I shouted before I could stop myself. "Mr. Darcy!"

I interrupted the not-so-private conversation before they could continue. Both host and hostess turned to stare at me. The head of the estate's expression hardened, and the hostess's mouth hung open a fraction. I stepped forward. "You are *the* Mr. Darcy?"

The man pressed his lips together. "I am quite sure I

don't know you, sir."

I turned to his wife. "You must be Elizabeth Bennet."

Mr. Darcy eyed his wife. The woman put a hand on the base of her neck. "I've never laid eyes on this man before in my life. My name is Elizabeth Darcy, but yes, I was baptized Elizabeth Bennet. How are we acquainted?"

"You had four sisters. I remember one was Jane, but I can't recall the others' names."

Pennilane stepped forward and put her hand on my shoulder. "Harold, stop being rude. How do you know these people?"

"*Pride and Prejudice* by Austen. They are the—"

I stopped myself in mid-sentence and cleared my throat. "I've heard of the Darcys before. Your courtship is quite the story."

Tilting her head inquiringly, Elizabeth said, "You have us at a disadvantage. You know much about my household, but we know nothing of you."

"My name is Harold Saturn." I bowed. "And this is my sister, Pennilane Saturn. We have come a long way seeking someone vital to the success of a...a campaign overseas. They have essential information."

Mr. Darcy remained stone faced. "I cannot believe my wife's maid would know something of value to you. What ruse are you perpetrating?"

"You would be surprised at how information flows around the world, Mr. Darcy." I took a deep breath. "I know, for example, your wife once asked you when you knew you were attracted to her. You replied you were in the middle of the attraction before you knew the feeling had begun."

Vexed, Elizabeth asked, "How could you possibly know this? Mr. Darcy and I spoke privately of this matter."

"The same source led me to believe your maid holds important information."

Mr. Darcy's attention turned to Pennilane. "You have been quiet, miss. Do you agree with your brother?"

"Adopted brother," snapped Pennilane. "His thoughts are fantastic, but he is a bit of an oracle, and will not hurt you, your wife, or your maid. If we could have a few minutes alone with your servant, we shall clear up this confusion."

Elizabeth shook her head. "I want to be in attendance. I cannot allow you to be alone with her."

I was about to protest, but Pennilane cut me off. "Agreed. Although I will warn you, you may not understand everything we say. I advise you to keep an open mind and recall my adopted brother's knowledge of your affairs."

I said, "There's more to life, Horatio, than what you can conceive of."

Mr. Darcy shook his head. "Shakespeare, and you misquoted it dreadfully. Americans!"

Someone tapped on the door and then slowly opened it. Cassie stepped into the room, blushing when she spotted me. Mr. Darcy left us to our conversation.

Cassie inclined her head and remained by the hostess, who closed the door behind them. Elizabeth put a hand on her domestic's arm. "Cassie, can you explain who these people are and how you know them?"

Cassie's eyes darted to Pennilane and then back to me. "I don't know the woman, ma'am. The man was in a dream I had."

"A dream?"

"Yes'um. He and I were at a dinner together, and we were…" Cassie beamed at me. Pennilane's eyes narrowed.

I finished her sentence. "Sweethearts. Can you describe the scene?"

"We were at a restaurant, and we were wearing funny clothes. The lights were low, and you told me I had the most wonderful eyes you had ever seen. Then you took my hand."

Delighted, Cassie came alive recounting the dream. "Was it real?"

I turned toward Pennilane and whispered. "This is a memory—not a dream. Cassie experienced it through

Sanders. Sanders did the same through Planet."

Elizabeth stepped forward. "Speak up. I want to know what you two are saying!"

I cleared my throat. "Sorry, we're trying to understand." I addressed the maid. "May I call you Cassie?"

Cassie grinned. "It would please me greatly, Harry."

"Harold. Cassie, were you an orphan?"

Cassie answered, "No. Do you want to meet my parents? My mother and father live not far from here. The Bennets know them. My aunt was my mother's midwife, and they described my birth to me. They kept my caul. I have both my parents, praise the Lord."

Pennilane scowled at me, broadcasting an "I told you so." "She is not the one, Hero...Harold."

The color drained out of Cassie's face. "What do you mean I am not the one? I am the one. Destiny has brought us together."

If she wasn't an orphan, then the daughter of the witch must be someone else. I had to switch tactics with her. "Cassie, I'm married. I'm not the person you think I am."

Cassie wrung her hands. "Your name is Harold Saturn. You think you're married, but in fact, you aren't. Not in your heart. You're deeply in love with me."

I showed her my wedding band. "My wife gave me this ring, Cassie. Not you."

"It doesn't matter. Dance with me. One dance, and you'll know we're meant to be together. The other woman is not right for you."

The room broke out in a cacophony of voices. Elizabeth tried to prevent her maid from making a spectacle of herself. I heard the fragment of a sentence: "...worse than Lydia." Pennilane grabbed my shoulder as if I had been the one to ask the girl to dance. Her words of "warned you" and "will tell Sanders everything" were drowned out by Cassie's protests. The maid talked over Elizabeth, explaining how she knew I was her one true love.

I remained silent and then asked everyone to quiet down. When they did, I spoke. "Yes, Cassie, I will dance with you."

Pennilane grabbed my shoulder. "One moment."

She dragged me to the furthest corner of the study while Elizabeth pulled Cassie aside for a similar private consultation. Seething, Pennilane whispered. "This is madness. I tell you specifically to stay away from her, and now you are going to dance with her. To be fond of dancing is a certain step toward falling in love!"

"What you said sounds familiar. It must be this place."

Pennilane poked me. "You are not listening to me. Do *not* fall in love. You hold Sanders' heart in your hands. Forget it, do not!"

I put up my hand. "Forget it, I won't, Yoda. I promise. It'll be like dancing with my sister. Or sister-in-law. My younger sister-in-law."

The selkie's shoulders tensed. "It had better be."

I said, "We need to get into the ballroom. While I'm dancing, you should ask people if they've heard of a witch in the area. Talk to the men as well as the women. You may make the women jealous."

Tucking a curl into place, Pennilane asked, "And why would they be jealous?"

"Because you're going to turn every man's head when you enter the ballroom."

Pennilane started to disagree and then threw her hands down in disgust. "Humans! What an insufferable lot!"

When we returned to talk to Cassie, the maid's joy was as palpable as that of a child observing a Christmas tree in Rockefeller Plaza, indicating Elizabeth's failure to prevent her from dancing. I extended my hand, but she refused it. "I must change. I cannot go out there in my maid's uniform."

Elizabeth and Cassie exited the study. The rain poured harder against the window, and lightning illuminated the room multiple times. Pennilane stood with her arms folded, and I observed her whiskers emerge. I pointed it out to her, and she retracted them, claiming they come out when she's agitated. The selkie said, "I will be telling Sanders about this."

"As you should, but the dance is harmless."

A little while later, the door opened again, revealing Elizabeth. She waved us into the hallway, and we followed her. Cassie stood in the hallway leading to the ballroom with her hands folded. She straightened her pink, floor-length dress, which complemented her eyes. She lifted the skirt, stepping toward me in elegant white shoes—the high heels Elizabeth had been wearing. Her expression radiated the glee of a bride on her wedding day.

I took her gloved hand while Elizabeth preceded us into the ballroom. The hostess walked through the doorway and stepped aside, allowing everyone to view Cassie and me entering holding hands. A small orchestra had just finished playing a lively dance, and the people on the floor stepped away from each other. The musicians announced the next piece they would play.

The crowd stopped and stared at the three of us: Cassie, Pennilane, and me. As expected, the men ogled the selkie, who squared her shoulders despite the leers and whispers. Others pointed at Cassie, asking each other if she was the maid they had seen moments before serving them. No one bothered to ask about me while I guided her to the dancing area.

When I stood close to her, she pushed me away. "Line up with the men."

I turned around. A line of gentlemen dressed in suit coats stood in a row behind me, arms at their sides. All at once, I realized the flaw in my plan. I could dance—if you could call it that—to modern music, but I had no idea how to move to a nineteenth-century composition. As a child, I had learned to waltz, but nothing else. Panicked, I gulped loud enough for Cassie to hear. She rubbed her hands. "You don't know how to dance?"

"Not at all."

Cassie widened her eyes in a Sanders-like way. "It is improper for a lady to lead, but I'll make an exception this once, sweetcake. Go line up and mimic the other men."

When the dance started, I found myself a half step behind everyone else, but Cassie gestured and whispered to me my next move. As I started to understand the pattern, I relaxed enough to take in my surroundings. A group of ladies ignored Pennilane's attempts to talk to them on one side of the ballroom. A short distance away, Mr. Darcy was standing behind Elizabeth with his hands behind his back, glaring at me.

I focused on Cassie instead. When we came together, palm on palm, I asked a question. "Do you know of someone around here, an orphan, who seems magical?" We parted, and I had to turn around in a full circle then return to her. "Perhaps someone may have called her a witch at one point?"

The twinkle in Cassie's eyes never faltered. "Why would this person interest you?"

"Do you know this someone or not?"

"Left foot forward, right hand up," she replied. "Perhaps I do. But let's talk about us. We both know what we shared was no dream."

I stepped forward. "We haven't shared anything but a dance."

"We have now shared you stepping on my foot."

I flinched. "Sorry."

I had told Pennilane that Cassie was like a sister, and in some ways, this was true. Sanders' real sister, Karen, couldn't be more different than my wife, but Cassie was not like Karen. Cassie was, instead, analogous to someone who had studied Sanders' personality, someone imitating my spouse. "You're similar to my wife, but I can't get used to your accent."

"I have no accent." The maid rolled her eyes. "You colonists! Admit it was not a dream, or you shall receive no help from this household."

I stepped forward and lifted her hand. "Blackmail, huh? My wife would never resort to blackmail." She and I circled one another. "Well, maybe she would. How about this? I know about your dream. You give me a name, and I'll tell you what I know."

She stepped backward in time with the music. "Why do I feel I won't profit from your knowledge?"

I stomped my foot a half-second behind the rest of the men. "The name?"

Cassie twirled around, her dress billowing out, and then turned back to me. "A colonist in England so soon after the war. Another reason why everyone is suspicious. I'm surprised they allowed you to lodge this far out in the country."

I hadn't thought of finding a place to settle in overnight, hoping Pennilane and I would've retrieved our quarry before the sun rose. "I don't have a place to stay tonight."

Cassie tilted her head in a way that differed from any of my wife's gestures. She pressed in close to me in step with the music. "I shall request the Darcys give you and your sister a room for the night." Cassie showed all her teeth, one slightly crooked. "Do you agree?"

The music ended, and I took her hands to end the dance. "Fine," I grumbled. "I agree."

I parted from her and made my way to Pennilane. I noticed she had been talking to a man at one point when I was dancing. As I approached, she said, "The other women will not talk to me."

"I'm not surprised. I saw you speaking to a man."

She waved her hand. "He knows nothing."

I said, "We have to spend the night here then. Cassie will only tell me if—!"

Cassie bumped into me from behind. "You two will share a room tonight. I arranged it. I will be back, sweetcake."

Pennilane watched her go, then turned her full attention on me. "Sweetcake! I warned you about this."

"What am I supposed to do? She knows her experience wasn't a dream."

"Typical man. She's younger than Sanders. You are enjoying this."

I threw my hands in the air. "In what way, precisely, am I enjoying this?"

"Human women batting their eyelashes at you. You are not trying hard enough."

"And you aren't trying at all. We need information, Pennilane. Why don't you bat your eyelashes at the guy who just left and get us a name if you think it's so effective."

"I told you he doesn't know anything. Shh...Cassie approaches."

Cassie and the Darcys strode toward us. Mr. Darcy halted and crossed his arms. "You don't have a place to stay tonight?"

"Turning them out in this rain would be unchristian," said Cassie.

"Perhaps, a good baptism by nature would do them good," countered Elizabeth. "However, Cassie has convinced us to allow you to stay."

I adjusted my breeches. "We don't need to stay. If you would provide me with the name of the local witch, we'll be on our way."

Mr. Darcy nodded. "Yes, Cassie told us you would ask us about her. It would be a high point of my life to give you directions to a neighbor who respects and admires me so you can go bother her."

Elizabeth peered out a nearby window. "I wouldn't advise going out in this storm. The river will overflow, and without a chaise, you may drown. Best to stay with us. I'll prepare a bedroom for you."

The Darcys summoned the majordomo, and he led us to the exit of the ballroom. While leaving, the man Pennilane claimed knew nothing strolled up to her. He had an oval face, long brown sideburns, and a cleft in his chin. He tipped his head and halted our progress. "Apologies. Miss?"

Pennilane leaned away from him. "I am leaving now."

The man focused on the selkie, ignoring me. "Eustacia Vye is the woman you seek."

The man bowed to her, and I noticed his hands shaking. Whatever Pennilane had said to him had made an impression —a bad one. Lacking information, we needed all the allies we could get. As he turned away, I nudged my selkie companion. She grimaced. "Sir?"

The man stiffened, and Pennilane took a deep breath, forcing the sentence out. "I am grateful. Thank you for being a gentleman and for giving me this name though I did not deserve it."

"Everyone deserves a chance before judgment." He turned on his heel and left her behind.

Pennilane and I exited the ballroom, and the majordomo guided us through the house. The servant led us to a thick paneled door and opened it. "You should be comfortable in the Hudson room."

We entered a compact room with a dresser and mirror on one side, a straight-backed chair, and a single double-sized bed. The majordomo lit two candles that illuminated the room, bowed, and left.

I touched my chin. "I recognize the name Eustacia Vye, too."

Pennilane threw her fan on the dresser. "Is she a character in this story you mentioned? *Eyed and Presumed Kissed*?"

I paced the room. "*Pride and Prejudice*. Potentially. Sanders reads these stories sometimes. I read a lot of genres but not many romances. I wish she were here."

Pennilane sat in the chair after dusting it with her hand. "Your pining for your wife is a good sign." She caught a glimpse of herself in the mirror and tisked. "These clothes are insufferable."

"If Cinderella could see you..."

Pennilane snorted. "I would never hear the end of it. And you will not tell her about it."

"If we get out of this mess and save Kingdom, I'll write it down for my world."

She yawned. "Then make something up where I behead

someone to preserve my dignity."

A knock on the door interrupted our conversation. Someone called out from the hallway. "It is I, Mrs. Darcy."

"Come in."

Elizabeth Darcy entered, holding a candle aloft. She addressed Pennilane. "A gentleman downstairs asked after you. The one you spoke to briefly? He wishes me to give you his card. Shall I convey your name to him? Miss Pennilane Saturn?"

Pennilane accepted the card and pretended to read it. "Yes. Tell him I would like it if he called on me on the morrow."

I eyed her with approbation. Elizabeth nodded her head and then stepped back to address both of us. "I don't know your true intentions and fear misjudging them. I have made terrible mistakes in the past accepting false testimony as the truth. It nearly cost me my husband. Therefore, I implore you to be gallant with your intentions for Cassiopeia." Elizabeth Darcy looked quite somber.

"She's a wayward innocent without a friend in the world beside me," the woman went on. "Cassie intends to marry you, yet she has no dowry, no prosperous relative, no skills to make it on her own. She lacks talent even as a servant. If I had not taken her in, I cannot say what she would have become. God has placed many obstacles in her way, and now her head is filled with a fantasy of running off with you. A married man! I foresee tragedy in every outcome I imagine."

I said, "I don't wish to hurt her. I swear."

"Oaths from strangers do not assuage my concerns. Whoever you are and whatever your purpose, if you're ill-intentioned, I will use my resources to discredit you across this great nation. As a lady, I do not engage in pugilistic endeavors, but I have a sharper sword than any soldier wields—my tongue—and beware the man who crosses it."

She turned on her heel and marched out of the room, slamming the door behind her. Pennilane laughed. "I favor her. She seeks to behead someone too. Never fear, Hero. If you are unfaithful, I shall decapitate you before she gets a chance. Now, to slumber."

Ungentlemanly as it was for me to take the bed, I laid down after Pennilane insisted, telling me she wouldn't have a good night's sleep on the mattress or the chair. Used to sleeping under the stars, she preferred the floor.

The night passed with the storm raging outside. I tossed and turned, then fell into a sleep of exhaustion. At the height of the storm, I had a dream.

I sat on my couch at home in my living room while Cassie, dressed in modern clothing, was next to me. At first, I mixed up Cassie with Sondra, but Cassie's youth convinced me of the identity of my companion. Cassie had on a blouse and jeans, complemented by a baby's burp cloth over her shoulder. Glowing as bright as a summer day, Cassie held an infant in her arms. Dream logic conveyed the little one was my son.

I leaned over and tickled the baby, and Cassie glanced at me, delight dancing in her eyes. The vividness of the scene convinced me this wasn't a dream but a glimpse into the future—a vision I was sharing with Cassie.

Cassie and I were interrupted when Sondra walked into the room holding a teacup. Sondra regarded us with surprise. The teacup slipped from her fingers and smashed on the floor.

I awoke, sat up, and released a long breath from the depth of my turmoil. Reflecting on the vision, I grabbed onto my wedding ring and twisted it, knowing I wouldn't fall back asleep that night.

19 - INCANTATIONS AND LAMENTATIONS

The queens celebrated when Celeste returned to the castle the evening of the witches' defeat at Pernissa Bay. Glinda warned the monarchs the crones would be back and ready for revenge and cautioned Penta, Helga, and Cinderella to leave the defense of Kingdom to the magic-wielders. "The witches will try to provoke and sow discord between you. The best defense now is to be indifferent to them."

Dinner was served in the royal dining hall, and Penta received a message from Exile through her magic ring. One of her contacts had spotted the witches, huddling in the shadows near the coastline. They had freed themselves from Glinda's cube sooner than the Good Witch had predicted.

Penta longed to teleport to Exile but instead relayed the news to Glinda who went with Celeste to seek out their adversaries there. In less than an hour, Celeste contacted Penta on her ring. She and Glinda had found the hags in the underbelly of the city and were surveilling their movements to discern the witches' next attack. Celeste urged Penta and her sisters to dine without them; the pixie would report in later on.

Though concerned for her magical allies, Penta entered the dining hall and told the royal families the latest information about their enemies. Helga, Danforth, Cinderella, Roger, and Beauty listened to the report while they awaited their dinner. Penta stood before them, hands clasped. "I do not want to eat while our friends are in danger, but Celeste is confident they will learn something valuable about the witches. If we join Celeste and Glinda, or if we act out of the ordinary, we may alert the hags to our friends' presence."

"Let us dine, then, and act merry," said Cinderella. "We'll pretend to be ignorant of their whereabouts."

Penta nodded and removed her gloves, revealing her hands, which were now pink due to Beauty's proximity. The eldest queen's floor-length, dandelion-yellow gown swished over the stone floor as she tread toward the table.

After everyone was seated, waiters and waitresses entered carrying large, covered platters, and the aromas of meat, vegetables, and fruit filled the hall. The servants placed the food on the long, rectangular table in banquet style, allowing the queens to serve themselves—a rare occurrence. The monarchs wanted an uninterrupted dinner, and the family began passing plates to each other.

Penta encouraged table talk, so Beauty said, "Grr and I plan to visit the gardener Tuck and his daughter, Kyla. They want me to read Paisley's last letter."

"Impossible," said Penta. "You must remain in the castle."

"But, Mother, I promised days ago that I would read it to them."

"Princess, use your brains. If you cannot go to them..."

"...may I bring them to me? May I summon them?"

Penta scooped vegetables onto her plate. "Of course."

Beauty spiked a pea. "I feel like a prisoner. Aunt Helga, have you been watching Aunt Valencia's squonk?"

Helga grinned at her niece. "That unfortunate creature nearly drowned itself in its tears again last night. He misses his adopted mother."

"I want to visit him. Remember your promise."

Helga replied, "Yes, my dear, you may come over. It will be our pleasure to have such an attentive niece watching your aunt's pet."

Beauty sipped her water. "Aunt Cinderella, after this is all over and done, may I babysit your son again?"

Cinderella dabbed her lips with a napkin before answering. "Certainly."

Beauty sighed. "I miss Cutlass John."

Penta patted her daughter's hand. "Use his given name, Beauty."

Roger grinned. "No offense taken from me, my niece."

Cinderella's voice had a hitch when she breathed in. "I... I miss Cuthbert, too, Beauty. I wish he were here."

Roger put a steadying hand on his wife's, and she took it. Cinderella squeezed Roger's hand, Helga lifted a spoon to her mouth, and Penta smiled at her sister's show of affection for her husband at the same time. And then everyone froze in mid-motion as if encased in amber. Two seconds, three, five. No one moved, spoke, blinked. Though the dining party could hear and think, they couldn't talk or act. They remained as still as fence posts when the witches stepped out of thin air in front of the dining table.

Picana observed those gathered around the table. "Is this not a scene of domestic tranquility?"

Tomana spoke to the paralyzed diners. "While your ignorant magic-wielders follow our illusions around Exile, we thought we would pay you a visit."

Mya stepped closer to the table, waving her hand in front of Penta's unblinking eyes. "Uninvited guests, wishing for a plate, looking for handouts, receive only hate."

"Quite, my dear Mya." Picana tugged on her hat. "Though they cannot move, I sense their enmity."

"Since they didn't invite us to dine, let's take something of theirs for their rudeness," said Tomana.

The crones cackled and swept around the room. Mya and Picana stooped down on either side of Cinderella and talked into each ear. Picana cupped her hand but yelled anyway. "Where's the little one? Where have you hidden him?"

Mya answered, "Take him with us. His prospects grim."

Mya put her hand on Cinderella's forehead while Tomana folded her arms in front of the queen. "Your thoughts shall betray you. To enter your vacuous mind, my dear, is but a trifling act for us."

Mya pulled her hand back. "Upon my word, she doesn't know. Her mind is blank—"

"Enough!" snapped Picana. She put her hand on Roger's head. "The child's location must be in the brute's mind."

Picana lifted her hand moments later. "Neither of them knows. They have hidden the child well, even from themselves. Clever. I wouldn't have thought it of them."

Picana returned to Cinderella. "Your sisters withhold their thoughts from you, believing you too ignorant to be of use. Will you hide behind your elders the rest of your life, my dear?"

Mya turned to Helga and placed a crooked, withered hand on her throat. She squeezed it lightly. Tomana placed her hand on Helga's forehead. "Ah! You should read this one's mind." She tsked. "Such violence! No, no, my dear. Those thoughts will never do for one who claims to be a Light-Bearer."

Helga's expression betrayed nothing.

Tomana stepped away and gestured. "We know your innermost doubt, warrior! Afraid for your soul, are you, Helga the Virtuous? Why not wear your shame on your skin for the rest of your days?"

With a flourish of Tomana's index finger, green spots

blossomed on Helga's skin as they had on her soul body. The three laughed while the pockmarks covered the brown of her skin, standing out like lichen on tree bark.

Picana put a finger next to her chin. "Sisters, we haven't accomplished what we have come here for. We desire distress, not resignation."

They regarded Beauty. Picana cackled. "Here is a bonbon worth stealing."

They released the princess from their spell, and Beauty leaped to her feet, knocking over her chair. She gasped. "Mother."

Smile etched on her face, Penta did not move or speak.

The witches rushed toward the girl, but Beauty was nimble. She ran around the table, avoiding their clutches. They feinted left and right, causing her to stumble her way toward the door. Her celerity outpaced their efforts, and she sprinted toward the exit, almost free from their grasp. And then, at the last moment, they materialized before Beauty and snatched her. She screamed when they dragged her to the table in front of Penta.

Picana cupped her hands around Beauty's face and squeezed her cheeks. The girl wailed in pain. "Now, don't be too hasty to leave your mother. She worries about you so, and with good reason, true?" The witch turned her attention to the queen. "Now what shall we do with our prize, Penta? Perhaps we will skin her alive, dismember her fingers, and feast on them tonight?"

Penta's frozen smile remained in place.

Maya clapped. "Bake her bones. Wheat and rye. Make our scones." She eyed Beauty's abdomen and added. "Kidney pie."

Tomana's nail scratched the girl's throat. "Perhaps we will turn her to our side, corrupt her soul, and force her to kill her mother?"

Picana released the child's cheeks. "For now, we will hide her in Kingdom until we decide, and when you see her next, you won't recognize her."

Mya giggled. "Incantation. Transformation. Deformation. Lamentation."

And then the hags disappeared, and the party regained its movement at the same time. Penta jumped up. "Beauty!" She reached out, grasping at the air as if to pull her daughter back from the witches' clutches. Her hands had returned to their silver sheen and reflected her wide-eyed, open-mouthed expression.

Helga buried her face in her green-spotted hands while Danforth leaped to his feet. Roger pulled Cinderella close, both trembling in each other's arms.

Penta spoke into her ring. "Celeste. They were here. They took her, and now they are gone. She is gone!"

Celeste's voice buzzed from Penta's ring. "They took who? Cinderella?"

Penta replied, "Helga or Cinderella can explain. Right now, I need Grr."

She teleported away before anyone could stop her.

Later that night, Helga and Cinderella gathered in the war room. They sat on two cushions beside an enormous unlit fireplace. After searching for hours, the two sisters had sent scouting parties out on a quest for Beauty. They decided to coordinate the effort from the castle.

Cinderella rubbed her hands together. "The hour of midnight approaches, and we've heard nothing from Penta."

Helga removed her buckler and set it on the table. "Have any of our scouts spotted her?"

"No. Do you think the witches have her?"

Helga reached inside her tunic and retrieved a chain with a gold ring, and placed it on her finger. "They wouldn't fail to gloat. I know you've been trying to call Penta, but you have to know how to do it."

Cinderella observed her ring. "Being the youngest as I am, Penta can afford to ignore me."

Helga lifted the ring to her mouth and squinted at her sister. "Not true, but observe. Penta, this is Helga. If you don't come to my chambers within a minute, I will assume the witches have kidnapped you and will take appropriate action."

In ten seconds, Penta stood before Helga. Her yellow gown was ripped apart at the knees and covered in mud, her mussed hair hung in clumps on her shoulders; boots replaced her slippers, and her eyes were circular like those of a jack-o-lantern. "Did you find Beauty?"

Helga put a hand on her sister's shoulder. "Slow down. You cannot be racing off by yourself for such an extended period. You had us worried."

Penta shook off the gesture. "Why aren't you searching?"

Helga dropped her arm. "As Celeste told you, her locator spell failed to detect Beauty's position. Glinda says to let the witches make the next move."

"Glinda says," spat Penta. "Doesn't she realize my daughter's in danger?"

"Penta—"

Stepping up to Helga, Penta shouted, "My little girl! You don't understand."

Though Helga stood firm, Cinderella recoiled at Penta's outburst. The golden-haired queen cleared her throat. "I am a mother," Cinderella said, "and I understand your plight."

Penta turned to her as if noticing her for the first time. "You were the smart one. You hid your son, or they would have taken him. They would have taken him…"

"…instead of Beauty, yes," finished Cinderella. Her

cheeks turned red. "You sound as if you would have preferred that they had taken Cuthbert."

Penta trembled and then cried. "I'm sorry, but she called out to me to help her. I hear her voice over and over in my head. No, Cinderella, I don't want them to take Cuthbert, but I have had those thoughts. God forgive me. I cannot help but think about it. I can't lose my daughter."

Helga put both hands on her sister's arms. "Penta, calm yourself."

"I must find her!"

"Penta, do not disappear. Take a breath. We are going to find her." After her reassuring words, Helga hugged her sister tightly, tears forming in her eyes.

Softened by Helga's embrace, Penta wiped a tear from her cheek. "You said it yourself—Glinda and Celeste have tried the locator spell. It failed."

Cinderella folded her hands together. "Celeste admitted magic cannot locate someone underground, in the sea, or on distant islands. She could be in any of those places."

Penta dismissed her sister's suggestion with a shake of her head. "Or the hags' spells counteract the good witches' power. I have teleported around Kingdom since dinner, from the Marsh of Wishes to Bremen, and haven't found a trace of her. Grr has sniffed the air, hoping to catch her scent. Again nothing. Where could she be?"

"Penta—"

Helga opened her arms to hug Penta again, but her elder sister avoided the gesture. "Helga, please leave me be," said Penta. "I promise to check in by half-morning tomorrow if you'll allow me to continue my search without returning here." Before the other queen could react, she vanished.

Cinderella said, "I'm worried about her."

Helga crossed her arms. "Valencia, where are you?"

While lying in bed next to Danforth, Helga reflected on her earlier prayers. She had kneeled on her ornate mat, chanting ancient verses, and listing her requests. Find Beauty, defeat the witches, bless Snow White's soul, remove the green spots, relieve Penta's anxiety, bring Valencia home, and grant her faith. Tears had poured from her eyes during her petitions.

Back in her bedroom now in the middle of the night, she prepared for slumber. Her emotions had exhausted her, and she needed to have energy in the morning if she was going to sally forth to find Beauty or confront the witches.

"Helga."

At first, she thought Danforth had whispered her name in his sleep, and she nearly ignored it. But someone, or something, had said her name. Danforth's snores then proved he wasn't the one who had called her, at least not consciously.

"Helga."

The second time the word hung in the air like a firefly glowing in the night. Helga pushed off her blanket and sat up, eyes darting around the room, expecting the witches. Though she was alarmed, her equanimity remained in place. The voice delivered a soothing aspect to its sound, similar to showering under a magically warmed waterfall. She rose from the bed and decided a whisper in the middle of the night was not the witches' style.

"Helga."

The heavenly voice beckoned to her as if it needed help. It sang its summons, imitating a tune similar to what her husband, a bard, would compose. She rounded the corner of the four-poster bed and entered the hallway, leaving Danforth behind.

Passing Cinderella's room, she didn't bother to wake her sister while treading after the captivating voice. The beckoning could be a trap, yet she stayed her course. Whoever called her sounded as hopeful as a singing angel on Redeemer Day.

Helga wandered down to the main floor of the castle, where Lyken crossed her path, holding a plate of cheese and bread. Guilt colored his expression after he turned a corner and just barely avoided colliding with her. An amiable man, he bowed when she approached him, holding the plate behind his back. "I apologize, my queen. May I assist you in some manner?"

"Lyken! My mentor and friend when we lived in Nor. Set the tray down and accompany me."

"Yes, my queen."

He left the tray on a nearby table and trailed after Helga. She stopped and gestured him forward. He stepped up next to her, glancing at her while they roamed the hallways. "Begging your pardon, my queen, but you do not look to be yourself. Are you sleepwalking?"

"No. A voice calls to me and grows stronger with every step I take."

"I do not hear anything."

Her eyes drifted to a hallway ahead. "It only wants me. Stay with me, Lyken. Something is about to happen."

"What?'

"I do not know."

They wandered into the trophy hall and then into the long corridor of portraits of famous past kings and queens of Kingdom. Trying to pull a knife without observable fuss, her companion reached for the hilt of his sharpest weapon. "My queen, shall I call Queen Cinderella or Queen Penta?"

Helga's eyes remained forward. "We will not need your knife tonight."

"I am worried about you."

Helga stopped in the middle of the hall and turned toward a portrait of King Leopold the Magnificent standing tall, holding the holy sword Cusp with its blade pointed down. The balding king boasted a walrus-styled mustache and steely blue eyes. Helga put her hands on her hips. "King Leopold was regal and stern, but fair and merciful too."

Helga extended an arm toward the portrait.

Lyken examined the likeness of the former king. "What is it, my queen? Has someone done something to the—?"

Lyken's words died in his throat when the painting of King Leopold moved. The king lifted his arm with the sword of Cusp and extended it through the surface of the picture. The hand holding the sword was as flat as parchment, but the sword ballooned into three dimensions when it crossed from paint to air.

Trembling, Helga reached for the sword, and the former king and current queen both held its handle for a long moment. The painted monarch released the hilt and pulled back his arm into the painting, leaving his weapon behind in the human queen's hand. The sword glowed in the night and then dimmed while Helga held the artifact.

The warrior queen examined Cusp in her green-tinted hand. Her voice quivered. "I can't believe what I'm holding. Lyken, am I dreaming?"

Amazed, Lyken couldn't construct an answer to her question, and a quick inspection of the painting by the two showed King Leopold now lacked his sword. Helga examined the weapon in wonder, her eyes pouring over the intricately carved handle and runes on the blade. Then she held it up to Lyken. "Is it? Is it truly Cusp?"

"The sword." Lyken licked his lips. "Legends say the bearer is immune to all magic, and one cut from its blade, however slight, is certain death to whoever receives it."

Helga shook, overwhelmed with emotion. In her hands, she held the only weapon they knew capable of killing the witches.

PART TWO

The Part Two Cast of Characters

Morbidum:
Count Brahm Cupsince: Peter's friend and séance participant.
Lyndon: Missing butler.
Lenore Marstings: Deceased cousin of Peter Marstings.
Peter Harcourt Marstings: Art collector, owner of Marstings Manor, not currently in residence.
Beatrice Rappaccini: Veiled art student, friend of Lenore, and séance participant.
Allan Usher: Art critic, Lenore's former lover, and séance participant.
Zariah Zephyr: Artist and art historian, friend of Lenore, and séance participant.

Janay:
Elizabeth Darcy: Hostess at Pemberley and friend to Cassie.
Fitzwilliam Darcy: Host at Pemberley and Elizabeth's husband.
Pip: A guest at Pemberley.
Cassiopeia (Cassie) Yarkus: A familiar-looking maid.

Cixxes:
07151823051212 (Julia): Resident of Centrania.

Quotes

The quickest way of ending a war is to lose it.

—George Orwell

To be fond of dancing was a certain step towards falling in love.

—Jane Austen

20 - BACK FROM THE DEAD

A sharp rap on her door woke Valencia the next morning, and she sat bolt upright in her bed. She called out to ask who had knocked, expecting a servant. The answer surprised her.

"Beatrice Rappaccini. I thought I would escort you to breakfast."

Valencia had slept in her clothes, and she now ran her fingers through her hair to remove any tangles from sleeping on it. Grabbing her cap and tying it under her chin, she opened the door and came face to face with Beatrice's veil. "I was up late and must have overslept," apologized Valencia.

"Who could blame you?" Beatrice replied in a calming Italian accent. "Did you find a nightgown in the bureau?"

"It was empty. I slept in my clothes."

Beatrice inclined her head. "Let me take you into Lenore's room. The Marstings wanted it preserved, so her clothes are still there. You're smaller than my friend, but I believe a few garments may fit you.

They entered a room at the end of the hall, and Valencia found herself in a large chamber with a four-poster bed, a vanity, and a large closet. Beatrice opened the closet door. "Take what you like."

Valencia hesitated. "Are you sure?"

"She can't use them anymore. Please."

Valencia found clothes her size and stepped behind a partition to change. She slipped into a vermilion dress—a velvet, plush, floor-length garment with a white belt and intricate lace around the collar—hiding her ruby pendant. While standing before the mirror to make final adjustments, she noticed a painting of a woman sitting on the grass with a lake in the background and examined it. "This painting is lovely."

Beatrice stepped next to her. "It's Lenore."

Valencia walked closer to admire the portrait. The fair-skinned, solemn woman had her hair pulled back and parted down the middle. The subject's placid eyes marked a point above the observer. Though the background exuded light and color, the painter had chosen muted, dull pigments for the person at the center. The downturn of the woman's mouth intimated a melancholic disposition.

Valencia twisted away, and she and Beatrice left the room together. Beatrice fingered her veil. "Zariah did superlative work capturing Lenore. Her portrait may be Zariah's best effort."

"She's a marvelous artist."

"*Si*. Zariah sometimes chooses to paint with her less dominant hand to vary her style. Even when she does, the result is still remarkable." Beatrice gestured for Valencia to proceed down the stairs. "Not to speak ill of the dead, but Allan was wrong about Zariah's artistic ability. She once accepted a challenge to paint with her feet. All agreed the result was better than what most people could produce with their hands."

Valencia filled a lapse in conversation to change the subject and learn more about her quest. "Zariah is young. Does she travel with a companion or her parents?"

Beatrice snorted, ruffling her veil. "Zariah's parents sold her to a traveling show. Lenore, Zariah, and I met there."

"How awful. My parents put me in an orphanage. Tell me, are any of the others here orphans as well?"

Beatrice's sure footsteps followed Valencia down the stairs. "I have a father, Giovanni. The count carries a picture he drew of his parents in his billfold. I'm sorry, my dear, but none of us are orphans. Why do you ask?"

"Trying to find something in common," she replied. "You and Zariah were in a show together?"

They reached the bottom of the stairs. "The show is where we met Lenore. The manager ballyhooed us as freaks, but it was all an act. Lenore would display feathers glued on her skin—reincarnated Egyptian goddess or some such nonsense. After we left, Lenore invited us here, and we became friends of the family."

Valencia asked, "May I inquire how she died?"

Beatrice lowered her head. "She and Allan had been taking a walk on the cliffs overlooking Lake Montresor. According to Allan, they had a minor disagreement. Lenore ran from him, and in her hurry to get away, slipped on the embankment and tumbled a hundred feet to the rocks below."

Valencia put her hand on the base of her neck. "How awful!"

"Zariah and I think he was drunk, and she confronted him about it then ran away, upset. Allan swore he didn't see her body at the bottom, unsurprising in his intoxicated state. Sad, sad affair. We put a headstone in the family plot behind the house but never buried the body."

"The lost Lenore," said a voice from behind the women.

Valencia startled. Count Cupsince had joined them as silent as a snake slithering through tall grass. He flashed a wry grin at the women. "Not long after, the raven appeared. Allan swore it talked to him, but he wouldn't reveal what it said. He called it *le démon*. A black thing from hell itself. It followed him around like a curse."

Beatrice said, "It must have some unfinished business. I find it handsome."

As they proceeded down a hallway, Valencia spotted a library through one of the open doors and thought of researching the local area for an orphanage. "If you'll excuse me, I'm not hungry. I wish to examine the library. I love books of all kinds."

"But of course. I'll have the cook set aside a plate for you," said Cupsince. "You're welcome to join us after you peruse the Marstings collection."

Except for a light lunch, Valencia remained in the room for hours, reviewing most of the collection. In the middle of the afternoon, she found an old registry and sat at a desk, hoping to uncover a reference to an adopted child. Turning page after page, faster and faster, she finally shut the book with a sharp thump and pushed it away. The sun struggled to shine through the window, casting the room in an ominous shadow. She stood and made her way to the window, reflecting aloud. "They wouldn't keep it on the bookshelves."

She returned to the desk, opened the drawers, and located a black, leather-bound tome—the family's Holy Bible. Placing it on the desk, she flipped it open and read the first page. With the title printed in cursive, the author had written "The Marstings." Lines extended down a family tree. Valencia's finger traced down its branches until she cried out, "Oh, no!" She put a hand to her mouth. "It cannot be!"

Lowering her head, Valencia reflected on her next move when a rustling sound caught her attention. She spied the raven sitting on a ledge with an empty jar and a broken stein. Motionless, the bird regarded her, reminding the queen of a sentry protecting an entrance to a building. Valencia had left the door open a crack, and in her absorption, hadn't heard the bird slip into the room. She approached the creature, her eyes locked on its features. The two remained frozen in the same position for a long time as if in a staring contest, each daring the other to blink.

Valencia broke the silence. "You're a person, aren't you? I noticed last night you watch people like a human being. Where I'm from, people can become animals. I know a woman who transformed into a frog. Are you cursed?"

The raven didn't answer.

"I recognize human characteristics in you. The others won't believe it. The idea is beyond them. But 'tis true, is it not?"

The bird slowly nodded.

"Very good. Can I help to restore you to your body?"

The bird leaped off the shelf and landed on the ground. The raven at that point spread its wings full and puffed out its chest, and then began to grow taller. As it enlarged, its legs filled out, its beak collapsed, and its shoulders broadened. The transformation took less than a minute before a young lady stood in front of Valencia. Feathers covered her body, but her head, hands, and feet were human.

The Match Girl's eyes widened, recognizing the female. "It's you."

"Lenore," answered the woman.

21 - CASSIOPEIA

Harold

In the morning, I sat staring at the knots in the wood on the floor, arms draped over my knees, reflecting on the vision. Across the room, Pennilane stood before the mirror, attempting to tame her hair with a brush. I looked up, and the selkie's reflection regarded me. "What is troubling you, Hero?" Pennilane asked.

"I want to leave this place with or without our witch."

Pennilane turned around. "Why the change of mind?"

"This place is affecting me."

Pennilane returned to viewing herself in the mirror and brushed at a tangle. "We have a name and a gentleman who may escort us to a local tavern. From there, we shall find her."

I twisted my wedding ring. "And then throw a bag over

her head and kidnap her?"

"I'm relying on your eloquence to convince her. Kingdom knows you as a most persuasive knight."

I was about to reply when a knock at the door interrupted me. Elizabeth asked if she could enter. After Pennilane responded affirmatively, our hostess marched in and observed Pennilane wrestle with another tangle in her hair. Elizabeth pointed to a chair in front of the mirror. "Sit."

"I do not require—"

"I said sit."

Pennilane sat. Elizabeth was not a pushover, that much I remembered from *Pride and Prejudice.*

Our hostess pulled a small box from the dresser, opened it and revealed multiple types of brushes, going to work on the selkie's hair. "We will feed you, and then the gentleman said he would return. I assume you will be departing with him."

"Yes," we both replied.

Elizabeth eyed Pennilane's dress—the same one she had worn the night before. "You cannot go out in the same clothes. Fortunately, you and my sister Jane have the same build. I will retrieve a dress for you to keep."

"You do not need to trouble yourself," said Pennilane, examining Elizabeth's quick work in the mirror.

"You will wear Jane's clothes," said Elizabeth. "And I will not take no for an answer. I won't be known in this county as inhospitable."

The women went to another room while I waited for them to come back. When they returned, Pennilane appeared in a tomato-red, ankle-length dress—presumably Jane's. Then our hostess escorted us from our room through the house to a nook tucked away in a back corner of the dining area. On our breakfast table there, someone had placed a small glass bowl of water with cut peony heads floating on the surface—an elegant decoration. Elizabeth left us, and a servant stepped forward and presented rolls and a half of an egg to each of us.

Pennilane and I ate alone, each lost in our thoughts, the fragrance of the peony surprisingly strong.

I should have been thinking of our mission, but my mind was fixated on the dream. What did the vision mean? Had someone arranged it? Did it predict the future? How could I be with anyone other than Sondra?

Elizabeth returned during the middle of our meal. "The gentleman is at the door for you, Miss Saturn."

Pennilane stood and followed Elizabeth from the room. While I stared out a rain-streaked window at the dawn of a new day, gray clouds passed over the manicured landscape, casting shadows on the water-soaked grounds. Lost in reflection, I didn't notice someone slip into the nook and stand by the table. "How was your sleep?"

Cassie, in her maid's uniform, stood next to the table.

"Troubling."

"I disagree. 'Illuminating' is what I would call it." She eyed the floral arrangement. "I set the peonies out for you. They're my favorite flower."

"My wife's is lavender."

Cassie hovered over the flowers, breathing in their scent. "Are you certain?"

"Of course!"

Cassie nodded to Pennilane's vacant chair as a question. I grimaced but gestured for her to take that seat. She sat down and regarded me with lively eyes. "You know what our dream means."

"It means now you're aware of my wife. Her name is Sondra. I call the two of you parallels."

"All three of us know each other now."

And a revelation dawned on me all at once. Cassie and I weren't the only ones who'd had that vision. Sondra had experienced it, too. What could be going through her head? I dreaded the thought of meeting up with her again. She would believe I had cheated on her when I hadn't.

I cleared my throat. "I'm devoted to my wife."

"Then why not have a baby with her?" Cassie asked.

I snapped, "Because she can't. Or I can't. We can't have children!"

Cassie leaned back. "It must be her, Harold."

I opened my mouth to respond, but Cassie held up her hand. "I am not unfeeling toward your wife, but you understand how this makes everything right? The dream said I could bear children. I was the mother."

Irritated, I pointed a fork at the maid. "You reason like a teenager. The situation is not so simple."

Cassie put her elbows on the table. "Did you come in a horseless carriage? Or one of those cylinders that soar through the air?"

I gaped at her, and she laughed. "I've seen your world in my dreams. I've always thought it a fantasy, yet here you sit. If you're real, then everything I dreamed is real, true?"

"Yes."

"I figure my visions must be of Janay in the future," Cassie said. "I cannot believe the dresses the women wear in your time. Scandalous! How I long to dress in them."

I drummed my fingers on the table. "The place in your dreams is not Janay. I'm actually from a different world."

Cassie tilted her head in her hands. "Another planet? Venus?"

"No. I can't explain exactly. You have to believe in a whole lot more than horseless carriages. You have to believe in fairies and real witches."

A fly buzzed past Cassie's ear. "I do believe in them. I know fairies watch over us."

I waved aside the fly. "I'm serious."

The bug landed on a window, and Cassie examined it. "As am I. I once dreamed I had wings and could fly like this insect, but I was a butterfly person." Her smile faltered. "For some reason, I haven't had the flying dream in a long time."

"The butterfly person was Planet, a pixie," I said. "I suppose I should tell you everything."

I explained about the different worlds, parallels, and the connection between her and Sanders. I went on to describe the quest to find the three daughters. "Now you know I'm not seeking a replacement for my wife but a witch. The daughter is the key. I'm not here because of you but for more important reasons."

"The woman with you. Is she one of your queens?"

"She's a guard and a selkie."

The maid clapped her hands. "A selkie! How exciting!"

"You don't believe me."

Cassie nudged a glass on the table thoughtfully. "Oh, but I do. I've experienced Kingdom as Planet. I've experienced Earth through Sondra. I live in Janay, and now you say other worlds exist? This Oz, for one?"

I nodded. "Yes."

Cassie dipped her finger into the bowl and spun one of the peony heads in the water. "Do you promise not to travel from this world without me?"

"But Sondra won't allow—"

Cassie held up her hand in a Sanders-like way. "We will have to discuss it. She must concede that you and I are supposed to be together, Harold. The baby proves it. You cannot leave me here. Not now. Think about it. You found this pixie named Planet, then Sondra, and now me. These events weren't merely coincidental. I have a part to play."

"I'm not convinced you do," I said. "Planet belonged to Kingdom and Sondra to Earth. Leaving a world may not be part of nature's plan."

Cassie slammed her palm on the table. "I cannot stay here and grow old as a maid. If I don't have you, Harold, I have nothing at all. My parents will die soon, and without Mrs. Darcy, no one will employ me. What if Mrs. Darcy turns me out for making one mistake too many? What will happen to me? Would you leave Planet's and Sondra's kin to destitution?"

Wincing, I reflected on her outburst. Cassie was similar to Sanders and Planet before her in many ways. For the

first time, I spied the scared girl behind the self-assured facade. She had been a flirt, a tease, an opportunist. But Cassie
had revealed her innermost fear—her destiny lay in my hands.
Planet had the freedom to run away, and Sanders was born
into a world that allowed her to flourish. But Cassie was a slave
and could descend into abject poverty if not for the charity of
Elizabeth Darcy. My choice was clear.

"You can come with me."

Cassie brightened, but I held up a finger. "I'm not attracted to you. Protective of you? Yes. I want you to have the
best chance for a happy life, but bringing you along doesn't
mean I'm in love with you."

"Sondra, you, and I shall come to a resolution. I understand a marriage vow, but if you've been to a fairy tale land,
you must understand something about true love."

I was about to disabuse her of the idea we were lovers,
but Cassie stood up and collected the plates on the table.
"We'll talk later."

"Only if you tell me where I can find Eustacia Vye."

Cassie balanced the plates on the crook of her arm. "You
won't find Eustacia Vye. She doesn't exist. I promise to lead
you to your witch, but not before we talk again."

Minutes after Cassie left, Elizabeth led Pennilane back
to the breakfast nook. The selkie had a hand over the lower
portion of her face when she took her seat. What now?

Pennilane nodded at her guide and thanked her through
her hand. After Elizabeth left, she removed her palm. Whiskers sprouted from her upper lip. Thankfully, we were alone.
"What's the matter with you? Retract them!"

"I cannot." She placed her hand over her whiskers again.

"What do you mean?" I asked.

Speaking through her fingers, Pennilane said, "They
emerged while I was talking to the gentleman. I immediately
hid them. Have you ever had a muscle spasm? 'Tis the same."

"Just relax then."

She closed her eyes, lowered her hand, and took a deep

breath. The whiskers pulled slowly back into her skin.

I leaned forward and whispered. "What brought that on?"

Pennilane's fingers brushed over her cheeks. "I don't know, but I will be more careful. No matter, I discovered another name. Eustacia Vye married and is now Eustacia Yeobright."

"Let's go visit her with your gentleman."

"We have to stay here until evening. Then Pip will return."

"What the hell is a Pip?"

Pennilane squared her shoulders. "Pip is the gentleman caller. Also, a heroic seal name, as it turns out. You instructed me to be nice to him, so I conversed with him."

I would've paid good money to watch Pennilane show kindness to a man. "You didn't frighten him off? You can be kind of...brusque."

Pennilane lifted her chin. "I also can act like a lady if the situation calls for it."

We stood and were about to leave when Elizabeth entered the room with Cassie in tow. Elizabeth regarded me crossly—her face a cardinal red. "Cassie now tells us you've agreed to take her away. I thought last night you were married and wanted nothing to do with my maid. And now you're absconding with her to God knows where!"

I glared at Cassie. She had told Elizabeth because of her strong bond with her mistress. Or perhaps, with her garrulous nature, she'd let the news slip out. "I made Cassie a promise to leave with her once my wife arrives. The three of us need to straighten out a private affair."

She frowned at the word "affair." Poor choice of words on my part. Elizabeth asked, "Why should I believe you?"

"If you must know, my wife and your maid could be twins," I answered. "They look exactly alike, which is why this situation is so screwy. Uh, highly irregular."

Elizabeth relaxed at my explanation. "You will not be

leaving with Cassie?"

Cassie scowled at Elizabeth. "Ma'am, I'm a grown woman. I know how to take care of myself."

"Cassie, you sound like a child at times," growled Elizabeth.

"I'm waiting for my wife, and the three of us will leave together," I said. "My wife and I will treat her as a friend of the family. Right now, I must speak to Mrs. Yeobright."

Mr. Darcy entered the room and leaned against the wall. His face was as pale as curdled milk. Elizabeth regarded him worriedly. "Fitzwilliam? What is the matter?"

"One of this gentleman's party has shown up at our front door on horseback." Glaring at me, he said, "Did you tell them all to come here?"

I gestured to Elizabeth. "This will be Sanders or Alice."

Mr. Darcy shook his head. "She said her name was Julia. She is dressed oddly and is behaving like a lunatic. I had to assume she was with you."

"I don't know a Julia."

Elizabeth eyed me with distrust. "We'll stable her horse."

Mr. Darcy said, "She calls him Bree."

22 - THE CLENCHED FIST

Sondra

Seconds after Julia disappeared on Bree, four people in nondescript uniforms with green lights encircling their chests charged into Julia's apartment. I screamed and ran toward the bedroom, scooping up my bag on the way, but they grabbed me and forced me to the floor. My chin struck the carpet with a jaw-jarring thud. A woman from the invading party, bald except for sandy-colored bangs, entered the bedroom and retreated a half-minute later. She spoke to a larger woman sporting a military haircut. "Two imprints when we entered, but the bedroom is clear."

Electricity skittered across my bones, accompanied by pain and a loss of muscle control. When the sensation stopped, a woman growled, "Who was here? Who was with you?"

Alice must have awakened and escaped to another world when these devils had blown the door off its hinges. Good! If we were both caught, we'd be in real trouble. She'd come for me and take me away from this madness.

A man said, "Come on, 07151823051212, you're going to The Soul." If snakes could speak, they'd have this guy's voice.

The woman with bangs for hair examined something in her hand. "But this isn't 07151823051212."

Military Haircut put her hands on her hips. "Who the zwork is she then?"

Sandy Bangs replied, "She's unregistered."

A momentary pause, and then I received a kick to the stomach. Unprepared, I cried in pain. Hands grabbed my shoulders and lifted me. Again, before I could prepare myself, a baton pushed against my hip. Military Haircut grinned, and a low charge exploded through my body. I bit my tongue hard enough to draw blood, moaning.

Military Haircut put her hand on my back. "We'll take her to The Soul anyway. They're expecting someone there. As long as we deliver someone, they won't care. This one is as good as 07151823051212. Grab the bag, too."

They marched me outside to a morning sunrise. No vehicles were parked on the roadway. Instead, the soldiers guided me down a set of stone steps to a subway discordant with the cobblestone streets and cozy storefronts above. Where was Alice? I had never read *Brave New World* or *1984*, but I knew I didn't want to go anywhere with these sadists.

The underground chamber, obviously once used as part of a subway system, no longer supported the cylindrical cars to transport people. At the bottom of the stairs, twenty high-tech elevators in a row, some open and some closed, awaited us.

Sandy Bangs shoved me into one of the elevator carriages with windows on all sides except the door. Three of my captors, the two women and a man with a bowler hat, stepped inside with me. When the doors shut with a sharp ping, walls surrounded the compartment. Bowler Hat typed on a keyboard near the door, and the elevator took off backward. I then realized the elevator was not an elevator but a vehicle. A few hours ago, I would've been fascinated by this new technology, but now I didn't care about anything but escaping.

Through the windows, I could see that numerous interconnecting tubes formed a massive maze beneath the city. My mouth went dry while the elevator-car rushed along at sixty or so miles an hour across the glass corridor, narrowly missing another speeding car in an intersecting channel. Cat's piss! The officers lounged against the glass walls, not caring that if the transport was a fraction of a centimeter too fast or slow, we would collide with another vehicle. I should've marveled at the precise engineering, but I instead focused on keeping the tuna in my stomach.

Our car turned a corner and raced toward a more constricted tunnel ahead. The elevator was too tall and wouldn't clear the smaller tube. I braced for the inevitable accident, but milliseconds before the car entered the second tube, the ceiling and floor adjusted so that the head of the taller woman in the car was flush with the roof.

Military Haircut crossed her arms. "I rode with 04211302011919 yesterday. The bilgehead's so tall we needed nearly a minute to travel downtown."

A voice from a hidden speaker in the car jarred me. "Stow it, 19010409192001."

A few seconds later, we stopped, and my captors pushed me out of the car. We were in a narrow hallway with no furniture and gray walls. A staircase led upward.

We walked up five floors, and though not out of shape, I began to tire. On the first floor, precise lettering on the walls indicated we had arrived at The Soul. More gray walls surrounded my ascent, and the guards directed me to a door on the uppermost floor. We passed through it into a sterile corridor with bright recessed lighting, momentarily blinding me.

Sandy Bangs grabbed my arms and shoved me forward.

Doors without handles stood at intervals along the passageway. While we progressed down the hall, a man with silver hair exited a room. My mouth dropped open when I observed he walked on a metal leg, not an ordinary prosthetic, but a thin, Tin Woodman leg. Fearing Military Haircut would hurt me again, I didn't turn around for a second look.

After we had all proceeded down four corridors, the guards forced me to halt in the center of a hallway, and Sandy Bangs fiddled with the lights on her shirt. Right in front of me, a hole opened in the floor, and a chair ascended from it. The panel in the floor sealed, and the chair, resembling a seat more for a dental patient, hovered before me, equipped with a headrest. I noticed multiple straps—not seatbelts, fetters.

The guards pushed me into the chair and secured me with restraints across my chest, arms, and legs. Now that I was trapped, the chair swiveled around, then moved on its own. It glided forward down the hallway.

The officers didn't accompany me while I rode around the facility, drifting along as if on a parade float. Other gray-clothed inhabitants of The Soul passed me without acknowledging my presence, avoiding my mobile prison.

The chair wheeled me down ramps until I came to yet another corridor in the same shade of bland slate gray. I rode along until one of the doors opened to my left, and I supposed I'd arrived at my destination. The experience reminded me of an indoor ride at an amusement park, but I knew this was no funhouse.

The chair entered a tiled room with a low ceiling and sound dampeners. It drifted to the center, where a spotlight shone on me. Certainly, they were watching me. Would they leave me here to starve? I blinked to block out the glare of the light.

After what could've been an hour, a man strolled into the room. He carried a stool in one hand, his other hand clenched into a fist. He set the stool down and sat on it, staring at his open palm, flexing his fingers. He lifted his closed hand within my peripheral vision, ignoring me. I didn't speak to him. He appeared to be reading the palm of his open hand. I took deep breaths to calm myself, but fear kept its icy hold on my spine.

As if suddenly noticing me, he turned my way. His eyes were as cold and dark as two black holes. The color of ripe bananas, his yellow teeth flashed. "You are 07151823051212?"

I didn't reply.

"No, you are definitely not."

His left hand remained closed. My attention shifted to it and then back at him, fearing he would strike me. He didn't.

"We scanned you while you rode around our facility. No record of you exists in Centrania. Our records show you're not a known resident of Sirling, Myrimodan, Frayda Narumbia, or any other continent. I'd ask you for your name, but names mean nothing to us. I'll call you Squatter." He grinned at the name 'Squatter,' pronouncing it like a profanity.

I didn't react. What was he going to do?

"Whether you talk or not doesn't matter. I know everything important about you. You aren't a Centrania's resident but likely a spy or renegade from outside. Hmm?"

I closed my eyes, but a loud cymbal crashed in my left ear. My eyelids jerked open.

He studied the palm of his hand. "Let's see here. Female. I have your age down to your date of birth, even the day, and your weight and length at birth. Removal of wisdom teeth, rather poorly done, I may add. Evidence of poor eyesight as early as five years old, but no evidence of eye surgery. Odd. Your blood pressure is a little high. You're married the old-fashioned way, indentation on your ring finger, which went out of style years ago. Signs of a fast-acting cancer. It will probably take your life in the next twenty years."

I had to tell myself to breathe. Breathe, dammit. I wasn't about to let this jerk get the better of me.

The interrogator continued, "The police were dispatched to 07151823051212's residence early this morning when her monitor went off for over fifteen minutes. We arrived to find you in her apartment, Squatter, but no owner of the residence. The resident has vanished from our surveillance equipment, and let me tell you, that is quite a feat."

I couldn't resist the temptation, and I chanced a glimpse at his left hand. Still tight-fisted.

"We had to tell the courts 0715 was sick. What a terrible loss of productivity. Worse, you are occupying an important room in The Soul. This room is booked months ahead of time, but I overrode an old associate's reservation to have this conversation. Take a look."

The chair twirled me around like a barber's chair, and I read Julia's number on an electronic display above the door. The first time Harold Traveled to Kingdom, he and the queens had all undergone tests set up by their adversary. To start their challenges, they had to enter a doorway with their names above it. The experience had nearly removed their hope. Now I sat in a similar room with a name above the entrance. Good God, my turn had come.

The seat rotated me back to face the man. He rubbed his forefinger and thumb together. "So, where is 0715? Hmm?"

Again, I forgot to breathe. I forced air out my nostrils. In. Out.

"If you tell us, we will let you go free outside of the borders of Centrania."

I doubted that.

"If you don't...someone has to do 0715's work, and you seem quite capable despite your lack of cooperation. Tell us where 0715 is, and we can put this unpleasant morning behind us both."

If only Alice would arrive to rescue me before he started to become violent.

He noticed my eyes shift to his closed hand. "The fist? Oh, you're quite concerned about it, aren't you? Do you think I mean to strike you? Don't worry. You're at The Soul, not The

Body."

The revelation calmed me for a moment. What could they do to me to break my spirit? I could pretend to be depressed or upset. I was a good actress.

The man examined a fingernail as sharp as a dagger tip. "We have different methods, no less effective. Still nothing to say?"

I kept myself from begging by saying the first thing that entered my mind. "You have yellow teeth."

"Pigment 33, thank you very much. It's my favorite shade, although the director thinks 24 compliments my eyes. Anything else?"

He tapped my nose with his abnormally long fingernail. He lowered it to my arm, and I awaited the pain across my skin, but none came. The finger moved down, and I stiffened. Grinning, he lifted his talon and wagged it in my face. "I don't know why you're acting so stubborn on this point. You've never been seen with 0715. What you hope to achieve with loyalty, I don't know. However, you've forced me to utilize this room for its intended purpose. My time is valuable, you know, and quite frankly, you aren't worth the bother."

I pressed my lips together.

"I have here a list of medications you're taking. It's clear what you're hoping to achieve."

Again, I held my breath.

"You want to be a mother, don't you? You want to be a mother so much that you carry a doll around in your purse."

"The doll means nothing."

"And there's your tongue." He consulted his hand again. "And you decide to lie. As if you could hide anything from me. I think, rather, the doll means everything. No question that the toy's an antique. Heart accelerating. I'm right again. A family heirloom, perhaps? Another yes."

I still hoped I could convince Glinda to change her mind about Pinocchio and the Powder of Life, and I could use the powder on the doll my father had given to me. The Pinocchio

I had been lugging around was *my* baby growing up. He was the doll I coddled—the little one I could protect. In turn, he comforted me in the face of a scary world by being something familiar.

"Since you aren't a Centrania resident, perhaps you don't understand. *You* don't own anything. The Center owns everything. And if the Center wants to destroy something, the Center does it."

What the hell did he mean?

"This includes your body. If the Center wants to prevent you from becoming pregnant, the Center does it."

Oh, God. No, no, no!

I shook my head from side to side, tears welling up. The man opened his fist, and particles of wood dropped to the floor. The slivers and paint flecks that had once made up my Pinocchio doll fell to the ground in a pile. Later, someone would no doubt sweep up the sawdust and dispose of it in the nearest trash bin.

At the sight of the doll's debris, I hyperventilated. The day my father had given me Pinocchio was been one of my most treasured childhood memories. Not a baby doll for me, but an inanimate doll I could bring to life with my imagination and will. And my connection wasn't just with the doll —but with what it represented. One day, I could be a mother too.

My self-control crumbled like a building imploding. My face became a watery mess, and I struggled to catch my breath. How could this happen? Where was Alice or Harold?

The man flicked a speck off his shirt with his long fingernail. "Well, this has worked out much better than I expected. Something transpired between you and 0715, and you atomized her before we entered her apartment. We had three life readings and then only one. We don't care about the third, but 0715 was performing a duty in Centrania. You'll take her place." His yellow teeth flashed in a wolfish grin.

I screamed while the chair backed away on its own.

Yellow Teeth wiped away the remains of my doll on his pants leg. "Our reservation is up. I hope you enjoyed your stay here and our tête-à-tête. I know I have. Don't worry. The chair will inject you with something to help you sleep before the surgery. We're not butchers, you know."

The chair wheeled itself down hallways while I called for help. But the people I passed ignored me. I recalled nightmares in my past where I couldn't control my actions. I couldn't escape, and no one would come to my aid. Now I was living it. My chest burned with the hope Alice would find me. She would appear, and then all would be fine. But as the chair traveled farther and farther into the building, my doubts grew. No one would rescue me. How could they when they didn't know I was here?

Tears blurred my vision. My thoughts swung back and forth—someone would rescue me; or I would become Julia and live her life; no, someone would rescue me. Perhaps Alice would come for me now, at the last minute, and teleport me the hell out of here. But then again, why bother with me when they were all too busy saving Kingdom? They had abandoned me.

I turned a corner, and a voice from a speaker in the chair spoke into my ear. "You have now entered the surgery wing."

A needle pricked my right arm. I flinched. Alice! Where were you?

Warmth enveloped my body, and the prickles of sleep my mind. The somniferous drug they had given me was working fast. To my surprise, the shackles retracted and freed my feet and hands, but that didn't matter. My limbs were as heavy as granite, too heavy to lift.

I reached up with all my effort. Must do something to remain awake. My fingernails dug into my face, but I didn't feel anything. The room wavered. I couldn't think...straight. Everything was...spinning and...Harold, help me! Please appear...and I need you. I can't...Harold...parallel...not my...

23 - ROYAL DECISIONS

"**P**enta, do you hear us?"

No response.

Helga's voice. "Penta Emily Corden, answer me! I have something important to tell you. I'm in my sitting room."

Five seconds later, Penta stepped out of nothingness into Helga's suite, brows creased and chin set. Dark circles surrounded her eyes; her dinner dress was splattered with mud, and her hair teased into a bird's nest level of unruly. "What is it?" she snapped.

Helga and Danforth sat across from each other in Helga's antechamber. The Norse-styled chairs were arranged in a circle around a long table used to hold books or a tea set. Now on the table lay a wooden sheath, as if on display. A golden hilt shone in the early morning light, decorated with gold lily-shaped markings.

Helga regarded her sister then spoke. "Did you rest at all last night?"

Penta breathed loudly out of her nose. "You're wasting my time."

Helga pressed together her lips and gestured a green-freckled hand to the sword's encasement. "I have something to show you."

She picked up the scabbard and unsheathed Cusp. The sunlight caught the shining sword, and the stunning filigree glowed. Helga presented the flat end of the blade to her sister. Penta's breath hitched as she stepped forward to view the weapon, and she no longer seemed eager to leave. She examined Cusp as might a monk study a holy relic.

Segments of the blade were flat and metallic, similar to any other sword, but twisted iron links held these portions together—Cusp's signature. Runes glinted from the flat sections of the weapon. The tip came together in a sharp, deadly point.

"Is that...Cusp?"

"The very same," Helga replied.

"But where did you find it?"

Helga related in detail the story of her prior night. "I haven't slept since receiving the holy blade. I had to try it in my sparring room."

"You didn't call me when you first received it?"

Helga bit her lower lip. Penta waved away her response. "Your penchant for weaponry made you eager to try it."

"I wanted to satisfy myself that the sword was genuine and not a trick conjured by the hags. Cusp is perfectly balanced. Its weight and length match my height and strength. I practiced all of my offensive and defensive maneuvers. I feel as if I've used this weapon my entire life."

While the sisters discussed Cusp, Danforth retrieved a lute from the floor beside his chair. He placed it on his lap but didn't play it. "Quite the birthday gift, eh?"

Helga stroked the flat end of the blade as if petting an animal. "This is no toy, dear one," she told her husband. "I admit I spent the last hour thanking the Creator before I called you. Only Lyken and Danforth know I have it."

Penta put a trembling, silver hand on the handle, gripped the sword, and closed her eyes. "We must use it but not to kill them. Cusp has other powers."

When Helga released her hand, the sword pulled down on Penta's arm, and she let it go. The blade clattered to the floor with a jarring, metallic noise. Helga said, "Danforth could barely carry it. The weapon is balanced only in my hands, making it unusable to anyone else."

With effort, Penta raised the end of the blade into the air. "I've no doubt you are its owner. This sword is our best defense against the witches."

"I agree, but all is not well. As you know from legend, Cusp talks to its bearer. The holy blade has been silent thus far. I wish it would speak to me before I use it. If an unworthy soldier brandishes this divine gift, it could mean her end."

Penta set down the artifact. "Like Jazlar the Thief."

Helga leaned over and lifted the blade effortlessly. "Indeed."

Danforth's fingers ran up and down the strings of the lute. "Who is Jazlar, Helga?"

"Jazlar broke into King Leopold's chambers in the middle of the night to steal Cusp. He planned to use the blade to cut the king's finger. All it takes is a scratch from Cusp to kill your opponent. But when the blade touched King Leopold's royal skin, 'twas Jazlar who melted into a pound of flesh."

Penta again examined the shape of the unusual weapon. "Helga, you are worthy of Cusp. Your virtue is unquestioned."

Helga held out her arms. "By Saint Peter's beard, my blemishes tell a different story."

Penta's eyes shifted from the artifact to Helga herself. "They mean nothing, dear sister. The sword doesn't present itself to one who cannot wield it. Cusp is a powerful weapon.

Are the legends surrounding it true?"

"I have not tried it yet. If it does indeed provide magical immunity for the wielder, the witches have much to fear from me."

Danforth said, "You shouldn't try it for the first time in battle."

Helga fiddled with the chain around her neck that held Penta's ring. "We'll practice with Celeste. We'll have her toss a minor spell on me to learn whether I'm immune to magic."

Penta's fingers brushed Cusp's handle. "Grr and I have not found Beauty yet, and we've been all over Kingdom. We've spotted the witches from time to time. They've been taunting us but not attacking."

Helga said, "They're prolonging your agony."

"But they will act soon, I'm certain."

Danforth's fingers touched the lute's strings at the bend in the neck. "On Earth, we would have no qualms about using Cusp to terminate the witches. The next time they show up to taunt you, cut them with it, and let the sword do its magic."

Helga lifted her chin. "From the onset, my sisters and I sought to rid Kingdom of its brutal violence. We have captured, not killed, many of our enemies. Taking their lives must always be our last option."

Danforth asked, "How about using Glinda's magic? They kidnapped Beauty when the Good Witch wasn't present. Perhaps they're afraid of her."

Penta ran a hand through her hair. "I think not, but because of her, I believe they've changed their strategy." She stopped regarding the sword and locked eyes with Helga. "Inform Cinderella. I will return to Grr and give him instructions and then teleport back here. I wish to convene a council in two hours."

Without another word, she vanished.

Two hours later, Helga and Cinderella sat in the throne room, waiting for Penta. The warrior queen had strapped Cusp to her belt, and her sister regarded it like a third presence in the room—a new but welcome guest. Every few minutes, Helga's hand patted its hilt—"to make sure I still have it," she claimed.

Penta had chosen destinations in the castle to target her appearance after teleportation. She materialized in one of her chosen spots and strolled to her throne.

Penta's sunken cheeks and weary eyes alarmed Cinderella. "You've not rested, sister?"

"My heart is ill over Beauty. I have been everywhere in Kingdom. From the nor in the unexplored lands, to the cuuth of the alleys of Tusk, and all areas in-between. Grr knows her scent but has not picked it up. He continues our search."

Helga drew Cusp and positioned it with its point touching the floor. She set her hands on the hilt. "I have confidence we will find her."

Penta sat and gripped her chair's stone armrests. "Glinda found me this morning and has confirmed the witches haven't traveled outside of Kingdom."

The tips of Cinderella's shoes brushed against the ground in her swinging throne. "Glinda has continued to train Celeste. Celeste confided in me yesterday that she has grown more in the last two days than in the last five years."

Helga leaned forward. "Yet they both confess they are weaker than the hags."

Cinderella folded her hands. "Danforth, Roger, Lyken, and I flew the wyverns across Kingdom earlier this morning and put the word out for Beauty. We searched everywhere for her." She regarded Cusp. "And now...this."

Penta followed her eyes to the object in question. "Cusp is a mighty weapon. The Creator bequeathed it to us in our time of need."

Helga regarded the runes on the blade. "Celeste and I have tested Cusp, and her magic was ineffectual against me when I wielded it."

"Perfect. Now at least one of us can strike the crones if they dare to come here again." Penta sighed. "If only you had possessed the sword when they arrived and took Beauty."

"I have thought the same, my sister," said Helga. "I regret that the blessing came too late for me to protect her sweet innocence."

The chains suspending Cinderella's seat moved when she shifted. "We can now defend ourselves, however. Perhaps with Celeste and Glinda's aid, we can capture the witches and ask them to reveal Beauty's location."

Penta sat back in her majestic throne, tapping an inlaid ruby affixed in the armrest. "I don't believe they will tell us. Or if they do, the destination will be her..." She struggled to say the next few words. "Final resting place."

Helga's hand tightened on Cusp's hilt, and Cinderella gulped. Cinderella asked, "What would they gain by killing her?"

"Why keep her alive when that gives them no advantage?" Penta countered. "Helga, as a battle leader, you know her death would serve to demotivate us. They don't need to bargain with us."

Helga didn't respond.

Penta closed her eyes. "The witches are perilous to all living within Kingdom. Every second they remain in our world, our people's lives are at stake. In the best scenario, if we were to capture them, where would we confine them? They could easily escape every prison here."

Cinderella shifted on her seat, causing it to move.

"Glinda—"

"Glinda has admitted she is not as powerful as the witches. So where would we put the hags? We could expel them to another world, perhaps, but we're not irresponsible monarchs. They are our problem now. So what do we do? We have three skilled queens, two powerful magic-wielders, and now Cusp."

Helga traced her finger along a carved serpent on the edge of her throne. "I do not favor your frame of mind, sister. I hope you're not suggesting what I'm thinking."

"I believe it has become an option," declared Penta. "Danforth spoke of it earlier. We have come to the point where we must at least consider killing the witches."

Helga snorted. Cinderella protested, "No! We are not murderers."

Penta tugged at the tips of her gloves. "This is not a question of murder. 'Tis self-defense. Our laws allow for it. If a murderer enters one's house and the owner is ill-prepared and has no other option, she may kill the intruder without fear of retribution. They entered our house, and we have no other recourse.

Helga's hand tightened on the serpent's head, her knuckles whitening. "You forget they've been killed twice before but have not stayed dead."

Penta ground her teeth, her jaw moving. "But not with Cusp. Cusp is immune to their magic. It will kill them."

Cinderella's eyes shifted to the vacant thrones in the room. "I miss Valencia's and Snow White's counsel now more than ever."

A vein throbbed in Penta's neck. "They aren't here, however. We cannot wait for Valencia, and Snow White will never sit on her throne again."

Helga regarded Snow White's empty timbered throne. "They targeted Snow for a reason, Penta."

"I call it to a vote," Penta declared.

Neither sister answered immediately. Helga drew Cusp

and held it aloft. "I suspect you will want me to do the deed?"

Penta shook her head. "Three witches. Three queens. We will each take a turn with Cusp."

Helga fingered the carvings in the blade. "You know that plan won't work. I'm the only one who may wield Cusp."

Penta glowered at her sister. "Glinda says Mya and Tomana are the most powerful, so we'll target them. Eliminating them should make Picana far weaker. For Mya, you will only need to hold Cusp steady. I will teleport her onto the pointed edge. You'll strike Tomana, and Cinderella will then push Picana toward the holy weapon's sharp edge."

Helga studied her reflection in the blade. "You know my thoughts on taking another's life. But I still feel their cold hand on my neck. And now I have Cusp. I agree that the holy sword coming to me means we must take action. The Creator has given us a weapon, not a spell or a means to vanquish them peacefully."

Cinderella brushed back a curl. "What are you saying, Helga?"

"Cinderella, I am saying 'aye.' If we have the opportunity, I will use Cusp."

Penta turned to the youngest sister. "And your vote?"

Cinderella pointed at Valencia's wooden chair. "She would disagree."

Penta replied, "We don't know how Valencia would vote. What if she had remained here and the witches had killed Graddock?"

Cinderella crossed her arms. "I abstain."

Penta tilted her head toward her younger sister. "I wondered if you would. However, you know our bylaws. We agreed at the start of our reign to be unanimous when ruling on the punishment of war criminals."

Cinderella closed her eyes and paused before speaking. "Aye."

Penta said, "And I vote aye as well. I will find the witches and invite them here on vague terms. We'll show them Cusp and hope they surrender. If they do not..."

Penta stood, and without another word, vanished.

After practicing with her newfound weapon, Helga mopped her brow and made her way across the training room toward Danforth, swinging Cusp one last time. The sword cut through the air with only a near-silent whistle. She gripped it in both hands, placed her forehead against it, closed her eyes, and whispered. When Helga opened her eyes, she joined her husband. He asked, "Are you talking to it again?"

"I am praying in gratitude. I'm worried, Danforth."

"What troubles you, Tootsie?"

"None of that now. I'm serious."

Helga examined Cusp in the midday light. "The legends state Cusp advised King Leopold. It hasn't communicated with me."

Danforth placed a hand on Helga's shoulder. "Perhaps the sword's biding its time."

"Doubtful. Why has it not spoken to me? Does it see my spots and know I am unworthy? When I go to strike the witches with it, will it vanish in my hands?"

Danforth leaned against the wall. "What if the sword's talking is a legend?"

"The tales say it sings with an angelic voice. I long to hear it, I confess."

Danforth eyed the weapon. "You're the most qualified to hear angelic voices."

The warrior queen examined her green markings again. "Are you certain? Others are more virtuous than I am."

"The sword sought you out. You fret too much on the

state of your soul."

Helga shook her head. "Confidence in one's salvation is the fastest way to hell."

Danforth touched the hilt. "Maybe it needs a trigger word or phrase?"

"A sound idea, husband," said Helga. "Powerful artifacts have been known to require words to reveal their magic. A sacred verse might loosen its tongue, but which one?"

"Abracadabra?"

Helga shook her head. "What kind of holy word is abracadabra? And Earth people make fun of our words." She held up the sword. "Please speak to me, spirit of Cusp. I am listening."

The sword remained mute.

Cinderella, Celeste, and Glinda sat in Celeste's magical study sipping tea while the queen related the events of the vote. The chamber, in a hidden location in a lower level of the castle, reflected Celeste's current mood. If the pixie was happy, the windowless room shone with sunlight on a clean and organized group of vividly colored jars. If Celeste was agitated or distressed, the area reflected a tangle of tomes, beakers, and bottled dangerous creatures. Today, the three huddled in a corner away from a mess of objects littered over the desks and floor.

The sorceresses listened to the queen, and both exclaimed when she told them the results of the vote. Glinda's usual serene expression darkened. "I won't participate in this strategy. You have asked for my help, and I will defend Kingdom with all my power, but I won't help if you act on this resolution."

Cinderella ran a hand through her hair. "And we wouldn't ask you to do anything against your conscience, but what choice do we have? Please tell me a witch prison exists somewhere, and I'll gladly call the council back and present an alternate plan."

Glinda set down her teacup. "No, I know of no witch prison. I understand your position and am grateful for your decision to deal with the witches within Kingdom's borders. Many other leaders would ask me to find a way to remove the problem from their world to another."

Cinderella stared dolefully at a jar of gray liquid on one of Celeste's shelves. "Then this remains our sole option. We know the witches won't hesitate to kill Beauty."

Celeste's aura dimmed. "Glinda and I sense they are planning a different devious deed, and Beauty is a part of it."

Glinda, adorned in leather armor, tugged on a fastener. "Cinderella, you and your sisters are acting too hastily. I have often found if you let events run their course, evil defeats itself, or good arrives at an alternate plan. Once, in Oz, the Nome King tunneled into the Emerald City with powerful allies. Our Scarecrow devised a strategy that defeated them without loss of life or limb."

Cinderella said, "Your scarecrows must be highly intelligent to come up with such a plan."

Glinda smiled. "This one is. The point is we are never out of options, though such may seem to be the case. My advice is to wait for your sister."

Celeste put a hand on the side of her face. "But if Beauty dies while we wait, any victory will be bittersweet. Penta will never recover, and Beauty is a future ruler of Kingdom."

Glinda straightened her posture. "Fair point. I will Travel to a dangerous land and find out how the witches have cheated death. Their avoidance of death disturbs me."

Cinderella set down her teacup. "Glinda, could the witches have thrown a spell to present Cusp to Helga? Is it possible for evil people to manipulate a holy item for their own purposes?"

Glinda's mouth was a thin line while she considered the question. "No one can corrupt Cusp. Forged by the Divine, the sword is the embodiment of virtue. Cusp is a living entity. However, they could corrupt its wielder."

Celeste's wings drooped, and all the liquids in the room turned black. "What advantage do they gain by introducing Cusp? They would not live long enough to witness the results of their handiwork."

A pile of crumpled-up scrolls rolled onto Glinda's feet, and she kicked them aside. "Maybe the end doesn't matter to them. Maybe they know they're dying, and they plan to embrace each queen in their descent to hell."

"Through the use of a holy artifact?" asked Cinderella. "How could they?"

"If the Creator has given Cusp to Helga, but the witches have manipulated her to do evil, the witches may survive the encounter. Imagine Helga goes to strike one of the hags. Cusp may fly away from her hand to await someone virtuous. If your sister has the means to defeat her enemies but uses it for ill-intentions, she will blame herself. Knowing her, she may allow her guilt to consume her, and the witches will use her devastation against her."

Cinderella asked, "Have the witches manipulated Penta into a state where she is not thinking clearly because of Beauty? And then turned Helga's doubt against her? Are my sisters being used to achieve the hags' purpose?"

"The destruction of their souls," said Celeste.

Cinderella whispered, "And mine. I voted aye."

24 - SOLUTION ON
A STAIRCASE

Valencia and Lenore stood apart, observing each other. The Match Girl regarded the other woman—her dark hair framing an oval-shaped face. Plumage covered Lenore's thin torso like a dress, dipping only at the neckline. Feathers spread down her legs to her ankles, and her fingernails and toenails were as long as needles.

The raven woman examined Valencia as well, standing before her in Lenore's own red velvet dress. The queen reached into a pocket and produced a match and began rolling it between her fingers.

Lenore's transformation from raven to young woman reminded Valencia of the shape behind Usher at his murder. She phrased her question carefully. "Did you murder Allan?"

Lenore walked over to the door and shut it, her nails clicking on the wood. "Not I. I was making sounds across the room when he was killed. I flew down to the table to take a closer look when I feared Allan was in trouble." She lowered her chin. "But no one will believe me now."

"I do. I asked because I wanted to hear you say it. I observed you pulling Allan's chair away from the table, but his blood pooled underneath it. Someone stabbed him before you transformed. Besides, a knife is too large for a raven to carry."

Lenore's shoulders relaxed. "The people around here are so superstitious. But your presence in this place isn't an accident, is it?"

"No. This will be quite a shock, but I'm from a different world called Kingdom," replied Valencia. "'Tis usually bright and cheerful there, unlike Morbidum."

The raven woman nodded. "I've seen a lot this world cannot explain. As a bird, I was there last night when you appeared on the path to the house. How could I deny you came from another world? I want to hear more about people like me. People who transform."

"Some cannot control it. Some can." Valencia continued moving the match between her digits. "Are you a magician?"

"Not at all."

Valencia returned the match to the pocket in Lenore's dress. "People would admire you in my world."

Lenore flexed her long fingernails. "They would burn me at the stake in this one. When I was twelve years old, I discovered I could change. My mother knew and warned me never to transform in front of anyone else." She snorted. "And then I ran away and joined a traveling show. Beatrice, Zariah, and I became close there. We were the three freaks—a contortionist, a poisoner, and an Egyptian goddess."

"A poisoner?" asked Valencia.

"Beatrice," Lenore replied. "She was a fraud. She would breathe on birds and kill them, or so the manager said. A ruse accomplished with gas."

Valencia walked over and showed the journal to Lenore. "The Bible says you are an orphan?"

"Yes, when I transformed the first time, I panicked, thinking a spirit possessed me. To calm me, my mother admitted she had found me on their doorstep."

"Then you're the one I'm seeking."

Lenore leaned forward. "Did my birth mother send you?"

"No. Your mother is an evil, powerful witch who is intent on destroying my world."

Lenore completed her alteration into a young woman, her feathers changing into an ebony, form-fitting dress. Her claws became long fingernails. She turned and sat on an overstuffed chair—the energy sagging from her body. "My mother gave me this accursed ability then rejected me. I'll have nothing to do with her. She abandoned me as a babe. Fortunately, the Marstings took me in as one of their own, calling me a cousin. Yet I've never quite fit into this world."

Valencia folded her hands. "You'd be most welcome in Kingdom, but my home will be destroyed without your help. Will you assist us and help capture your mother?"

Valencia described Kingdom, her position as queen, and the threat of the three witches. Appearing enraptured, Lenore listened without interrupting, imbibing every sentence the way a connoisseur enjoys her favorite wine. When Valencia trailed off, Lenore gazed at a painting of a field of reeds on the wall. "Queens and witches are quite a difference from Morbidum. Kingdom sounds like a simple world."

Valencia walked over to a globe in the corner of the room and tapped her finger on their current location. "My friends will arrive soon, and I'll take you there. If you'd rather, we can return you here when the witches are defeated."

Lenore bit the ends of her nails. "No! I am dead in this world. Allan loved me, but he loved his writing and alcohol more. I destroyed him by faking my death, throwing myself off a cliff, and becoming the bird. I followed him, not precisely knowing why, perhaps hoping he would come to his senses instead of mourning me, but he wouldn't. And last night, he met his end before I could be honest with him. This world is nothing but a tragic play for me. I'll gladly follow you and start over again."

Placing her hand on the globe, Valencia spun it. "When my friends come, we shall go together." Valencia trailed her fingertips on the spinning sphere. "We'll wait for them in the meantime."

The raven woman gripped the edge of her chair's armrests. "You mentioned two others were abandoned as babies and taken to other worlds?"

"Correct."

"I want to meet them," said Lenore. "I have something in common with them, at least. I would hate to leave, though, without knowing who killed Allan."

"Perhaps I could help." Valencia moved closer to Lenore. "Who do you think cast the levitation spell on the knife that killed him?"

Lenore blinked. "Levitation spell? We have no such thing in Morbidum. No magic exists here."

Valencia crossed her arms. "Says the woman who can turn into a bird."

"Curses, dark dealings, yes," Lenore replied. "And do not forget, I don't belong to this world. I've always thought of myself as accursed. Mark me! Someone killed Allan without speaking an incantation. His death is a murder mystery."

Valencia uncrossed her arms and twirled a long strand of hair around her finger. "A mystery? Like a puzzle? With magic available in Kingdom, subterfuge of this nature is less common there. I wonder…"

Laughter came from the direction of the hallway, and Lenore turned her head. "I should return to my bird form lest anyone spy me."

Before Valencia could respond, Lenore shrank into the form of a raven. Valencia opened the door, and the raven exited and flew off to the far recesses of the house.

Valencia marched in the other direction and encountered Count Cupsince and Beatrice exiting a room. The count bowed. "Ah, Valencia! We have only now finished a game of quadrille, and the women wanted to retire before dinner. Will you accompany us?"

The count had surprised Valencia this morning, and she hadn't had time to recall the scene with the maid. Now, with his arm around Beatrice, the memory came back to her. She bit her lip and didn't respond.

The count asked, "Are you ill, my lady?"

Valencia's cheeks flushed. "No."

She offered her arm. The count took it, his other arm around Beatrice, and he led the way down the hallway to the stairs. Cupsince glided around the balustrade and paused to allow the women to lift the hems of their skirts. They proceeded to their rooms, arriving at Beatrice's first, where she left them with an "*arrivederci*." The count moved with Valencia to her room. He bowed and turned to go, but she detained him by placing a hand on his shoulder. Valencia led him to a remote corner of the hallway next to an oblong window.

Count Cupsince beheld the young woman, his eyes dancing with curiosity. "You are trembling. Do you fear me?"

"No, but I have a confession," answered Valencia. "Please accept my apologies, but I witnessed an interaction between you and a maid last night when you wished her good night. I didn't mean to eavesdrop, but I couldn't turn away."

The count smiled. "A minor indiscretion, I assure you. It's of no consequence to me. And what the maid, Miss Ligeia, doesn't know won't hurt her."

Valencia peered at her companion through the gloomy gray of the hallway. "I have a...a friend who could learn from someone like you. I wondered if I could visit you later and discuss it in detail?"

The count's eyebrows rose at the word "discuss." He lowered his eyes to her necklace. Valencia wasn't sure she had made her point, but the count spoke next. "You surprise me, my mysterious maiden. You are not the coquettish young lady

I took you for yesterday. *Certainement*, I hope to see you to-night."

His answer didn't ring true, but before Valencia could question him further, the count stepped back.

He swung around, cape swirling, and marched down the hallway without another word. Valencia watched him, her heart beating hard at their conversation.

Dinner passed without incident, after which Valencia found herself pacing in her room. She paused and stared out her window to the sky above, marking the moon crossing the sky.

The queen removed the necklace from around her neck and held it in the glow of both moonbeams and candlelight, fingering the ruby. She spoke to it as if it were an old friend. "'Tis frustrating to wait for Alice! While I'm detained, I will question Count Cupsince. He knows about delirious passion. Perhaps I could use his advice on Graddock and ignite a flame I know exists in Graddock's heart." She pointed at the jewel. "But I don't favor how the count looked at you, *ma chere*, so I'm going to hide you in this room until I return."

The ruby glinted in the flickering light like an angry, red eye resenting her for leaving it behind.

Valencia opened a drawer and hid the necklace. She noticed a thin, used bit of lipstick and rouge, cosmetics she knew from her visit to Earth. Bored, the queen carried them to a small, oval mirror on one wall and applied the makeup to her face. Satisfied with the results, she pocketed the lipstick and marched into the hallway.

There, she twisted around the banister at the stairs, gripping the railing while she made her way to the floor below. A shadow flew over her shoulder, overtaking her, and landed on the stairs halfway down. Valencia nearly missed a step while the dark form elongated and turned into the figure of Lenore. The plumage-dressed woman folded her arms across her chest. "Where are you headed, Valencia?"

Valencia raised her chin. "It's a personal matter. Let me

pass."

Lenore followed the queen's focus and eyed her destination. "Count Cupsince's room?"

"Indeed."

Lenore paled. "Don't go to him. His guiles are not worth whatever you hope to satisfy. His passion is an itch better left unscratched."

"I don't think you understand," replied Valencia.

"Valencia, my newfound friend, I won't prevent you from going to his room, but heed me first. If you follow this path to its inevitable end, you cannot return to the beginning and start anew. If a horse tosses you the first time you ride him, you will approach all other horses with trepidation. I think highly of you and hope you'll return to your room. I once stood where you now stand, and I made the wrong choice."

Valencia had wanted to interrupt the confession, but she intuited Lenore needed to reveal these secrets about herself, and she waited for her to finish.

Lenore bowed her head. "Cupsince was my first. I ran into his arms, seeking the thrill of a first encounter. His tenderness made me think he loved me, but he rejected me the following morning. I ran away to the traveling show, and while there, I broke the heart of someone whose love I could not return. Then I came back here and became enamored with Allan, but his longing for drink and the pleasures of the world were greater than his preference for me. My love life has been one of lust, unrequited longing, and dissipation."

Valencia bent her head forward and placed her hand on her chest. "Oh, Lenore."

Lenore's long-nailed hand wiped tears from her face. "I want a simple love, a young, uncomplicated attraction."

Valencia put her hand on Lenore's feathered arm and steadied her. "I'm sorry. But I am not visiting Cupsince's room for the reason you think. I want advice for my relationship with my true love, Graddock."

Lenore blushed when she realized her mistake. "But Cupsince invites young women to his room for one purpose. Are you sure he understood your intentions? You spoke specifically of your lover?"

Alarmed, Valencia retreated one step back up the staircase. "No."

Lenore put her hand on top of Valencia's. "Then perhaps the count thinks you were referring to a liaison with him?"

Valencia replayed the conversation in her mind from this perspective. She realized how he could have misinterpreted her request. And was he looking at her necklace? Hardly. She closed her eyes. "I shall go to Cupsince and clarify my intentions."

Lenore tapped her long fingernails against the staircase rail. "Do not visit the count tonight. He is a gentleman, but I'd allow his blood to cool for a bit and approach him in the morning."

"I don't want to be here in the morning," Valencia said. "I hope my friends come tonight, and you and I are in Kingdom come daybreak. But I shall heed your advice and return to my room." The queen beamed at Lenore. "Saved by an Egyptian goddess. What would my sister Helga think, I wonder? Her own tale has roots in Egypt. She'd be fascinated by you, a wereraven. Beatrice too."

Lenore said, "You've figured it out. She does breathe poison."

"I suspected as much."

"Please keep it a secret. Using her power disturbs Beatrice."

Valencia nodded her head. "I will. Thank you."

Valencia ascended the stairs. Behind her, she heard the rustle of the woman transforming into a bird and flying away. The queen stopped on the top step. To herself, she said, "I wonder...something Beatrice said this morning."

Valencia's eyes widened with a revelation. She turned around and headed down the stairs.

At the bottom of the staircase, she marched to the end of the hallway, halting before a pale green door and rapped on it. Zariah, dressed in a kimono with yellow lilies printed on the front, opened the door and peered out at her. "Well, well. What do we have here?"

"I have something to discuss with you regarding last night. May I come in?"

Zariah's expression hardened, and she flung open the door. Valencia entered confidently, and the woman shut the door behind her.

Zariah crossed her arms. "What about last night?"

"I must ask you an important question." Valencia reached into her pocket for her match, but instead, her fingers brushed the stone she'd found in Oz. "Why did you murder Allan Usher?"

Zariah remained motionless. "We both know the servant murdered him."

"Lyndon is innocent," said Valencia. "I found blood under the table. 'Twas the first spilled that night because you stabbed him while we were all distracted by the séance. I confused the issue when I said the butler could have snuck in, but I thought he threw a spell to murder his victim. However, no one casts spells here, do they? If the killer was Lyndon, he would've had to sneak into the room, crawl under the table, stab Allan, and creep back out without anyone noticing. Impossible."

"And yet, he fled the scene. Where is he?"

Valencia answered, "You went to find him alone and claimed he ran away. I suspect you know his whereabouts. Regardless, he was not in the room with us."

Zariah clicked her tongue. "You're an ignorant beggar. We all sat with our hands on the table. What third arm did I extend to commit this murder?"

Valencia shook her head. "Not a hand. I heard what I had thought was a footstep, but it was an object someone seated at the table had dropped to the floor. This person had a knife hidden in her belt under the flap in her dress. Before you set your hands on the table, you balanced your hidden dagger on your knee. And then, at just the right moment, you flipped the murder weapon off your leg, allowing it to fall to the floor."

Zariah shook her head. "And then what? How did the knife stab the ratbag?"

Valencia regarded her with a puzzled expression. "Beatrice told me your talent in the traveling show. Contortionist. She also told me you paint with your feet. With such flexibility, you slipped out of your shoes and lifted the knife with your toes. You positioned your leg under the table, aimed for Allan's stomach, and extended your leg."

A sneer stole over the artist's face. "You think you know everything. Tell me, why would I commit such an act?"

"You killed Allan because he criticized your work."

Zariah bent her head, and her neck cracked. "How little you know. Allan stole *her* from me and then killed her. Now, do you understand? She was my love. If only..."

Valencia stepped back, realizing the subject of Zariah's desire. "You're the one Lenore rejected."

"She never gave me a chance. 'I do not love women, dear Zariah,' she said. 'Let us be friends instead, Zariah.' After debasing herself with that odious Cupsince? And then what does she do after rejecting *me*? She falls for a poor excuse for a lover, Allan Usher. How could she? None of this would've happened if she had embraced her true nature."

Valencia's eyes narrowed. "Or what you wanted her to be. And now you must go to the constable and confess. I have discovered your deed. 'Tis your only option."

Zariah lifted her arms. "'*Tis not* my only option."

25 - JULIA AND EUSTACIA

Harold

I hoped the news of Bree's arrival signified Alice calling herself by a different name, but I had a sinking feeling when I walked to the front of the estate. Why would Alice give a false name? Was Sanders with this Julia but then had separated from her for some reason?

Cassie, Pennilane, and I followed the Darcys down a long hallway to the study's doors. Before we went in, Mr. Darcy blocked the entrance. His untied cravat hung out of his suit coat. "You seemed unperturbed that she arrived out of nothingness," he commented to me.

I regarded the tips of my boots. "It might be best if you forgot about that."

Mr. Darcy put his balled fists to his eyes and then

lowered them. "I knew you were behind this. You have a lot to explain."

"Let me talk to her first," I said.

We four entered the room to find Elizabeth and a dark-haired, wide-eyed girl standing on a chair and touching the pelt of a mounted deer's head. She stepped down from the chair and spoke in a clipped British accent. "Hello, I'm Julia. Have I arrived in the nineteenth century?"

When Cassie made a sound, Julia turned to the girl and the visitor's face drained of all color. Julia's hands trembled. "How did you get here?"

Julia mistaking Cassie for Sanders set off alarm bells. I marched across the room and stopped in front of her, leaving little private space. "Where's Sondra?"

Julia blinked multiple times and peeked around my shoulder. "Sanders is behind you."

"She isn't Sanders, just someone who looks like her. Where's my wife?"

Julia snapped her attention back to me while Mr. Darcy closed the door. Five pairs of eyes stared at the newcomer dressed in a silver shirt and platinum pants. Purple electricity flowed through her clothing, flashing at times. Her black hair shone in the daylight streaming in the window. She tapped a small device in her ear. "Have I really left Cixxes?"

I grabbed her arms. "Where *is* she?"

Julia pulled back, attempting to free herself, but my grip was iron. "She's in Cixxes with the other one. The redhead."

"How is she going to get out of there without Bree?"

Julia's jaw trembled. "Sanders said the other one was a Traveler."

Sanders would never loan Bree to a stranger. I didn't know how this woman had activated Bree without my wife, but I was going to find out. Sensing my anger, Pennilane grabbed my arms and yanked me away. I strained against her grip. "Let me go."

Elizabeth edged me out and took the newly arrived

woman's hand. "I don't know where you think you are, but we have no place called Cixxes here. You're at Pemberley estate in Great Britain."

Mr. Darcy put out a hand and steadied himself on a chair. "What devilry caused you to appear from nowhere? I witnessed your arrival when I happened to be looking out a window."

Julia ignored the owners of the estate and addressed me. "Have I truly escaped?"

"You're in a world named Janay," I said. "Now tell me, where are Sanders and Alice?"

"Is that the redhead's name? They wouldn't tell me. They're in Cixxes."

"Without Bree. What happened?"

Julia twisted a short strand of hair with her forefinger. "You don't know how it is in Cixxes. To flee, one would sacrifice her children. Many have. So what if I left two strangers behind?"

I shook with rage. Pennilane dragged me away from Julia. The selkie blocked my view. "Do not panic. Alice is with her, and she is a Traveler."

My shoulders lowered a fraction. "Then they should be here, too. Something's not right. I'm going to them, and I'm taking Julia back there."

Julia shook her head. "No! You can't take me back. I'll die here, in Elysium, rather than return."

Mr. Darcy said, "Will someone tell me what in the name of God is going on?"

I pointed at Julia. "This woman somehow stole my wife's horse and raced off with it here. She's left my wife and my friend in a very dangerous place."

Julia crossed her arms and backed into a corner. "If you go there, *they* will capture you. They imprisoned me once." Her eyes clouded over. "I was a hollow woman for years. Then your friends came, and I felt something I haven't felt in a long time."

Rocking back and forth on the balls of her feet, Julia said, "Hope. Is that the right word? My granddad explained the concept to me when I was a child, but I never dared to use the word 'hope' in public."

Cassie turned to me. "What is this place she's talking about?"

"Neither Pennilane nor I have ever been there," I replied.

Julia swallowed and stepped forward. "Don't go there. Cixxes is a place full of pain of misery."

I straightened my shoulders. "Maybe you can go with me and help me sneak around."

"I won't go back," said Julia. "Sanders said I was a witch's daughter, and you had to keep me safe."

At this revelation, Mr. Darcy leaned toward his wife and whispered in her ear. I didn't care any longer if Darcys found out about our secrets. I gripped the back of a chair. "You're one of the three."

Julia clasped together her hands. "I dreamed about my mother last night—one of my special dreams. I'm Tomana's daughter. She's the one who left me behind." She glared at Mr. Darcy. "And I am not demented. I can hear you quite clearly."

Mr. Darcy scowled. "We were whispering."

She tapped a tiny device in her ear. "I can hear everything." She turned to me. "I used the amplifier to listen in on your wife and Alice debating whether to leave me behind in Cixxes. Why do you think I escaped without them?"

Mr. Darcy straightened his cravat. "Before this goes further, I demand to know what is going on." He pointed at me. "You show up ready to attend my wife's ball and frighten my maid to death. Then you plan to run off with my maid. And now this one, talking nonsense, appears from thin air. I will not allow anyone to remain at Pemberley until I have a full explanation."

Cassie grabbed my shoulder. "You must tell them. Mr. Darcy, please, I beg your forbearance to listen while this man explains."

Mr. Darcy tugged on his waistcoat. "At this point, why not?"

I began my narrative in earnest, leaving out details the others didn't need to know. I explained the worlds, the witches' arrival, and their threat to Kingdom. I skipped Oz but explained the three doors to Morbidum, Janay, and Cixxes, and our quest to find the three witches' daughters.

Mr. Darcy sat in the chair behind his massive desk and grew more and more resolute through the entire discourse. As I finished, he lifted his head. "Sir, are you familiar with the term poppycock?"

"Yes."

"This story and you people are pure poppycock."

Julia said, "We say bilge in Cixxes."

Pennilane came to my rescue. She stepped in front of Mr. Darcy and let her whiskers emerge. Mr. Darcy pushed back his chair in alarm, and Elizabeth's jaw dropped open. Cassie grinned. "A real selkie."

"Indeed," said Pennilane, eyeing me. "And no sister of his."

"I can do better," said Julia. She presented her tattoo, and the cougar reared up on its haunches. The host and hostess cried out a second time.

When the Darcys had recovered from their initial shock —Cassie had retrieved a teapot of their favorite tea—the couple came to grips with their new reality. Mr. Darcy held his head in his hands. "You are telling me this woman is from another world? Your world has written a novel, and she is a character in it?"

"Maybe a combination of characters," I said.

Elizabeth's eyes lit up. "Characters are based on us too, Fitzwilliam. How else would Harold know what we've said in private?"

I nodded. "A famous novel. Revered by many."

Mr. Darcy lifted his chin. "No doubt an adventure novel, or a work of fiction of all my accomplishments."

"Actually, your story is more of a romance, and you don't come off too well at the beginning." I nodded at Elizabeth. "Your wife is the main character."

Elizabeth smirked.

I sat in a chair, holding out my hands. "This is why Pennilane and I are desperate to meet Eustacia Yeobright. She is another witch's daughter. But if Alice and Sanders have found Julia, why have they not returned? Alice should be able to Travel with Sanders between worlds. Julia is here. So, where are they?"

Pennilane brushed her whiskers with her hand. "We shall give them until tomorrow, and then Harold, you and I shall travel on Bree to Cixxes. Let us finish our quest here first."

Mr. Darcy regarded Julia. "And what of this one?"

Julia said, "I'll stay here. I'll give up all modern conveniences to live free. If you like, I'll help around the house."

I stood. "It's time we visited Mrs. Yeobright."

Mr. Darcy splayed his hands on his desk. "I'll save you from a wasted chaise ride. I called on Eustacia's husband, Clym, myself this morning. Becky Sharp was there."

Elizabeth flinched at the name. "What did *that* woman want?"

"Being a friend of Eustacia's, she came to inform Clym that Mrs. Yeobright had left him.

"What?" exclaimed Elizabeth and Cassie together. Elizabeth placed a hand on her heart. "Eustacia left Clym? Where did she go?"

Mr. Darcy put together the tips of his fingers. "Not far. Eustacia wanders the moors at night. Mr. Saturn, I'm surprised you didn't encounter her on the way to Pemberley. Anyway, I'm nearly certain Eustacia is plotting a rendezvous with Damon Wildeve."

Cassie's mouth formed a circle. "The innkeeper?"

"So Eustacia is somewhere on the moors." I approached a window. "We should go out this afternoon and find Eustacia before—"

A loud rumble of thunder interrupted the end of my sentence, followed by large raindrops striking the windowpane. Seconds later, water streamed down the glass. I shut my eyes. "Before the rain gets too heavy."

Everyone agreed to participate in the search and donned the appropriate weather garments. We split into three groups: Mr. Darcy and Cassie; Elizabeth and me; and Julia and Pennilane. We left the Pemberley demesne in the downpour and headed toward the moor—a swampy area already in dry weather—where Eustacia often strolled. The moor was split into sections by a turbulent river.

We searched everywhere for Eustacia, regrouping when evening descended. Agreeing to spend one more hour outside, we continued our search, calling Eustacia's name and shining a lantern when we could keep it lit. The torrential rain beat down on our hats and coats, drenching us to our bones. No sound but the roar of thunder assaulted our ears.

At the end of the hour, Mr. Darcy shouted over the heavy rain to return to the mansion, and I reluctantly agreed. While we retreated, the river beside us began to swell and started to flood the moor. We all had difficulty staying on higher ground as the water lapped first our ankles and then our shins. The gushing waterline rose across the heath.

Thunder rumbled and brought with it the roaring sound of a rising tide. Mr. Darcy turned around and then cried for us to hold onto anything sturdy. "This oncoming current is not from the storm and river. The dam must have collapsed. This flood must be excess water from the weir."

The water poured over and pummeled us while we held onto trees and bushes. Nature's wet fingers tried to gain purchase on us and sweep us to a watery grave.

During the turbulence, we noticed the flood carried the bodies of a man and a woman. Motionless, they floated along on the surface of the water. I judged it too dangerous to rescue them, but Pennilane let go of her tree and dove into the rushing water. She swam to the woman and grabbed her body around the shoulders. Keeping the woman's head above the water, Pennilane rode the current and dragged the woman from the water to higher ground.

The flooding of the moor ended soon after Pennilane's rescue. When the swell of the river receded and we could all let go of our safehold, we hurried to Pennilane. The selkie held onto a young, waterlogged woman in her mid-twenties.

Elizabeth lifted her bonnet. "Eustacia Vye Yeobright."

"Is she alive?" I asked.

Pennilane strode toward Pemberley, Eustacia in her arms. "She is breathing."

Mr. Darcy tipped his hat to Pennilane. "Your rescue of this gentlewoman was both inspirational and courageous.

Pennilane's features remained impassive at the compliment. "I am a seal. Water is my natural home. Where you slide, I glide."

We returned to Pemberley, and I was never happier to step out of a rainstorm in all my life. As we removed our coats and bonnets in the back room, Pemberley's major-domo approached Mr. Darcy. "We have a visitor."

Mr. Darcy ran a hand through his hair to rid it of excess water. "Another one?"

"The young gentleman who asked last night if he could return this evening."

Elizabeth's eyes sparkled. "The man who gave our visitors Eustacia's name."

Pennilane handed Eustacia to the major-domo for him to carry into a bedroom to recover. Pennilane turned her head, keeping her features from the rest of the party. Mr. Darcy shook his raincoat. "Why the deuce is he back? And in this storm?"

The major-domo adjusted his hold on Eustacia. "His chaise became stuck in the water on its way here. He says he has walked five miles in the rain."

Elizabeth spoke to no one in particular. "Quite a distance for a social call. Isn't it a wonder?"

The Darcys made sure Eustacia was made comfortable in one of the many spare rooms. While her chest rose and fell, she remained unconscious, despite efforts to awaken her. Pennilane sat in a chair next to Eustacia's bed. "I shall watch over her. If she regains her senses, I will detain her."

Elizabeth started for the door. "And I shall send the gentleman in here to assist."

Pennilane opened her mouth to protest, but the hostess slipped out. Mr. Darcy regarded me. "The rest of us ought to sleep. Hovering over her will not achieve anything. I shall send for a doctor when the rain lets up."

"But, I think—"

Mr. Darcy grabbed his lapels. "I'll wake you, Harold, if her condition changes."

Lowering my shoulders in defeat, I returned to the room Elizabeth had assigned me the night before and went to bed. I didn't want to leave Pennilane, but I was dead tired. I slept without dreaming.

In the morning, I hurried down to the spare bedroom and found Elizabeth standing in the hallway at the door. She held up a hand as I strolled up to her. I paused, and she took my arm and led me away. "Eustacia has not regained consciousness yet, but she mumbled a few times last night, an encouraging sign."

"Where are we headed?"

"To the morning repast. You must be hungry after missing dinner."

"I was going to talk to Pennilane." I looked over my shoulder.

"She has company. The man, Pip, has been a companion to her most of the night."

I arched an eyebrow. "And she didn't kill him?"

"They have been getting along splendidly. Furtive glances, long stares when the other is not looking, all that sort of thing."

I stopped dead in the hallway, forcing Elizabeth to turn

to me. The owner of Pemberley smirked. "You can't tell me you haven't noticed."

"We're talking about Pennilane. The one with whiskers."

"She hasn't revealed that to him, poor devil." Elizabeth's light-hearted expression remained in place. "You seem surprised. I find bad temper and loneliness to be companions more often than not. From the little I've observed, Pip has made her quite at ease."

Elizabeth led me to a breakfast room, and I sat. My mind drifted to Sanders while I formed a plan to retrieve her from Cixxes. But Pennilane had asked me to stay. Was that because she wanted to spend time with this Pip guy? I decided I had had enough of Janay. I would retrieve Bree today and travel to Cixxes. Though Bree was Sanders' totem and might not work for me, I had to try.

While I finished breakfast, Pennilane and Pip entered. Pip was a straight-backed man with boyish features and curly hair. Normally stone-faced, Pennilane beamed at me when she entered the room. "The second daughter woke up for a moment, Hero. We should take this opportunity to talk to her."

I threw my napkin next to my plate. "You're quite happy."

Pennilane narrowed her eyes. "And why shouldn't I be? If *you* can now convince her, then we are assured of success. My queen won't fail us. I have the utmost faith in her."

"You're ready to leave Janay then?"

Her brilliant eyes lost their luster. "Yes."

She lied. Plain and simple. I was at a loss for words.

"Miss Pennilane has been by the side of Mrs. Yeobright all night," said Pip. "Did you know she saved the drowning woman by herself? Mrs. Darcy recounted the story to me in detail. I have tried to be Miss Pennilane's companion but am no match for her in conversation."

I regarded Pennilane, who averted her eyes. "Yes, she's quite the chatterbox," I remarked.

Elizabeth offered Pennilane and Pip breakfast while everyone else went and gathered in the bedroom around Eustacia. She sat up in bed, sipping tea. As each person entered her room, her scowl deepened. Eustacia complained of a headache, but I ignored her and sat in a chair by her bed. Mr. Darcy introduced me, and Eustacia nodded her head.

Mr. Darcy placed his hands behind his back. "Mrs. Yeobright, you are at the center of an intriguing tale, but not the one you think."

The recovering woman set her teacup down. "Where is Damon Wildeve?"

Mr. Darcy's features hardened. "He's dead. They found his body this morning."

Eustacia put her hands over her face. "I'm ruined. We were going to go to Paris!"

I scooted my chair closer to her. "Eustacia, did you know your mother was a witch?"

"I must be tired." Eustacia blinked rapidly. "I'm quite sure I didn't hear you correctly."

I proceeded to tell her about the worlds of Janay, Earth, and Kingdom and explained the concept of Traveling. I paused, and she glared at her host.

"I don't find this jest at my expense at all funny, Mr. Darcy."

"Do you know me to be a jesting man?" Darcy asked.

Eustacia clenched the bedsheets in her hands. "You cannot expect me to believe what this man says is true."

"You have my word that he's speaking the truth, and my word is more substantial today than yours," replied Mr. Darcy. "Listen to his story, and then we'll talk."

I continued and explained the coven, the danger to Kingdom, and the mission. Eustacia scowled through the entire discourse. "And what has this to do with me?"

Julia cut off my reply. "As Harold said, you're one of the witch's daughters, Stacy."

Eustacia turned her attention to Julia. "Impossible.

True, my mother abandoned me. My grandfather told me my mother's name—Mya. But we aren't from another world."

Julia sat down near Eustacia. "My name's Julia, and two days ago, I was the same as you. I lived in a different world when I met this man's wife and her friend. The difference is I saw them Travel. I stole their horse and came here. It's all true."

"And why should I believe you?"

"Because I am a witch's daughter as well. Think, Stacy! You must be able to do something that is unusual. My gift is my dreams. I can transmit dreams into others' minds. It helped me stay alive in my home world."

Eustacia frowned. "Susan Nonsuch is more of a witch than I am. She creates items to curse people."

Elizabeth crossed her arms. "She also believed you bewitched suitors before you married Clym. We all know why you were out last night with Damon. Nonsuch will claim you ensorcelled him."

Eustacia put a hand to her breast. "I never influenced Clym."

"Influenced?" Mr. Darcy asked.

Eustacia spread out the bedsheets she had bunched together. "I make friends by projecting emotions into their heads that I want them to feel."

"I find no magic in this," said Mr. Darcy. "It's a credit to your figure more than the supernatural."

Eustacia turned her attention to Elizabeth, and their eyes locked for a few seconds. Elizabeth turned to Mr. Darcy, tensing her body. "You are quite impertinent. How dare you attack this poor creature before us who is never at fault?"

Mr. Darcy stepped back at his wife's remonstration, and Elizabeth gasped and put a hand to the base of her neck. She turned to her husband and apologized. Mr. Darcy held his hand up. "No need. Mrs. Yeobright is an accomplished sorceress."

"I'm not a sorceress," Eustacia said. "I've had this ability all my life. My near-death experience last night has heightened it. I could never influence people with so clear a mind as Mrs. Darcy before."

"So why are you finding believing you're a witch's daughter so hard?"

"I don't cast hexes."

"I don't either," said Julia. "But I have a gift. I hate my mother for abandoning me in Cixxes, and if her defeat means my freedom, then I'm willing to risk it."

Elizabeth touched Julia's shoulder. "Unlike you, Mrs. Yeobright is attached to people here."

I stood. "Mrs. Yeobright is dead. She drowned last night. At least, this is the story we'll tell. We witnessed her dead body float by us while we were out searching for a friend. Eustacia Vye, on the other hand, has her entire life in front of her."

Eustacia regarded me with wide eyes. I leaned toward her. "You can go anywhere and do what you want. Save Kingdom, and the queens will reward you with overflowing riches. And they'll return you right here, in Janay's Paris, with a new identity if that's what you'd like."

Eustacia's eyes brightened. "Away from here? From the heath? Say no more. I accept. I don't believe any of this. But if this is all nonsense, do you swear to take me to Paris anyway?"

I nodded. "Of course."

Mr. Darcy said, "I will pay for the transport, Miss Vye. And you know my word is my bond."

Eustacia gripped the bedsheets. "Very well. I shall accompany you to this Kingdom place."

I sighed. "Good. Now we need to find my wife and the third daughter."

26 - REUNION MISFIRE

Sondra

A nurse in gray scrubs and purple teeth smiled at me when I came around. "I see you've rejoined us in Recovery. I'll download a list of instructions for your discharge."

Disoriented, I tried to sit up but failed. Had Harold rushed me to the hospital? I couldn't remember. "What happened?"

Odd. The nurse didn't inquire how I felt. Weren't they duty-bound to ask?

The nurse ignored my question. "Your surgery was completely successful."

"What procedure did I have?"

The nurse regarded her palm. "Since the Center ordered

the surgery, we can avoid all the paperwork."

Oh, God! My breath lodged in my throat.

The nurse flashed violet-colored teeth. "You don't have to pay a pence."

I released my breath through my nose. "I don't control my healthcare?"

"Of course not. Lie still for fifteen minutes, and then I'll help you out of bed."

My thoughts cleared, and I remembered where I was and what had happened. Images of the self-propelled chair, the room with Julia's number, and the man with yellow teeth paraded through my brain. I trembled and shook my head, refusing to believe that what I saw in my mind's eye had actually occurred.

The only pain I felt other than a dull ache in my abdomen was a stinging sensation on my left cheek. I put my hand to my face and discovered multiple scratches.

"Oh, you cut yourself before you went into surgery. The doctors stopped the bleeding but thought you'd like to see what you did to yourself. It should heal in a day."

My hand reached down to my waist. Maybe the surgeon didn't go through with it. Maybe the nurse was bluffing.

I hung onto this frayed thread of hope while the purple-toothed nurse assisted me from the bed and into my silver clothes. The woman placed a pillbox hat on my head and then made me sit in the visitor's chair. Staring at my rumpled bed-sheets, I knew. I just knew.

Numbness followed. They had cracked me open, scooped me out, and left behind a shell. I was absent of substance as if I had switched places with my own shadow. All at once, my tears broke through my stuporous dam. Water streamed down my face, and I wept harder than I ever had in my life.

After another thirty minutes, the nurse asked if I could walk. My head had cleared after my good cry, and I didn't want to stay here. I nodded, and the nurse gestured to the door.

"Good day."

As I left the recovery room, not recovered at all, a man in a gray uniform intercepted me. He had Asian features, bushy eyebrows, and mutton chops. The lights on his clothing swirled around. "Miss?"

I opened my mouth. Nothing emerged.

He held up his palm, faced inward, and read aloud. "You may select any vehicle upon leaving The Soul. Once you touch its handle, the transport will return you to 07151823051212's apartment. Or if you prefer, take the underground. We coded the door to the apartment to your biometrics. You'll find you have a new door, and everything is tidied up and returned except for the disruption device. Naughty. Naughty." He grinned. His incisors were blood red.

Why was he scolding me? The device wasn't mine.

He continued, "Tomorrow, select any vehicle, and it will take you to the courts. They'll train you there, ensuring our society's ongoing success." He lowered his palm. "Welcome to Centrania, 07151823051212."

He turned on his heel and left. They wanted me to become Julia.

Now what? When I thought about it, what choices did I have? If I ran, they'd put me back here or in one of the other places Alice described. What if I ended up in The Body or The Mind? My only course of action was to replace Julia for a time. But taking her place was impossible. How could I?

But then again...why not? I was barren. Why would Harold want me now when he could choose the other girl— certainly a parallel—and have a family? Even my sister and brother wouldn't know the difference. The queens would find a way to kill the witches without me. Happy endings all around for everyone. Except for me.

Tired of crying, I wanted to go home, or to Julia's home, and sleep forever. I didn't want to be myself. Being Julia, I could escape my life.

I wandered the halls of this floor of The Soul, having to

ask for directions three times to find the stairs. On the way out, I passed a woman in her twenties screaming and crying, strapped to a mechanical chair similar to the one I'd traveled in. She begged for help. How could I do anything? They'd throw me right back in a room here. I walked past, avoiding eye contact. I was no hero.

I eventually found the front doors. I expected guards to accost me before I exited, but they didn't notice me. I was an insignificant speck to them now.

When I exited, the morning light hurt my eyes thanks to the glaring sun. Couldn't the future control the damn weather? Lights activated on my shirt and swirled around through the cloth.

A few boxy vehicles were parked on the streets. No one owned cars here, I realized. No one owned anything.

I approached a white car shaped like a U.S. mail truck and reached for its handle. Before I could clasp it, someone behind me took my arm and steered me toward the entrance to the underground. I tried to shrug him off, but he was a tall, muscular man.

I tried to pull away a second time. "I don't want to go down—"

We arrived at the top of the stairs together. "Miss, you just asked me to help you."

"But—"

We approached the first step down the cement stairs, chipped with wear. The man's grip tightened. "Watch your step here. Alice-oop."

His saying "alice-oop" instead of "allez-oop" prompted me to examine the man. Had Alice sent him? He had short hair, a weather-beaten face, and a steely gaze. His eyes focused forward while we proceeded down and stepped into a line of people waiting to board any one of a series of cars. When our turn came, we had the vehicle to ourselves.

The man took control of the steering panel. I didn't ask questions, knowing in this God-forsaken place we must be monitored. Someone was likely sounding an alarm right now. I didn't want trouble; I wasn't going to help him. I leaned back against the side of the car while we rocketed off through underground tubes.

The ride lasted a few minutes while the car rushed along at a dizzying speed. When the capsule opened, the mysterious man gripped my hand and pulled me toward the stairs. I didn't want to run; after all, they would catch us anyway. What was the point of this? And sure enough, two men were gathered at the top of the steps, both sporting military cuts. They smirked as they shook their batons, crackling with electricity.

My guide pointed at the two men. I noticed then his hand was a prosthetic, and I jumped in alarm when the tip of the index finger popped off. Twin beams of light flashed from the end of his digit, and the guards collapsed to the ground. Completely baffled, I allowed him to lead me upstairs.

We emerged onto another nondescript Victorian street in this damned city. Three more figures in the distance advanced toward us. My guide dragged me into an alleyway —sending my hat toppling off my head—while footsteps pounded on the pavement behind us. Wonderful. Now we were doomed.

After we ran a few feet into the alleyway, Alice emerged from the shadows. She reached out and grabbed our wrists, and an Oz plain replaced Centrania. In front of us floated the three doors. The man let go of my hand.

I kneeled on the ground, passing my hand over the grass in disbelief. "Am I really here?"

Alice put her hand on my shoulder. "You're safe."

I wouldn't ever be safe again.

Alice said, "You've been in The Soul about a day and a half. I'm going to take you to Janay to see Hero now."

The man nudged Alice. "I have to go back. You know I can't be gone for long. They'll suspect."

I started shaking violently at the thought of being alone

if Alice left with the man. My stomach roiled, and I dry heaved spittle all over the grass.

Alice swore at my reaction. "Give me a minute," she said to the man. She crouched down by me and took my hand. "I promise. I'll be right back. I'm not going to take you back with him. He belongs in Cixxes, and I'd rather you waited here."

Oz! Oz was safe. I wasn't *there* anymore. I nodded. "Come back quickly."

Alice squeezed my shoulder. "I promise." She turned to her companion. "How did they get to her so fast?"

The man put his hands on his hips. "It's The Soul." He pointed at me and spoke as if I weren't there. "She's communicating. Coherent. Remarkable, all things considered."

Alice took his arm. "Let's go, Deckard."

She disappeared. I closed my eyes and tried to imagine I was someone else for a while. Maybe pre-Cixxes Sanders. My old self. Yes, that might work. I'd block out as much as I could.

A few minutes passed before Alice was again at my side, but I was starting to panic at the thought of being deserted once more. Alice kneeled and took my arms.

"Let's go to Janay."

I shook my head, unable to form words.

Alice asked, "What do you want to do, Sondra?" The fact she used my given name didn't escape me.

I started to rock back and forth and cry. Alice sat down, threw her arms around me, and laid my head on her chest. I had thought Alice was a bit of a cold fish, but I welcomed the gesture and now understood how she and Penta were such good friends. Alice stroked my hair and whispered. "It's okay. It's okay."

When I was able to form words, I said, "I want to go back home. I want to go to Earth."

"Not a good idea, Sondra. I can't leave you alone, and I can't abandon the others."

"You can leave me at home. I'll go to my mother's."

Alice asked, "And tell her what?"

I had no more tears at the moment. Alice continued, "You know I'm right. I'm so sorry. Really, I am, but I need my friend Sondra back. Come back to me. A frustrated or sad or pissed-off Sondra, but I need you back in the game."

I swallowed. Something Alice had said struck a chord. "How about pissed-off Sondra?"

"Sounds good. And listen, I'm not going to leave you again. No matter what."

I shook my head and wiped the tears from my face. Was crying a good sign? Did it mean I could feel something at least? "Can we remain here a while longer?"

Alice pulled me closer, tightening the embrace. "Absolutely."

Harold

I spent my third morning and early afternoon in Janay riding Bree around Pemberley in an attempt to travel to Cixxes. Every effort failed, although I sensed Bree tried with all his might, missing his owner. Whispering the name of the world in his ear and getting him to gallop only resulted in us crossing a field. After three hours, I gave up and led Bree back to the stable.

I thought about the dream of Sanders walking in on Cassie. What if Sanders was lost in Cixxes and we couldn't find her for years? Did the vision predict that I would begin a new life with Cassie on Earth? And after Cassie and I had started a family, would Sanders escape from Cixxes to come home to my new wife and child? Impossible. I would never abandon Sanders. We had our problems, but I loved her. Always had. Always would.

I crossed Julia's path while strolling to the mansion, and asked her how she'd managed to ride Bree across worlds without Sanders.

"When your wife first arrived in Cixxes, I saw Bree transform on his own. I guessed Sanders could transform him and others could use her horse without her."

"No, Sanders has to be mounted on Bree."

Julia spread her hands. "The two of you have this all wrong. How many times have you Traveled on him?"

"Not many."

"Proves you don't know everything."

I resolved to try again after a break. I had to leave Cassie behind and show the woman I loved that she meant everything to me. I excused myself and searched for Pennilane until I found her on the back porch with Pip. The two of them were standing across from each other. Very close. Too close

Neither noticed me at first. Pip was talking. "...feel before. Estella taught it to me, but I believe it all led to this moment. I have never been more at ease in the presence of a woman and hope I can call—"

Spotting me, the selkie interrupted Pip. "We are not alone."

I clenched my jaw and stepped forward. Pennilane was out here flirting with him while my wife was God only knew where. "May I talk to you in private, *sister*?"

Pip blushed while Pennilane passed him, holding up her chin. I led her into a nearby music room adorned with gold trim and providing a large pianoforte. We stepped up to the instrument, away from the door. When we knew we were alone, Pennilane accosted me as if I was a seal hunter. "How dare you interrupt a private conversation."

"How dare I? My wife and Alice are in danger, Valencia hasn't contacted us, all of Kingdom is at stake, and I catch you making goo-goo eyes at a Janay stranger."

Pennilane slammed her fist on the piano, and it played a jarring note. "If I follow your meaning, you insult me by thinking I have forgotten my duty. In the first place, Alice is a Traveler and knows Cixxes. If they are in danger, I'm sure they have left."

"You just said I'm instead of I am, Pennilane. You never used to speak with contractions. You've been talking too long to your little boy-toy out there."

Pennilane pointed to the interior of the mansion, ignoring my comment. "Julia and Eustacia are here. If we go to Cixxes, all we do is endanger the quest by leaving the daughters alone. And Valencia gave me a strict order not to follow her to Morbidum. I have no reason to believe she is in danger. She is more resourceful than you give her credit for. And as far as Kingdom is concerned, I feel its peril more than you. Kingdom is my home, and all my friends live there. I am doing my duty by following the instructions my queen gave me to stay here until the others show up."

"Are you sure you aren't remaining here for *him*?"

"I thought you knew me better. Pip is a man, and men are my sworn enemy. True, he is a businessman and not a fisherman, and he detests seal-hunting. The only men I will listen to with any regard are Prince Roger and Graddock. All other men, including yourself, I treat with disdain."

"Your little display on the porch was not disdain."

Pennilane bit her lip. "Was it goo-goo?"

I snorted. "Yeah. I'd say it was. Now take how you feel for him, multiply it by a million, and you have how I feel for Sanders. I need to find my wife."

"Hero, this seems a poor choice of action, even for you."

"I must leave, Pennilane. You said you wanted to protect my marriage. If I leave Cassie here and go after Sanders, you'll have accomplished your objective. You remain and guard the daughters."

Pennilane realized the logic in the statement and nodded her head. I turned on my heel and marched out the door.

With new resolve, I strolled across the grounds to retrieve Bree from the stables. I stopped when someone shouted my name from behind. I recognized the voice, and for a moment, turned and hoped to find Sanders. However, the speaker's accent gave her away as Cassie. How could I mistake the Cockney accent for my wife's? I was becoming desperate.

The maid ran across the grounds to me like a lover in

an old-fashioned movie. I wanted to ignore her, but I knew she would climb on Bree with me if I did. Instead, I waited for her while she rushed up to me, breathless. "My dear, a servant overheard you inform your sister of your intent to leave."

"Please address me as Harold."

"But, sweetcake, we are bonded together."

"No, we aren't. I think I know a way to reach Sanders. I have to go."

The maid circled in front of me. "You promised to take me."

I shuffled. "Cixxes is too dangerous. I'll return to pick you up."

"If you promise, seal it with a kiss of affection. If you kiss me, I'll be able to tell if you're lying." She pursed her lips.

Her limerence was starting to annoy me. I recoiled. "No way. Come on, act your age!"

Cassie's eyes welled up at my remonstration. "You mean to desert me. I can tell you do not have any intention of saving me or the baby."

I threw my hands into the air. "There is no baby!"

"Not yet."

Just ahead were the stables. I wished I had slipped away before Cassie had found me. "I give you my word that I will return. Every relationship starts with trust."

Cassie blushed. "I do trust you. If not a kiss, then embrace me. Not as a promise but in consolation. Believe it or not, I'm worried about you. I know you intend to return, but I fear you may not be able to."

She trembled, and I realized acutely at that moment her affection was genuine. I had viewed her preference for me as an infatuation born from her desperation in wanting to leave her bleak future behind. Yet her speech touched me—she had allowed me to peek behind her self-assured facade. If Planet and Sanders loved me, she might be attracted to me too.

I wrapped my arms around her, and she placed her head on my shoulder. I embraced her to protect her from the world, which can be cruel to an innocent. The maid put her arms around me, and I knew she was listening to my heart. In the brilliant sunshine of the day, among the beautiful garden of Pemberley, I connected with her. Not romantically but as a guardian. When she lifted her head and stared into my eyes, I resolved to help her. I had no intention of kissing her, and she was true to her word as well. Yet we shared a moment of tenderness—the protective knight, the innocent waif.

"You're getting on well without me!"

I released Cassie in a panic and turned around. I recognized the speaker. Standing twenty yards away with her hands on her hips, Sanders glared at me with eyes full of fire.

27 - WE HAVE PROPER MANNERS HERE!

Harold

I hated to admit this, but this wasn't the first time Sanders had come upon me in the arms of another woman. Even worse, this wasn't the first time she'd caught me in the arms of another woman who looked exactly like her. Perhaps being in the arms of a duplicate version of her wasn't as terrible as finding me in some stranger's arms. At least I've only embraced women who resemble her.

On second thought, it wasn't better.

Alice stood beside Sanders, eyes bulging at my indiscretion. Sanders' glasses were missing. Both were dressed in light silver garments with lights crossing back and forth around the surface. What a spectacle. Two women wearing Christmas tree lights, a twin of one in a maid's uniform, and me in the middle, all standing on the manicured lawn of Pemberley estate.

"I can explain." But really, I couldn't. Who could explain this?

Sanders' mouth changed from grimace to a thin line. Resignation? She asked, "Is Julia here? I told Bree to go to Janay when she tricked me."

I fumbled for words. Alice gaped at Cassie. "What is a parallel doing here in Janay?"

I didn't know who to answer first. Abashed, Cassie eyed Sanders but wouldn't let me go until I shrugged her off. I addressed Sanders. "I was about to ride Bree to find you."

Sanders tilted her head in a way I knew too well. She repeated, "Is Julia here?"

When she moved her head, I noticed Sanders had scratches on her cheeks. "My God, Sondra. What happened?"

Sanders' expression was inscrutable. "None of that matters, Harold. Answer my question."

An unpleasant pause filled the air like a sulfur smell in an enclosed room. Sanders had experienced the vision too, and now she had caught me in Cassie's arms. I hadn't even hugged Sanders yet, and I regretted the faux pas. Something else was going on. "What happened in Cixxes?"

"We're not going to discuss it now, Harold!" Behind her, Alice shook her head.

I stepped back at the outburst. I knew better than to press, so I answered Sanders' question. "Yes, Julia's here."

Alice grabbed Sanders' arm. "We can't hurt her, Sanders. She's a daughter and vital to Kingdom."

Sanders gritted her teeth. "I make no promises."

I jerked my thumb back to the mansion. "I'll take you to Julia and the one we found."

Sanders wrested her arm away from Alice's hold. "You found yours? Good. Let's go and get them."

As she passed me, I reached for her hand. Sanders pulled it away and wagged her fingers between Cassie and me. "We'll discuss this and the dream later." Cassie shrank back from Sanders' Medusian glare.

We marched toward the estate with Sanders in the lead. I questioned Alice. "I thought you had never Traveled to Janay?"

"I haven't. Glinda told me how to get here, remember? We spotted the mansion, and before we went to the front door, Sanders spied Bree grazing. The stable boy directed us to you. Said you had been riding him all morning."

While we advanced toward the back entrance, Sanders stopped and examined the estate. "Where are we?"

Austen was one of Sanders' favorite authors. Her response ought to be good. "Pemberley."

The tension drained out of Sanders' body. "Pemberley estate? Mr. Darcy's home? Is...is Elizabeth Bennet inside?"

If I wasn't in such trouble, I would've laughed. Sanders' wide eyes and open mouth anticipated meeting a celebrity. "Elizabeth Darcy, yes."

Sanders grimaced and continued her march forward. "Figures. You end up in *Pride and Prejudice*, and I end up in Dante's playground. Is Elizabeth the witch's daughter?"

We traversed the grounds toward the back door and caught sight of Pennilane and Pip on the porch. I answered, "No. It's a woman named Eustacia Vye."

Alice spoke from behind us. "A Thomas Hardy character from *The Return of the Native*. Interesting. He wasn't a romantic novelist. Harold, you should read more than fantasy."

Sanders' eyes lit up. "Is Emma Woodhouse here?"

"I haven't met her."

"Too much to hope for," Sanders said. "Elizabeth will do nicely. I can't wait to meet her. Wow, look at Pennilane's getup. Who's that with her?"

"Some nobody. He's Pennilane's source of information."

Pennilane waited at the door with Pip. She read the

look on my wife's face and lowered her head. "I take responsibility for Harold's indiscretion, Sanders."

My wife turned to Pip. "Are you related to the Darcys, my good sir?"

Again, I had to suppress bursting out laughing. My good sir? Was she for real?

Pip shook his head. "Sorry, I am not so illustrious. My name is Pirrup, but everyone calls me Pip."

Alice nodded toward the house. "I expect the Darcys are waiting for us with *great expectations*, Harold. If you get my meaning."

Sanders whispered to me. "You are zero for two."

"I got the Darcys."

"Oh...that was *so* hard."

Pennilane led the way to Eustacia's room. Pip followed along and whispered to his selkie companion—"clothes" being the only discernible word.

Alice and Sanders stood out like sore thumbs. When they passed the maids, the servants stared at the women in silver suits as if they were creatures from the netherworld. Pennilane eyed Pip and cleared her throat. "Perhaps you should excuse us."

"Please, I wish to accompany you," replied Pip.

Uncharacteristically, Pennilane hunched her shoulders and opened Eustacia's door.

We entered Eustacia's room and found both Eustacia and Julia seated together. When Sanders stomped in, Julia stood and backed up to the wall. Her face turned as pale as the sheets on the bed. "I can explain—"

Sanders stopped in the middle of the room, shaking with rage. She rasped, "No, you can't."

Julia twisted a strand of hair around her forefinger. "You lived in Cixxes for two days. Imagine spending your entire life there and then finding an opportunity to leave."

Sanders hollered, "We told you we were going to take you away! Why didn't you trust us?"

"They were coming! I had no time! Better I escaped than all of us were captured."

Sanders screamed, "There *was* time. You removed the interference device on purpose!"

"You had Alice."

Sanders lunged forward, screeching obscenities and stretching out her hands. Alice and I sprang into action and held her back. While we restrained Sanders from bloodying Julia's nose, the Darcys appeared in the doorway.

Mr. Darcy stepped in front of Sanders and straightened his waistcoat. Sanders blinked at him and stepped back in awe. The Darcys regarded Sanders and then Cassie. Realization dawned in Elizabeth's eyes. She beamed. "Mrs. Saturn, at long last."

"Elizabeth Bennet!"

Sanders curtsied, a sight to see in a silver jumpsuit. I snorted. "They aren't royalty."

Sanders flashed her mask of hatred at me. "Some of us have proper manners here!" She turned back to Mr. Darcy. "I am most pleased to make your acquaintance too, Mr. Darcy." She again curtsied.

"Despite her absurd clothes," said Mr. Darcy. "This one I favor."

Sanders said, "I know all about you. I've read—" She stopped.

I leaned against the wall. "You can tell them how many times you read it. I've explained everything."

"Tell me you didn't," said Alice. "They aren't supposed to know."

Sanders ignored her. "I've read *Pride and Prejudice* four times. More than the three times for *Wuthering Heights* and twice for *Jane Eyre*."

Elizabeth touched her chin. "Jane has a novel too?"

Alice held up her hands. "No more. Stop talking about this!"

"'Tis far too late for that," muttered Pennilane.

Sanders cupped her hand as if confiding to Elizabeth, although everyone in the room could hear her. "I like your novel the best. I must meet your sisters one day."

"Enough!" shouted Alice. "We have Julia and Eustacia. We should go to Morbidum to find the third."

Pennilane stepped next to the bed, examining her patient from the night before. "Eustacia is still recovering from her recent episode."

Eustacia raised her hand. "The headache has subsided. I feel well enough to leave."

"We promised to meet up with Valencia once we had completed our mission," said Sanders. "With luck, she has the third daughter, and we can be in Kingdom tonight."

Pip turned to Pennilane. "I am at a loss as to what is happening here. Are you going somewhere?"

"Yes. Far away." Pennilane wrung her hands.

"May I inquire where?"

Pennilane flushed and pressed her lips together, unable to answer. Alice interjected. "I'm afraid you'll never see her again."

Pennilane swallowed hard. Casting his eyes down, Pip shuffled his feet. He took her hand and bowed. "I am exceedingly sorry to hear you say so, dear lady, but in all fairness, you have warned me. The Darcys have been very gracious to have me as their guest, but I must take my leave now."

When he reached out to hold the selkie's hand, Sanders and Alice rocked on their heels as if about to faint. Pennilane allow a man to touch her? Absurd. Yet when he pressed his lips to the back of her fingers, she covered her mouth with her other hand. I realized at once what was happening.

She spoke through her hand. "Don't leave."

"Pennilane!" hissed Alice.

I put a restraining hand on Alice's shoulder then placed a finger to my lips.

Pip straightened up and allowed her to continue. Pennilane's face distorted. "Words cannot express how I feel right now. I hate nearly all men, but I cannot help but admire you."

The room was quiet enough to hear a bird glide along the air outside. Everyone who knew Pennilane was stunned; everyone else was amused. My mouth was dry. "Pennilane..." but I couldn't continue. Watching this scene unfold was like witnessing an automobile accident moments before the crash.

Pennilane trembled. "I cannot prevent what is about to happen. I have no control over it. It is the reason for my frequenting the water closet so many times during our talks. I'm not what you think I am. You think the creatures we discussed, the selkies, are imaginary. I warned you to keep an open mind. You shall see selkies are far from imaginary."

She dropped her hand and revealed her whiskers. Brown fur emerged from her face, and her hair grew into a pelt. Her arms flattened and shortened into flippers while her clothes ripped apart and fell off. Her legs merged, and she plonked onto the floor, gazing up at him as a lovely seal.

Pip backed up until he struck a wall. His eyes were as large as their sockets.

Pennilane spoke with a wheedling voice, though still hers. "This is who I am. When I was a young pup, hunters murdered my parents for their pelts in front of me. I had to abandon mine to escape the fur traders. I've spent my life searching for my pelt to return to the sea, never dreaming I could grow a new one. The fondness I have for you have restored my pelt. 'Tis a miracle I never thought possible."

Pip put a hand to his head. "I must be dreaming."

Pennilane reared up on her haunches, and her pelt parted along her stomach. Her fur sagged like an ill-fitting costume, and everyone marveled when a naked leg followed by its twin stepped out of the brown covering. In less than a minute, a human Pennilane stood in front of Pip, pelt wrapped discreetly around her. She lifted her chin. "I don't know if I ever will reconcile with mankind, but you have made such a difference in my life, dear Pip, that I will never be the same seal

I once was."

Pip rubbed his eyes with his fists then blinked. "A delusion. It must be."

"If you must tell yourself you are deluded, so be it," said Pennilane. "Farewell. I don't belong here, and you know too much. We shall never meet again."

The whiskers reappeared, and Pip stood motionless. Elizabeth approached him, took his arm, and guided him from the room. Pip never took his eyes off Pennilane as he left, allowing his hostess to lead him away. Seconds later, Pennilane rushed through the doorway in the opposite direction.

Sanders turned to me. "Did the two of you think you were on vacation here?"

Alice said, "It's this world. How could Hero remain immune if Pennilane fell victim to it?"

I spread my hands. "I never faltered, Sondra."

Mr. Darcy cleared his throat. "I fear you may have to delay your journey until Ms. Pennilane is quite recovered. Mrs. Darcy will attend to her."

"Let's not be hasty," said Julia. "I love it here."

We remained in the room while I told the story of how we rescued Eustacia, giving props to Pennilane. When the sun began to set, Elizabeth returned with Pennilane dressed in her first night's clothes. She avoided everyone's attention, keeping her swollen eyes to the ground. None of us dared to talk to her.

Alice observed the darkening sky out a window. "Morbidum is full of creatures of the night. Travelers know it's not safe to be out after the sun goes down. Going there now may be dangerous. If we don't find shelter quickly, something may attack us."

"Something?" I asked.

Alice turned from the window. "I would feel better if we slept a night at the local inn."

Mr. Darcy sat on a chaise-lounge. "You're welcome here. Future women, witches, selkies. The past two days have to be the most interesting episode of my life, and I confess I'll be disappointed to see you off."

Before anyone could answer, the major-domo opened the door and asked for the master of the house. Mr. Darcy stepped outside to talk to the servant and came back. "Another of your party has presented himself."

He threw open the door, and Sanders shouted, "Graddock! What are you doing here?"

Graddock stepped into the room, dressed as if he just stepped out of a tavern in Kingdom. Eustacia nudged Julia. "Is he wearing medieval clothing?"

Alice tilted her head. "How'd you get here? You're not a Traveler."

Graddock examined us, ignoring Alice's question. "Where is Valencia?"

Sanders clasped her hands. "She's in another world searching for the third sister."

Graddock strode over to Alice. "We need to go to her immediately. She is in danger."

Alice asked, "How do you know?"

"'Tis a long story. A mermaid named Rhapsody told me."

Confusion registered on everyone's face except Alice's. Mr. Darcy put a hand in his vest pocket. "Mermaids now? Why not?"

Alice stiffened. "Rhapsody came to you? But she is not a Traveler."

"But the White Rabbit is."

"What the hell is he talking about?" I asked Alice.

Alice explained, "Rhapsody is an ally and inspired the Little Mermaid fairy tale. She must have contacted the White Rabbit to bring Graddock here. No matter where I am in the worlds, the White Rabbit can always locate me. He Travels by digging holes connecting one world to another. He must have dug a shaft for Graddock to bring him to me so that I can take him to Morbidum. We must go right now!"

Sanders touched Alice's arm. "Valencia's in danger?"

Surprised, I raised my eyebrows at Sanders' familiarity with Alice. Alice didn't shy away from her touch. "Rhapsody has the gift of prophecy, especially for sweethearts. Her approach to someone signifies their lover is in peril. If she sought out Graddock, Valencia is in trouble, and only he can save her. We must hurry, including the two daughters. We leave no one behind."

"I'm going too," said Cassie.

Elizabeth said, "Cassie, the Saturns are united. This is their story, not ours."

I eyed my wife. Sanders' mask of indifference remained in place. We hadn't talked while waiting for Pennilane to compose herself. Sanders murmured, "She comes with us."

No one debated the declaration, though I expected Alice to object. Instead, she said, "We'll need to take Bree, so we'll have to go outside. We Travel straight to Morbidum."

We progressed out of the room and through the mansion to the yard behind the Darcy estate. Mr. Darcy went to retrieve Bree from the stable. In the growing darkness, we made our way at once to a broad field behind the house.

As we gathered, Sanders broke away from us to approach Mrs. Darcy. She touched Elizabeth's hand and curtsied. "One day, I hope to spend more time here if you'll have me?"

Elizabeth pressed her hand on top of Sanders. Her expression was complacent, and I realized the perceptive woman sensed something had upset my wife. "Of course."

Alice told us to form a circle and hold hands after Mr. Darcy arrived, leading Bree. Sanders pointed at Eustacia. "You. Gloomy Gus. You're with me on the horse." She and Eustacia mounted Bree.

The rest of us held hands, and Alice closed her eyes. Cassie somehow managed to end up beside me, despite my efforts to distance myself from her. She squeezed my hand, and we Traveled.

Neither

After they had gone, Mr. Darcy turned to Elizabeth. "As interesting as my life was two days ago, I think it far more fascinating now. Don't you, my dear?"

"Delightfully so. Multiple worlds, fairies, it all exceeds my highest expectations. And I'm the centerpiece of our novel, Mr. Darcy."

Mr. Darcy frowned. "Women's literature, eh? I suppose some young man has to make a living."

Elizabeth took his hand and turned him toward the house. While they strolled across the grounds, she remarked, "Sanders whispered to me that a woman wrote *Pride and Prejudice.*"

Harold

Outside of the Marstings mansion, my companions and I appeared on a forest trail. Cassie's hand gripped mine—her lips bloodless. I said, "You're fine, Cassie."

But she wasn't. Unladylike, she leaned over and threw up a small portion of her last meal on the dirt. She gulped and closed her eyes, wearing the expression of a person stepping off a rollercoaster she had underestimated.

Julia asked, "Where are we?"

"This world is called Morbidum," answered Alice.

Morbidum had a different vibe than Janay, for sure. In Janay, one could stroll around and enjoy the sounds and sensations of a calm night. Here, the frogs croaked dire finales, the cicadas sang dirges, the wind didn't whistle—it keened. The air bit you, the clouds hung lower, and the leaves skirted across the road like enlarged, hostile insects.

Bree galloped up behind us, bearing Sondra and Eustacia. When the horse stopped, it vanished and left the two women straddling a stick pony. Eustacia yelped at the sudden transformation and fell to the side of the road. "What is going on? Where's the steed?"

The maid reclaimed my hand and wouldn't release it,

so I had to drag her to Eustacia and extend an offer to help the Janay witch's daughter up. "We've Traveled to a different world. I explained it to you."

Eustacia took my other hand. "Hearing a fantastic story is not the same as experiencing it. What is this world?"

Alice eyed the mansion across the way. "We are in a time period similar to your own, but this world is markedly different. You'll find Morbidum more oppressive and threatening. Travelers have recorded supernatural events here, and magicians, though rare, exist."

A raven soared down from the air and landed on the path in front of us. Right after Alice claimed magic was rare, the raven enlarged, its body expanding outward. We stepped back until the lithe figure of a woman in her twenties, feathers covering her body, stood before us.

The feathered woman said, "Do not yell. I'm Valencia's friend."

Despite her words, Eustacia yelped.

The woman held up her hands. "I am Lenore. Follow me to the cemetery. Valencia may be there."

She transformed once again into a bird and ascended, hovering over the road. Everyone looked at me to make the decision. This could be a trap, but I had no better idea.

When we arrived in the middle of the cemetery, we called out for Valencia, but no one answered our summons. Lenore returned to her human form in a black dress, and we gathered around her. Graddock asked, "Where is Valencia?"

"I have been flying around the estate, trying to locate her. The last I saw of her, she was coming from the direction of the woodcutter's cabin. She waddled as if inebriated, and my friend Zariah was supporting her."

Graddock said, "Valencia would not drink to excess while on a quest. Something is not right."

"Who's Zariah?" I asked. "Perhaps she knows where Valencia is."

"Zariah is my friend. In my raven form, I overheard her

telling the guests in the manor that Valencia left by herself without saying good-bye. Something's amiss because Valencia identified me as a witch's daughter."

Alice regarded the mansion. "Valencia wouldn't leave you."

"Curiouser and curiouser," I joked, at which Alice rolled her eyes.

Lenore reached into her pocket. "I returned outside and have been searching in my bird form. I didn't find her, but I did discover something interesting."

She held out her hand to reveal five matchsticks. "As a raven, my eyesight is heightened. I spotted a trail of these matchsticks from the direction of the woodcutter's cabin to this spot. I remembered Valencia carried this type of match. The last match I found was here."

Looking down, we realized we were standing on a grave. I asked, "Whose is this?"

"Mine."

"Your grave?" I stepped off the patch of dirt. "You're dead?"

Her long fingernails tapped the headstone on the grave. "It's empty. But everyone here thinks I'm dead."

Alarm bells rang in my head. I turned to Alice. "This world would contain the works of what authors?"

"On the American side? Hawthorne, Bierce..."

"Poe?"

Alice put a hand to her mouth. "Definitely! Oh, my God!"

I turned to Lenore. "Do you have a shovel or a pick?"

"Tools are in a shed next to the graveyard." Lenore pointed to a small wooden structure twenty yards away. "You may help yourself. What is it?"

I turned to Graddock. "I think Valencia is buried alive in Lenore's grave."

28 - AN INTERRUPTED COUNCIL

Two days after the witches had kidnapped Beauty, Penta stood in front of her bedroom window looking over the front courtyard of the castle, gloved hands clasped behind her back, an open box lying on her bed. A servant had found the box at the entrance of the palace with Penta's name scrawled on a tag. Fearing another one of the witches' tricks, the royal guards had tried to open it, but they couldn't lift the lid.

After Penta had returned to the palace, a servant had presented the box to her. The queen retreated into her room with it. She was afraid the present was a trap and didn't want others around when she tripped it. With trembling hands, she removed the lid of the box and observed with horror the contents inside. She suppressed a scream, standing over it for a full minute. Tears streamed down her face.

When Penta turned away, she strode to her closet to retrieve new clothes. Once she'd dressed, she stepped up to a full-length mirror and observed herself. Penta stood before her reflection adorned in black armor, form-fitted to her body.

Her obsidian-colored leather vest over a similar black, long-sleeved tunic fit her torso like a second skin. The tunic's neckline hugged her throat, and sharp-edged epaulets crouched on her shoulders the way gargoyles sit on cathedral walls. A thick belt with sheaths to carry multiple knives encircled her waistline, securing tight-fitting, navy-blue trousers. She had pulled her hair back into a bun and tied it with a sloe-colored bow, ribbons hanging down like the legs of a dead spider. To complete her ensemble, Penta slipped on thick, black gloves.

The mirror shifted, and instead of reflecting Penta, it displayed red-haired Alice dressed in her Kingdom garb. She eyed Penta's choice of garments. "A bit dark for you, girl-friend."

Penta crossed her arms. "I wish Celeste had never given me this Reflecting Glass. I thought it delightful at first, but now it's annoying."

"Reflection is good for the soul," answered Alice.

"I have no use for your double-entendre talk today," snapped Penta. "I know you're me but in Alice's form. I thought you'd be on my side. Didn't you see the odious gift the witches sent me? Hasn't it moved you at all?"

Alice's shoulders sagged. "How could it not? But, Penta, your latest idea is one you'll never be able to take back. Some actions cannot be undone."

Penta's nostrils flared, and she walked to her bed and snatched up the box. She returned to the mirror and shoved the container toward the glass. Inside lay a severed, brown hand. Penta said, "I worried she was dead, but 'tis far worse."

"You don't know—"

"They are torturing her!" wailed Penta. "Cutting off her hand. Mocking me by maiming her as I once suffered. They know I understand best the agony associated with losing a hand. And now they've inflicted that same pain on the true treasure of my life."

Penta shut the box and laid it back on her bed. She put her hands in her hair and lowered her gaze. "I hear Beauty's voice in my head. 'Why didn't you save me? Frozen at the dining table, doing nothing, will be my last memory of you.'"

Alice refuted her other self. "She wouldn't say that."

"Go away," Penta whispered.

Once she'd wiped her tears, she saw Hero standing in the glass. Wearing a checkered shirt and jeans, he put his hands in his pockets. "I'm sorry, Penta."

Penta didn't answer him.

Hero said, "Please, Penta. You haven't slept in two days. You aren't thinking clearly."

"I don't know what to do," whispered Penta.

"It's why I'm here."

"You're not Hero. You're still me."

"But you listen to Hero. He's a best friend you'd never let down."

Penta ground her teeth and glared at the mirror. "He doesn't have a daughter who is being tortured. I wished that Beauty were dead. At least she'd be at peace. Her suffering would be over."

Hero put his hands in his pockets. "You plan to kill them. You'll wait until Helga brandishes Cusp and swings her weapon, and then you'll teleport around the room as fast as a wink of an eye. You'll touch each witch and put an arm, a shoulder, any body part that won't resist the momentum, in the path of the holy blade. With one slash, Helga will cut them all at once because of your action."

Penta growled, "Once Cusp's blade touches their skin, the witches will die. The sword's divine nature against their profane souls should make short work of them."

Hero stepped toward the mirror and put his hands on the glass. "And what of you? After you use your sister to kill the witches, what kind of a queen will you become?"

Penta stepped back and lowered her eyes. "I will abdicate, of course. I will live in a cave in the mountains of Grok's Teeth."

"Penta, please. You'll ruin your life."

Penta closed her eyes. "I'm already dead, Hero. They killed me when they took my dearest, Beauty. They left my mind and body but killed my ability to love. I'm a hollow woman. Go away."

She opened her eyes. Alice and Hero had disappeared from the reflection. In their place, the pixie Planet cocked her head. "Do you recall what happened the last time you failed to listen to a friend?"

Penta cursed the mirror and touched it, teleporting it to a room far away in the castle. She wailed in frustration, then took several deep breaths. Her eyes glazed over, and she turned to the door and marched out of her room.

Penta proceeded downstairs. When she passed servants, they stopped and bowed, regarding her with their mouths hanging open wide enough to insert a hen's egg. She progressed to the southernmost spire of the castle and up the circular stairs to the highest room. The queen didn't hesitate before the oaken doors but grabbed their handles and pushed open the portal, the last to arrive into what the queens called the Planning Room. The others all stood around a large table in the middle and stared at her while she advanced.

Her knee-high, black boot heels clicking on the stone, Penta strode across the room, swinging her hands by her side. Appearing shocked, Helga struggled to put into words her reaction to her sister's clothes. The princes eyed each other and looked at their hands, choosing silence as their response. Cinderella managed to squeak out a sentence. "Penta! Your clothes!"

Penta rejoined, "Helga, your bone armor should suffice for the battle with the witches. And Cinderella, the red dress." Her command to her sisters was absolute.

Penta sat at one side of the square table, which was large enough to accommodate twelve, three on each side. On the tabletop, Helga had recreated a dollhouse-sized replica of the throne room with tiny, carved stone walls and furniture. The small statues representing the queens stood before miniature thrones.

Penta licked her lips and described the plan in detail of how she and the others would engage the witches. She included that, if necessity insisted, the queens would kill the witches. Roger, Danforth, Rose Red, and Celeste all nodded. They focused on the model on the table, readying their minds for the oncoming violence. Celeste folded her hands, not questioning the decision. Pale and restless, Cinderella drummed her fingers on the edge of the table. Helga, on the other hand, gripped Cusp's hilt at her side.

Penta turned to Rose Red. "You have Lycrotta's Arrow?"

Rose Red reached into her jerkin and produced the arrow, holding it out.

"As to the plan, no one must know of it. This includes Glinda."

Cinderella blinked. "I told Glinda." Everyone else shifted uncomfortably.

Red splotches of anger arose on Penta's face, and her expression was similar to the appearance of a disturbed cobra. "And why did you inform her of our plans?"

Cinderella remained placid. "No one said I shouldn't. And I am a queen and can make my own decisions."

"And what did she say?" asked Penta.

"To refrain, and let events unfold."

Penta shook her head. "I'm tired of waiting. They are vermin. We shall deal with them as such."

Helga lowered her eyes, cheeks coloring at the harshness of Penta's voice. Cinderella stopped drumming her fingers and folded her hands on the table, her delicate fingers interlaced. "You are Penta, my sister, and not a changeling? Have the witches assumed your form or captured your mind?"

Penta rubbed her temples with both hands. "I won't willingly take another life after these three, but I assure you I am indeed your sister."

Before Cinderella could respond, the door swung open, and everyone started at the sound of wood scraping across the stone floor. For a brief moment, Penta's pulse quickened in anticipation of the witches' presence. Helga unsheathed Cusp so quickly she seemed to have magicked it into her hand. But two familiar people stood in the doorway—neither a magic-wielder. On the left, his hand on the doorknob, Lyken nodded to those gathered. Sylvia marched past him into the room. Lyken announced, "Miss Swonewith requested entry."

"This is a closed meeting, Lyken!" barked Penta.

Before shutting the door, Lyken responded, "I thought Sylvia would be a worthy addition."

Pale as an eggshell, Sylvia advanced across the stone floor. Her slippered feet made a sound like leaves falling as she proceeded to the table. Grim-faced, she stopped near Celeste and Rose Red to the right of Penta.

Penta picked up a miniature of a woman soldier and examined it, not meeting Sylvia's eyes. "Do you wish to join us in defeating our enemies? If so, you may remain."

Sylvia lifted her chin. "Someone told me of your plot to kill the witches."

Everyone regarded Rose Red, who shrank under their scrutiny. Sylvia said, "Do not blame her. I'm grateful she told me." Pausing, she looked around at the gathering and glared at them. "Am I the only one around here with any common sense?"

Helga had sheathed Cusp when Sylvia entered and now took a seat. "We plan to offer them terms of surrender."

Sylvia's eyes darted around the table. "We call that a cover story on Earth. You're going to kill them, and you know it. They'll never surrender merely due to a sword."

No one objected. Penta pointed to the door. "Sylvia, leave before you force me to escort you out."

Sylvia put her hands on her hips. "Really, Penta? Is this you? Has everyone lost their minds?"

Helga said, "'Tis a desperate time, Sylvia."

Penta started toward her, but Sylvia held up her hand. "I will leave, but I'll also have my say. How dare you consider murder? You, whom I admire. You, who represent the opposite of what's wrong with my world."

Cinderella said, "We are not the clichés your world makes us out to be."

Sylvia swung toward her. "Cliché? People in my world look to Cinderella with hope. You're the queen who beat all odds to end up with her prince. You lived with abuse and never turned to evil yourself. What would the people of Earth think of you now?"

Cinderella narrowed her eyes. "My earthly portrayal hasn't met these devils and has not a young son. They'll torture and kill my beloved Roger and find where Ozark has hidden Cuthbert. They will do the same to Ozark." She swallowed nervously. "And then they'll kill my son, tear out his heart, and force me to watch while they eat it. I doubt Earth's version of Cinderella has ever encountered such a dilemma."

Penta reached for Sylvia, but Sylvia avoided her touch.

"Or you could find a way to defeat them," Sylvia countered. "Have you no hope? And what about the virtuous Helga, daughter of the Marsh King? And the maiden without hands? Planning to kill people?"

After taking a deep breath, Penta said, "Sylvia, you don't understand. This situation is different than the ones we've faced in the past."

"No, it's not." Sylvia turned to Rose. "You were willing to lay down your life before to defend doing what's right. Have you forgotten? My world knows you as Rose Red, sister of Snow White, but also as Little Red Riding Hood."

Rose flinched at the name. "I never favored that depiction."

"But you are Red Riding Hood. Where has that innocent

girl gone? She's turned into—"

"Enough!" Penta stepped forward, and before Sylvia could defend herself, she grabbed the other woman's hand. Sylvia vanished. Penta, face flushed, released a deep sigh. "I sent her to the aviary. She will be safe there."

Cinderella took a step away from the table. "I'll go to her."

"Remain where you are, Cinderella," commanded Penta. "We need to ensure everyone understands their place in the upcoming battle."

The entire time Sylvia had addressed the council, Rose had avoided looking at Penta, keeping her eyes locked on the table. Now she raised her head and drew herself up. "I cannot be a part of this."

Everyone gaped at her except for Penta. The gloved queen shook with anger. "But part of the plan is for you to pin them to the wall with Lycrotta's Arrow. We know the arrow works on them. My sisters and I will do the rest."

Rose held the arrow in her hands and then let it fall to the table, clattering against the wood. "I will not make this mistake again. Syl is right. I *am* Red Riding Hood. She stopped and admired the flowers after being told not to do it. She knew it was wrong, but she did it anyway. Not me. I will carry out my duty to Kingdom."

She turned to go. Penta said, "Rose. Don't do this."

Rose stopped and drew her cloak around her. "For a moment, Syl reminded me so much of *her*. Syl's voice doesn't sound like your sister's, but briefly, I had Coal back again." Rose turned and strode from the room.

After the door closed, the assembly remained still, not daring to break the silence. Before any of them spoke, someone summoned Penta from her ring. The shrill, nasally voice belonged to Picana. "Queen Penta, oh, high queen, your majesty and eminence, and all that sort of dung. Are you present?"

After recovering from her initial shock, Penta lifted her hand to her mouth. "What is it you want now?" she hissed.

Picana cackled. "Oh, deary, I want you to talk to one of your beloved dwarfs—the one whose ring I just stole." Her voice became distant. "Speak!"

Fox's voice. "Queen Penta?"

"Fox?"

His unsteady voice answered her. "The witches are here in our cottage."

Penta gasped. "I shall be there in a second."

"If you come, they said they would kill us," said Fox. "Please remain at the castle."

"What do they want?" Penta ground her teeth.

A cry answered her, and then Picana's voice rang through the ring. "Queen Penta, are you ready yet to accept our terms?"

Penta glared at the ring on her finger. "If you hurt him, I will twist your ears until they fall off."

"Really, such brutality. The terms, Penta. Are you willing to come to terms?"

Penta observed her sisters. "Yes, we are ready. Come to the castle tomorrow, and we shall discuss the subject of surrender."

"Well done, my pet. Sleep with the knowledge that no more harm will come to your people. We shall arrive when the sun is at its highest point. In your castle's throne room, you will kiss our hands in obedience, and then all shall be well."

Penta forced out one word. "Indeed."

"We shall abduct the dwarfs just in case you plan to betray us. If you do, we shall leave the castle with a snap of our fingers and return to them. And with our nails, we shall cut open their torsos and string them up by their gizzards."

Three cackles. And then silence.

29 - A GRAVELY
ROMANTIC GESTURE

Sondra

I was acting like a bitch, and I knew it.

I hated giving Hero the silent treatment, glaring at him and snapping at him whenever he asked anything. Harold's stiff embrace of my parallel didn't upset me. If that hug was romance, let's give love a funeral and put it out of its misery.

Alice's advice to me, to become pissed-off Sanders to keep my thoughts off the—Lord, even thinking the word made me want to weep—was the right advice. I wanted to cry a river of tears, but with Valencia's life hanging in the balance, I had to focus on the present.

I would have to tell Hero what had happened when we were alone, but for now, he would receive the brunt of my anger. One thing about my husband, he knew when to press and when to hold back. Though we hadn't been married long, we understood each other. That was why the dream was so confusing.

Shovelful of dirt by shovelful of dirt, Hero and Graddock dug up Lenore's grave. The rest of us surrounded them. Behind us, a weeping angel sculpture stood with one hand held high in supplication to the heavens. Her other arm had broken off, yet another reason to cry. The wind came in bursts, annoying because a second statue, one of a crooked man in a cloak, held a real bell. Every wind gust would ring the bell, jarring the diggers and disrupting the rhythm of their task at hand. Lenore's headstone, a rectangular affair with a simple stone cross on top, displayed the words "Beloved Lenore." Merely this, and nothing more.

While Hero removed dirt with as much speed as he could muster, Graddock threw dirt aside as fast as a frontloader. His muscles bulged, and I bet the others were admiring his sculpted deltoids. Let them look; Valencia ruled his heart. She loved him for far more than his body, but I had to admit his physique was easy on the eyes.

Standing next to Eustacia and Julia, I tapped Lenore on the shoulder. "So you're the third daughter?"

Lenore curtsied. "At your service."

Julia said, "My name is Julia, and this is Stacy. Our mothers abandoned us too. Our three mothers are the ones destroying their world."

Julia and Eustacia nodded to the bird woman as a greeting. Lenore didn't return the gesture but curtsied instead. Eustacia laid a hand on her hair to keep the wind from ruffling it. "The three daughters are found. Shouldn't we be leaving for this fairytale land?"

Grimacing, Pennilane turned to Eustacia. "My queen lies beneath the soil of this accursed land and must be rescued.

Much as I saved *your* life."

"But she is dead, surely." Eustacia hugged her arms, glancing around the graveyard. "Why linger here?"

Graddock wailed. "She cannot be dead. Do not stop, Hero."

Cassie leaned and peered into the hole. "I don't understand this. Sweetcake, why can't we go?"

Sweetcake? No one calls Hero a stupid-yet-endearing name but me! Before I could snap at her, Alice spoke. "Valencia started the quest. We cannot return to her world without her."

"But she's dead," whined Eustacia. "She must be. And I'm tired of this place and wish to see this fairyland."

Cassie turned to Eustacia. "But she must be important."

"What would you know, *maid*?" Her tone was biting, and Cassie lowered her head.

I scowled at Eustacia's remark. Though I was furious with Cassie, I thought back to the girls in high school who looked down their noses at me. No one had ever stuck up for me, and clearly no one had ever defended my parallel either. I understood now why Hero wanted her to come along. He had a soft heart for outcasts.

I said, "She's no longer a maid here, you hoity-toity bitch. Cassie's one of us now."

Cassie's mouth dropped open when I came to her defense, and for a moment, I didn't despise her...much. Eustacia gave me a look that I returned in spades. She wanted a catfight? I would beat the cat piss out of her.

Cassie interrupted our glaring contest. "I understand, Miss Vye. Though we could be in another part of Britannia, I feel as though I don't belong." She rubbed her arms up and down with her hands. "Something's wrong here."

"A common occurrence with people who Travel for the first time," said Alice. "But you're right. Travelers report heightened anxiety all the time in Morbidum."

Lenore turned to the mansion. "I know a man who can aid us. When he comes, don't tell anyone I'm the bird. I'll reveal my secret when I'm ready."

She returned to her raven form and flew around the other side of the house to the second floor. Graddock had removed his shirt, much to the delight of Julia and Eustacia, and was drenched in sweat. Hero's shovel struck him on the back. Irritated, Graddock said, "Hero, get out of the hole and let me clear some of this dirt."

The hole was only waist-high when Hero climbed out and brushed off mud from his pants, throwing his shovel aside. Cassie marched to my husband's side and took his arm. I gritted my teeth, refusing to go to his other side, and moved a clump of dirt with the toe of my boot.

Lenore returned and became a woman once more. "I had to appear as a ghost, but the count is on his way." She turned back into the bird and flew over to a nearby bust carved at the top of a tombstone and perched on it. While Graddock removed more soil, a well-dressed man in a black cloak and hiking boots emerged from the house. He ran toward us with a lantern in his hands. "Someone is truly here? Lenore's visit was not a dream? How may I offer my services?"

He had an awesome French accent. Graddock ignored him, but the rest of us regarded the newcomer with interest. The count examined us, his attention on the women the longest. Pennilane's jaw hardened. "If you look at me like that again, I will put out your eyes."

The count said, "Lenore said you were trying to help Valencia."

"You know who she is?" I asked. "Do you know if someone buried her here?"

The count's head swiveled from me to Cassie and back again. Smiling, he bowed. "Twin visions of beauty. Impossible to determine which one of you is the loveliest."

Cassie blushed, but I couldn't be bothered with his nonsense. Since I didn't react, Cupsince eyed her. "Twins would be most interesting..."

I swallowed my disgust. Hero blurted out, "What do you

know about Valencia?"

The count's attention turned to the grave. "She's my lover."

Graddock stopped shoveling, and his head snapped to the man. The raven squawked on the headstone. "Nevermore!"

She didn't really say that, but I couldn't resist.

The count smirked. "She came to me seeking intimacy."

A single tear rolled down Graddock's face. He resumed his digging without speaking.

Hero crossed his arms. "I don't believe it. Who do you think you are?"

The count bowed. "My name is Count Brahm Cupsince, of France, here in the colonies visiting my friend Peter Marstings. The more interesting question is who are all of you, and why are you desecrating my dear friend's grave?"

Oh, cat's piss! A vampire is all we needed now! I asked, "Count? As in Dracula?"

The count touched his chin with his forefinger. "A curious name. It sounds Eastern European, not Western, but I am not familiar with this count. Should I be?"

With Cassie in tow, Hero made his way to me. "We believe someone may have buried our friend Valencia alive in this grave."

The count snorted. "Why should I believe a group of trespassers who are engaged in digging up Lenore's grave?"

The raven transformed into Lenore. The count stepped back in shock as she said, "Because I know something is amiss, Brahm."

The count cowered. "Lenore! Will you haunt me for the rest of my days?"

Lenore pointed to her grave. "I'm very much alive. No questions. Just help them."

At that moment, Graddock's shovel hit wood, and he cried out. "I have reached the casket."

Hero let go of Cassie's hand and dropped to his knees, peering down. "Graddock, punch a hole in the top so she can breathe."

Graddock flipped the shovel so that the top of the handle faced downward. He used the wooden end of the tool like a jackhammer to puncture the coffin lid. Leaning down, he called inside. "Valencia? Valencia, my love."

Hero and Count Cupsince cleared more dirt around the shallow ditch. Hero said, "We'll have to make sure the hole is large enough before we lift out the coffin."

The box wasn't buried deep, and I helped to remove the rest of the dirt. Cassie didn't. Within ten minutes, Graddock and Count Cupsince raised the coffin out of the grave and placed it on the grass beside the hole. Graddock leaped from the shallow pit and ripped open the lid. Inside lay Valencia, eyes closed, arms folded over her chest, still as a statue.

Graddock put his hand on the side of her face. "Valencia?"

She didn't budge. Everyone formed a circle around her, and I held my breath.

Graddock leaned down and listened to her heart. He moaned. "Her heart is not beating."

No one moved to assist Valencia. Time for Sanders to take charge. I kneeled next to Graddock. "Stand aside. I have to give her mouth-to-mouth resuscitation."

Graddock hugged Valencia tight. "No! No! I cannot be too late. She was my second chance when I had lost everything. She was the best of the queens. I was not worthy of her."

I attempted to pry Valencia from him. "Graddock! Let me help her."

Graddock ignored my request. "I have failed you, my queen. I do not deserve to live. I will ask for the executioner's block when I return to Kingdom."

I lost patience with the forlorn idiot. I reached over and grabbed Valencia's arms to pull her away. "Graddock, give her to me! She's— Wait. What's this?"

Someone had scrawled words on Valencia's left arm. I squinted but couldn't make them out in the dim light. The count swung his lantern over, and I read the hastily written message aloud. "Sleeping curse."

The count bent down, studying the writing himself. "Curses now? What manner of people are you?"

"Her left hand is clenched," said Lenore.

Graddock pried an object from her fingers and held it to the light. "'Tis a stone and a red stick."

"The rock is a wishing stone Valencia found in Oz," remarked Hero.

I asked, "Alice, do they have sleeping curses in Morbidum?"

"They're mostly found in Kingdom. You'll find manias here, not sleeping curses."

Graddock wiped away his tears. "I have seen a sleeping curse before. One can mistake it for death, but a sleeping curse preserves the body. The cursed person does not breathe, does not require food, and does not age."

I nodded. "Makes sense. I always wondered how Sleeping Beauty blipsie doodled."

Everyone looked at me, and I gave it right back at them. "Oh, you wondered about it too."

Alice crossed her arms. "No one in Morbidum could cast a sleeping curse."

No one spoke. The wind blew, and the bell rang in the distance. Hero touched his chin. "I think I know what happened."

"What?" I snapped.

Hero pointed at Valencia. "She wished it on herself. She awoke buried underground with the wishing stone and lipstick in her pockets. She was running out of air and had to think of a way to get out of the casket. Instead, she wished herself into a sleeping curse to avoid death, certain we'd come along and find her."

Graddock hugged her tighter. "Surely the cleverest of queens."

Alice gestured to the stone. "But then why not wish herself out of the coffin?"

"My guess is she had one wish," answered Hero. "One shot. If she wished herself above ground, the person who put her here might have caught her a second time. She dropped the matches as a trail to lead us here, then waited for us to rescue her."

I eyed my husband. "Maybe she had another reason."

Cassie asked, "What reason?"

I turned my attention to Graddock. "She knew we would come here and figure out her location with Lenore's help. Maybe Valencia expected us to take her back to Kingdom still under the sleeping curse. There, her true love would awaken her with a kiss. She cursed herself for you, Graddock, not realizing you'd come here for her."

Graddock paled in the lantern light. "You mean...I should kiss her?"

The count rubbed his hands together. "Now this is getting good."

Graddock leaned down to Valencia and brushed a stray strand of hair from her face. "I am not worthy of the title of prince. I am not a soldier and am not renowned for heroic deeds like Roger. Nor am I wise and even-tempered like Danforth. They are two legendary princes."

"Come on, Graddock. They were a farmer and a musician," remarked Alice.

Hero put a steadying hand on Graddock. "Planet once told me those in Kingdom set no limits on who can fall in love. Even a bodyguard and a queen can have a happy ending."

The count turned to Cassie. "I have no idea what's going on, but I like it."

Graddock set Valencia down on the grass and bent over her. He hovered over her, and then he brushed his lips against hers. His sign of affection was over in a blink of the eye. Graddock reared back. He had hoped the queen would open her eyes.

She didn't.

Graddock covered his eyes with his hand. "I am not her true love, and now I have ruined everything for her. I have sullied her character."

Eustacia grunted. "All you did was kiss her."

She was getting on my nerves. Hero said, "His reaction may seem a bit extreme to you, but in Kingdom only lovers are supposed to kiss. And kissing a queen without her permission is a big no-no."

We had all been certain Graddock would awaken her. Stumped, we struggled to think of our next step when the count spoke. "What is the matter with you? Give the woman a real kiss. What you did would turn a frog into a toad, not into a woman. Be passionate, *monsieur*."

Graddock lowered his hand. "I am not a passionate man."

The count folded his arms. "I cannot help you with that."

Graddock was not passionate? Not true. I cleared my throat. "At the risk of making present company really angry. Like really, really angry. Like so pissed off that—"

Hero gritted his teeth. "Spit it out, Sanders."

I said, "You don't give yourself enough credit, Graddock."

Graddock still shook his head.

I blushed, forcing the words out. "Remember Oz? Let yourself go, Graddock. Don't be so uptight."

Thoughtful for a moment, Graddock closed his eyes, and then he lifted and turned the little queen around to face us. He held her under her arms and positioned himself behind her, lowering her to a sitting position. Valencia's head lolled down, eyes shut. Graddock kneeled behind her, hugging her to his breast with one arm. He took his other hand and parted the hair hanging down the back of her neck, massaging the base of her scalp. Graddock pressed his lips to the sensitive skin on her neck.

Valencia's eyes shot open. She took a deep breath and

blinked to come to her senses. Not realizing who was behind her, she focused on us instead of her guard. "Hero and Sanders, you came for me. I knew you would when I made the wish. And I see a second Sanders dressed as a maid but holding Harold's hand. I must have double vision. Lenore! You're here, too. No longer a bird. And I'm still in Morbidum. I thought I'd be revived in Kingdom. Who has saved me? Someone's lips on my neck." She purred the last sentence. Actually purred it.

Valencia pulled away and turned around in one sudden movement. Graddock beamed at her, tears rolling down his cheeks. Valencia squeaked, "You?"

"Me."

She put her hands on either side of his face and flattened his cheeks. She tilted her head and leaned in close, and then halted. "You made me wait."

"I am sorry. I—"

Before he could continue, she lunged forward and kissed him. Her motion knocked him backward until they both landed on the grass. She held the kiss for a long minute and then pulled away. "Don't you *ever* make me wait again."

"Never, on my honor."

"And only me."

"Always you."

Valencia looked over her shoulder at everyone and blushed. "I suppose we have a lot to explain. Some of you I haven't met yet, but I can guess who you are, except for the duplicate of Sanders." She pointed at Julia and Eustacia. "The two other daughters, right?"

They nodded.

"A woman named Zariah drugged and buried me, but I'm not concerned about her right now," said Valencia over Lenore's gasp. "We must be off to Kingdom."

Valencia pressed her hand to the base of her neck. "Oh, I need my ruby necklace from the mansion first. Wait for me. I shall return promptly."

She hurried off, and Hero asked, "Is a necklace important now?"

Graddock watched her rush out of the graveyard as the bell rang again. "Indeed, it is."

"I'll go help her." I glared at Cassie. "Stay away from my husband. Someone fill in Nosferatu about what's going on."

I caught up with Valencia when she emerged from a room on the second floor with the jewelry in her hands. I asked, "What's the deal with the necklace, Valencia?"

She didn't answer my question but looked down the hallway at a figure rushing up the stairs behind me. I turned around, and a lithe woman in a nightgown approached us. Valencia hissed, "Zariah!"

Zariah put a hand in the pocket of her robe. "How are you here?"

Valencia's nostrils flared, and she raised her voice. "How dare you kidnap, drug, and then *bury* me! My friends are here now, and the count knows what you did. I saw the butler's body in the woodcutter's cabin, though you thought I was unconscious. 'Tis further evidence of your misdeeds. I won't waste any more time with you. Go to the constable. You have no choice."

Zariah threw back her shoulders. "You are such a naïve creature. Always talking of surrendering. I don't plan to do anything." She produced a revolver from her robe. "Your friends will find you and your companion dead." She nodded at me. "This one will have a bullet hole in her chest. You will have one in your temple. Murder meets suicide."

Zariah aimed her gun at me, and Valencia and I raised our hands into the air. People had pointed guns at Hero in our prior adventures, not me.

Another woman emerged from a room behind Zariah, distracting our adversary. The newcomer wore a nightgown and a hat with a veil. I didn't know what the hell was up with her but didn't care at that moment. The veiled woman screamed, "Zariah!"

Zariah's loss of focus allowed Valencia a couple of seconds to slip her hand in her pocket and retrieve something. The queen then lifted her hands back up. "Zariah, lower the gun, and let's talk. Beatrice, return to your room."

Zariah put her back to the wall to keep us in her purview, directing her gun from me to Valencia. "No more time for talking. I don't know how you survived. I was careful. I made sure everyone was asleep when I carried you out to Lenore's grave and buried you."

Beatrice's veil fluttered. "You're insane."

"Insanity? No." Zariah licked her top lip. "This Valencia isn't one of us. She talks of spells and magic items. She's not from this world. I heard of these other worlds during my time in the circus. Beatrice, attend to me. Valencia is a creature in the form of a young woman. She came out of the darkness when we needed someone for the séance. What happened? Murder."

"You are the murderer," snapped Valencia. "You buried me. All because of your misguided love for Lenore."

"How dare you judge me for whom I love?" Zariah snorted.

My cheeks burned. "Oh, hold on a minute. You don't get to play the judgment card on me, missy. My friend Tanya has a wife."

Valencia looked as incensed as I was. "And my dear friend Lyken prefers men. I don't think any less of him. The truth is you couldn't bear Lenore's rejection. Even if Lenore fancied women, she wouldn't love a killer like you."

Beatrice advanced toward Zariah. "Zariah, let me help you."

"I don't need your help!"

Beatrice grabbed the netting in front of her face. "Look at me, or I'll raise my veil."

Zariah's eyes went round. She glanced at Beatrice while keeping her gun trained on Valencia. "You wouldn't! Beatrice, I'm the victim—"

Suddenly, something flared in Valencia's hand. My brilliant friend had retrieved a match. And a match in the hands of Valencia is a weapon of its own. Valencia flicked the match at Zariah, and it flipped through the air and landed on her hair, aided by both the queen's luck and skill.

The fire didn't catch but served as a distraction. Zariah tried to snuff the match, pointing the revolver at the ceiling. I took advantage of the situation. I released my pent-up hostility and punched Zariah on the chin. The gun went off when she fell backward, looking upside down at Creepy Veiled Lady. Beatrice stepped forward, lifted the heavy lace, and blew a little bit of air on Zariah's face.

Zariah whimpered, "No, Beatrice. What have...?" Her eyes rolled up, and the tongue of fire on the ends of her hair snuffed out.

Beatrice, Valencia, and I gathered around the murderer, and I nudged her with my shoe. Veil back in place, Beatrice stooped down and set a hand on Zariah's cheek. "She'll be out for the rest of the night. My breath can kill, but small amounts will only render people unconscious."

Ooh. I'd love to get a sample of her breath and analyze it, but this was neither the place nor the time. Valencia briefly explained the details of Allan's murder and instructed Beatrice to fetch the constable. "Zariah was right about one thing," said Valencia. "I don't call Morbidum my home. My companion and I must leave, but will you refrain from telling anyone about us?"

Beatrice took Valencia's hand. "Your secret is safe with me, my dear. Go, and I shall summon the constable."

Valencia and I hurried down the stairs and out the front door. I said, "Lyken's gay?"

"He's happy, but my guess is the meaning of that word differs on Earth. We tried to pair Snow White with him before we knew. What a mess, but I'm glad he told us. I find it disconcerting how Earth labels people, Sanders. To me, he's Lyken, my friend. That's the only label I need."

Her observation made me reflect again on the differences between Earth and Kingdom. We hurried to the graveyard where the rest of our party waited for us. Valencia slipped on the necklace. "We're ready."

Cupsince's gaze lingered on Cassie and me. "I do so love beauty and being in the company of women. Allow me to offer my services to whoever needs them. I can accompany you on this Traveling, did you call it?"

I awarded him points for calling me beautiful, especially in present company. Hero's jaw hardened. "You're not going anywhere."

"Would you mind if he came with us?" asked Lenore. "I'm a bit nervous about Traveling, and he's an excellent swordsman and a friend."

Hero, Alice, and Graddock all protested at the same time. When the clamor died down, I eyed the count. "He's a fighter, and we could use the help."

Hero frowned. "Is this your way of getting back at me? Inviting Dracula to Kingdom?"

Alice interjected. "He's not Dracula. I've met *that* man. But this guy's a native and may not Travel across worlds."

Valencia caressed her necklace. "I have one of my intuitions about him, and I think he should join us."

Alice threw her hands in the air. "I give up! Should I send out invitations for everyone in Morbidum to accompany us?"

I was about to suggest taking along the poison-breath lady too, but Alice's face was cherry-soda red. Valencia said, "We are wasting time. We need to hurry back to Kingdom. Hero, mount Bree behind your wife. The rest of us, join hands."

Hero moved to mount the stick horse, but Cassie fastened onto him. Hero called over to the aristocrat. "Count? Will you take my place?"

Count Cupsince sidled over. "It would be my honor to escort your wife's beautiful younger sister to this Kingdom world." He extended his hand to Cassie.

Cassie held onto Hero's shoulder, but my husband pulled away. "Please, take his hand."

The maid sighed. "Fine."

Hero mounted the stick pony behind me, and my good boy Bree enlarged from his toy state. My steed then galloped away from the graveyard while everyone else joined hands.

30 - CONFESSION

When Penta approached Celeste's magical study, she had to hold onto the doorway or risk stumbling into the room. Celeste, sitting at her desk and reading a fairy-sized tome, looked up wide-eyed. Instinctively, the pixie wrinkled her nose, but her reaction didn't matter to the queen. Penta had decided to speak to Celeste before starting drinking.

Penta cleared her throat. "I came to tell you something important. If my sisters and I die tomorrow, I want you to run and hide. Save as many people as you can from those odious hags. Resist them, but only defend. That is a royal command."

"Yes, my queen."

Penta stepped in and shut the door behind her. She leaned against it. "This wasn't my only purpose in coming here. I need to tell you something woman to woman, so please do not interrupt me."

Celeste closed her book and gave Penta her full attention.

"Before I became queen and I was a barmaid, and your sister, Planet, worked for me, an elf came to my tavern. He ordered an expensive port but couldn't pay for it. I was furious, but he offered something in return." Penta removed her black gloves, revealing her silver hands. "Fully flexible hands."

Penta's hands shone in Celeste's magical lamplight. "My original hands had motion thanks to a magical friend of mine, but they were stiff, and my friend had to keep applying the spell. I knew I was one of the prophesied queens. With the hands the elf offered, I could fulfill my destiny as queen—or so I thought. Before I struck the deal, your sister, being the busybody she was, listened in and recognized my patron. She called him a delfling."

Celeste gasped. "Demon elf."

"Yes. Planet told me not to make the deal but run him out instead. She didn't know I was a princess when she instructed me, didn't know what was at stake, so I ignored her. I took the hands, and he cast a spell to affix them onto my wrists."

Penta said, "Planet and I had quite a row. She said I had treated her the way everyone did, thinking she was a silly pixie. She had a point. She left that night, saying she had lost faith in me."

Tears rolling down her face, Penta lowered her head. "The next time Alice visited, I showed her my new hands. She was horrified. Alice told me hands like these are commonplace in Oz. They belong to a set of residents who identify as tin woodpeople. Former Travelers turned brigands sneak into Oz, cut off body parts, and sell them to other worlds." Penta stopped for a moment to regain her composure.

"So that I might hide my shame, Alice helped me cover the tin with silver. But the coating only made my condition worse. I can see my reflection in my hands, and it reminds me of how I let down your sister. Because Planet left, she met Hero and joined him on his adventure. And due to her love for Hero, she died. If she had stayed in my tavern, safe and sound, your sister would be alive today."

Celeste stared at the queen, speechless.

"You understand now," said Penta. "You have served the person who caused your sister's death all these years ago."

"No, I have not," spoke Celeste, loud and clear. "I have served Penta, one of the greatest queens in Kingdom's history."

"No, I—"

Celeste cut her off, something she had never done before. "I know in my heart Planet was destined for Hero. He would have shown up at your tavern, the closest inn to where he arrived in Kingdom. There, he would have met Planet and have fallen in love. As certain as a wyvern flies eft at sunrise, they were meant to be together. Do not blame yourself."

Penta put her gloves back on her hands. "Do you honestly believe Planet and Hero would've fallen in love?"

"I do."

Penta let out a long sigh. She opened the door to slip back out, but Celeste stopped her. "Yet, my queen, you are guilty of something."

"And what is that?"

"You should have listened to Planet about the delfling instead of thinking you were right," said Celeste.

Penta bit her lip at Celeste's audacity. The fairy opened the book and returned to her studying. "Good night."

31 - MAGNUS

Sondra

When we appeared in Kingdom, I saw that those of us who were Traveling for the first time were experiencing a variety of reactions. I was amused to witness the count's knees wobble and then give way. Lenore, with her bitchin' plumage, popped into her bird form and flew in a circle. Eustacia and Julia, having Traveled before, handled the situation better than they had the first time. I was still itching to slap Julia, but now was not the moment.

Though she had Traveled once before, Cassie dropped to her knees and retched again. Ha! Served her right for trying to steal Hero away. Her chunk-blowing distracted the count from his predicament, and he walked over and stroked her back to help her regain her composure.

I closed my eyes and sensed the current of magic floating through the air. I relaxed, and my pixie wings appeared. "There. That's better."

Eustacia cried out and scrambled away from me while the count swore in French. Cassie approached me, hand reaching out toward my wings. "How do you have wings? Can I have wings?"

My wings fluttered at her touch. "No, you can't. And without magic, wings are useless to humans. Biologically, our bodies aren't equipped for flight."

Cassie examined my petal-shaped purple and green wings. "You can't fly?"

"Of course I can fly, but it's my magic that allows me to fly, not my wings. Don't be silly. If I could use these wings to fly, my shoulders couldn't move in the directions they can currently. The muscles for my wings would crowd out my arm muscles. And I'd probably have to lose a lot of body weight to get off the ground. No way could these small wings provide enough lift to counteract gravity. Unfortunately, my internal organs weigh—"

Hero interrupted, "Sanders, you're over-explaining again." He continued in a lower voice. "I still think your wings help you fly."

I glared at him. "Squids fly, Hero. Not people."

"Wait, squids fly?" he asked.

I turned to Cassie. "And I didn't get my wings when a bell chimed. How I got them is a long story."

"I'd like to hear it." Cassie blinked expectantly.

Her sincerity took me by surprise. "Another time."

We had arrived in a place called the Circle of Counsel, the midpoint of Kingdom, where large stone seats faced each other. Valencia peered west toward the royal palace and touched her chin. "What I wouldn't give for Penta's teleportation ability right now. I wonder if Glinda made it here?"

The instant Valencia said Glinda's name, a slip of paper appeared in the air in front of her and floated toward the ground. Catching sight of it in the moonlight, Valencia snatched it in midair and read it aloud. "Will join you in less than an hour. Stay where you are. Glinda."

I rubbed Bree's handsome face while Lenore restored herself to her human form. The raven woman observed the plains surrounding the circle. "We're in fairyland now?"

Before anyone could answer, Julia hugged her arms. "Are we safe here?"

Valencia placed a hand on Julia's shoulder. "Yes, we're here and safe for the moment, but we need to talk to a magician before we reunite with my sister queens. While we wait, we should introduce ourselves. I shall go first."

Once the eye-rolling pleasantries were made, Valencia took Graddock's arm and draped it around her shoulders. She then described the entire tale from start to finish for the newcomers. Alice recounted our journey to Cixxes, excluding most of what happened to me at The Soul. Hero described what had unfolded in Janay. Lucky ducky. I noticed he skipped over Pennilane's little tryst, though.

While Count Cupsince was convinced he had teleported somewhere, he maintained he was still in Morbidum. He believed my wings were human-made. To convince him our stories were true, Pennilane let her whiskers grow, and I soared into the air, alighting with a bow.

"Which brings us to the present," said Valencia. "You three are the witches' daughters, and you have powers to defeat the coven."

Hero chewed on a blade of grass, crickets chirping in the background. "And how do we do that precisely? We don't have a plan."

"Hero, we'll devise a plan when we return to the palace and inform my sisters of what we've learned." Valencia crossed her arms. "If only Glinda would appear."

As Valencia said Glinda's name, another note materialized and drifted to the ground. The queen picked it up and read it aloud. "Will return in fifteen minutes. Glinda."

Valencia approached Count Cupsince with Graddock and touched his arm. "We had a conversation last night concerning a certain friend."

Cupsince's attention darted to Graddock and back to Valencia, eyes widening with revelation. "I take it my advice is no longer needed."

"All I ever wanted was advice. Do you see why now, Count?"

He put his hands on Graddock's and Valencia's arms and moved them closer. "I may be more of a romantic than you think. I wish you both blessings."

This scene reminded me of my own unfinished business with Cassie and Hero. I marched to Hero and Cassie and grabbed their arms. "We three have something to discuss."

I didn't want to talk about this at all but now was as good a time as any. We had a few minutes to ourselves, and Cassie was irritating the hell out of me. And then I thought of the dream, which had been hanging over us like a cloud itching to rain.

After we three had walked out of earshot of everyone else, I said, "We all had the same dream two nights ago. Julia's power triggered it in me. And it extended to you." I indicated Hero. "And *you*," I added, indicating Cassie. I emphasized my last "you" with the narrowed eyes I reserved for our villains, and for Hero when he leaves the toilet paper roll empty.

Cassie put her hands on her hips, mimicking my style. How dare she! She said, "You're awfully hostile to your parallel."

I stiffened. "That you're my parallel makes the betrayal that much deeper."

"You think I am stealing him. I'm not, Sondra." That she used my real name didn't escape me. "I was destined for Harold, but he met you first."

"Are you for real? Maybe my being first is destiny too." I glared.

Hero said, "Perhaps it—"

Cassie poked me on the collarbone. Ouch. She said, "Planet was first. You were second, and I'm third."

Hero tried again. "But if you—"

"This isn't Spin the Bottle, Cassie! Harold isn't instantly attracted to the person he meets last. Poor Planet died! I didn't steal Harold from her."

Cassie crossed her arms. "But the baby, Sondra. The baby."

I turned away my head. I knew this argument was leading to the final scene with the infant. Hero licked his lips. "I've been thinking. The baby could be yours, Cassie, and not mine. The dream was rather vague."

Cassie shied back as if Hero had said something nasty. "But we were holding it on the couch together." She pointed at me. "She's the one who barged in."

Hero kicked at a piece of dirt. "That doesn't mean it's our child, Cassie. Who knows? Maybe the baby was Sondra's and mine?"

And though Hero didn't know it, his words squeezed my lungs with icy fingers. I took a deep breath. "Harold, I have something I should tell you. I—"

And who decided to show up at the moment I was about to confess? Glinda rode our way on a gust of wind. She stepped off and beckoned for everyone to gather around her. I would have to tell Hero later about what happened in Cixxes, and in a way, the interruption was fine with me. I didn't want Cassie around when I spoke to my husband.

As the three of us walked back to the others, Glinda observed the daughters and the count with a curious expression. "Who are these people? Where did you go?" I forgot she had erased her memory.

Instead of waiting for an answer, Glinda held up her hand. "Don't tell me. I have been focusing on a different problem. Namely, why don't the witches die when they are killed?"

Valencia asked, "What have you learned?"

Glinda's eyes flashed. "Something important. Fortunately, I know where demons keep the dark archives! I will tell you how I broke into it some other time. I was lucky to escape with my spirit intact, but the risk was worth it. The witches are performing a ritual called Magnus."

"What's Magnus?" asked Hero.

Glinda clasped her hands. "Magnus is a profane spell cast to prolong a mortal life. Once enacted, the witch must tempt a pure soul to murder her. The spell acts at the point of death. Just before the first murder is complete, the magic plucks the recipient from her agony and extends her life by one year. The second time by ten years. And the third time, one hundred years. The witches must have cast it on themselves."

Valencia put her hands to her mouth. "Rose Red."

Pennilane added, "And the dwarves."

Hero's shoulders slumped. "So, the witches have already added eleven years to their lives."

Valencia lowered her hands and stroked her chin, calculating. "They want us to kill them to activate the spell the third time. Then they will want to stay in Kingdom for one hundred and eleven years and outlive all of us."

Glinda said, "Yes, and I think they will do anything to lure the three queens of Kingdom into being the ones to attempt the murder. If the rulers of Kingdom fulfill the requirements of Magnus, they score a double victory. They live one hundred and eleven years, and the monarchs will have brought this misfortune upon their people. The queens will never forgive themselves."

Valencia crossed her arms. "My sisters shall never kill them."

Glinda clasped her hands. "I'm afraid the witches are doing everything to coerce your sisters to do just that. Before I knew about Magnus, your sister Penta commanded me to refrain from arguing with her, Helga, or Cinderella on the witches' punishment. As I'm here at their invitation and didn't want her to expel me from Kingdom, I acquiesced."

Valencia shook her head. "She would want to know."

Glinda nodded. "I agree, but your sister won't talk to me, fearing I'll sway her from killing the hags. Valencia, the witches kidnapped Princess Beauty."

Valencia's eyes widened. "No! Tell me it isn't true."

"It is. Cinderella and Helga will defer to your sister's judgment. The witches will do anything, anything at all, to force your three sisters to try to murder them. When people are desperate, they do foolish things." Glinda's eyes settled on Cassie. Interesting.

Valencia received the warning loud and clear. "We must go. We must return to the palace immediately."

Glinda stepped in front of Valencia. "Before we do, I must inform you of their state of mind. Penta has been frenzied since the hags took Beauty. Your sister Helga has received Cusp."

"Cusp!" exclaimed Valencia. "What a boon for her!"

"Helga believes herself corrupted beyond hope and now has received a weapon of significant power. I fear what she may try to do with the holiest of holy blades in her hands."

"And Cinderella?" asked Valencia.

"Cinderella frets unceasingly about her hidden child. Your sisters need you right now."

Hero rubbed his chin with his knuckle. "Hold on. Right now, the witches are trying to make the queens attempt to kill them the third time. Glinda, can we consult in private without you for a moment? I have an idea."

Glinda nodded and walked out of earshot.

Hero turned to us. "If the coven suspects their daughters are in Kingdom, the witches will kill them. But if we find the hags first, they won't recognize their daughters, and we'll be able to approach them."

Valencia shook with excitement. "Excellent, Hero. We'll warn my sisters while we form a plan to infiltrate the witches' coven."

Hero paced back and forth. "But if we tell the other queens about Magnus, your sisters will back off, and the witches will sense something is up. If they figure out we know about the daughters, they won't trust anyone to come close. The hags will read someone's mind and learn our plan. They'll try to murder their daughters, and we'll lose our only leverage. However, if we keep what we know from the queens, your sisters will continue to fight them, and the crones will think they have the upper hand. If they're overconfident, the three daughters can present themselves to the coven."

Eustacia reared back. "You mean…meet our mothers?"

My hubby was in his element. He regarded Julia, Eustacia, and Lenore. "Yes. Each of you has a special ability. I believe your abilities are the witches' undoing, and they know it. By abandoning you to different worlds, your mothers completed their apprenticeship to the devil and became pure evil, but they could've left you anywhere. Why keep you at such a distance?"

"Because the daughters can harm them," said Cassie.

Hero pointed at her. "Exactly."

I grimaced. "I was going to say that. But how will the daughters defeat their mothers?"

Hero bowed his head. "I haven't figured it out yet."

I waved Glinda back to our circle. "We have the start of a plan, but is it possible the witches will read our minds?"

Glinda shook her head. "Mind-reading is a costly spell. They'll only expend the energy on those they believe are a threat. In their arrogance, they wouldn't pay attention to any of you except Valencia. And me, which is why I keep erasing my memory."

Hero said, "Except for Valencia, we're all safe to be around them. Including the daughters."

Glinda looked back at the castle. "We don't have much time. Valencia's sisters are meeting the witches tomorrow to discuss terms, but I've learned from Sylvia and Rose Red that the queens are secretly planning to kill them."

Again, my husband paced around the site. "We can work with that. When the witches arrive at the castle, we have to pretend we're on the hags' side."

Appalled, Valencia stepped back. "My sisters will never believe I turned against them."

Hero stopped walking and frowned at the queen. "Which is why you must remain hidden."

Harold

Glinda disguised us so we could spend the night at the Inn of Five. As a bonus, she also conjured glasses for Sanders. The Good Witch said she would return in the morning and teleport us to the royal castle in time for the queens' encounter with the witches.

The party separated, and Sanders and I went to our room for the night. I asked her about what had happened on Cixxes, but Sanders only shook her head. "Not yet, Harold."

She didn't want me to hold her. Heck, she didn't want me in the room at all. We spent the first hour in silence. I tried to think of a way to defeat the witches while Sanders reflected on another subject, apparent by the expression on her face.

We lay in bed, next to each other, lost in our thoughts. I decided to make conversation to put Sanders at ease. I knew giving her a chance to explain a bit of science worked to relax my wife. "If you don't use your wings to fly, why have them?"

Sanders didn't make eye contact and spoke in a monotone resembling the speech of a bored college professor. "Pixies are small. Wings are defense mechanisms to tell larger predators to lay off. I suspect they evolved from the soup of all Kingdom life forms. However, the number of chromosomes existing in beings here is higher than Earth's *homo sapiens*, allowing for countless possibilities."

"Fascinating."

"Wings also serve as visual stimulation to attract a mate. That's why so many pictures of pixies with their wings expanded are of them nude."

I highly doubted artists depicted pixies nude in an

effort to be scientifically accurate.

"Can you explain all of Kingdom's magic with science?" I asked.

"No. Magic and science can be found side by side in this world. Gravity, chemistry, all the building blocks of matter exists here, but so does magic. I don't limit myself, scientifically speaking, to think of something as this or that. I'd rather think in terms of this *and* that. I find inclusivity far more insightful."

I pondered this when, to my surprise, Sanders put her head on my shoulder. "What time is it?"

"Around ten o'clock?"

"Hold me."

I wrapped my arms around Sanders and kissed her on the ear. My wife took a deep breath and recounted the lachrymose events of the day before. She wouldn't let me interrupt, so I listened in shock.

After she finished, I hugged her closer. "We can use magic. Celeste can fix this."

Sanders wiped her eyes. "Always thinking of fixing it. Just listen to me, will you?"

"I'm listening." I cleared my throat. "But I think she'll be able to help."

"Harold!" Sanders pulled away and lay on her side. "You overheard what Glinda told me. A fertility spell is an advanced incantation, and Glinda is more powerful than Celeste and doesn't want to try it. Besides..."

"Besides?"

Perhaps your destiny is with Cassie."

I regarded her through tear-filled eyes. "Absolutely not. How does that solve anything?"

Sanders sighed. "I admit, I'm not thinking straight. But, Hero, I'm a galaxy away from rational now."

I looked her in the eye. "I would have to be—I don't know the right word—wicked, I guess—to abandon you. If this is our fate, and our family is only you and me, then so be it."

Tears slipped down her cheeks. She put her index finger on my face and wiped away a similar teardrop. "Maybe we could adopt. We talked about it, but perhaps it's time we seriously consider it."

I used my thumb to rub her cheek. "Adoption. Foster care. Without children we're still us. We're still a family." I put my hand under her chin. "I love you. For better or worse, remember?"

She placed her hand on my cheek. For a moment, she gave me a wistful look, and then the expression metamorphosed into thoughtfulness. She narrowed her eyes. "You said something important."

I thought back. "About your wings?"

"No, you said you would have had to be wicked to abandon me." She paused and looked off at a point in space. "Hero, what if we cause the witches to turn on each other?"

I liked where she was going. "And why would they turn traitor?"

She placed her attention on me again. "Because they're wicked. They don't trust each other. Loyalty and honor aren't strong points for wicked witches."

And taking Sanders' nascent idea, lying in bed at the Inn of Five, Sanders and I devised a plan. We discussed it for ten minutes, replacing one proposal with a better one, sitting up and staring at each other, complimenting the other's contribution. The scheme had nearly congealed when a scream from outside broke the stillness of the night.

We leaped out of bed, and my wonderful wife turned pixie and flew through the window. I climbed from the same window and jumped to the ground. When I rose to my feet, I followed my wife around a corner of the building.

Back there, a troll, olive-skinned and eight feet tall with stringy black hair tied back, roared a horrid noise through a protuberant mouth and swung a club toward Count Cupsince. The club was twice as large as the count's weapon, and it missed the man by inches. Cassie was gesticulating like a hypnotist who had just drunk eight cups of coffee. "Yes, that's right. I'm a legendary pixie about to spread my wings."

When the troll saw my wife, he stepped back, mouth agape. He pointed his club at her. "Who is she then?"

Sanders crossed her arms. "Go on, beat it."

I pulled up short of the creature. "If you hurt anyone, I'm going to kill you."

The troll grunted and backed off with his eyes glued on my wife. "Sanders the Pixie."

"Yeah," said Sanders, not debating her name. "And I'm pissed."

The troll stumbled-ran back to the hill and over it while Valencia and Graddock, in disguises, exited the inn. In the darkness, I almost didn't recognize them.

I turned to Cassie. "Did he hurt you?"

She ignored me, rushing to Cupsince and hugging him, nearly knocking him down. "Thank you."

Sanders landed and returned to human size. "Hey, what about us?"

Cassie released Cupsince and turned around, her cheeks flushed. "He saved me while you took your sweet time."

Sanders balled her fists, but Cassie grimaced. "Thank you, too," Cassie said. "I'm surprised. I thought you'd let him hurt me. You hate me."

Sanders put a hand on her hip. "If you'd leave my husband alone, we'd get along fine. You're my parallel for God's sake. Believe it or not, you and I have a lot in common."

I took a deep breath. "What the hell are you doing out here so late at night?"

Cassie shuffled her feet. "The count and I were talking on the ground floor of the inn. We decided to go outside for some fresh air."

"Why outside?" I gestured to the field behind me. "I told you Kingdom was dangerous. It's not all kitten milk and wayward butterflies."

Cassie straightened her frock. "Your concern for me is

unwarranted."

Sanders stepped toward her. "Then stop pretending to be a helpless ding-dong. You're giving Planet and me a bad name."

I put my hand on Sanders' arm. "She's scared of going back to Janay as a maid."

Cassie went pale. "I'll end up destitute. I have no skills to speak of."

Sanders rolled her eyes. "Cassie, do you believe Hero and I would send you back without helping you? You're like a sister to me. Or a cousin. Or the relative no one will tell you about."

"Sanders!" I cautioned.

Sanders said, "With a little bit of foreknowledge of the future, you could build a fund. When you have enough money, you'll hire someone to educate you, and then you'll be on your way."

"But I'm not smart," protested Cassie.

Sanders' wings beat with agitation. "You think you're not intelligent because you've grown up a poor woman in a world where education is mostly available for men. Trust me, we share genes. Knowledge doesn't come easy, but if you try, you can learn anything."

Cassie looked unconvinced until I jerked my thumb at my wife. "She has more education than I do."

Cassie's eyes lit up. "Really?"

"Let's discuss this some other time," Valencia said. "I haven't been able to sleep. I keep going over different strategies in my mind. Hero, I disagree with you about warning my sisters. I think Sanders should turn me invisible. Then, I will enter the castle to tell my sisters about Magnus."

I shook my head. "Hear me out. Sanders and I have a better plan."

32 - AN INTERRUPTED
BATTLE

Penta led her family and Celeste into a small antechamber across the hall from the throne room, sensing the
hesitation from the two princes, Roger and Danforth.
The princes followed the monarchs, scuffling their boots on
the floor. Danforth shut the door after everyone had entered.

Penta gestured to a standing mirror in the center of the
room like a shopkeeper presenting valuable merchandise. Celeste raised her hand and twisted it, as if swatting away a
fly, and the mirror clouded over, then displayed the castle's
throne room.

Penta touched the glass. "In the throne room is the twin
of this mirror. Whatever it reflects will display here and show
you the battle in the throne room. As we discussed, you men
are to remain here while we fight the witches—unless we call
for you."

Danforth crossed his arms and leaned against the wall. "I don't like this. You will need every ally when you face them."

Helga set a hand on Danforth's arm. "Roger and Cinderella know they cannot be in battle together. If one of my sisters…" She paused, then said, "Falls…then the rest of us will do their duty as queens of Kingdom and continue to fight. If the witches kill you, they pierce my heart as well. We try to be queens first, but we are also wives and mothers. We cannot allow it."

"I would instruct Beauty to remain in this room too." Penta lowered her head. "If she were here."

The two married queens kissed their husbands, then the trio of monarchs and the fairy left the chamber, crossed the corridor, and entered the throne room. The enormous chamber hosted the five thrones raised on a dais. Penta swallowed down a golf-ball-sized lump in her throat when she eyed Snow White's chair.

The throne room, the largest enclosed space in the castle, had been cleared out of its other furniture and decorations. At intervals throughout the room, iron stands bearing illuminated glass spheres lit the hall. The mirror to the princes' room stood to the side, and a small, standing rack held a few weapons. The three queens took positions in front of their thrones and readied themselves for battle. Penta set her hand on the hilt of a dagger with a twisted blade, and Helga had her ball-and-chain flail with Cusp in its sheath. They waited while Celeste turned pixie-sized and flew above them. All eyes focused on the double doors leading into the room.

Penta ground her teeth, eyes focused on the entrance, leaning forward one moment and back the next. She had confidence Cusp was renown throughout many worlds, though not on Earth. Was she leading her sisters into a battle they could not win and dooming Kingdom?

They heard the sound of something toppling outside. The witches entered not long after the disturbance, accompanied by two allies, surprising the Kingdom monarchs.

Picana—dressed in a gray tunic and black leggings tucked into ragged, leather boots—had acquired a black bird somewhere since the last time they had met. The witch's familiar perched on her shoulder and glared at the queens with red eyes. Tomana wore her battered, shabby black coat, which trailed on the ground, and Mya had on a funeral shroud with a hole cut out to reveal her face.

Penta drew in a sharp breath at the two other women who had followed them into the room. With a haughty expression, the first carried herself like a lady, her full, brown hair swaying behind her. She wore a pale-blue, floor-length dress with cinched wrists. Her eyes blazed with hatred toward the queens. Her hunched-over companion hop-stepped beside her. This female wore a bonnet on her head, covering all but a few wisps of dark hair. Dressed in patched-together pieces of disparate clothing, the stooped woman kept her eyes down while she twisted a curl of her tresses with her forefinger.

Penta hadn't accounted for extra enemies. They didn't appear to be prisoners—a good sign—but she wondered what role the witches would have them play in the upcoming battle.

Picana noticed the high queen's nervousness and laughed. "Two defectors from your realm joined us in the middle of the night. Meet Eustacia Vye. She aspires to become a great witch. The other is her slave, Julia. Aren't you pleased to meet them?"

Eustacia peered down her nose at the queens, and her servant's head jolted at the word "slave."

Penta released a long, steady breath. "We will deal with them later. I heard a sound before you entered."

Picana brushed rubble off her shoulder. "Oh, that! Eustacia told us of your so-called heroes as we entered. She said they were the statues of the pixie Planet and the lovers Sanders and Hero. We destroyed them on our way here. No heroes shall be saving you this time, I'm afraid."

Celeste balled her hands into fists. "You shall answer to

me for those statues! They are my family!"

"Pay? Fear not, dimwitted fairy. Our magic reserves are deep. Witness." Picana twirled her fourth finger, and the plaque holding Snow White's name affixed to her throne cracked in two. Half of the placard fell to the ground.

"We can restore nameplates and statues." Penta gripped the hilt of her knife, knuckles whitening. "But the lives you've taken are another matter."

Helga and Cinderella stepped next to the eldest queen. Penta continued, "My sisters and I are of one mind now."

While Picana and Mya chuckled at Penta's declaration, Tomana's expression remained dour. She leaned away from the other two, a scowl affixed to her face. "Are you ready to agree to our terms and surrender?"

Picana eyed Tomana as if she had spoken out of turn. Penta stepped forward, spine straight, chin upraised. "We shall never surrender to you."

Mya danced in place. "Now for us, a fight we'll have. Your next home, an unmarked grave."

Cinderella muttered, "Doesn't even rhyme."

Color rose in Picana's cheeks. "You cannot possibly think you will win."

With her free hand, Helga unsheathed her sword. "This is Cusp, the holy sword of the archangel, and capable of killing anything mortal and wounding the immortal. It shall protect me from your spells."

The witches' expressions didn't change. Penta had hoped they might step back in fear, possibly flee. She knew the chances they would retreat were small, but her hope died at their impassive reaction to Helga's weapon. Perhaps where they came from, they didn't know Cusp's power? Their lack of familiarity would be to their detriment.

Tomana raised her hands and curled her fingers, preparing a spell. "Well then…let us have at it."

Before they started, someone charged into the room, pushing the door open with the force of a strong wind. The wood hit the wall with a sharp sound that echoed through the chamber.

Roger stepped back from the mirror, hand on his sword. "'Tis Hero! What is he doing here?"

Danforth never had a chance to answer him. The door swung open in the princes' room, and four women slipped inside: Rose Red, Sylvia, Alice, and Pennilane—still in her Janay garments. Alice addressed the princes. "We need your help. Form a circle."

Before they could protest, Alice took Danforth's hand and Rose Red's. Rose grabbed Roger's hand, and Sylvia gripped his other hand, closing the circle and leaving Pennilane outside. Alice made sure all hands were linked and nodded. "Now."

Before Alice could complete her action, Roger tugged free of Sylvia's grasp. "What is going on?"

Alice screamed, "No!"

But it was too late. Sylvia, who understood the danger of a broken circle when Traveling, grabbed Rose Red's hand. Danforth, Sylvia, Alice, and Rose Red vanished in a blink.

Pennilane turned toward the prince. "Prince Roger. That was unwise."

Roger crossed his arms. "Where did they go?"

Pennilane eyed the mirror and watched Hero step into the throne room. "Everyone knows full well if Helga or Cinderella is in danger, their princes would never stand by. We came to ensure you do not interfere."

As Hero strolled across the throne room, he held up his hand. "Stop!"

For Penta, creases in her forehead replaced her small grin at Hero's entrance. He strutted into the room wearing a stiff white shirt, mauve waistcoat, and breeches with black boots. A blue pixie wearing glasses floated in behind him, enlarged to form Sanders, and stepped in stride next to her husband. Sanders' outfit of a silver jumpsuit with lights zipping up and down the sides stood out like a bichon frise at a sphynx cat reunion. A gentleman with smartly parted hair dressed in a cape entered the doorway next with his rapier drawn.

The queen didn't recognize the swordsman, but the person trailing him caused her to blink multiple times. Sanders, dressed as a maid, snuck in, eyes enlarged. If the second Sanders surprised Penta, the last figure to march into the throne room doubled her astonishment. A seven-foot-tall female knight covered in golden armor with a helmet whose top was an upside-down funnel lumbered in behind the maid. Hero and Sanders had brought a fighter, a hero from another world, to help them.

Penta expected Hero to address the witches, but he surprised her by stopping in front of the queens and ignoring the hags. "Penta, Helga, Cinderella. Surrender to the witches immediately."

For a moment, the only sounds were Sanders' and Celeste's wings rustling in the air. Penta had to compose herself and make sure she had heard him right, that she hadn't mistaken his command. "Hero? What are you doing here?"

"I'm here to negotiate the terms of surrender."

The witches, also shocked by the third party's presence, regained their humor. Mya laughed and clapped. Picana grinned, but Tomana narrowed her eyes and spoke to the eldest queen. "What trick are you playing on us?"

Penta lowered her knife. "'Tis not my trick, I assure you. Hero, upon my life, I will never surrender to them."

Hero took a deep breath. His steady voice rang throughout the chamber. "Penta, listen to me. You can't win. We found this out in Oz. They are more powerful than you can imagine. I won't have you throw your life away."

"Where's Valencia?" asked Helga.

Hero kept his eyes locked on Penta's while answering. "Valencia learned what we know, and she refused to return to Kingdom. She has fled to another world."

Helga stepped back in shock. "I don't believe you."

Picana cackled. "She is the smart one, after all."

Sanders lifted her chin and glared at Helga as if daring her to call her a liar. "It's true."

The queens eyed each other. Penta knew they were lying; Valencia would never abandon them. Before she could protest, Sanders pointed at the queens. "We know you planned to kill the witches if they didn't surrender. How dare you even think of such a thing? You of all people! You are the women Planet died for."

Penta's bloodshot eyes burned into Sanders' own. "They took Beauty. You don't know anything about raising children, Sondra. When your child is in jeopardy, we shall see how you act."

Sanders flinched. Hero frowned and resumed the conversation. "Will you surrender?"

Penta, Helga, and Cinderella answered as one. "No."

Hero observed the dagger in Penta's hand. "You've chosen the knife you gave me when I first arrived in Kingdom, Penta. Will you kill me with it if I stand between you and them?"

Penta hadn't given her weapon much thought. She

glanced at it, and the reflection of her tired eyes stared back at her. "Harold, you're asking me to subjugate my people to these three—as Earth would call them—terrorists. I can't do it. I refuse!"

Helga sheathed Cusp but lifted her flail with a spiked ball. "Enough! Stand aside, Hero. Witches, I call us to arms!"

The queens didn't anticipate any more trouble from Hero and his party. They expected them to scurry away after voicing their disagreement. Instead, Hero stepped in front of Penta, Sanders faced off against Celeste, and the knight assumed a battle-ready pose before Helga. The man in the cape moved toward the witches and bowed, turned his back on them, and drew his rapier, protecting them. Surprisingly, the maid didn't square off against Cinderella but stepped out of the way.

The count called to the queens. "I am Count Cupsince. I do not plan to kill any of you lovely ladies but beware...I do more than bark. This count bites."

Celeste glowed a brilliant blue, illuminating her hair, and gestured to Sanders. "You are not my equal. Step aside before I hurt you, dear sister-friend."

Sanders spread her pixie wings. Her blue aura turned purple. "I may not be your equal, but I have a trick or two up my sleeve."

Celeste's eyes darted to the maid. "A moment. Is she the real Sondra?"

Helga gripped her weapon, staring down her broad-shouldered opponent, yet addressed Sanders. "Sondra, give up this foolishness. You face Celeste the Extraordinary, and she will not let a friendship as close as family get in her way. You are outmatched."

"Yeah, well, I'm Sanders the uh...the...Implausible. I've faced magicians trained by the Devil and made it out of Cixxes. Miss Extraordinary has her hands full with me!"

Helga shook her head then aimed her flail at the knight in gold. "I do not know who you are, but you should know I am the premier warrior in Kingdom. Stand aside."

Sanders answered for the knight. "She is known in Oz as the Silent Knight. Don't underestimate her."

Across from Penta, Hero removed his waistcoat and let it drop to the ground. "Please, Penta. I beg you to stop."

Penta held up Hero's dagger. "I love you like a brother, Harold. You know it. But she's my daughter. You and Sondra do not understand how it is with children. One day, you will know."

Hero's voice wavered. "You're wise, Penta, but you don't know everything."

Cinderella unclasped her hands from behind her back and pointed at the witches. Observing the queen, Picana laughed, "Your ability won't work on us. You tried it before and—" She swallowed the rest of the sentence and grimaced.

Cinderella growled, "I'm not holding back this time. No more asking you to play nice. I'm going to command you."

Sanders gestured at Cinderella, and the queen's hands went straight up in the air. Cinderella cried out, "Someone has a hold of me. I feel hands around my wrists. An invisible assailant."

Celeste's jaw dropped. "Conjuring an invisible companion is an advanced spell. The cost of such powerful magic will drain you, whoever you are."

Sanders grinned. "Blue-dy-locks, it didn't cost me anything."

Mya's head jolted. "Not a spell. Not a curse. Someone's here. Someone worse." The other witches ignored her ravings.

Picana ribbed Tomana with glee. "Watching them fight each other is great sport, is it not?"

Tomana folded her arms, displeased. "The queens will win. This conflict is pointless."

The battle diverted Mya's attention from the invisible intruder. Focused on the upcoming fight, she danced. "Strangers might. Strangers grin. Strangers fight. Strangers win."

The combatants came together with weapons clashing,

with spells sparkling, with hands clasping. Helga's flail met the knight's golden shield. Dagger brushed against an arm. Offensive struck defensive magic.

Penta started the mêlée. She teleported in front of the witches, her dagger drawn, reaching out for Mya. With cat-like reflexes, the count knocked Penta's arm away before she touched the witch, and the queen swung the sharp end of her weapon toward the count. He dodged the blade.

The maid shouted across the room. "Be careful, count."

He turned and smiled back at her. "Do not worry, my nougat! I'm quite capable."

Cinderella struggled against her invisible captor. "Release me!"

Sanders leaped out of the way of Celeste's latest spell, a purple cloud of confusion. Turning to Cinderella, she said, "Commanding people is not your style, Cindy-Loo-Who. You used to let people follow their consciences, not yours."

Hero's hand landed on Penta's shoulder, pulling her away from the witches. Penta thought of Valencia escaping to another world, a lie she didn't believe for a second. Valencia was a bit of a rebel, but she would defend Kingdom to the death. Yet if Valencia hadn't left, where was she? Why wasn't she here? Valencia was intelligent, and Penta suspected ulterior motives of Hero's party. They must have a reason they want the queens to surrender.

Helga and the Silent Knight fought each other to a stalemate. Both female warriors knew how to battle hand to hand, and each anticipated the other's tactics. Helga's purpose was to stun the knight, not kill her. Helga's flail, though, met the knight's shield every time she advanced. The queen spun her spiked ball around in her hand like a fan blade.

Unexpectedly, Helga let the weapon fall to the ground and swung the blunt edge of her shield at the neck of her opponent. The Silent Knight seemingly expected this, ignored the flail, and blocked Helga's attack with her golden kite shield.

The knight's defensive move pushed Helga back. She used the opportunity to retrieve the flail from the floor while observing the knight. "Only a handful know my flail diversion. Certainly no one from Oz," she charged.

The knight didn't answer but inclined her head toward the warrior queen. Helga lifted the flail and swung the spiked ball over her head like a helicopter propeller on Earth. The queen declared, "I know who you are."

Celeste threw three magic projectiles at Sanders while her opponent created a shield and deflected them away. "Magic bolts, Celeste? Is that what you've been reduced to?"

Celeste put her hands together and revealed a flock of birds, zeroing in on the silver-suited opponent. Sanders drew a rectangle in the air with her index finger, and the birds splatted against a crystal-clear, plate-glass window. Penta caught this defensive measure out of the corner of her eye. She had hoped Celeste would overpower Sondra (or now Sanders?) quickly and help the others, but she had forgotten what made Sanders so dangerous.

Sanders wasn't as skilled as Celeste, but she tapped into her imagination and her knowledge of Earth and science to create spells on the fly as unthought-of by any trained magician. In this case, the birds of Kingdom typically flew unhampered through windows as few glass windows existed here. Not so on Earth. Kingdom's magic-wielders were used to casting spells and counterspells on each other all the time. Sanders didn't know these patterns, so she was able to let her imagination run wild and create unexpected and disruptive magic. While over the long haul, she was no match for Celeste, her creativity stymied the best of spellcasters.

Sanders flipped her wrist and made a rope materialize. "I leave for a little bit, and you dye your hair blue? Where's your fashion sense, sis?" She lassoed Celeste, but the fairy shrank to avoid capture.

The rope reduced in size with the fairy, keeping her arms pinned to her sides. Celeste asked, "You do not like it?"

Sanders smirked. "It highlights your eyes."

In seconds, Celeste grew giant-sized and ripped the rope apart, startling Sanders with the backlash.

Without taking her eyes off Celeste, Sanders pointed at Penta. Across the room, the black dye of Penta's dress drained to the hem and dissipated, turning the cloth a bleached white with gold trim. Her gloves also dripped off their obsidian color. Sanders nodded in her direction. "You look better in white, Penta."

Hero reached for Penta's knife, but she teleported away. Penta said, "Will you give your friend your full attention, Celeste?"

Sanders turned back to Celeste. "The spells you prepared for the witches protected you and the queens against human magic, but you didn't expect to face pixie magic today, didja? You're off your game, and it'll take all the blue in your hair to defeat me!"

When Penta turned around, Hero was bearing down on her again. She aimed and swung her knife, slicing a thin line across the back of his arm. Penta had already cut him on his shoulder when he had grabbed her clothing before. Neither were deep cuts, and she hated herself for doing it, but she wanted to let him know she meant business. If she had to, she would wound him sufficiently to move forward. "Let me pass, Hero. My daughter's life is at stake."

"I can't. I—"

She didn't allow him to finish but teleported beyond him, just a foot away from the witches. Distracted, the count observed Helga and the Silent Knight's sword fight, leaving Penta with an opportunity to approach the devilish women. She reached out to touch them, but an adversary grabbed her other hand and squeezed, forcing her to drop her weapon. Hero again! Someone must have prepared him for this fight —someone who knew her moves. "Cinderella, a bit of assistance."

"Indeed," answered her sister. "I smell sweat. A conjured

rival would not give off body odor."

Cinderella leaned forward and delivered a mule kick. Her heel hit a shin, and a grunt escaped her unseen opponent, freeing her wrists. Cinderella lowered her hands, glared at the witches, and extended her index finger. However, before the hags fell under her control, Tomana brought her hands together, and Cinderella's body stiffened. The spell constricted her body as if a giant, undetectable serpent coiled around her. The queen screamed.

Penta raced toward Tomana, murder in her eyes. "You will not kill my sister!"

Penta drew back her arm, but a hand came down on her shoulder, pulling her back. Without thinking, she slashed her knife to ward away the person detaining her but miscalculated the distance. The knife's edge sliced into the abdomen of her opponent.

Hero dropped to his knees, blood staining his white shirt.

33 - DELIVER US...

Roger eyed the mirror in horror. Reflecting from the glass, Cinderella was screaming in mortal agony. "Enough of this. I am going to her."

Pennilane stepped between the prince and the door. "You will remain here."

Roger drew himself up, towering over Pennilane. "She will die!"

Pennilane spread out her arms. "They will not kill her. 'Tis not why they are here."

Roger stepped forward. "Pennilane, you have as much chance of stopping me as loving a man."

Pennilane's eyes widened. She dove at Roger and wrapped her arms around his chest. "You shall find I've learned much in my short travels."

Roger stiffened. "God's heaven, woman! What is this?"

Pennilane didn't answer. Whiskers grew from her face, and, in a blink of an eye, a brown pelt spread over her body.

Her torso flexed and grew short and round. She shoved Roger. He toppled backward, and Pennilane, a fully transformed seal, landed on the prince, pinning him to the ground.

Harold

Along with "This hurts!" and a string of expletives, another thought ran through my mind. I'm always the one who gets seriously injured in Kingdom. Both times I've visited, something awful happened to me, and I ended up on the brink of death. What had I done to deserve this?

The wound burned and dribbled blood, and if I didn't receive attention soon, I would lose consciousness. Holding my hands against my stomach wasn't stemming the tide of the flow of blood. While the puncture didn't hurt like a bullet wound or multiple blows to the stomach—read my last adventures—I had the pleasure of experiencing a new kind of pain all its own.

Quite obviously distraught, Penta dropped the knife and kneeled, extending her gloved hands. I leaned against a column of the throne room, removed from most everyone's line of sight. The sound of battle rang out around me while I slid to the floor.

Out of the corner of my eye, I observed something circular fly across the room. The object, one of the glowing spheres providing light to the chamber, fell to the floor and shattered at Tomana's boots. The glass ball didn't harm the witch, but the effort was enough to break her concentration. Cinderella stopped screaming and placed a hand to her heart, relaxing her posture.

Though in peril, I had to discover who dared to launch the globe at the witch. To my astonishment, I spied Cassie backpedaling into an alcove in the room, trying to hide.

You go, girl!" shouted Sanders, still unaware of my predicament.

I clutched my stomach and groaned. Penta fumbled around her jerkin. "I must have something here to help you, Hero."

With surprising celerity, Cinderella sprinted to my side, pulling a vial from a pouch on her belt. "I came prepared. Wyvern tears."

Cinderella nudged Penta aside and stooped down, unstoppered the small container, and dumped its contents on my wound. With a gulping sound when it left the vial and sizzle when it landed on the gash, the liquid healed the cut. The relief was instantaneous, and I blinked in gratitude at Cinderella.

Sanders and Celeste, realizing now what had happened to me, had stopped for a moment. They both started to move my way but halted when I took a deep breath. Cinderella's pale countenance went from panicked to relieved. She placed a hand on my shoulder, and I put mine on top of hers. She smiled. "Hi, Hero."

I realized then we hadn't properly greeted each other yet. Cinderella's winsome features darkened. She stood and addressed Penta. "This is bonkers! We must stop. Now!"

Penta's face hardened. "I didn't mean to hurt him. We resolved to kill the witches, Cinderella."

Cinderella swung her arm around the room. "Until we accidentally kill everyone here? No, I'm not resolved, Penta."

"Cinderella—"

"No! I will have my say. I have deferred to your judgment for too long."

Cinderella turned around, arms at her sides. Facing the

witches, she declared, "I surrender."

Sondra

Trying to keep Celeste busy was a full-time job. I'm glad I didn't see Penta stab Hero before Cinderella healed him because Celeste would've taken me out of the game. Keeping up with her, even with a boost of Glinda's magic protecting me, was more challenging than I had supposed. I figured she might go easy on me because we were soul sisters. She was *not* going easy on me. Despite the goofy conversation we were having, Celeste was throwing one complex spell after another. The plan was to hold her off until the others convinced the queens to surrender. First Penta, then Helga. Cinderella would fall in line. As it turned out, Cinderella went first.

This was the way with plans. They didn't always work out the way you thought they would.

Celeste gestured at me. "Sondra would never fight me. She would defend Kingdom."

"Wouldn't that statement be silly if I was Sondra?" I retorted.

From her fingertips, a series of small pebbles dropped to the ground. They rolled at me and grew larger when they came closer. "I am convinced you are Sondra no matter what name you have given yourself. I have no idea how you threw a replication spell, but *you* are my dear sister, not the maid image of you over there."

The stones were the size of basketballs when they reached the halfway point between us. This spell was too easy to avoid; she had something else up her sleeve. She would expect me to fly over the rocks, so I guessed they would lift off the ground as well. I had to come up with a different defensive maneuver.

I said, "If I am your dear sister, then stop fighting me and surrender."

An idea formed while the rocks tumbled closer. What

would a magic bowling pin do? Divert the bowling ball into the gutter, of course! I spread my arms wide, and the floor parted before me to create a trench. I continued my motion, and the channel encircled me and then sloped upward behind me. I watched with satisfaction when the stones fell into my makeshift gutter and rolled past.

"Celeste, you should come to Earth. I could teach you a thing or two."

My fairy sister-friend grunted at my creative counter-spell. Celeste raised her hands and materialized a giant slug next to me. Cat's piss! Slugs are cute when they're little things, but when they're humongous, they're creepier than a weirdo following you on social media.

I kept my cool and cupped my hands, then raised them. "Above my left hand, may I introduce sodium." A white metal appeared. "And on my right, a proper amount of chlorine." A yellow gas floated. "Mix them, and you have the perfect slug killer."

A flare of light, a wave of heat, and salt rained down on the slug. The poor creature curled up on itself. Celeste waved at the mollusk, dispelling her creation and releasing it from its misery.

I put my hands on my hips. "Really, Celeste. I have degrees in chemistry and biology. You need to up your game if you—ulp."

Celeste swiped her finger, and my feet and legs turned to stone with the transformation starting at the floor and working its way upward. I gestured to counteract the magic, trying to turn the rest of my body into gas, but the spell was beyond me and fizzled. The hardening spell consumed my waist while I failed to come up with another solution. Scowling, I asked, "Tell me, Celeste. Have you ever heard of the Headless Horseman?"

Celeste tilted her head. She hadn't.

I cast a quick spell and removed my head from my shoulders. Throwing something when your eyes aren't connected to your neck anymore is an odd experience. I don't recommend it.

I hurled my noggin at Celeste. Surprised, she screamed when the top of my skull hit her on the chest. Then my head fell to the floor. Ow! Hitting your head on the ground hurts no matter how much you've braced for it.

Celeste bent down. "Dismemberment spell on oneself. How very pixie." She picked up my head and pointed at my nose. "But you are defeated."

I bit her finger.

Neither

Helga twirled her ball-and-chain flail while announcing to the room, "I have found Graddock." She stepped to the side, circling to gain an advantage.

The knight didn't react to the name but matched her opponent's steps in perfect unison.

The whump-whump of the flail spinning continued while Helga feigned to take another step but then reversed her direction. "You are cunning, Graddock, wearing a female's breastplate. Even Rose Red doesn't know the spinning flail diversion, but I used it on you when we last sparred."

Helga's maneuver hadn't fooled the knight. She adjusted her motion, not giving Helga an inch.

"You cannot win, Graddock. I know your fighting style. My next move will disarm you. Though you've battled better today than ever before."

The knight slashed her sword in the air in anticipation.

Helga advanced, and the two shields clashed against each other, emitting a clanging sound. The tactic produced the desired effect for both of the brawlers—the loss of the other's shield. Both instruments of defense fell to the ground in a clatter. Only Helga's flail and the knight's sword remained in their hands.

They engaged each other again, striking with their

weapons, sparks igniting every time the spiked ball met the sword. Frustrated, Helga threw her flail at the knight, who knocked it aside effortlessly. But Helga's motives were never impetuous. With one swift motion, she drew Cusp. The sword shone like sunlight, dazzling the knight in gold, who stepped backward.

Helga grabbed Cusp's hilt with both hands. "You are a worthy opponent, but I have a divine sword. I do not wish to harm you, but I have killed before. Stand aside. If this blade touches your armor, it will bring about your demise."

The Silent Knight sheathed her sword and threw her shoulders back. She spoke loud and clear. "Helga the Holy One."

Helga gasped, lowering Cusp. "My dead sister gave me that title. Who are you?"

The knight responded with two words.

"Deliver us."

A celestial voice rang out. "Hark, Helga Helvys."

Cusp had spoken, and Helga's trembling hand nearly dropped the artifact. She lifted the sword's blade to her eyes, and the throne room dissolved and then reappeared. She stood looking at herself, a few minutes into the future perhaps, before three beheaded witches, gripping Cusp awash in blood. The vision revealed her secret plan to keep her sisters' souls pure. The hilt of her sword caught on fire with green flames, and Helga screamed in torment. The blade, and her hand, dissolved into thin air.

The scene rippled then became clear again. This time, Helga viewed the hallway outside of the throne room. A young soldier spoke to a white-bearded, older Lyken. The soldier asked, "What must I say to keep her from being angry?"

"Be brief and direct."

"Will she ever return to the ways of her youth?"

Lyken stroked his beard. "I pray for it daily, but my hope is fading."

The soldier entered a darkened throne room. Shadows

enshrouded the dais like a bat folding its wings around its prey. As the man approached, a cling-cling of metal on stone sounded across the cavernous chamber. He shook when he kneeled before a singular throne, the other chairs removed.

Clink. Clink. "And what news do you have, servant?" wheezed a voice from the darkness.

"They searched the Lost City. Many of my party died."

"I care not about our casualties. Was it there?" Clink. clink.

"The sword Cusp was not among the treasures, but we found other powerful—"

The sound stopped, and the figure leaned out of the darkness. Helga observed an older version of herself, every inch of her body covered in green up to her olive-colored eyes. She pointed a hook for her right hand at the soldier. "What care I for trinkets? I am Helga the Darkness-Bringer, Helga the Sister-Banisher, Helga the Profane. I must find Cusp at all costs!"

The room dissolved again, and Cusp's chiming voice sounded in her ears. "Choose your future, Helga."

"But I do not have a choice," Helga whispered.

A gentler voice whispered to her. "Helga the Holy One always has a choice."

The warrior queen took a deep breath and dropped Cusp to the floor. The holy blade clanged like a bell when it struck the stone.

Helga lowered her head. "I surrender."

Harold

When Helga surrendered, my heart quickened. Other than Penta skewering me like a pig, the plan was, for the most part, working. Cinderella healing me had gone in our favor—better than an invisible Graddock whispering about Magnus in her ear. And the Silent Knight had needed to wait for Helga to unsheathe Cusp to speak the words to activate it.

Helga had stood still, focused on a point in space, and surrendered. Whatever she had experienced had resulted in taking the warrior queen out of the battle. My brilliant wife had preoccupied Celeste long enough. The situation was up to me now. The time had come for me to unveil my trick on Penta.

She had retrieved her knife. I reached for it, and she drew it back over her shoulder. She held out her hand to ward me off, and I grabbed the tips of her fingers. Because of her teleportation power, she didn't anticipate this move, and her confusion gained me a few seconds of holding her hand. Unable to conceive why I would put myself under her power, she remained still.

I yanked off her glove.

Penta stepped back in alarm and hid her silver palm behind her body, but everyone had seen it. I had exposed her tin woodwoman's hand. The sight reminded her of when she had failed to listen to those who loved her the most. Keeping Oz a secret, she had confessed to me the story the last time I was here, ashamed of her argument with Planet. I had hoped her silver hand would prompt her to recall that what had seemed right at the time was dreadfully wrong.

Haggard, furious, and upset, Penta stepped forward and grabbed the glove from my hand. She clenched it in her silver fist in front of me, taking a moment to stare at her reflection on the back of her hand. Without a word, she lifted her eyes beyond me. Penta marched toward the witches, ignoring everyone else in the room.

My heart lurched when Penta held out her knife. Cupsince swung his rapier at her, but she touched his hand and teleported him across the room. Penta stood full height before the hags with her dagger pointed at them. Hand shaking, she released the knife. It clattered when it struck the floor.

"I surrender."

34 - ...FROM EVIL

Sondra

I must admit, I had trouble viewing everything from my vantage point. My head, on its side and on the floor where Celeste had dropped it after I had bitten her, wound up looking at everyone sideways. Without my hands, throwing spells was impossible. Fortunately, Glinda's durable glasses had stayed on my head all this time. Score one for magic.

After Penta surrendered, the three hags' sneers were wiped away as if a giant rubber eraser had removed them with one swift stroke. Shock and disbelief replaced their condescending expressions. Tomana's eyes shifted to her coven sisters. "I told you two this was a mistake."

Eustacia, the haughtiness apparent on her face, straightened her shoulders. "This is all of your fault, Tomana."

Tomana turned to the newest member of their party

her coattails swinging like blades. "How is it my fault?"

"Kidnapping Beauty was your idea. Any fool would have known you ought to have killed her and left her body for Penta to find. Your restraint caused this result."

My heart leaped at the news Beauty was alive, and relief coursed through my veins...those in my head, not in my body.

Picana and Mya nodded their heads in agreement with Eustacia. They narrowed their eyes at Tomana, and Picana flexed her fingers.

Tomana stepped forward, her boot heel making the sound of a knife on a chopping block. "We all agreed to kidnap her."

"But the idea to sever her hand was yours," retorted Eustacia. "If the plan had been up to me, if I had joined your party before you kidnapped her, I would have advised you to kill her."

Picana's attention shifted from Tomana to Eustacia and back again. "The girl has a point."

"No one suggested killing her," Tomana screeched.

"You are soft, Tomana." Eustacia crossed her arms. "Picana said so last night. She didn't propose murdering Beauty because you are so damned weak."

Well, Eustacia's bitchiness was coming in handy. Picana and Mya's stares hardened at the third in their coven. Eustacia wasn't only exerting her power but had picked up a minor disagreement among the hags in the short time she had spent with them.

Julia clapped. "Mistress knows what's best. Always has."

Penta started at the slave's use of the word "what's." Julia had forgotten the general population of Kingdom avoided the use of contractions. I held my breath.

The witches hadn't noticed. Picana and Mya glared hard at Tomana as she took a step backward. Giddy humor gone, Mya stood rigid and observed Tomana as a guard views a trespasser. Picana raised her hands. "Stand down, Third."

Tomana began to gesture. "I dreamed that you were

planning to replace me with *her*! She's but a simpleton, incapable of the slightest whiff of magic."

Picana said, "Lower your hands, Tomana."

But the long-faced witch ignored her leader and cast a spell at Eustacia, knocking her off her feet. The daughter flew back against the wall, hitting the stone with the sound of a boxer hitting a punching bag, crying in pain. Eustacia would feel that in the morning. Tomana readied a second spell, murmuring the words "agony" and "torment," when Picana and Mya started gesturing.

The first and second witches drew on their magic together; energy crackled around them, and a heat haze manifested and moved in front of Eustacia. A split-second later, Tomana's spell coursed through the air at Eustacia but struck the shimmering barrier and dispersed with dwindling lights.

The raven on Picana's shoulder flapped its wings, and the lead witch addressed it. "There, there, Ravenous. We shall set this a-right." She turned toward the third member of the coven. "Apparently, Tomana, our shared dream is coming true. Now Mya!"

Tomana shouted, begging them to stop, but Picana and Mya hit her with a spell at the same time. The magic wrapped around her and the third witch wailed, raising her arms to deflect the curse—but her resistance had no effect.

The third witch writhed while the streams of black spiderweb-thin tendrils the other two had sent flew into her body and out of her mouth, her ears, her nostrils. In the end, filaments of dark magic poured from her eye sockets, and Tomana shook as if someone had pressed a charged defibrillator to her chest. She fell to the ground, the black goop escaping from her eyes and slinking away like an errant earthworm.

Mya laughed and danced. "Prophetic dreams. Witches scry. We see through it. Tomana *lies*."

Picana crossed her arms over her chest. "True. True. Our divination proves the two of us are loyal to each other, and that Eustacia is our real third sister. Eustacia foretold the coming of the raven, and the vision showed us Tomana's turning against us in her drive to rise to First Witch."

I held my breath. The count had lowered his rapier, and Cassie had slid behind Hero, peeking around him. Out of the corner of my eye, I observed Cinderella and Helga watching the proceedings. Penta caught my eye, and I blinked my reassurance.

Tomana lifted her head. "What have you done?"

Picana petted her raven. "Removed your magic, didn't we? Mya and I dreamed you took my position away by becoming First Witch and planned to form a coven in your own image."

Tomana groaned. "I dreamed you turned on me and killed me as you almost did."

Picana's smirk disappeared. "You had a dream, too?"

"Aye, almost the same as what has happened here."

"Something is not right in Denmar—"

But Picana broke off when Mya started to convulse. She had turned a ghostly white once the black mist had dissipated, and the rhyming witch put her gnarled hands to her head throughout the exchange. She had trembled at first but now thrashed like a woman possessed. Uh-oh. Hero and I hadn't anticipated this—whatever it was.

"What's happening to her?" asked Penta.

Tomana glared at Picana. "Daughter of a halfwit! Do you know what you have done? Mya will destroy all of us without my intervention, but it only works when I am a witch."

Picana moved toward Mya. "Tomana, you're so presumptuous about your power. I was too busy with important things to control Mya's little episodes, but now you shall see how a First Witch rules her coven."

She slung her arm forward, and a purple band of light, the color of a bruise, whipped around Mya. At first, the energy seemed to calm her, but a sharp crack echoed through the throne room. The violet magic snapped back like a rubber band and struck Picana, knocking her back a few steps.

Tomana screamed at Picana. "Goose of a woman. Only family magic can contain it now. If she continues, she shall disperse and kill everyone here."

At the warning, Celeste sprang into action and wove a net of gold around Mya, but its tendrils fell apart. "I need help. I'll call Glinda."

Glinda appeared next to her. "Here I am."

Picana and Tomana paid no attention to their rival who had just materialized, instead focusing on their perilous situation. The two crones quarreled while Glinda and Celeste strung together a net of golden light to surround Mya—but her body resisted it and spasmed. Sparks and bolts of lightning spurted from her head as if it were a defective transformer exploding. A jet stream of magic bolted upward and smashed the ceiling, loosening the stonework and raining down debris.

Picana gritted her teeth, ignoring the efforts of Celeste and Glinda. "You are a liar, Tomana. If you have been able to control her all of this time, how did you do it with dark magic? Only light magic calms and heals."

"Because I am her family." Tomana managed to sit up. "Before I became a witch, I secretly married her brother when he was under Mya's love spell. She and I are sisters-in-law. Only family can restore her now...or the touch of a blood family member, but we killed everyone in our families." She gestured at the ropes of light springing from Celeste's and Glinda's fingers. "Their golden net won't hold. Mya will erupt, and her dark magic shall consume us. Even Magnus won't save us this time."

Hero pointed at Cusp. "If Cusp strikes her, will it stop her?"

"No!" shouted Picana, Tomana, Celeste, and Glinda together. Celeste added, "She will disperse if you kill her."

Tomana held her head in despair. "We're doomed. Without one from her bloodline here, the net will fail eventually."

Holding her ribs, Eustacia stepped forward and held out her hand to Mya.

Picana shouted, "Stop, Eustacia. Follow me. Let us flee this world, and leave the rest of them to their fate."

Eustacia reached through the sparks and electrical discharges unharmed and grabbed Mya's hand. In a gentle voice, she simply said, "Rest easy."

At first, Eustacia's gesture didn't seem to accomplish anything. The tormented witch cackled and flung her body around. Eustacia grabbed the hag's other hand, unaffected by the squirming, and stepped toward her mother, embracing her. "I'm here. No more death. Wake up from your nightmare, Mother."

Picana scowled, eyes blazing. "Who do you mean by 'mother'?"

Mya's violent tremors slowed while Eustacia hugged her, and the golden nets held.

Tomana scraped backward on her rear end and licked her lips. "The resemblance. Why didn't I notice it before?" Her head turned toward the servant, and her eyes went as round as a full moon. She strangled out a further single word. "Daughter."

Julia straightened up. "It was I who sent the dreams to you three while you slept. Did you enjoy the feeling of abandonment, *Mother*?"

Hero pointed at Picana. "The jig's up, everyone. Someone needs to take out that one."

Glinda, holding the golden net like a fishing line, nodded to Celeste. "I almost have it covered, Celeste. Give me a few more seconds."

Music to my ears. Maybe I could spark up Picana, though first I needed one thing. "Hero, attach my head."

Hero came my way with Cassie using his body as a shield. Picana, now realizing what was going on, pointed toward us. "How dare you! Worms and excrement! Nobody touch me. I shall cast a curse that only I can undo and then depart. If you follow me, I'll ne'er reverse it."

She positioned her hands like claws, and a pea-soup

green mist rose from the floor around Hero and Cassie. They both turned to step out of its reach, but their eyes rolled up instead. They collapsed to the ground like marionettes whose strings had been cut.

Picana laughed. "Ha! I've put the lovers in a sleeping curse. Neither true love can save the other while they are both asleep. And now I will take my leave. I shall return with a new coven, one more powerful and much more wicked. I shall have time to plot my revenge, and you will see—"

But Picana forgot about the raven on her shoulder, and Lenore had had enough of her flagitious mother's diatribe. She leaned down on the word "see" and used her beak to pluck out both of the witch's eyes in two swift strokes.

Picana screamed and put her hands up to her eye sockets. With an economical gesture, Celeste sent Picana flying across the room against a pillar. The former leader of the coven slumped to the ground at the same time Lenore transformed from raven to her human form, a few feathers floating to the floor.

Across the throne room, Glinda retracted the net into her hands. With a flourish from the Good Witch, the powerful dark magic evaporated.

Eustacia trembled while holding her mother's hand, but Mya's convulsions slowed to a gentle rocking. When the older woman stopped moving, she opened her eyes, looking around. "Where am I?"

Eustacia answered. "You're in a castle."

Mya blinked multiple times as though she was trying hard to remember something she had forgotten. "And who are you?"

"I am your daughter, Eustacia. Don't you recall?"

"I remember being a child and being stung, but nothing afterward. Who am I?"

Eustacia patted her hand. "You're my mother, Maria Vye, and we're touring the French countryside."

Mya smiled. "Maria Vye. What a wonderful name.

Thank you, my dear daughter. You've always been a good child."

Julia rushed over to Eustacia and Lenore and slung her arms around their shoulders. Julia addressed Mya. "That she is. We're all good children."

35 - THE FRAGRANCE
OF LOVE

Sondra

Picana shook her head and started to rise to her feet. Celeste shrunk Picana, created a cube out of thin air, and trapped the evil witch inside of it. My fairy sister's magical energy reserves seemed endless. Picana, now with her coven in pieces, was a much weaker sorceress than my extraordinary sister-friend.

Picana pressed her hands against the glass of her cube cell, but the walls held, entombing the evil hag. Glinda, taking a cue from Celeste, encased Tomana in a similar prison. With a snap of her fingers, the fairy made both the first and third witches disappear. Celeste reported to Penta that she had imprisoned Picana and Tomana. They were in magically secured cubes as well as a chamber in the dungeon. She had also removed Picana's magic.

I cleared my throat. "Sis, a little help here?" My eyes gestured to my body.

Celeste jumped at my voice. "Absolutely."

Seconds later, my friend had reunited my head and neck and freed my body from its stone encasing. While Celeste restored me, Helga sheathed Cusp, and Penta asked Mya about Beauty, but the former witch only shook her head. A side door to the throne room opened, and Roger, Alice, Danforth, Rose Red, and Sylvia stepped into the room, all smiles. More solemn than her companions, Pennilane, in her human form, strolled in behind them.

Roger rushed to Cinderella and wrapped his wife in his arms. Meanwhile, Danforth also embraced Helga and kissed her. Helga, after two more kisses, parted from her husband, then turned to the Silent Knight. "You are a worthy opponent, Graddock."

A laugh originated near Cinderella, and Glinda twitched her fingers, causing Graddock to appear. Cinderella blinked at him in surprise, and he bowed his head to her. "You have a mighty kick, my queen."

Helga put a hand to the side of her face. "By St. Peter's beard!" She now examined the knight. "My heartfelt apologies. I was certain you were someone I knew."

Her opponent replied, "'Tis certainly someone you know."

The knight shrank two feet from a seven-foot-tall height. The shoulders compressed and arms and legs thinned out. The knight reached up and twisted her helmet, first one way and then the other. The helmet came off and revealed the freckled face of Valencia, grinning from ear to ear.

Helga shook her head. "'Tis impossible."

Valencia embraced her sister Helga. "No, 'tis me. In armor supplied by Glinda."

Penta and Cinderella rushed to their returned sister and joined in to hug her, welcoming her back home. After they finished, Helga reached for her a second time. The warrior queen held Valencia at arm's length. "Valencia, you have never been a fighter before. What accounts for your sudden increase in skill?"

Valencia eyed her sisters. "Graddock and I have continued seeking the gems of fortune and recently found the Ruby of Resolve in Mount Voyle."

The Kingdom residents nodded knowingly, but the rest of us exchanged baffled glances. Valencia explained, "Often known as the fighter's wishing stone, the ruby's natural ability brings a steady resolve to its bearer and entitles its owner to a fault-free wish. The gem was perfect for boosting my determination to complete this quest. This morning, I wished on it to become your equal in combat. I cannot defeat you, but we are now likewise matched.

Valencia pushed back a lock of hair and went on to explain the Magnus spell and how her sisters had nearly added another hundred years onto the witches' lives. At the end of her summary, she regarded Helga. "And our quest was more in peril with the sword Cusp in your hand."

"But you said 'Deliver us,' and then Cusp spoke to me."

Valencia set her helmet on the ground. "Recall that I was researching arcane artifacts to try to save Snow White's life. Naturally, I read about Cusp. In the third volume of the Epiphanies of Saint Lewis the Good, he clearly states to engage in conversation with Cusp—"

Helga held her hand up. "I'll take your word for it. The phrase is in the Good Book."

Valencia peered at the holy sword. "May I see it? This time not aimed at me?"

Helga pulled the divine artifact from her sheath. "I am unworthy to hold it in my hands. I almost killed you with it."

Cinderella shook her head. "Hardly, sister. The blade spoke to you, didn't it?"

Valencia examined the runes. "I recognize some of these symbols. I may be able to translate—"

She was interrupted when the sword gave off a burst of light and blinded everyone for a moment. After the spots floating before our eyes cleared, Helga said, "I don't think Cusp wants you to translate its runes, Valencia."

Cinderella touched Helga's shoulder. "You misinterpret what it did. Look at your hands."

Helga flipped her palms up and then down. The sword had removed all of her green blotches.

Valencia ran her index finger along the hilt of Helga's sword. "Cusp is a sword of healing, as the legends say."

After Cusp removed the spell on Helga, Celeste moved over to me. Tears formed in the pixie's eyes when she took my hand. "I know you are my dear sister. I am very sorry for battling you."

I squeezed her hand. "I expected it. And yes, Glinda helped me out, or you would have defeated me too quickly. Hero and I planned every detail except your dye job—that threw me. What the hell, Celeste? Blue?"

The pixie ignored me. "The other cannot be a duplicate spell. You cannot throw a sleeping curse—as Picana did—on magic. She is a parallel."

I headed over to the two sleepers while Celeste floated along beside me. Eyes on my husband, I marched forward. We halted in front of a slumbering Hero and Cassie.

Celeste swallowed. "What is her name?"

"Cassiopeia."

Everyone gathered around the two cursed victims. Graddock touched his chin. "I do not understand why the witch cursed those two instead of Hero and Sanders."

Valencia replied, "Picana observed the statues outside the throne room and noted a pixie and a pair of lovers. She made a mistake and thought Sanders was the pixie, and Cassie and Hero were the lovers. If she had thrown her spell on Sanders and Hero, we would be in trouble as only true love's kiss would awaken them."

I kneeled. "No big deal, you could've just positioned our lips together to wake us up."

Penta shook her head. "No, it's a big deal, my friend. For true love's kiss to work, it must have two elements. True love, of course, but also intent. 'Tis not only two lips touching each other."

I paled at the revelation and leaned over Hero. He wasn't sleeping. I've seen him asleep a hundred times with his mouth half-open, and this was different. The word "stasis" popped into my mind, and I couldn't help thinking of Carl Neumann's theory that an unalterable body exists as a reference for theories on mechanics. What would Neumann think of Harold as a physical example of the *body alpha*? Oops, no time for theoretical science. I puckered up, and my heartbeat increased in volume when I leaned down. Stupid organ! Couldn't it be quiet for once when I was crushing on Hero? I was supposed to be the rescuing heroine, not the lovestruck maiden.

I planted my kiss firmly on his lips, and energy flowed and ebbed like a tide going in and out, from me to him and back. I watched as his eyes fluttered open, and he regarded me with recognition. His arms reached for me, and he pulled me on top of him, deepening the kiss and moving his hand along my thigh. None of that now, *Hero*. I grabbed his wandering fingers and interlaced them with mine while my heart continued to loudly betray me. Thump. Thump.

We parted, and everyone around us beamed. Hero blushed while we rose to our feet. I clasped his hand, not wanting to let him go.

My husband asked, "Picana defeated?"

Celeste rushed over and embraced him. "Yes."

After Hero finished the gesture of affection, Penta pulled him in. He said, "About the glove, I'm sorry, but it was the only way I could get our message across to trust us."

Penta released Hero and held up her silver hand. "Perhaps I should go without gloves. Maybe it's time I—"

She broke off speaking when the silver polish of her right hand transformed to flesh. She gasped, knowing the change signified Beauty was near and had used her ability. She turned toward the main entrance of the throne room. Framed in the doorway stood Beauty and Grr, and the princess called out. "Mother."

Penta teleported over to her, flinging her arms around her daughter. "My Beauty! Oh, I'm so glad you're safe."

Beauty cried on her mother's shoulder. "You won't believe it. They hid me in a giant clam at the bottom of the ocean for days, and then the witches came and transformed me into a monster. I couldn't speak. The witches set Grr on me to kill me!"

After a long embrace, Penta reached out to Grr and pulled him into their reunion. When she released them, she regarded Beauty's left hand—a stump at the wrist. "I'm so sorry."

Beauty held up the end of her arm and lifted her chin. "Don't be. They wanted me to renounce you, Mother. I wouldn't do it. I slapped Tomana across the face, and she took my hand as punishment."

Penta's tears rolled down her cheeks while she kissed her daughter's wrist. "We'll have Celeste heal you, my poor darling."

Beauty tilted her head. "We'll talk, Mom. Perhaps others will spot it and remember not to cross me." The princess peered around the room and spied the gathering. "Why do two Sondras exist? And why is one on the ground?"

Penta teleported them back to the crowd around Cassie. Hero looked at Helga. "Wait a minute. Your power is to remove curses. Reach out and touch her, Helga."

Helga folded her arms. "In this regard, my power is limited. I'm afraid true love's kiss is the only way to remove a sleeping curse."

Celeste bobbed up and down and returned to pixie size. "True, Kingdom's sleeping curses were created as part of this world. Picana knew what she was doing, for a sleeping curse is core magic to Kingdom. Kissing is the sole remedy. Neither Glinda nor I can awaken her."

Duh! The answer was obvious. I touched my husband's shoulder. "Kiss her."

Everyone turned to me except Hero, who examined the sleeping maid. His nostrils flared. "I won't do it."

"Of course you will." I swung my arm toward Cassie. "We can't leave her in this condition. How could we live with ourselves?"

Hero turned to me. "But I'm not her true love. My kissing her won't matter."

I spun him around to face Cassie. "Then do it."

"By 'matter,' I mean it won't wake her up. But if I kiss her, it will matter a great deal to me and you." Listening to him, I put my hand on my hip.

"You won't do it because you're afraid you'll wake her up."

Hero stepped back. Pixies must be fools—well, at least Kingdom pixies—because Celeste rushed in where angels would certainly fear to tread. She spread her arms wide. "But that is absurd." She pointed at me. "Hero loves you, Sondra Sanders, not this woman. How could you think such a thing?"

I opened my mouth to respond, but Hero held up his hand. "Don't."

I pushed aside Hero's arm with one hand and Celeste's pointing finger with another. "I must."

I took a deep breath. "Hero and I have been trying to start a family but without much luck. Hero, this woman, and I —the three of us—had one of Julia's prophetic dreams about a baby. It turns out, the baby belongs to Hero and Cassie."

All eyes bored into Hero, and he shifted uneasily. "The problem is I don't love her, Sondra. I love you. I've told you that about a hundred times in the last twelve hours. Cassie's more like your kid sister." He grimaced. "Thinking of it that way, I really don't want to kiss her."

I folded my arms and shrank into myself. "But Cassie's

your destiny."

Hero's cheeks flushed with anger. "Who says? Why don't I get a choice of who I love? I won't leave you for her. My life would be a total lie. I won't do it, child or no child."

Again, my heart beat loudly, and everyone looked around. Pennilane asked, "What is the beating sound? I heard it before."

My cheeks reddened. "It's me. When I feel close to this guy, everyone can hear my heartbeat."

Celeste nudged me with her hip. "Planet glowed when she loved Hero."

I patted my chest to get my ticker to shut up. "Yes, I guess we Sondra parallels do something weird when we're in love." I turned to my husband. "Hero, we can't leave her like this without you trying to awaken her. It isn't right."

Animated, Hero gestured beyond the throne room's entrance. "Have you noticed we're in a country of handsome knights? If someone's going to fall under a sleeping curse, better here than anywhere else."

"I could be the one on the ground now. A fancy-dancy knight is no guarantee. I know I've had my differences with Cassie, but she's still my parallel. I'm literally looking at a younger version of myself lying on the floor. If you're her true love, and maybe that won't be until the future, we owe it to her to give her her life back."

Everyone held their breath for him to answer. Hero said, "If I do this, it doesn't change our relationship. We may not have children, but our marriage is just as loving as everyone else's."

I closed my eyes. "You once tried to convince Rose Red's husband to awaken Snow White with a kiss, and now karma's coming back to kick you in the ass. Just do it."

Hero took a deep breath and kneeled beside Cassie. His lips hovered over hers then he spoke out of the side of his mouth. "There's no one like you, Sondra."

Hero's lips brushed Cassie's and pulled away. She didn't

stir at all, and Hero scratched his ear. My husband must have assumed his kiss would awaken her. When her eyes didn't open, he shook her shoulder. "Cassie?"

Hero turned around and squinted at me. "I don't understand."

Despite Cassie's situation, a flutter rose in my chest. "You idiot. I feared she was your true love, but she's not. I am."

"But that's what I've been saying all along."

Count Cupsince snorted with disdain. "You people! No wonder this Eustacia wants to go to Paris. You all kiss without passion, without life, without *l'amour*. You gave her a peck on the lips, a kiss I reserve to seal an envelope, not to awaken a woman. Permit me."

And before anyone could stop him, the count kneeled and took Cassie in his arms. He tilted his head and pressed his lips on hers with a hunger for a woman's skin, longing not only for her to rouse but arouse. Everyone expected him to part from her within a few seconds, but he didn't, and the kiss went on far past the modest time frame of a Kingdom kiss. He moved his lips over hers without ever breaking contact.

Reading the body language in the room, I suspected Roger and Danforth would receive a gentle reminder of what true passion looked like later. The count's kiss made me wish I had spent a little more time awakening Hero.

Before he released the kiss, the fragrance of peonies filled the chamber, wafting over everyone present. Pennilane, with her extra-sensitive sense of smell, had to cover her nose. We were all about to remark on it when Cassie's eyes flew open. Her hands went up to the count's head, and her fingers kneaded his hair. When they parted at last, both of them stared at each other as if seeing a new person in front of them. The large group of people standing around didn't matter at all.

And then the rest of the group clapped and cheered. Cinderella wolf-whistled—that will never be recounted in a bedtime story—and the count helped Cassie up. Bashfully, they continued holding hands. I couldn't believe it, but the count blushed!

Cinderella threw her arms into the air. "'Tis time for a festival!"

At the word "festival," Penta's shoulders slumped, and she cast a weary expression at her younger sister. "Cinderella, I don't know if I can celebrate. Perhaps the rest of you are more at peace, but I've never properly mourned Snow White."

Cinderella took Penta's hands. "You need to sleep. When you rise, you'll put on this dress Sanders bleached white for you. She is right. Black is not your color. Then you'll come down and join us. We won't start without you."

Penta sighed. "But Snow White—"

"Snow White would want this. This festival is not to forget but to honor her."

Helga, Valencia, Sylvia, and Rose approached, overhearing the conversation. Rose nodded. "I think she'd be pleased to celebrate now."

Valencia put her hand on Penta's arm. "Kingdom needs this. We need this."

Penta nodded. "Maybe a small celebration."

"Totes!" Behind her back, Cinderella crossed her fingers in front of us.

The whole crowd dispersed to prepare for the festival except Cassie, Cupsince, Hero, and me. Cassie ran her toe along a crack in the floor. "Um, sorry about the dream. I thought you were the one, Harold."

"It's fine," said Hero. "I told you I wasn't, right? Now we know."

Cassie's forehead wrinkled. "But the dream? I still don't understand."

Hero pulled me closer. "We aren't bound by our dreams but by our choices."

Cassie nodded at him, still puzzled. The count, sensing her uneasiness, led her away to the three daughters. I smirked and spoke in a funny voice meant to mimic his baritone. "'We aren't bound by our dreams but by our choices.' Thank you, swami, for your fortune cookie bit of wisdom." I shook my head. "You're hilarious."

"It sounded good."

"Hero, you crack me up."

"That's an important thing in love, *Sanders*."

We laughed and kissed, my heart beating loud enough for him to hear. When we parted, he cocked an eyebrow at me. "I have to admit. Cassie's true-love scent thing was pretty cool."

"Oh, come on. She farts, and everyone draws hearts in the air."

36 - ANNOUNCEMENT

Cinderella allowed Penta three hours to sleep while she bossed the best hall decorators, dress designers, chefs, and custodians to prepare for the festival. She instructed Celeste to teleport the couriers all over Kingdom with news of the witches' defeat. Glinda, although longing to return to Oz, agreed to stay for the celebration and leave the next day. The three witches' daughters went to free Snow White's dwarfs from where the witches had hidden them.

After Julia, Eustacia, and Lenore returned, servants escorted them into chambers and measured them for elegant gowns. Everyone except Pennilane, who never attended Cinderella's celebrations, gussied up for the night. Penta wore her white dress, dazzling in the chandelier light. The rest of the queens chose gowns Snow White had favored on each of them —a memorial to their fallen sister.

The queens started the celebration with an announcement of the witches' defeat. Cinderella then asked Hero and

Sanders to open the dance floor for their role in constructing the victorious plan.

While Hero and Sanders joined hands and began to dance, Valencia walked away from her sisters and stood next to Graddock. He leaned down and whispered to her. "You made contributions to the hags' defeat too. You knew the catchphrase for Cusp."

"It doesn't matter, Graddock," she responded. "They deserve the credit, and this dance is their reward. And speaking of rewards, I believe you are due one for rescuing me in Morbidum. Shall we dance?"

Valencia took Graddock's hand and led him onto the floor. The pair stepped around Helga and Danforth, finding a corner to themselves. Graddock placed his left hand on Valencia's waist, and they joined right hands. The queen lit up with a luminescent smile as they moved together. "Now, I can think of a thousand places better than a cemetery to continue where we left off in Morbidum," said Valencia.

Graddock twirled Valencia. When they resumed dancing, he said, "About that. We should talk."

Valencia's forehead creased with wrinkles. "Do tell, Graddock."

"You know the depth of my love. I have been holding back my passion for you, but we are in a doomed relationship. I cannot be a prince. You do not know me."

Through this inauspicious opening, Valencia's grin never faltered. "Oh? I don't know you occasionally threaten people behind my back for information when we're on quests? I don't know you stole an amethyst-inlaid dagger from the Ghost Pirates of Pendragon and told Helga said knife fell overboard?"

"How did you—?"

Valencia rolled her eyes. "I don't know you frequent The Thirsty Wench at least once a fortnight, sometimes have too much to drink, and always cheat at cards while you're there?"

Graddock broke off dancing. "Have you been spying on

me?"

Valencia tugged him back and swayed toward the center of the dance floor. "I cannot tell you the number of people who have come to me complaining about your misdeeds. They know I favor you. And I noticed the dagger on our quest for the Ruby of Resolve."

Graddock stopped dancing again, but Valencia urged him to continue. His face fell. "I am sorry, Valencia."

"Don't be," she said. "I know my heart belongs to a swindler and a rascal. I also know it belongs to a card player who avoids the women at the Wench, and a guard who defends my honor and would stick with me if the whole world turned against me. You're the man who would give his life for me without a second thought."

"Valencia, I—"

She drew closer to Graddock. "I love you. I cannot change you, I know, but I also can't change the way I feel. My choice is to either love you or settle for something less. I'm not settling."

Graddock met her eyes. "And I love you more than anything, but I cannot be a prince. I would not enjoy the trappings of royalty, and it would be bad for Kingdom."

Valencia squeezed his hand. "I agree."

"Therefore, we should separate."

"But why?" Valencia's eyes sparkled. "No Kingdom law says you have to be a prince if you become my husband. Marry me, then renounce the title. I'll be Queen Arkenson, and you'll be Mr. Elston. But we'll also be Valencia and Graddock, husband and wife."

Graddock considered her idea, slack-jawed. "Truly? You would allow such an unconventional union?"

Valencia squinted at him. "Do you promise not to cheat poor people at cards? Only those who can afford to lose?"

"Yes."

Her eyes narrowed further. "And to continue to avoid the dancing women at the Thirsty Wench?"

"What dancing women?"

Valencia patted his arm. "That's the right answer. I may be small and weak, but don't forget…" She leaned up and whispered in his ear. "I play with matches."

He pulled back, and Valencia flashed a mischievous grin. "Now, you will notice I've maneuvered us to the center of the dance floor, kiss me for the first time in public. Let us make our courtship official."

Valencia tilted her chin upward. Graddock leaned down and hovered his lips over hers but then changed direction. He pressed his lips against the nape of her neck instead. He then proceeded up to her jawline, kissing her along her face to her ear, where he nibbled at her earlobe. Valencia sighed when he moved toward her mouth, and when he reached it, he lifted her off her feet and pressed his lips against hers. Valencia made a small, pleased sound in the back of her throat.

When they parted, Valencia slowly opened her eyes. "Graddock, you brigand. You always take more than you're allowed. I love you."

The couples around them had stopped dancing and witnessed the display of affection, most beaming with joy. Helga blushed, but Cinderella leaned in, whispering. "Marvy. Now get a room."

"Cuthbert! Are you enjoying the festival?"

"She's beautiful, Mama."

"Who is beautiful, Cuthbert?"

"The woman over there. The lady with dark hair."

"Lenore's a little old for you, Cuthbert."

"I wanna dance with her. I look growed-up."

"Now, Cuthbert, please. You are a prince. Act like one."

"She is as beautiful as a princess, and I want to marry her."

"Cuthbert, I'm sure she's a nice—oh, what is it, Roger? Quit tapping me on the shoulder!"

Roger leaned over and whispered in Cinderella's ear. She grimaced and leaned back from him. "Did you say Pennilane?"

Roger nodded.

Cinderella lifted her skirts to scurry away. "Talk some sense into your son. I shall go and find her."

Cinderella rushed across the dance floor to her best friend's side. Pennilane stood with her back to the festivities, examining a large painting of the sun going down over the town of Tusk. When she noticed Cinderella approaching, she wiped her eyes.

Cinderella stepped between the selkie and the painting. "Pennilane, my dear. What has happened?"

Pennilane swallowed hard. "Nothing has happened, my queen. I thought I would come down and admire the festival." She tipped her head at the picture on the wall. "And this painting."

Cinderella put her hands on her hips. "You're acting strange. You never attend my parties."

Pennilane rubbed her hands together. "I was admiring how elegantly you and Roger dance. Do you know what they say about dancing? They say it is—"

Pennilane faltered and walked away toward the grand staircases at one end of the ballroom. The queens often used a second-story balcony to arrive at Cinderella's celebrations. Two sweeping staircases curved outward and down from the balcony, forming two large alcoves—a private place for people to conduct a conversation. Pennilane stepped under the stairs and placed a hand over her eyes. Cinderella followed and put her hand on her friend's shoulder. "Are you ill? Do you want me to help you to your room?"

Cinderella gasped when Pennilane removed her hand.

Tears filled her eyes. "I have lost..." She stopped herself and shook her head. "'Tis nothing, my queen."

"Don't give me that 'my queen' nonsense, Whiskers. I am your dear Cinderella. First, you refuse to tell me how you grew your pelt back until after tonight. Now you won't share what's wrong. Tell me what's troubling you, or I will end our friendship right here." She stomped her foot for emphasis.

Pennilane released a shuddering breath. "I cannot believe what I have become. I refuse to give in to it, yet I cannot help but be sad."

"What are you talking about?"

Pennilane fingered a stray curl. "I have lost...my Roger."

Cinderella tilted her head. "What do you mean by 'my Roger,' Pennilane? You aren't making sense."

Pennilane dropped her eyes. "In Janay, I met someone."

Fortunately for Cinderella, her jaw was hinged to her mouth, or it would've dropped to the floor. When she recovered from her shock, she presented a warm, Cinderella-patented smile to her friend. "You must go to him. Immediately. No matter where he is."

"But I am your guard and—"

Cinderella said, "Do not make me command you."

From around the corner, Hero and Celeste stepped in front of the entrance to the alcove. Often polite, this time Cinderella turned her back on them. "This is a private conversation. I must ask you to leave."

"But—"

"Hero, I won't ask again. Nothing could be more important."

Hero ignored her. "A gentleman's requesting your presence on the dance floor."

Cinderella waved him away. "Whoever it is will have to wait. Pennilane and I must have our privacy."

"Not your presence, Cinderella." Hero turned to Pennilane. "Yours."

His words flew at Pennilane like tiny darts. She stepped

backward and fell against the wall. "Who?"

"Alice went to Janay," said Hero. "She said she was breaking every Traveler rule in the book, but she thought this was the right thing to do. I agree."

Cinderella and Pennilane both understood the intent of Hero's message, and the queen and the selkie peeked out from behind the staircase to where Hero pointed. A young gentleman stood at the side of the dance floor in nineteenth-century clothes. Pennilane inhaled a sharp breath. "I cannot go out there. I did not dress for a dance."

Celeste stepped forward. "This is why I am here. Cinderella, will you guide me?"

The queen rubbed her hands together. "I would be glad to."

Two minutes later, Pennilane stepped out from underneath the staircase, dressed in a gold and blue, floor-length gown with a sequin belt. Elegantly styled, her hair lay on her shoulder with one strand curling near her neck. She stepped across the floor on daffodil-colored slippers, replacing her normal stride with a more elegant saunter.

Pip stood on the side of the dance floor with Alice, holding onto her arm, observing the room in amazement. Shuffling his feet, he removed his stovepipe hat when he spotted Pennilane. His expression blossomed into joy when she approached. He held out his palm for her, and she stepped across the floor and took it.

Pip, his eyes never leaving hers, cleared his throat. "I don't understand any of this. Alice tried to explain to me about worlds and fairy tales. She said someone here is Cinderella? And she's the host of this festival because of witches? I'm utterly baffled."

Pennilane pointed at her friend. "Cinderella is over there. Here in Kingdom, the queens and princesses are all beautiful. You could take your pick of any of the pretty women here."

Pip's attention remained focused on Pennilane. "Then

I choose the one modeled after the most gorgeous of all life forms...the lovely seal."

Color rose on Pennilane's brown complexion at his small flirt. They stepped out in the middle of the dance floor, and Pip took her hands. She lifted her chin. "I am a seal. Does it bother you?"

"I'm a human. And a man. Alice tells me you're a bit bitter toward my kind. Does what I am bother you?"

She blushed again, and the music started. "Perhaps I have been somewhat judgmental."

They moved together in rhythm to the music. Pennilane gulped. "After this dance, would you care to take a stroll in the garden?"

Pip listed his head toward her, his breath on her ear. "I'd be delighted to."

Pennilane's whiskers emerged. "Oh, always at the wrong time." She removed her hand from his and put it over her mouth.

Pip retrieved her hand, kissed it, and interlaced his fingers with hers. "I rather fancy the bristles. I wish to dance with the most beautiful whiskered woman in the room." Pennilane's eyes crinkled.

Pip said, "Please, don't turn into the seal."

Pennilane wiped away a joyful tear. "I make no such promise."

Across the room, Cinderella stood at the edge of the dance floor with Hero next to her. She shook her head in awe. "I would've wagered my scepter against Pennilane dancing with a man. Of all of the things I have seen today, this one takes the pie. Is that the right saying, Hero?"

"I couldn't have said it better myself."

Harold

A couple of hours later, I sat in a corner of the ballroom with Penta. She described all the events in Kingdom after Valencia left. When she finished, she stopped and observed Beauty and Grr dancing together, her daughter's new golden hand on her partner's furry neck. "I meant it when I said I loved you as a brother, Hero. Will you forgive me for not listening to you?"

"No worries, sis. But you should also apologize to Sanders," I replied.

"I don't recall insulting Sanders specifically."

I fiddled with a button on my sleeve. "The comment about knowing how it will be when we have children of our own. The truth is something bad happened to Sanders on Cixxes, and I'm afraid we won't have any babies in our future."

Penta put a hand to her mouth. "They sterilized her?"

"Yes."

"Alice told me sterilization is common there. She said corrupt governments start by offering the choice of sterilization to women, subtly influencing them to think this is *their* idea. They convince women babies are a burden. When they have their population convinced, they alter a woman's body to conform to their wishes, not hers."

I didn't know what to think of her statement other than that sounded like something Cixxes would do. "Maybe for us to be parents isn't in the cards. I'd make a lousy dad anyway."

Penta squinted at me, and then slapped me on the back of my head. Ouch! Metal hands hurt. "Hey, what's that for?"

"You'd make a wonderful father," Penta replied. "Good

fathers are loyal like you and patient like you. And they stand up for their families."

"Like me?"

"Two out of three isn't bad." She grinned. "Yes, good fathers stick by their family as you did with Sanders."

Celeste floated over the dance floor, towing a pixie Sanders in her wake. They landed and enlarged to human size next to our table. "Sorry to interrupt, Penta, but I would like a word with Hero and Sanders."

The blue-haired fairy nodded to a smaller room off the ballroom, and I excused myself. Sanders and I followed Celeste into an empty antechamber. I glanced at Sanders. She shrugged.

When we were alone, the fairy brushed back blue locks from her eyes. "You are my brother and sister. If not by blood, then in spirit. Now, Hero, I do not want you to be angry at Sondra Sanders when I tell you we had an intimate talk today. We discussed what happened in Cixxes."

Sanders stiffened, and I frowned. "Celeste, let's not talk about this now."

Celeste reached behind to where her right pixie wing membrane met her back. She retrieved two vials of a pink liquid and handed them to each of us. "This will solve *that* problem. Drink this and then..." She raised her eyebrows.

Did I hold the solution to our fertility problems in my hand? "Is it guaranteed to work?"

Celeste winked, an obvious one with her mouth open. "As long as you do your part!"

Sanders said, "But I asked Glinda about it, and she said this spell demands too much from a magician. You cast it?"

"And made a potion from its results." Celeste rolled her eyes. "And what does Glinda know? Am I not a great magic-wielder? The spell's cost is small compared to the love you two have shown me."

"Hey, we love you 'cause you're family," I said. "Like it or not, you're stuck with us."

"I would not trade our friendship for dragon magic." At our confused expressions, she added, "Dragon magic is powerful magic. Now, the festival is over for the two of you. Observe the pennies behind me. I set out forty coins. They will lead you to a special room I prepared just for you. Once you enter, the pennies and the door to the room will disappear from the outside. You shall not be disturbed for the rest of the night."

Sanders hugged Celeste. "How can I ever thank you?"

Celeste released her and held her at arm's length. "By leaving."

We left.

The next morning, Sanders and I turned down a hallway and halted when it dead-ended. Sanders grimaced, "This isn't the way to the dining room."

I retreated a few steps to the corridor we had just been in and counted the hallways we passed. My wife shook her head. "'Follow me,' he says," she mocked. "'I know the way,' he says. And now we're lost."

What a crab. "Why don't you cast a spell or something to find the breakfast room?"

Sanders shook her head while we doubled back. "I used up all my magical essence for the day when I cast that spell on myself this morning. I had to know, Harold." She widened her eyes and grinned like a cat who has eaten three canaries.

We rounded a corner and came to the front of the castle. Outside, several guests lined up to mount their steeds and leave for the four corners of Kingdom. I spotted a familiar face. "Lyken! Can you direct us to the breakfast room before everyone leaves?"

Lyken bowed to us. Though we weren't royalty, he treated us with the respect due to a prince and princess. "I would be glad to be of service. You do not want to miss the queens' declaration of the new royal advisor. They sent out proclamations and will announce it at midday."

The new royal advisor? I straightened up. "Me? The queens are going to give me a title? Sir Hero does have a nice ring to it."

Lyken strolled to one of the many doors in the massive hall. "No. They chose someone who they believe of the highest moral caliber and the sharpest conscience."

"Jiminy Cricket?" I guessed.

Lyken led the way down a hallway. "I do not know a cricket named Jimmy. I am speaking of the esteemed elf of Blar, Turducken."

Turducken! The weaselly little elf who always worms his way into my stories? He wasn't even *in* this story at all, probably hiding when the witches first came here! I hated that little braggart. "Really? Turducken?"

Lyken opened a door and entered a large chamber. "He is a noble, and a dear friend of the queens."

Sanders nudged me. "He's so cute."

She was trying to irk me, I know. I couldn't help but take the bait. "Turducken didn't do anything this entire adventure. I risked my life and friendship—"

I had to be careful in front of Lyken. "Er, and that *fine* gentleman wins the prize."

Sanders took my arm. "Don't worry, Hero." I expected her to say that we won our prize, but she surprised me with: "You'll always be my Turducken."

She wasn't funny.

Moments later, Sanders and I entered the breakfast room with the massive bay window. The queens and royal family were finishing their breakfast as we hurried inside. Celeste floated out of her chair at the sight of us, her aura radiating a brilliant blue.

Penta, not knowing what had transpired the night before, stood and leaned on the table. "Where have you two been? Celeste told us not to worry, but I couldn't help it. What's wrong?"

I put my arm around Sanders. "Everything's fine." I raised my voice and looked around. "Everyone? I have an announcement."

The people in the room stopped what they were doing and regarded me in anticipation. I swallowed and opened my mouth to speak, but Sanders shouted it out before I could, using the Kingdom way of announcing such news.

"I'm with child!"

37 - THE END OF THE LETTER

Harold

In my office, I reread the last paragraph I had written on our adventure in Kingdom. As I was about to type the next passage, Sondra called to me from the kitchen. "Hey, Harold. Come here."

Grumbling a bit at my broken concentration, I strolled into the kitchen to find Sondra standing with her back to the sink. She waved an envelope in front of me so I couldn't read it. "Guess who it's from?"

"Alice?"

"Bingo." She handed me an envelope. Alice frequently Traveled to Kingdom and carried back letters for us, sending them in the regular mail. I ripped open the envelope while Sondra put her hand on her hip—her classic pose. Same posture, except for her large abdomen. Any day now.

She had called me out of my office after retrieving the mail. When I pulled the letter out of the envelope, I noticed the creases weren't aligned, as if the writer had folded and unfolded it multiple times. My focus went to the kettle on our stove and then to Sondra. "You didn't."

Her eyes went upward—the picture of an angel. In reality, more devil than angel. "How could you?" I asked. "Penta addressed this letter to me."

She sat down and grabbed a baby catalog, which had apparently arrived in the mail with the letter. "I've been waiting for Celeste to write to me. She may be Celeste the Extraordinary, but she's not Celeste the Pen Pal. I couldn't wait any longer."

I sat down across from her. "That's low. Reading your husband's mail."

"Don't worry. I won't spoil it for you." Sondra flipped through the catalog. "The beginning describes how miserable Picana is in her dank cell on the bottommost floor of Kingdom's dungeon, waiting to die after her eleventh year."

"Penta says here Picana has lost the will to live," I said. "Funny how the Magnus spell she wanted so much has now become a curse. And quit spoiling the letter!"

Sondra tapped something on the catalog's glossy page. "Mya has changed her name to Maria and has settled into a lovely dwelling in a quaint corner of France in Janay, the elderly companion to her free-spirited daughter. Eustacia lives close by in Paris and only goes to the best parties. She calls herself Iviana Eye now."

I lowered the paper. "Will you stop?"

"Tomana lives in a small dwelling in the Forest of Death near the northern coast. She gardens and sews. Her daughter, Julia of course, watches her, making sure she's not into mischief."

I set the letter on the table. Sondra widened her doe-like eyes at me. Large and innocent eyes like those in an anime illustration. "Keep reading."

"Why don't you just tell me the rest?"

She grinned. "If you insist. My favorite part is the Guild is investigating the disappearance of a certain man with yellow teeth from Cixxes. Let's just say Picana has a cellmate to her left."

I blinked. "I'm surprised Alice would do something so risky for you."

My wife's lower lip protruded. "Alice didn't do anything." Then she smirked. "That you know. Glinda returned to Oz the afternoon after the celebration and ran the Belligerent Battlecocks out of her world."

"Take a breath." I had to remind her sometimes.

"Pennilane and Pip got married! For the winter and autumn, they'll live in Janay's London, visiting friends at Pemberley and other mansions. And then for spring and summer, Pip magically transforms into...well, I'll let you read that part."

"Hmm...maybe a seal?"

"And they live under the sea with Pennilane's uncles and aunts."

I cupped my chin and rested my elbow on the table. Sondra had wound herself up now.

"Julia remained in Kingdom and joined Ozark's realm in the Forest of Death. Lenore has settled in the other forest, the Forest of Blood. Her 'nest' of wood in a tree is magnificent. When Lenore visits Valencia, a certain young prince—Cuthbert, duh—can't keep his eyes off her."

I was about to say something, but she kept talking like a train rolling downhill. "Count and Countess Cupsince are residing at the Netherfield estate in Janay where the best instructors are teaching Cassie history, literature, and science, naturally. While their estate is a good distance from Pemberley, they visit the Darcys often. I guess the count has settled down, and the countess is known far and wide as more than a match for his antics. That's my parallel!" She leaned over the letter and pointed at the bottom of the first page. "Read this part."

I started to read, but she blurted out the news. "Elizabeth and all the Bennet sisters visited the count and countess. Cassie's lucky."

Sondra had changed her attitude toward Cassie once she'd come up with an idea to recreate the visionary dream. After we have our baby, we'll have Alice bring Cassie to Earth and let her hold our newborn. Sondra is planning every detail; she's even picked out the teacup to drop just as in the dream.

I returned to the letter while Sondra flipped another page in her catalog. "Oh, and Helga talks to Cusp all the time now," she said. "It drives the rest of them crazy to listen in on their one-way conversations. She's used the holy sword to restore Neighsayer, the horse, to his proper age. And of course, Valencia and Graddock became publicly engaged soon after we left."

I folded the paper and slapped it on the table. "Thank you for ruining my letter."

Sondra tilted her head and folded her hands. "I didn't ruin all of it."

"Are you sure?"

"I—" She broke off. "He kicked. Harold, our son kicked." With a bit of effort, she rose to her feet and started from the room. "I need to write down what he's telling us."

My wife has gently tapped and rubbed her belly for weeks in an attempt to teach our unborn child Morse code. Already convinced our bundle of joy will be a genius, she's written down most of the babe's kicks and movements, interpreting them as messages to us. My wife is brilliant, but sometimes I worry about her.

As she left the room, she shouted over her shoulder. "I didn't spoil the final piece. And I wouldn't. Read it."

I picked up the letter and skimmed the parts Sondra

had already revealed. When I arrived at the end, I grinned and called out. "She agreed to do it. We have our second godmother."

"Was that ever in doubt?" Sondra responded from the other room.

Two godmothers instead of a godfather and godmother pairing was unconventional, but nothing Sondra and I did, seemingly, was ever normal. I picked up the letter and started rereading it. Our little adventure to defeat the three witches had too many deaths of loved ones. Also, too many people smooched others they shouldn't be kissing, yet in the end, true love prevailed. I've written most of our adventure down to remember it, but I won't publish it. The experience was too personal and too painful. I'll send my only copy to Kingdom for safekeeping. Yes, not a perfect ending but a good one. I'll take it.

Sondra rushed back into the kitchen. "Four dots followed by two dots. Our son says 'hi'. What do you want to tell him?"

Yes, I'll definitely take it.

Neither

And now, godson, we have come to the end of our little narrative from so many years ago. Your parents never questioned their wonderful miracle, which, my dear godson, Fitzie, is you. I know you dislike your younger name, but you understand I can't help using it and will call you Fitzie the rest of your life. I wrote at the start about a secret, and I will uphold my promise. You now know the longing your mother had for you, and your father's unfailing fidelity to both you and your mother. But another sacrificed much for you, my dear, and you should be aware of that and honor her.

After seeing off Hero and Sanders at the Circle of Counsel, Penta searched the castle for Celeste to discuss the matter of restoring the monuments the witches had destroyed. The queen wanted the statue of Celeste's sister, Planet, reconstructed first. Hearing Celeste's voice from a side annex of the throne chamber, she approached the doorway. She halted when she heard Glinda's voice and decided to do something out of character for the high queen—eavesdrop. Glinda's first sentence made her curious.

"Sanders' pregnancy is impossible, and you know it, Celeste. I discerned instantly when we reunited in Kingdom what they did to that poor woman in Cixxes. She shouldn't be with child."

"Yet she is." Celeste's voice.

A pause. "You threw the spell. The one I dared not throw."

Celeste didn't answer her.

The rustling of a dress. "Did you tell the Saturns?"

Celeste said, "No!"

"They have no idea you sacrificed your ability to have children to Sanders," declared Glinda.

"And they do not need to know," answered Celeste. "Perhaps one day, a long time from now, I will tell them only because keeping secrets from those you love is a dangerous thing. When they look in their baby's eyes, they will know, as I do, I made the right decision."

Glinda gasped. "Celeste. Your title truly fits you. You are extraordinary."

I have reviewed this entire manuscript multiple times for accuracy. Your mother has denied for years she had said "fart" when poor Cassie awoke from Picana's curse, but she did. You yourself have traveled to different worlds and can confirm with Mrs. Darcy what happened in Janay. Tell Miss Woodhouse and Miss Everdeen to distract your mother, and I'm sure Elizabeth will be glad to answer your questions.

And so, my tale has come to an end, but my affection for you will never do so. I'm not your fairy godmother—that honor belongs to Celeste—but because we're both from Kingdom, your world thinks the best gift we can present you with is spells or magic trinkets. They have it all wrong. Magic, as you've read in this book, can destroy or impart life. No, the greatest gift a godmother can give to her godchild is a steady and irrepressible love. It's my gift to you, my child. My love for you will never falter, my dear Fitzwilliam Saturn.

Love & blessings,

38 - POSTSCRIPT

Cinderella unfolded the package wrapped in cambric in front of Roger, Rose Red, and her sisters. She had received it after attending the funeral of Ozark, surprised he had bequeathed anything to her. Returning home with the gift, she had unwrapped it in private and recoiled, stunned by his dying legacy. Carefully wrapping it a second time, Cinderella had assembled her sister queens and friends who watched her unravel the cloth around the package once more.

When Cinderella set aside the cambric, she lifted the object enclosed inside for all to view. Everyone uttered exclamations of surprise and shock, similar to Cinderella's when she had first unwrapped it. The contents of the package matched an item in a painting in the castle.

Paintings of the queens' lives hung throughout the palace. Cinderella's present matched an article in the background of a depiction of Snow White sitting on the grass. Behind her, through a window in her childhood home, her evil stepmother is staring at a mirror. Snow White herself oversaw the painting for its accuracy and approved every detail.

Cinderella held the mirror belonging to Snow White's stepmother.

A black, wooden rectangle framed the mirror's warped glass, which bent like heat haze coming off the sands of a desert.

Hands shaking, Cinderella almost dropped the mirror. Her eyes sought out Rose Red. "Is it?"

Rose Red nodded. She regarded the mirror as a person on Earth might view a hand grenade without its pin. "How is the glass restored?"

Cinderella leaned forward and examined the reflective surface. "We know you and Hero encountered Snow White's stepmother in Grok's Teeth, and he smashed the mirror. Her stepmother went insane after Hero broke it and remained in the caves trying to recover the pieces and reassemble the looking glass. After my sister ascended to the throne, Snow White searched for her stepmother. You, Rose Red, assisted Snow White and brought her to the exact spot where Hero shattered the glass."

Rose Red nodded. "We never found her."

Valencia asked, "How did this come into Ozark's possession?"

Cinderella shuddered. "I don't know. Perhaps Snow White's stepmother gave up and went to Ozark to ask him to help her."

Valencia reached into her pocket and retrieved a match. "Or Ozark sought her out."

Cinderella lifted her chin. "He would never cross into Kingdom without asking my permission."

Helga folded her arms. "Yet he harbored an item of dark magic. I know you loved Ozark, but he guarded his secrets jealously. Even from you."

Cinderella's nostrils flared. "I will never think less of him."

Penta put her hand on Cinderella's shoulder. "However he obtained it, 'tis good news it's in your hands, kid sister. We know it belongs in the vault with the other evil artifacts we guard."

Everyone at the council agreed with Rose Red who was standing in for Snow White. Hers was the most emphatic "aye."

Cinderella nodded. "I agree too, but something troubles me. Ozark bequeathed me the mirror with a note. 'Use it when all hope is gone.' Why give me such an abhorrent item and then tell me to use it?"

Rose Red sucked in her breath. "You are not seriously considering using such an evil object, are you? I would rather you smash it and scatter its pieces. Let us be rid of it once and for all."

Cinderella rubbed her hands together. "But then why give it to me?"

Roger cleared his throat. "If I may, Cinderella. As a parent to Cuthbert, I find myself changed in a certain way in regard to him. When it comes to my child, my judgment is often not objective."

Penta interceded, "As I was with Beauty."

Roger nodded to Penta. "And I understood your distress at the time, my queen. Cinderella, would we have been any different if the witches had taken Cuthbert?"

"But what has it to do with the mirror?" Cinderella set the looking glass face down on a nearby divan.

"I once argued with an admirer of Snow White's over who was the fairest in Kingdom. Then, and now, you remain the most beautiful to me. Now that Snow White is gone, 'tis no competition. Excusing the queens' pardon, as your husband, I have the right to proclaim you 'the fairest.' Ozark, being a father, likely thought so too. If you use it, you will prove it."

Cinderella scowled. "But why would I care? Why give me such a dreadful gift to prove something I have no interest in?"

"Not a drop of vanity exists in you, sister." Valencia rolled the match between her fingers. "Yet, Roger's reasoning is sound. Ozark wanted you to know you are the most beautiful in Kingdom."

Cinderella stomped her foot. ".No! I knew Ozark. He loved all of his protected ones and not because they were fair. Gruesome and handsome creatures inhabit Ozark's area. Ozark knew I didn't care for beauty. He saw my heart."

Rose Red glared at the back of the looking glass. "Then why give you the mirror?"

Cinderella closed her eyes. "You will think me insane. I do not have the acuity of mind you possess, dear Valencia, but I know Ozark and trust him, even after death."

Penta fiddled with the hem of her shirt. "You do not mean to use it?"

"That is exactly what I mean to do." Cinderella's lisp was evident.

Roger spoke over everyone's protests. "You do not need the mirror to proclaim what we all know to be true. Cinderella, if Ozark wanted you to use it, he must have meant for you to use it against the witches."

Cinderella said, "Ozark knew my despair regarding a specific subject we spoke of in private. It doesn't concern the witches. I hesitate to say it aloud as I'm afraid I may be wrong."

Roger set his hand on her shoulder. "What did you say, love?"

Recalling her words to her father, Cinderella closed her eyes. "I had said, 'My sisters may have accepted Snow White's fate but not me. I must know for certain if all hope is truly gone, father.'"

The room went silent, and Rose Red put her hand to her mouth.

Cinderella returned to the present and addressed her gathering. "I wish to use it right now."

Rose Red said, "While I understand your desire to use this odious gift, this mirror nearly killed Snow White. Do you think it wise to employ it again?"

"The mirror works on the vain. Do you think I am so self-absorbed as to be ensnared by its promises?"

Rose Red frowned. "No. But that does not mean it is not dangerous."

Cinderella said, "I'll use it once, then lock it away in the vault and promise never to retrieve it."

Helga turned away. "I will retrieve Cusp."

"No!" Penta said. "Cinderella. I trust you."

Cinderella nodded toward her. "I could have done this in private but wanted you all here with me. I'm scared too, and I need your support. Please, let's not tarry. Let's use this horrific relic and then lock it away."

Cinderella hung it on a wall, and her sisters and Rose Red gathered around her. Roger stood behind her with his hands on her shoulders. Cinderella looked at her distorted reflection in the glass and steadied herself. She shivered when she realized the mirror reflected only her image. Everyone else in the room was absent. Cinderella lifted her chin and called out in a loud voice. "Looking-glass, upon the wall. Who is fairest of us all?"

The answer came loud and clear.

"A fair question from the queen of ashes
Second-best of pretty eyelashes.
Not fairest yet, for there lives another
Hidden from all, no parents or brother.
One who has lost memory in her mind
And yet remains true, gentle and kind.
Fairest of face, natural beauty not faux
Dark-haired maiden, skin white as snow."

AFTERWORD

The fun doesn't have to stop here. If you want to learn more about Kingdom and its inhabitants, read *Kingdom Come*, and *On Earth, As It Is*.

Kingdom's Advent is a prequel of short stories to the novels.

Furthermore, please check out jimdorantales.com to find more short stories and blogs about Kingdom. Wonder what happened to Graddock after he left Oz? Seek out *Bonhomie Rhapsody* with password "DeliverUsRhapsody." Or what happened to Beauty after she left with the witches? Look for *It's A Beautiful Thing* with password "DeliverUsBeauty." Future stories will be a combination of "Deliver Us" and a name in parentheses (e.g. *The Magnificent Seven* (Dwarfs) is "DeliverUsDwarfs).

If you'd be so kind, please leave a review of this novel.

If you would like to contact me directly, please email me at jim.doran.author@gmail.com.

BOOKS BY THIS AUTHOR

Kingdom Come: A Fantasy Novel

When times are dim and full of woe / And devils threaten maidens low...

Harold Tray is haunted, not only by his past, but by a ghost as well. After he agrees to a request by the ghost, Harold is transported to a land of fairy tales called Kingdom. He partners with a pixie in search of a way home when he discovers a scroll containing a prophecy. The prophecy predicts the rise of five queens to overthrow an illegitimate king. Harold, armed only with the knowledge of the stories he read as a child, encounters famous and obscure fairy-tale characters as he journeys around Kingdom. He is unaware of the villain who has set traps for the princesses...someone who will correct his past only if Harold chooses to go home.

Kingdom Come is not only a fantasy but also a drama that explores the potential of the human heart to live, grieve, and love.

On Earth, As It Is: A Kingdom Fantasy Novel

Three years after the events of Kingdom Come, Harold and Sondra are struggling to establish a lasting relationship. When a friend from Kingdom travels to Earth, she tells Harold that someone has abducted the realm's five queens. Harold assumes he will travel to the world of elves and dragons, but the messenger has a different idea—one in which Earth itself will play a vital role.

In this whimisical fantasy tale, Harold, Sondra, and other characters set out on a new adventure spanning not only one, but two, worlds.

Kingdom's Advent

Welcome to Kingdom, a fairytale world of grand fantasy consisting of endangered pixies as well as industrious giants, wishing wells and imprisoned towns, sorcery and swordsmanship—and cursed corsets too. This collection offers up an ambitious young fairy who learns a secret that will change her life, a virtuous girl trying to make a living in a community harboring evil creatures, outcast dwarfs with loving hearts, and a princess who despises anyone who would save her life. The legends of triumphant heroes and foul villains are captured within these six short stories.

ACKNOWLEDGEMENT

The following would like to acknowledge certain people for their contributions to "Deliver Us."

Valencia would like to thank you, our faithful reader, for coming along on our journey, and remind you that a review on sites like Amazon and Goodreads really does make a difference.

Harold would like to acknowledge editor G. Mikki Harden for her wonderful suggestions, for her attention to detail, and for keeping his wife's cursing to an acceptable level. Furthermore, Harold would like to point out the fact that Turducken didn't do anything of significance in this entire novel.

Sondra would like to acknowledge Nyssa Rae for being a fantastic critique partner and sticking with her through her narrative. The input Nyssa provided for Sondra's references to science, and for all the characters' motivations and key plot points, elevated the novel. Sondra stresses to blame the author and not Nyssa if any technical information is inaccurate.

Cinderella would like to acknowledge the contribution of artist Daniel Johnson for the cover and interior art. She believes her throne is the best depicted royal chair ever and is—in her words—"amazeballs."

Penta would like to acknowledge T. M. Doran for his review of an early revision of Deliver Us and for his remark that Penta is "the queen among queens" which played a large role in the plot. Note that the other queens are not amused.

Helga would like to acknowledge Kristiana Sfirlea for her unwavering support. By Saint Peter's beard, Helga would have never received her new gift if not for Kristiana's plea to "include more Helga."

Sir Turducken would like to acknowledge Cynthia Payne, a wonderful beta reader, without whom he would not have been knighted.

Snow White would like to acknowledge no one for this dreadful novel and believes author Jim Doran ought to be outlawed from ever touching a writing instrument again.

Jim Doran would like to officially apologize to Snow White. He would also like to thank the people above with similar sentiments. Furthermore, he would like to thank the following without whom this novel would not be possible: Ed Hosmer, John Doran, Judy Malecke, Jayne Doran, Paxton Doran, Phillip Doran, Eliza Luckey, Ellen Doran, Katherine and Joe Dovey, and Carla and Ken Graham. Thank you also to artists Lauren Nalepa and Desiree Johnson for depicting scenes in prior novels. And with special gratitude to Mary Celeste Lareau, Jim's godmother.

Jim would also like to thank someone with all of his love, Hope Doran, for being an inspiration, and for her fidelity in all of his projects.

Lastly, Jim realizes he, and all of creation, comes from the imagination of the Creator. So a huge shout-out to God.

PRAISE FOR AUTHOR

Kingdom Come:
Hit all the right spots for a work in this genre.

- LAURA

On Earth, As It Is:
This book is a great read for fans of the first story, KINGDOM COME, sweeping high fantasy plots, surprising urban fantasy influences, and multi POV.

- KRISTIANA SFIRLEA, AUTHOR OF THE STORMWATCH DIARIES SERIES

Kingdom's Advent:
Kingdom's Advent is a great read for anyone who enjoys fantasy, fairy tales, and fun.

- LISA CASKEY, AUTHOR OF THE FARMED TRILOGY

ABOUT THE AUTHOR

Jim Doran

Jim Doran is a genre writer who enjoys transporting his readers to unique destinations filled with wonder and spectacle. Within his novels, you will meet fascinating characters such as a queen who is always lucky, a beauty who visually projects her emotions, and three witches who won't remain dead. To learn more about Jim and his writing, visit jimdorantales.com.

www.ingramcontent.com/pod-product-compliance
Lightning Source LLC
Chambersburg PA
CBHW051437260626
47162CB00001B/130